THE CRAB CANNERY SHIP

AND OTHER NOVELS OF STRUGGLE

THE CRAB CANNERY SHIP

AND OTHER NOVELS OF STRUGGLE

KOBAYASHI TAKIJI

Translated by
ŽELJKO CIPRIŠ

With an Introduction by
KOMORI YŌICHI

UNIVERSITY OF
HAWAI'I PRESS
Honolulu

21 20 19 18 17 7 6 5 4 3

Library of Congress Cataloging-in-Publication Data

Kobayashi, Takiji, 1903–1933, author.
[Novels. English. Selections]
The crab cannery ship and other novels of struggle / Kobayashi Takiji ; translated by Željko Cipriš ; with an introduction by Komori Yoichi.
pages cm
Includes bibliographical references.
ISBN 978-0-8248-3667-2 (cloth : alk. paper) —
ISBN 978-0-8248-3742-6 (pbk.)
1. Political fiction, Japanese—Translations into English. I. Cipris, Zeljko, translator. II. Kobayashi, Takiji, 1903–1933. Kanikosen. English. III. Kobayashi, Takiji, 1903–1933. Yasuko. English. IV. Kobayashi, Takiji, 1903–1933. Toseikatsusha. English. V. Title.
PL832.O3A2 2013
895.6'34—dc23

2012029634

University of Hawai'i Press books are printed on acid-free paper and meet the guidelines for permanence and durability of the Council on Library Resources.

Designed by Julie Matsuo-Chun

To **Shane Satori Cipris** and
Ljubomir Ryu Cipris, and
to a better world in which
the free development of each
is the condition for the free
development of all

Contents

Translator's Preface

Incorrigible internationalism and love of travel take me to various points of the globe; so it was that I happened to be in Montevideo, Uruguay, in May of 2008 when a Japanese friend—a single mother and newly unemployed factory worker—informed me by e-mail that Japan had a brand new best-selling book: *Kani kōsen* (The Crab Cannery Ship) by Kobayashi Takiji. This was astonishing news in light of the fact that the book was almost eighty years old—it had been written in 1929! How did a famous anti-establishment book from the early twentieth century become a best-seller so many decades later? What enabled it to sell hundreds of thousands of copies and to generate a number of *manga* (i.e., comic book) versions, theatrical productions, a remake of the movie, and new words like *kanikō suru*—meaning, roughly, "to slave away?" Clearly, something about the old novel struck its many new readers as most timely.

Not that Takiji's novel had ever been entirely forgotten. It occupied a secure position in Japan's modern history as the best-known literary product of the proletarian movement, a major cultural and political current of the 1920s and early 1930s—a time when labor activism, socialism, feminism, and antimilitarism were briefly in the ascendant, while paintings, posters, prose narratives, poetry, and plays depicting the lives and struggles of the dispossessed enjoyed a considerable degree of popular interest and critical esteem. By the mid-thirties, however, as the country's elites led the nation ever closer to an all-out war on the Asian continent, this progressive groundswell had been largely obliterated through a combination of internal dissension, government propaganda, and intensified repression: arrests, beatings, imprisonment, and censorship. Though the proletarian movement made somewhat of a comeback at war's end, it lacked its former scope and eventually faded amid the officially encouraged consumerism and conformism that came to dominate much of postwar Japan. Takiji's novel lived on in libraries, bookstores, and school curricula, often as little more than a worthy historical curiosity and a reminder of the bad old days that would never return, as the country's economy kept on growing and its citizens seemed to bask in the glow of corporate-induced prosperity.

By the early 1990s, a number of factors including sheer industrial overcapacity brought decades of economic growth to an end, ushering in the "lost decades" of recession, marked by insecurity, unemployment, a drop in the standard of living, and a rise in the number of suicides. In 2008—the year Takiji's novel skyrocketed to fame—over thirty thousand Japanese people killed themselves, tens of thousands were homeless, some three million were unemployed, twenty million were living in poverty, and more than a third of the active labor force comprised irregular workers who were poorly paid and could easily be fired. This does not explain why a fiercely anticapitalist novel burst into light at this particular moment, but it does provide a highly receptive background of frustration, outrage, and smoldering rebellion that warmly welcomed its fiery call for united, collective action. (For the fascinating conjunction of circumstances that triggered the boom see the Takiji-related articles by Norma Field and Heather Bowen-Struyk in *The Asia-Pacific Journal* at japanfocus.org.)

Suddenly, the infernal atmosphere of *The Crab Cannery Ship* struck millions as a fitting metaphor for their own predicament—that of human beings trapped within a soulless system totally dedicated to the accumulation of profit, a system that deems them valuable only so long as they can be utilized to help maximize that profit, but otherwise considers them disposable. For many, Takiji's novel offered eye-opening insight into the core of a profoundly chilling status quo. Takiji's standpoint is neither conservative nor liberal. To a conservative, capitalism is the best of all possible worlds; to a liberal, it is the worst economic system except for all the others. Though both conservatives and liberals essentially agree with Baroness Thatcher's proclamation that "There is no alternative," liberals commendably strive to make the dominant system humane, as—had they been born in a different age—they might have heroically striven to do for slavery, feudalism, or Stalinism. Takiji, however, goes beyond this: for him, a socioeconomic system that divides most of humanity into those who own and control life's productive resources—factories, plantations, mines, etc.—and those who are compelled to sell themselves daily on the labor market in order to survive is inherently inhumane. Though it can and should be reformed to the greatest possible extent, it must ultimately be transcended through solidarity and struggle, to be superseded by a worldwide cooperative commonwealth in which emancipated humanity can for the first time begin to live to its fullest potential.

Japan, once widely looked up to as demonstrating one of the most successful forms of capitalism on earth—a veritable paradise of happy salarymen, content housewives, boisterous gangsters, and a beaming emperor—now began to resemble an angry purgatory, as the foreign press printed articles with titles like "Japan economy angst boosts sales of Marxist novel" (Reuters, August 11, 2008), "Japan's young turn to Communist Party as they decide capitalism has let them down" (*Daily Telegraph,* October 18, 2008), and "Communism on rise in recession-hit Japan" (BBC, May 4, 2009). And playing the role of catalyst in this tentative turn to the left was the *engagé* work of Kobayashi Takiji, a revolutionary organizer and writer come startlingly back to life.

IN JUNE 2008, on a stroll through the sloping grounds of a lovely Buddhist temple in Kyoto's western hills, the subject of Takiji came up in a conversation with Professor Gunilla Lindberg-Wada, Chair of Japanese Studies at Stockholm University. Somewhat to my surprise, Professor Lindberg-Wada stressed that there is a strong need for a new English translation of Takiji's classic novel. A partial English translation of *Kani kōsen,* based on a heavily censored edition and done by an anonymous translator—who turned out to be a young New Zealander named Max Bickerton—had appeared as early as 1933, and the first to produce a complete translation (along with another work by Takiji) was Professor Frank Motofuji of University of California at Berkeley, in 1973. I had enjoyed both translations—as well as a lively online rendition of Chapter 1 by Matt Treyvaud—but my Swedish colleague's comment gave me something to think about. The extant English versions of Takiji's novel had become somewhat difficult to come by and, even more importantly, a prominent novel surely deserves multiple translations. When Professor Norma Field of the University of Chicago, a scholar of proletarian literature and author of a book on Takiji, told me that she too would welcome a new translation, I resolved to move ahead. I was already working on two other Takiji novels—*Yasuko* and *Tōseikatsusha* (Life of a Party Member), both included in the present volume and never before translated into English—so now *The Crab Cannery Ship* would join them to offer a peerless introduction to Takiji's literary work: *The Crab Cannery Ship,* the most famous of the three, is experimental in avoiding individualized characters; *Yasuko* is the culmination of a series of works about tenant-farmer workers, poor women sacrificed to rich boys, and their sisters at the dawn of a political awakening; *Life of a Party Member* shows the cost of life in the party for a man—and his family—but also continues to explore female participation, depicting both the fulfillment and the agonies that involvement in revolutionary activism brings to women. The trio of novels can also be seen, as an anonymous reader for the University of Hawai'i Press pointed out, as a virtual how-to primer on raising consciousness, organizing, and engaging in focused local political actions. Possibly, in addition to being enlightening, Takiji's highly readable oeuvre may even inspire some readers to action!

My approach to the translation has been extraordinarily simple: I have tried to imagine and construct the sort of literary text that Takiji himself would be most likely to produce were he writing now, and in English. Takiji's style tends to be unadorned, dynamic, and cinematic, with frequent paragraph breaks that enliven the reading pace. The text, though not oversimplified, is accessible and inviting to a broad audience, and possesses a vigorous vitality that grips the reader. It can be read "on the run," and one suspects that some of its early readers—many of them members of the then-illegal Communist Party—had no other way of reading it. German writer Erich Kästner, whose books were burned by the Nazis as "contrary to the German spirit," once noted that his own writing aims at sincerity of feeling, clarity of thought, and simplicity of expression. The same qualities, I think, characterize Takiji's work, and it is my ardent hope that this translation will do him justice. For, to paraphrase Victor Hugo's preface to *Les Misérables,* so long as there shall exist artificially created hells on earth, books like this cannot be useless.

THIS BOOK OWES much to many people, so now for some words of heartfelt gratitude: first I wish to thank the Takiji Library (2003–2008)—especially to Mr. Sano Chikara, its founder and director, and Mr. Satō Saburō, its curator—for a magnanimous translation grant and for their continuous encouragement. (Additional thanks to Mr. Satō for identifying Takiji's first English translator, Max Bickerton!) Outstandingly constructive has been the selfless and tireless support of my colleague Norma Field who has read the manuscript in its entirety, and made countless suggestions toward its improvement. Many thanks also to Professor Komori Yōichi of Tokyo University for his wonderful introduction, and for taking the time out of his hectic schedule to write it. Thanks too to Ms. Aiko Kojima who kindly transcribed Professor Komori's beautifully handwritten manuscript into printed form, making it so much easier for me to translate. I am most grateful to Professor Gunilla Lindberg-Wada of Stockholm University who first gave me the idea of translating *The Crab Cannery Ship,* to Norma Field who did the same for *Yasuko,* and to Professor Chia-ning Chang of University of California at Davis, a specialist in modern Japanese literature, who suggested I translate *Life of a Party Member.* (With colleagues like this, the book almost writes itself!) I am also tremendously thankful to my fabulous editors at the University of Hawai'i Press, Pamela Kelley and Ann Ludeman, to the keen-eyed copy editor Wendy Bolton, and to the two readers for the Press, who all provided excellent counsel in making this book as good as it could be. I would like to thank Shoko Hamano for sending me a copy of *Yasuko* that I used for the translation and to Mutsuki Miyashita for first calling my attention to the astounding Takiji boom—and for everything else. A special and loving thank-you goes to Chiba Sen'ichi Sensei whose boundless thoughtfulness and erudition will always be of greatest inspiration to me. To the consistently supportive J. Thomas Rimer, a superlative scholar and lovable patron saint of Japanese literature, a deepest bow of affection and admiration. Infinite thanks to my parents Dr. Divna Popović-Cipriš and Dr. Marijan Cipriš for bringing me into a most fascinating world, and to my sons Shane and Ryu for making their old man euphorically happy. For being my muse, a big thank-you and a kiss to Kobayashi Ryōko. Solidarity and gratitude to the people of Japan—may you never experience another Fukushima! Warmest thanks also go to friends and comrades around the globe, too numerous to mention by name, who are doing their powerful utmost to change the world.

INTRODUCTION

KOMORI YŌICHI

Kobayashi Takiji was born on October 13, 1903, in the village of Shimokawazoi in Akita Prefecture, a snowy agricultural region of northern Japan. It was the year before the outbreak of the Russo-Japanese War. His father Suematsu was the second son of a small landholder, but his older brother Keigi had invested family funds in business and failed, leaving Suematsu to deal with the consequences after he himself moved to Hokkaido. In the Kobayashi family history we see that stage in the capitalist development of Japan when small landowners and independent farmers, driven into bankruptcy and loss of their lands, were being sent into the industrializing cities and colonies to become wage laborers.

In 1907, when Takiji was four, his family emigrated to Otaru in Hokkaido—Imperial Japan's first colony—to earn a living helping Keigi who had gone into business baking and selling bread under a sign that read "Mitsuboshidō Co of Otaru, Purveyors to the Imperial Navy." After completing elementary school, Takiji continued to work at his uncle's bakery, in exchange for which he received financial assistance that enabled him to enroll in the municipal Commercial School. It was there that Takiji developed a strong interest in literature and the arts. Graduating fifth in his class in 1921, he entered the Otaru Higher School of Commerce. From this point on Kobayashi Takiji's life was riven by multiple conditions, which at times coexisted in a state of contradiction, at others in outright conflict or disjunction: his family were former landholders and ruined farmers; once mainland farmers and now colonial wage laborers; close relatives of the owner of a bakery but part of that bakery's proletariat. Consequently, he himself belonged both to the proletariat and to the intelligentsia that aspired through elite education to join the petty bourgeoisie. Awareness of these cleavages in his existence became deeply etched in Kobayashi Takiji at the time he began his higher schooling. He himself would later compare such a condition to "holding dual citizenship."

While serving on the editorial board of the school's alumni magazine, Takiji began to publish stories in journals such as *The Novel Club* and *New Literature*. Still full of literary aspiration, he nonetheless took a job upon graduation in 1924 with the Otaru branch of the Hokkaido Colonial Bank. This bank began as a semigovernmental, semiprivate enterprise whose object was the colonial development of Hokkaido and Karafuto (southern Sakhalin Island). Its initial capital was three million yen, and it extended long-term loans using as collateral the agricultural and residential land that the immigrants had plundered from the native population. From the time of the Russo-Japanese War, before Takiji's family had moved to Otaru, the bank began issuing bonds and during World War I, it grew into a trust company. Beginning with the "cultivation of Hokkaido," a euphemism for a war of colonial aggression, and with each subsequent war—Sino-Japanese, Russo-Japanese, World War I—the Hokkaido Colonial Bank expanded its operations and increasingly became an institution dedicated to financing imperialist ventures.

Six months into work at such a bank, the twenty-one-year-old Kobayashi Takiji met sixteen-year-old Taguchi Takiko at the Yamakiya, a small eatery whose principal business was in fact prostitution. The experience of falling in love with a woman from the lowest stratum of capitalist society's class system—a woman who had been driven to commodifying her own sexuality—while working in a bank at the center of that system, imposed manifold disjunctions on Takiji. It also provided the germ of what would grow to become the core of his literature.

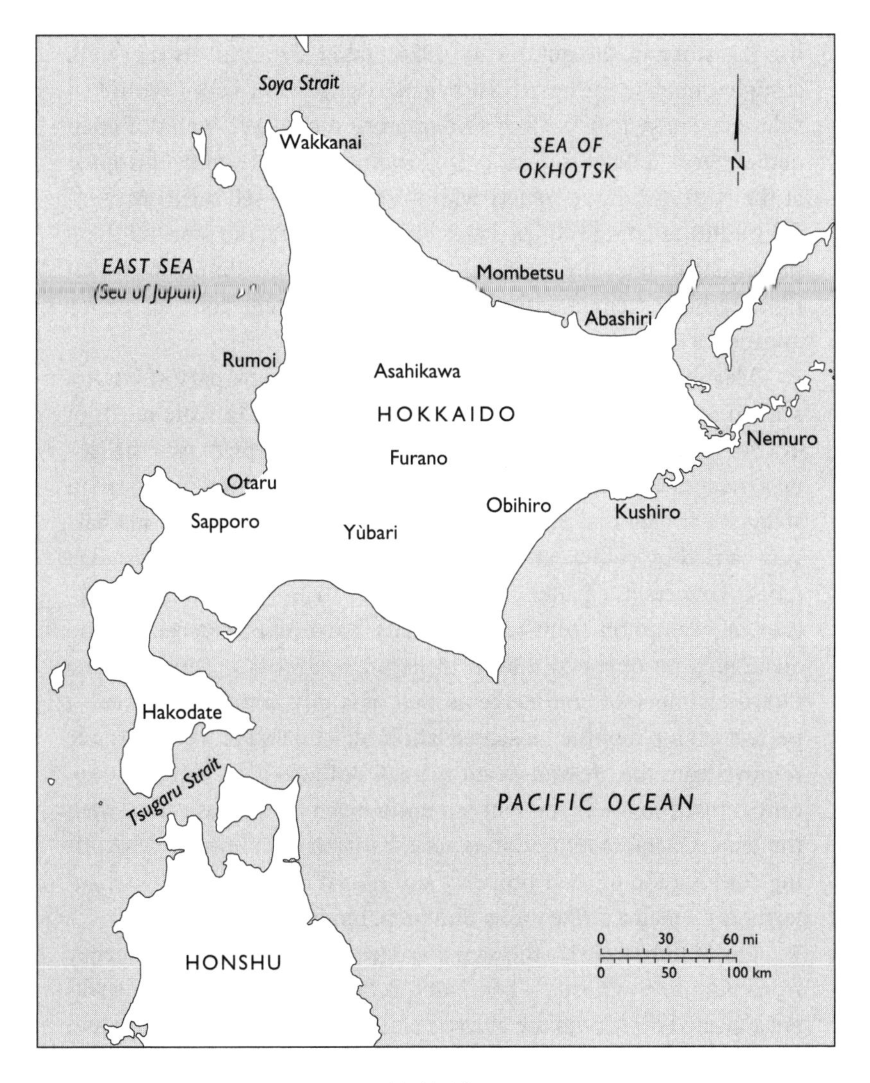

Hokkaido

Just about the same time, in 1925, a young writer named Hayama Yoshiki published a story called "The Prostitute" (Inbaifu), which became a virtual manifesto of the proletarian—i.e., working-class—literature in Japan: it made possible the linkage of prostitution with the growing class-consciousness of workers that labor power entailed the coerced transformation of their bodies into commodities. Reading the story in the autumn of 1926, Takiji wrote in his diary: "A straight punch to the heart!" He began to write short fiction with such titles as "Those Left Behind" (Nokosareru mono, 1927) and "Takiko and Others" (Takiko sonota, 1928), dealing with the reality of women at the bottom rung of society who were forced to sell their own sexual bodies as commodities. Later dubbed "the Takiko stories," these pieces depict not only a refusal to surrender to conditions in which fighting back seemed all but impossible, but a tenacious search for avenues of opposition and resistance.

Meanwhile, in 1927, three thousand people took part in Otaru's second May Day celebration, making it the largest in scale north of Tokyo. A key impetus for this upsurge in the movement was the Isono tenant farmers' strike, a signal event within the growing agrarian struggles in colonial Hokkaido. The previous year's disastrous harvest caused by cold weather had led to a grave crisis for Hokkaido's tenant farmers. One after another, furious strikes demanding reduction or exemption from tenancy rents broke out. A certain Isono Susumu, who operated a farm in Furano and was president of the Otaru chamber of commerce as well as a city council member—a perfect example of the "absentee landlord," situated at a comfortable remove from the life-and-death struggles of his tenant farmers—not only refused to lower the rent but announced an increase, and when the tenant farmers refused to accede, he initiated a lawsuit demanding confiscation of their property and return of the land. The tenant farmers formed a strike group and prepared for action.

On March 3, 1927, the strike group made the arduous journey from Furano to Otaru. When Isono refused to negotiate, the strikers appealed directly to the citizens of Otaru, distributing leaflets and giving speeches, generating a flurry of verbal activity. All the speeches attracted overflow crowds, with thousands of people showing up.

In response, the citizens of Otaru sought every conceivable form of action in solidarity with the strikers. The result was an arbitration signed on April 9 that actually exceeded the strike group's demands, extending to guarantee of the tenant farmers' right to cultivate their rented land. That year, in other words, the slow spring days leading to International Workers' Day—May 1—were marked by a historic joint struggle by tenant farmers and the united labor union that produced victory in the international port city of Otaru.

June saw the beginning of the Otaru harbor strike, the first general strike by an industrial union in Japan. It started with a demand by 36 barge stevedores for a wage increase. The workers of Otaru, however, had already tasted victory achieved by waging a united campaign. Harbor workers of various occupations, indeed the majority, began to join the strike. Their families organized mass meetings, elementary school students went on strike, and the contents of the workers' demands were widely publicized among the citizens. Drawing on the experience of the joint farmer-worker struggle during the Isono strike, the Japan Farmers Union called on all its Hokkaido branches to act in solidarity with the Otaru workers.

Kobayashi Takiji was directly involved with the strikers, helping to write publicity leaflets on his way home after work at the bank. He began taking part in study classes with labor and farmer activists. This experience of a revolutionary struggle by an alliance of workers and farmers would bear fruit in his novella *The Absentee Landlord* (*Fuzai jinushi*), published January 1930, in the prestigious magazine *Central Review* (*Chūō kōron*), an indication both of his rising stature as a writer and of the general public's interest in proletarian literature.

The general election held in the year following these strikes marks the next step in Takiji's growing political engagement. In 1925, along with the draconian Peace Preservation Law, a General Election Law was enacted, providing for Japan's first general election based on universal male suffrage. It was announced for February 20, 1928. Takiji actively involved himself in the electoral campaign of the Communist Party member Yamamoto Kenzō, who ran as the Labor Farmer Party's official candidate from Hokkaido's first district. That experience was to find vivid expression in the novella *Journey to East*

Kutchan (*Higashi Kutchan kō*), published in the December 1930 issue of the mainstream general-interest magazine *Reconstruction* (*Kaizō*).

The proletarian parties won 8 seats out of 466 in the general election. The government authorities took a grim view of the open electoral activities by the supposedly outlawed yet reorganized Communist Party that had evidently reconstructed itself. Beginning at dawn on March 15, they launched a nationwide wave of mass arrests directed against activists affiliated with the Communist Party and the Labor Farmer party. More than 1,600 people were arrested overall, most of them in Tokyo, Osaka, and—third in the number of those detained—Hokkaido. Kobayashi Takiji portrayed this act of massive repression as one of psychological and physical violence in his story "March 15, 1928" (1928-nen 3-gatsu 15-nichi). He paid particular attention to depicting the distinct psychological responses to interrogation and torture on the part of his characters, who differed from one another in terms of class origins and way of life.

The preceding year, 1927, Takiji had taken the initiative to join his abiding interest in literature with his strengthening commitment to the labor movement by taking on the responsibility of serving as executive secretary of the Otaru branch of the Worker and Farmer Artists Federation. The following spring, after the March 15 Incident, he took time off from the bank and went to Tokyo to meet Kurahara Korehito of the Japanese Proletarian Arts Federation (NAPF). Kurahara was the leading theorist of the Japanese proletarian literature movement. It was that meeting on May 5, 1928, that led to the submission and publication to instant acclaim of the novella "March 15, 1928" in the November and December issues of *The Battleflag* (*Senki*), the organ of NAPF. In February of 1929, Takiji was elected to the central committee of the Japanese Proletarian Writers League, formed through a reorganization of NAPF, and quickly followed up with the publication of *The Crab Cannery Ship* in the May and June issues of *The Battleflag.*

THE CRAB CANNERY Ship (*Kani kōsen*) was written on the basis of a painstaking investigation into an actual incident that took place in 1926. In a letter to Kurahara Korehito, dated March 31, 1929, Takiji provided a detailed discussion of seven points concerning the novel's "intent." First, its protagonist was not a single character, but rather a *group* of workers. Second, there was "no depiction of *individual personality* or psychology" (emphasis in the original). Third, "various efforts had been made with respect to form" in order to facilitate "popularization of the proletarian arts." Current efforts in this direction had the air of a superficial intellectual attempt at popularization; this work, by contrast, sought to be "overwhelmingly worker-like." Fourth, it "dealt with a *unique* form of labor," taking place aboard a crab cannery ship. Such labor involved "a type of exploitation typical of colonies and undeveloped areas," and it had "the advantage of making transparently clear" not only "the conditions of Japanese workers" but also the "international, military, and economic relations" constituting those conditions. Fifth, the novel "dealt with *unorganized* workers." Sixth, it showed how capitalism, while "seeking to keep the workers unorganized," was ironically "causing the workers (spontaneously) to organize." Seventh, even though it was said that "the proletariat must unconditionally oppose imperialist wars," few workers understood why this was so. To meet this need the novel had to touch on "the economic foundation of imperialist wars, the machinery of imperialism that sets the army itself in motion." For this purpose, a "crab cannery ship offered the best setting."

In my judgment, these seven points provide the most systematic and precise commentary on the basic characteristics and structure of the novel. Nonetheless, I must underscore the significance of Takiji's recognition that the crab cannery ship presented "a *unique* form of labor." This was none other than the discovery of the crab cannery ship as a temporal and spatial zone in which the rule of law had been suspended.

> Crab cannery ships were considered factories [factory ships], not ships. Therefore maritime law did not apply to them.
>
> . . . Moreover the crab cannery ships were factories pure and simple. And yet factory laws did not apply to them either. Consequently, no other site offered such an

> accommodating setting for management's freedom to act with total impunity.

Neither ships nor factories! The novel's narrative makes clear to the reader the double sense in which the rule of law had been suspended. What is more, since the ships were operating around Kamchatka, along the boundary of the Japanese and Soviet territorial waters, neither country's domestic laws applied. Thanks to its nature as a time-space zone absolutely beyond the constraint of law, the crab cannery ship made possible unlimited exploitation and plunder in "an accommodating setting," with "total impunity."

Takiji discovered the crab cannery ship to be a battleground—the site where, as Carl Schmitt points out, the rule of law is suspended. Yet because this battleground was not the site of a war being waged between nations, even the laws of war failed to apply on board the crab cannery ship. At the same time, however, a naval warship accompanied the cannery ship. The workers on board did not have the option of surrendering and withdrawing from the front. It was these characteristics of the crab cannery ship that Takiji identified as rendering the "international, military, and economic relations" transparently clear.

In the crab cannery ship, none of the laws pertaining to ordinary society apply. The workers aboard are not treated as human beings. "The Stuttering Fisherman," a man singled out among the fishermen by this linguistic feature, had first begun to stutter when the radio operator confronted him with the reality that manager "Asakawa doesn't think of you fellows as human beings." Being stripped of every shred of dignity that should be supported by law and confronted by conditions of constant exposure to naked violence had triggered a disorder in that very ability to use words that defines a human being.

Of the "group" controlling and managing the crab cannery ship, the only individual given a proper name is the fishing operation's manager Asakawa. The character who falls victim to his homicidal violence is a youth belonging to the factory hands, the weakest "group" among the workers. He too is given a name, Miyaguchi. In other words, proper names are accorded only to the highest and lowest members of the strata wherein naked violence is exercised by the strong over the weak. The others are only indicated by attributes that distinguish them within the group.

A personal name is used, however, to mark an important turning point at which the formerly "unorganized workers" begin to organize themselves. A fisherman who "had come through an agency in the Nippori section of Tokyo together with ten or so of his friends" and "who had long been bedridden with beriberi" dies. "*Everyone,*" we read, "resolved to stay up for the wake." The incident occurs after everybody has taken "turns offering incense," and the sailors and fishermen are sitting about "gathered in small groups."

The Stuttering Fisherman steps up to the body and declares, without stuttering:

> I don't know the sutras. I can't console Yamada's spirit by chanting sutras. But I've been thinking a lot, and here's what I think. I've thought about how much Yamada didn't want to die. . . . No, to tell the truth, I've thought about how much he *didn't want to be killed.* There's no denying that Yamada was killed.

It is when this fisherman breaks out of the naked violence and proceeds to correct his choice of words from "to die" to "*to be killed*" as a declaration of his anger, that the sailors—members of a different group—respond in agreement, calling out, "You're right."

By 1933, *The Crab Cannery Ship* had been translated into Chinese, Russian, and English, and came to be read throughout the world. Since then it has been buffeted by the vicissitudes of history: suppressed during the years of intensifying repression and war, revived in the postwar years, and increasingly neglected in the depoliticization of society from the mid-1970s. Then, in twenty-first-century Japan, where the systematic dismantling of laws regulating employment had begun in 1995, *The Crab Cannery Ship* sparked a great boom. This boom reached a peak in late 2008 and early 2009, when activist groups that had previously campaigned separately combined into an "Anti-Poverty Network" and organized a "Dispatch Workers' New

Year Village" in Hibiya Park, right in front of the Ministry of Health, Labor and Welfare. At Hibiya Park, unorganized workers gathered together for the first time, helping each other to organize, creating anew a social community in the form of a "village," and giving rise to a movement that directly confronted the state with the demand to heed the constitutionally guaranteed right to life. Kobayashi Takiji's theory of collective action continues to be valid in the twenty-first century.

DURING THE SECOND wave of repression directed against the Communist Party and its supporters known as the "April 16 Incident" of 1929, forty people were arrested in Otaru. Takiji himself was taken into custody on April 20 and his house searched. In September the Hokkaido Colonial Bank demoted Takiji from researcher to teller, and on November 16 he was fired. In March of 1930, Takiji moved from Otaru to Tokyo and became deeply involved in the activities of the Writers' League. From the middle of May, together with Eguchi Kiyoshi, Kishi Yamaji, Kataoka Teppei, and other writers, he took part in a lecture tour of Kyoto, Osaka, and Mie Prefecture to raise funds for the defense of the journal *The Battleflag*. Suspected of financially assisting the Communist Party, Takiji was arrested on May 23 by officers of the Shimanouchi police station in Osaka and kept in detention for two weeks, during which time he was tortured. On August 21, charged with violation of the Peace Preservation Law, Takiji was incarcerated at the Toyotama prison, and released on bail on January 22, 1931.

In July, having been elected member and secretary general of the standing central committee of the Writers' League, Takiji rented a house in Mabashi, in Tokyo's Suginami ward, sent for his mother from Hokkaido, and set up a household with her and his younger brother. From August 23 to October 31 he serialized his first newspaper novel, *A Portrait of New Women* (*Shin josei katagi*), in sixty-nine issues of *Miyako Shinbun*. This novel, whose title was later changed to *Yasuko*, was never suppressed and was published without a single word censored.

The narrative begins with a court scene in which Taguchi Sango, a poor tenant farmer and older brother to the sisters Okei and Yasuko, is sentenced to six months' imprisonment. A love triangle involving a girl named Kiyo has caused Sango to stab landlord Yoshimine's son, a fellow coordinator of the Sunada Village Young Men's Association. In the course of the investigation, a court officer closely questions Sango, insinuating that more was involved than resentment at having a girl taken away. "Didn't your hatred of him as your landlord also play a part?" The officer is trying to ascertain whether Sango had committed a simple criminal offense, or whether there was the possibility of a political offense.

At this point Sango recalls being told by a woman from his village—who with no land to till even as a tenant, lives as a day laborer and works in a "cheap noodle restaurant" in town—that "love affairs demand the luxury of free time." In order to pay overdue rent to the landlord, Sango had been toiling at all sorts of manual work to earn wages: performing hired labor, piling up gravel, cutting timber, digging irrigation ditches, and fishing for herring. Consequently, he does not possess "the luxury of free time" that he could devote to "love affairs." Under wretched conditions of employment, wage laborers cannot even have a love life. This fact exposes the exploitation and plunder that characterize the class relations between landlords and tenant farmers. Yet it had never occurred to Sango to demand a rent reduction from the landlord Yoshimine. When a strike of tenant farmers broke out in the neighboring village of Tsukigata, he had gone as coordinator of the Young Men's Association to conduct arbitration.

The person most dissatisfied with such a brother is his younger sister Yasuko. She was an excellent student and head of her class at a school attended by pupils from Sunada and Tsukigata villages, but she had been confronted with the reality that only a rich child can go on to a higher school. It stands to reason that when, in the course of the Tsukigata strike, night soil is thrown at the house of a landlord whose daughter is one of the group going on to middle school, Yasuko ends up dreaming that she herself had done it. Around the time that the rich children advance to middle school, Yasuko begins work at an eatery that is frequented by workers in Otaru's factory district.

A different experience makes her older sister Okei confront the reality of being a woman. While her brother is being interrogated,

Okei notices that "little Yamagami Yoshi," daughter of a family that lost the tenancy dispute in Tsukigata, has been arrested for engaging in prostitution to earn "one yen and fifty sen." A policeman tells her that with Yoshi's father punished for the strike and unable to find employment, the family is making a living with the money that the young woman brings in. As Okei wonders what kind of life lay ahead of her now that her brother was to be gone, she cannot help thinking that selling one's body might become a part of it.

When men who support a family by selling themselves as labor power become unable to sell that commodity, the only way for that family to survive is for its women to take on much cheaper forms of wage labor agonizingly close to prostitution. The only choices are working at an eatery or a cheap noodle restaurant, and after that, selling one's body. Okei and her mother, having been driven out of Sunada, move to Otaru where Yasuko is living. With the help of the owner of the restaurant where Yasuko works, Okei gets a job on a piecework basis at a pea-sorting factory where green peas are handpicked for export. As a wage laborer doing her best to support her mother, Okei works from six thirty in the morning until five in the evening to earn about seventy sen, or as much as one yen when she works until nine.

Meanwhile, Yasuko, who has been receiving an education about the labor movement from Yamada, the "union man" who comes to the eatery, is asked to persuade her sister to allow the room shared with their mother to be made available for clandestine meetings. Having permitted the union people to use the room, Okei comes to agree with Yamada's view that working-class women must be liberated from the "double chains" of men and capital. She is thrown into turmoil when she hears Yasuko's confession that she is "moving in" with Yamada and devoting herself full time to the union.

Yamada thinks that unless millions of women like Okei can be helped, the movement will not truly take root. As Okei tries to give Yamada and Yasuko's activities what support she can, she receives a declaration of love from Yamada's fellow activist Sasaki. While she tries to find a way to participate in the movement without abandoning life with her mother, the ensuing wholesale arrests throw the characters' relationships into chaos.

The novel *Yasuko* explores the whole range of literary subjects that Kobayashi Takiji had taken upon himself to pursue as a writer: state power and the legal system, criminal offenses and political offenses, resistance and slavery, cities and farming villages, class conflict and class consciousness, wage labor and prostitution, men and women, production and reproduction, spiritual love and sexual love, political consciousness and political practice. These subjects are delineated in the vivid changes taking place in Okei's body and mind, and they are constructed so that readers take them on as their own issues.

IN OCTOBER 1931, while in the process of completing *Yasuko,* Kobayashi Takiji joined the illegal Japanese Communist Party. The invasion of Manchuria, a vast region of northeast China, by the Japanese Kwantung Army was in full force. On January 28, 1932, the war of aggression expanded to Shanghai, and the puppet state of Manchukuo was "founded" on March 1. Between late March and May, two leading figures in the Japanese Proletarian Culture League, Kurahara Korehito and Nakano Shigeharu, were arrested. Around this time, Takiji supported a campaign to revoke the dismissal of temporary workers at Fujikura Industries in Gotanda, which would become the setting for *Life of a Party Member* (*Tōseikatsusha*). On April 3, after consulting with Miyamoto Kenji and other comrades, Takiji made the decision to engage in underground activities in order to rebuild the culture movement in the face of ever intensifying repression. Toward the middle of that month he married Itō Fujiko, who had helped to connect him with the workers at Fujikura. At the end of August, he completed *Life of a Party Member.*

In postwar Japanese society, this work became the basis for a negative evaluation of the novelist Kobayashi Takiji. Literary critic Hirano Ken charged that the treatment of "Kasahara" in this novel reflected the existence of a "housekeeper system," and that it revealed "a contempt for human beings whereby the end justified any means." Detecting within the text "the supremacy of politics" of the Japanese Communist Party, Hirano expanded his critique into a debate on "politics and literature." Critic Ara Masahito also condemned the "masked egoism" of the protagonist, who, lacking a "personal life of his own," was willing to sacrifice Kasahara for his causes.

Such criticism holds true only on the basis of a most peculiar premise: that among the novels by Kobayashi Takiji, a writer who did not use the "I-novel" technique that treats the author and the protagonist as one, only *Life of a Party Member* equates the protagonist with the author, and moreover makes the author identical with the organization that is the Japanese Communist Party. What cannot be overlooked, however, is that *Life of a Party Member* is structured in such a way that the first-person protagonist's narration is subjected to the criticism of other characters and relativized by their words.

In the course of a conversation between the first-person narrator/protagonist Sasaki Yasuji, a male comrade called Suyama, and a female comrade named Itō Yoshi, the talk turns to Itō's marriage. Suyama says, "I hear she's planning to wait till after the revolution. When our comrades marry, even though they're Marxists, a three-thousand-year-old consciousness still latent makes them try to turn Yoshi into a slave." To this, Itō icily retorts: "You're just making a confession about yourself!" It is here that an important theme of *Life of a Party Member* manifests itself.

A "slave" is an instrument capable of speech, whose human rights and liberties have all been stripped away, who under a master's rule and command performs compulsory labor without compensation, and who moreover is bought and sold as a commodity. Itō sees through to the desire concealed in the men's joking, and "with a chilly expression," rejects it. Though the change in her expression lasts only an instant, "I"-Sasaki does not miss it. Should we deal with our fellow human beings sympathetically as individuals like ourselves, or should we utilize them only as implements to serve our own desires? The very relations among the novel's characters pose this fundamental question to the "party members."

What is important is that the activities that "I," "Suyama," and "Itō" are engaged in within "Kurata Industries" constitute a movement demanding workers be treated not as implements, but as human beings who possess individuality and dignity. When the war against China began, the factory "stopped manufacturing the electric wires it had been making, and began to manufacture gas masks, parachutes, and airship fuselages." In view of the war's expansion, the hastily improvised war plant hires six hundred temporary workers and after supplying the army with the products, plans a mass dismissal of as many as four hundred. At this point, party members "I," "Suyama," and "Itō" move in, and while using the factory newspaper to protest the long hours and low wages that prevail at the plant, seek "to clarify the substance of imperialist war through everyday dissatisfactions."

Of course, war turns human beings into instruments of murder, namely soldiers, and suspends the enforcement of laws. The party members make it clear that a similar thing is occurring on the home front, too, right there at the factory. At first they try planting assistants in order to turn the words and human relations manifested in everyday conversations at the factory into instruments for the purpose of organizing the workers. One time, the "assistant" at a gathering of women workers remarks that under the present working conditions "we can't even whisper words of love!" and other voices chime in with "That's right" and "That's true!" As they continue, these voices begin to change into voices of human anger and demand: "Not that we can do much with the kind of daily wage we're getting!" "This company is heartless, and that's the truth!"

> Even Itō was surprised by this. Before she herself had noticed it, the talk of "whispering about love" had transformed itself into a discussion of the workers' treatment by the company. The "assistant," too, was astonished. Without any prodding, the conversation had turned into an attack on their maltreatment by the company.

The intent of the party members to try to turn words, logic, and women workers into instruments is completely overturned. The remark "we can't even *whisper words of love,*" deploying humor to denounce conditions that disavow human individuality and dignity, causes a shift in the logic by which the women workers themselves perceive those conditions. Through words that prompt them to recall that they are human beings endowed with individuality and dignity, the women workers acquire on their own the logic to denounce the company's treatment of people. The party members are astonished by this process.

Let's compare this scene with the one in which Kasahara has lost her job, and the narrator's life with her has reached a dead end. "I" proposes that she consider "becoming a café waitress." Kasahara, "not looking at me, her voice surprisingly calm and low," says "You mean, for the sake of your work, don't you?" And then she screams, "I'll do anything, I'll become a prostitute!" There is no question that Kasahara's outraged scream is a thoroughgoing criticism of the narrator. It is a denunciation of his regard for her only as an instrument, of his refusal of mutual understanding.

The word "sacrifice" that "I" uses in relation to Kasahara when he reflects "I, too, was sacrificing nearly my entire life" is in fact a central concept in the dispute between the company men and the party members over the collection of money for comfort packages to be sent to the front, and as such is positioned at a pivotal point in the novel. A reformist leader, who is using such money collecting as a screen for "Red hunting," points out that "on the factory floor our comrades were exploited by capitalists, but once on the battlefield, they are being sacrificed to enemy bullets." Therefore, given that soldiers were fellow workers, "collecting money for the comfort packages was a legitimate response."

Sacrifice denotes offering one's life for the benefit of others. The "enemy" having been established, it comes to mean that the soldiers at the battlefront are fighting for the people, in other words "for the whole nation." Itō and Suyama make it clear to everybody that such an assertion is nothing but "a trick to make us think" that something is true when in fact it is not. Suyama declares, "In every single situation, we are sacrificed for the benefit of the capitalists." He positions this question as "a turn from quantity to quality." What is being challenged is the quality—the actual substance—of "sacrifice": for whose benefit, and for the sake of what, are we to offer our lives? Furthermore, as "I" himself realizes, "we must conduct our struggle not through dogma, but through consent." Logic that concerns itself only with the quantity and greatness of sacrifice and ignores its substance is bound to lead to an affirmation of war. This is at the heart of the novel's criticism.

How Takiji might have developed the theme of the antiwar struggle in relation to solidarity that insists on human dignity and individuality can never be known. The text as we have it concludes with the words "End of Part One" and a dedication to "Comrade Kurahara Korehito." Takiji was tortured to death at the Tsukiji police station in Tokyo on February 20, 1933. His novel was published in the April and May issues of the magazine *Central Review* under the title *Tenkan jidai* (*Times of Change*), for there was no way that Takiji's preferred title could be printed under the circumstances. As it was, the handwritten manuscript, comprising 80 pages of 400 characters each, was censored in 758 places, with nearly 14,000 characters suppressed.

The editorial postscript to the April issue of *Central Review* contains the following words: "In our literary section, we are publishing a posthumous masterpiece by Kobayashi Takiji, a leading light among our country's creators of working-class literature! As we remember Takiji's years of hard struggle and his heartbreaking death, it is precisely this interrupted work that we regard as his truly monumental achievement."

THE CRAB CANNERY SHIP

1

"BUDDY, WE'RE OFF TO HELL!"

Leaning over the deck railing, two fishermen looked out on the town of Hakodate stretched like a snail embracing the sea. One of them spit out a cigarette he had smoked down to his fingertips. The stub fell skimming the tall side of the ship, turning playfully every which way. The man reeked of liquor.

Steamships with red bulging bellies rose from the water; others being loaded with cargo leaned hard to one side as if tugged down by the sea. There were thick yellow smokestacks, large bell-like buoys, launches scurrying like bedbugs among ships. Bleak whirls of oil soot, scraps of bread, and rotten fruit floated on the waves as if forming some special fabric. Blown by the wind, smoke drifted over waves wafting a stifling smell of coal. From time to time a harsh rattle of winches traveling along the waves reverberated against the flesh.

Directly in front of the crab cannery ship *Hakkōmaru* rested a sailing ship with peeling paint, its anchor chain lowered from a hole in its bow that looked like an ox's nostril. Two foreign sailors with pipes in mouth paced the deck back and forth like automatons. The ship seemed to be Russian. No doubt it was a patrol vessel sent to keep an eye on the Japanese cannery ship.

"I don't have a damned penny left. Shit, look." One of the fishermen moved closer to the other, gripped his hand and pressed it against the pocket of the corduroy trousers beneath his jacket. The pocket seemed to contain a small box.

The other man silently watched his mate's face.

"He, he, he," chuckled the first man. "They're cards."

The ship's captain was smoking a cigarette and strolling along the deck like an admiral. The smoke he exhaled broke into sharp angles as it passed the tip of his nose, and flew away in shreds. Sailors dragging wooden-soled *zōri* were bustling in and out of the forward cabins, food pails in hand. Preparations had been completed and the ship was ready to sail.

The two fishermen, peering down through the hatch into workers' quarters in the dim bottom of the ship, saw a noisy commotion inside the stacked bunks, like a nest full of birds' darting faces. The workers were all boys of fourteen or fifteen.

"Where're you from?"

"X District."

They were all children from Hakodate's slums. Poverty had brought them together.

"What about the guys in the bunks over there?"

"They're from Nambu."

"And those?"

"Akita." Each cluster of bunks belonged to a different region.

"Where in Akita?"

"North Akita." The boy's nose was running with thick, oozing mucus, and the rims of his eyes were inflamed and drooping.

"You farmers?"

"Yeah."

The air was stifling, filled with the sour stench of rotten fruit.

Dozens of barrels of pickled vegetables were stored next door, adding their own shit-like odor.

"From now on you can sleep hugging your old Dad here," smiled the fisherman lewdly.

In a dim corner, a mother was peeling an apple for her son who lay prone on his bunk. The mother wore a triangular scarf and a laborer's jacket and trousers. She watched the child eat the apple, and ate the spiral peeling. While talking to him, the mother kept untying and retying a small cloth-wrapped package that lay next to her child. There were seven or eight mothers. Children from the main island whom no one had come to see off stole occasional glances in their direction.

A woman took caramels out of a box and handed two each to the nearby children, saying, "You be good to my Kenkichi, and work together like friends." The woman's hair and clothes were covered with cement dust. Her hands were ungainly, large and rough like roots of a tree.

Other mothers were blowing their children's noses, wiping their faces with hand towels, and talking to them in subdued voices.

"Your boy looks so strong," said one of the mothers.

"I guess."

"Mine's so weakly. Wish I could do something . . ."

"We're all worried."

With some relief, the two fishermen drew their faces back from the hatch. Suddenly mute, they returned sullenly to their trapezoid-shaped "nest" situated closer to the prow than the hole that held the workers. With each rise and fall of the anchor everyone in the nest was tossed up and then thrown together, as if dumped into a concrete mixer.

In the dim interior, fishermen lay about like pigs. The nauseating stench itself was that of a pigsty.

"Damn, it stinks here!"

"It sure does, thanks to us."

A fisherman whose head resembled a red mortar was pouring sake from a half-gallon bottle into a chipped teacup. He munched on a cuttlefish as he drank. Next to him a man lay on his back eating an apple and looking through a pulp magazine with a torn cover.

Four men sat drinking in a circle. A man who hadn't yet had enough to drink wedged himself among them.

"Damn, we're going to be at sea for four frigging months. I knew I'd have no chance to get laid so . . ." The sturdily built man licked his thick lower lip and narrowed his eyes. He raised a shrunken money-pouch that looked like a dried persimmon and swung it at eye level. "Look at my wallet. That widow might be a skinny little slut but she sure knows how to fuck!"

"Hey, just shut up about that!"

"No, no, we want to hear."

The man laughed merrily.

"Look at those two over there. Isn't that a sight for sore eyes?" A drunken man pointed with his chin, fixing his bleary eyes on a bunk directly across. A fisherman was handing money over to his wife. "Look at that!"

The two had laid out crumpled banknotes and silver coins on a small box, and were counting them. The man was writing something in a small notebook, repeatedly licking his pencil.

"For crying out loud, can you believe that?"

"I got a wife and kids myself!" growled the fisherman who had spent his money on the prostitute.

A young fisherman spoke up loudly from a bunk a little way off. His face was swollen with a hangover and his hair hung long over his forehead. "I thought I wouldn't set foot on a ship this time. But I got a runaround from the employment agency and ended up penniless. They'll keep me at this till I drop dead."

A man with his back to him, evidently from the same region, whispered something to him.

A pair of bowlegs appeared at the top of the cabin stairs, and a man shouldering a large old-fashioned cloth bag came down the steps. His eyes darted around. Spotting an empty bunk he climbed into it.

"Hullo," he said, bowing to the man next to him. "I'll be joining you." His face was oily and black, as if dyed with a dark substance.

Later on, they were to learn the following story about this man. Shortly before coming on board, he had been working as a miner at the Yūbari coal mine and had almost got killed in a recent gas explosion. Similar things had happened many times before, but this time the miner had suddenly grown frightened and quit the mine. At the time of the explosion, he had been at work pushing a coal car along the rails. He had loaded the car with coal and was shoving it toward a man at a relay station when it happened. He thought that a hundred magnesium flares had burst before his eyes at once. In a fraction of a second he felt his body float up into the air like a scrap of paper. Several coal cars blown by the blast flew past his eyes more lightly than matchboxes. That was the last thing he knew. After some time, the sound of his own groans woke him up. Foremen and miners were building a wall across the shaft to keep the flames from spreading. At that moment he clearly heard other coal miners' voices from beyond the wall, pleading for help. Their cries tore unforgettably into his heart. There was still time to rescue them! He suddenly rose, jumped into the middle of his comrades, and began madly to scream, "Stop, stop!" (In the past he too had built such walls, but it hadn't bothered him then.)

"You damned idiot! If the fire gets to us, we're dead."

Couldn't they hear the voices growing fainter and fainter? Hardly knowing what he was doing, he began to run frantically along the mineshaft, waving his arms and crying out. He stumbled and fell countless times, struck his head against overhead beams, grew soaked with mud and blood. Finally he tripped over a railway tie, somersaulted like a thrown wrestler, and crashed against the tracks, losing consciousness.

Hearing the miner's story, a young fisherman said, "Well, things are not much better here either . . ."

The miner gazed at him with the yellowish, lusterless eyes common among people who toil underground, and said nothing.

Some of the "fishermen farmers" from Akita, Aomori, and Iwate sat around with legs loosely crossed, arms akimbo, ignoring everyone. The rest leaned against pillars, hugging their knees, innocently watching others drink and listening attentively to their idle chatter. The task of feeding their families, impossible despite working in the fields from before dawn, had forced them to come here. They had left the oldest sons behind, still short of food, and sent the daughters to work in factories. Even the second and third sons had to go somewhere to work. Masses of such surplus people, like beans scooped up in a pan, were driven away from the countryside and flowed into the cities. All of them dreamed of saving up a bit of money and returning home. But once they began to work—in Hakodate, Otaru, and other cities—they struggled like fledglings trapped in sticky rice-cake until they were thrown out of work as stark naked as the day they were born. They could not go home again. To survive the winter in snowy Hokkaido where they had no relatives, they had to "sell" their bodies as cheaply as dirt. Though they had done it over and over, they would calmly (if such a word is appropriate) do the same again the following year.

Three people now entered the workers' quarters: a woman with a box of sweet bean-jam buns on her back, a druggist, and a peddler who sold small daily necessities. They spread out their respective wares in the center of the cabin, in a place marked off like an outlying island. The workers in all the surrounding bunks, high and low, leaned forward to joke and tease.

"Got something sweet for me, honey?"

"Hey, what're you doing?!" The woman jumped up with a scream. "Don't grab my butt, you pervert!"

The man, embarrassed at drawing everyone's eyes to himself, roared with laughter. "This here woman's a real sweetie," he mumbled through a mouthful of sweets.

A passing drunk, tottering back from the toilet with one hand holding onto the bulkhead, poked the woman's plump sunburned cheek with his finger.

"What do you want?!"

"Don't get all sore. . . . I just want to get hold of you and show you a good time," he clowned, to general laughter.

"Hey," shouted someone loudly from a distant corner. "Hurry up and get me those buns!"

"Coming right up!" The woman—a rarity in such a place—replied in a clear, penetrating voice. "How many would you like?"

"How many would I like? How the hell many do you have? Just get your buns over here!"

Everybody burst out laughing.

"The other day a guy called Takeda dragged that woman someplace there was nobody around," said a young drunk man. "It was so funny. No matter how hard he tried, he couldn't get anywhere with her. She was wearing drawers, so Takeda ripped them off with all his might. But there was another pair underneath. Would you believe it, she was wearing three pairs!" The man shrugged and began to laugh.

This man worked in a factory during winter, making rubber boots. When he lost his job in the spring, he went to work in Kamchatka. Because both jobs were "seasonal work" (as was nearly all work in Hokkaido), whenever there was night work it went on without a break. "I'll be thankful if I can live on for another three years." His skin was the lifeless color of coarse rubber.

Among the company of fishermen there were some from Hokkaido's cultivated interior, others who had been sold into railway construction, wanderers who had gone broke in countless places, and still others who were content so long as they could just get enough to drink. Mixed among them were also farmers from around Aomori who had been chosen by worthy village heads and were honest and ignorant as tree roots. It was highly convenient for the employers to assemble such a crew of unorganized migrant workers. (Hakodate's labor unions were desperately trying to place organizers on crab cannery ships and among the fishermen who were heading to Kamchatka. The Hakodate unions were connected with the Aomori and Akita unions. This sort of thing worried bosses the most.)

A cabin boy in a gleaming-white starched jacket stepped busily in and out of the saloon called "Friends," carrying beer, fruit, and glasses of foreign liquor. The saloon was filled with corporate honchos, the cannery ship's captain, the manager, the commander of the destroyer charged with keeping an eye on Kamchatka, the chief of the maritime police, and one or two walking briefcases from the seamen's union.

"Sons of bitches are drinking their heads off," said the cabin boy sulkily.

The fishermen's shit-hole was lit by feeble electric lights. Its air was thick with tobacco smoke and the odor of crowded human bodies; the entire cabin stank like a toilet. People moving about in their bunks looked like squirming maggots. With the fishing company's manager leading the way, the ship's captain, the factory agent, and the foreman came down the hatchway stairs. The captain kept patting his upper lip with a handkerchief, fretting about the tips of his upturned moustache. The passageway was strewn with discarded apple and banana skins, a crushed hat, straw sandals, and wrappers stuck with grains of rice. It was one clogged gutter. The manager glanced around, and unceremoniously spat. The visitors all seemed drunk, their faces flushed red.

"I'd like to say a word," declared the manager. He had the powerful build of a construction worker. Placing one foot on a partition between bunks, he maneuvered a toothpick inside his mouth, at times briskly ejecting bits of food stuck between his teeth.

"Needless to say, as some of you may know, this crab cannery ship's business is not just to make lots of money for the corporation but is actually a matter of the greatest international importance. This is a one-on-one fight between us, citizens of a great empire, and the Russkies, a battle to find out which one of us is greater—them or us. Now just supposing you lose—this could never happen, but if it did—all Japanese men and boys who've got any balls at all would slit their bellies and jump into the sea off Kamchatka. You may be small in size but that doesn't mean you'll let those stupid Russkies beat you.

"Another thing, our fishing industry off Kamchatka is not just about canning crabs and salmon and trout, but internationally speaking it's also about keeping up the superior status of our nation, which no other country can match. And moreover, we're accomplishing an important mission in regard to our domestic problems like overpopulation and shortage of food. You probably have no idea what I'm talking about, but anyhow I'll have you know that we'll be risking our lives cutting through those rough northern waves to carry out a great mission for the Japanese empire. And that's why our imperial warship will accompany us and protect us all along the way. . . . Anyone who acts up trying to ape this recent Russky craze, anyone who incites others to commit outrageous acts, is nothing but a traitor to the Japanese empire. And though something like that could never happen, make damned sure all the same that what I'm saying to you gets through to your heads . . ."

The manager sneezed repeatedly as he began sobering up.

THE DESTROYER'S INTOXICATED captain, stepping jerkily like a spring-loaded marionette, tottered down the gangway to a waiting launch. Supporting the skipper from above and below as if he were a canvas bag filled with rocks, sailors barely managed to get him on board. The captain was waving his arms, bracing his legs, shouting random nonsense, and repeatedly spraying the sailors' faces with saliva.

"Always making fancy speeches," murmured a sailor, glancing at the captain while untying the rope from the gangway, "and look at the sorry sack now."

"Do we toss him overboard!? . . ."

The two caught their breath for a moment . . . and then simultaneously burst into laughter.

2

Far off to the right the light of the Shukutsu lighthouse, flashing each time it revolved, penetrated the gray expanse of sea-like fog. Its long and distant silvery beam swept mystically for miles around as it pivoted.

Off the coast of Rumoi a thin, drizzly rain began to fall. Fishermen's and laborers' hands grew numb as crab claws as they worked, forcing them to thrust them occasionally into their pockets, or to cup them over their mouths and blow on them. Endless threads of brown viscous rain fell into an opaque sea of the same color. As the ship neared Wakkanai, raindrops turned into grains, the sea's broad surface began to wave like a flag, to swell, and to grow jagged and restless. Wind struck at the masts with an ominous howl. The ship creaked endlessly as though its rivets were coming loose. Entering the Sōya Strait, this vessel of nearly three thousand tons began to move jerkily as if seized by a fit of hiccups. Hoisted high by a wonderful force the ship floated in space for a moment only to sink abruptly to its original position. Each time this happened it triggered a disagreeably ticklish sensation, an urge to urinate such as one experiences at the instant an elevator drops. Workers wilted, their eyes looked unhappy and seasick, and they vomited.

The hard outline of the snowy mountains of Karafuto could be glimpsed now and then through the round porthole windows streaked with spraying waves. But the sight was soon obscured by swelling waves that rose like icy alpine peaks. Deep cold valleys formed and rushed up to the portholes, crashing against them and breaking up into torrents of foam, then flowing away, sliding past the windows like a diorama. From time to time the ship's entire body shuddered like a feverish child. All sorts of objects fell smashing from shelves, things bent and squealed, the ship's sides boomed colliding with the waves. The constant throb of the motors ringing out from the engine room transmitted its vibrations through the motley utensils and sent mild tremors through bodies. Sometimes the ship rode the back of a wave, making the propeller spin in the air and stabilizer fins slap at the water's surface.

The wind continued to grow stronger and stronger. The two masts whistled and kept bending like fishing poles. The waves, like a band of rampaging thugs, swarmed unopposed from one side of the ship to the other. The cabin's hatchway abruptly turned into a torrential waterfall.

Mountains of water rose up in a flash lifting the ship like a toy to the top of a huge slope and turning it slightly sideways. Tumbling forward, the ship pitched to the bottom of the ravine. It was sure to sink! But in the depths of the valley a new wave heaved up high, slamming with a thud against the sides of the ship.

As the ship reached the Sea of Okhotsk, the color of the water became a clearer gray. The chilling cold penetrated the laborers' clothing and turned their lips blue as they worked. The colder it became, the more furiously a fine snow, dry as salt, blew whistling against them. Like tiny shards of glass, the snow pierced faces and hands of the laborers and fishermen who worked on all fours on the deck. After each wave washed over them, the water promptly froze, making the deck treacherously slippery. The men had to stretch ropes from deck to deck, and work dangling from them like diapers hung out on a clothesline. The manager, armed with a club for killing salmon, was roaring like mad.

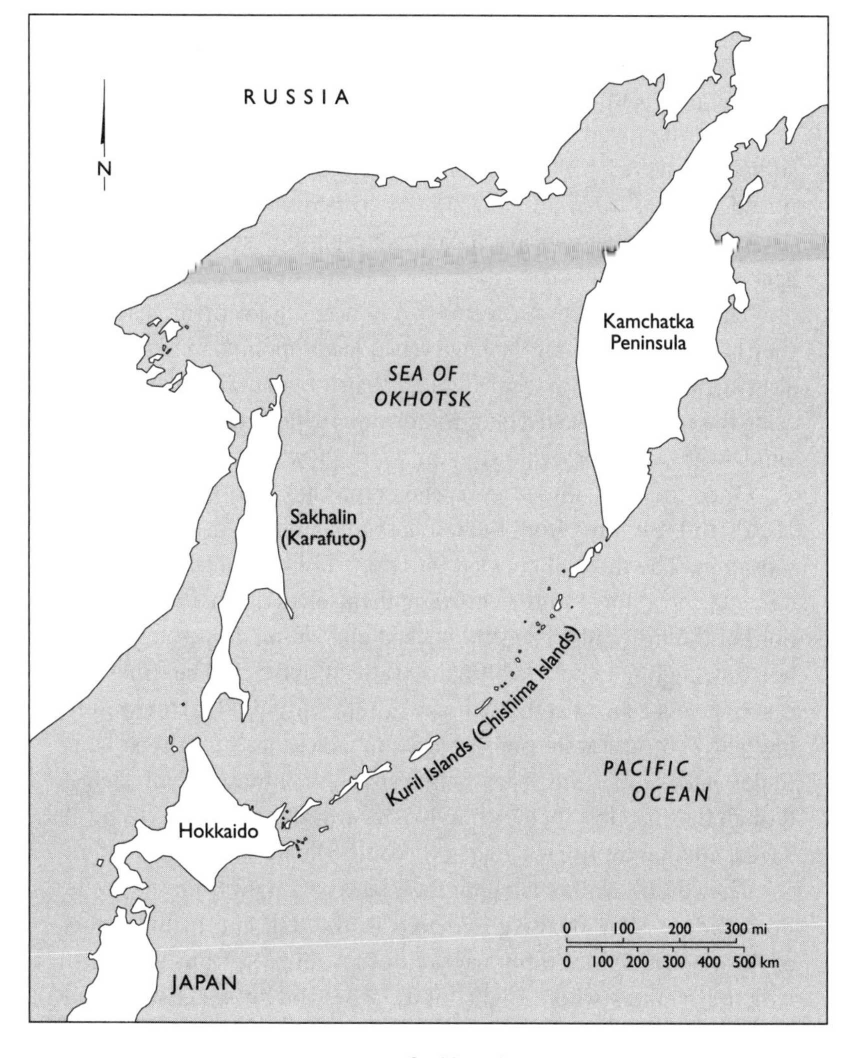

Sea of Okhotsk

Another crab cannery ship that had sailed out of Hakodate at the same time had gotten separated from them. Even so, whenever their ship surged to the summit of a mountainous wave, two masts could be seen swaying back and forth in the distance like the waving arms of a drowning person. Wisps of smoke torn by the wind flew by skimming the waves. Intermittent howls of the other ship's whistle were clearly audible amid the waves and shouts. Yet the next instant one ship rose high and the other fell away into the depths of a watery crevasse.

The crab cannery ship carried eight fishing boats. The sailors and fishermen were forced to risk their lives tying down the boats so that the waves, baring their white teeth like thousands of sharks, would not tear them off. "Losing one or two of you won't matter a damn, but if a boat gets lost it can't get replaced," shouted the manager distinctly.

The sea of Kamchatka seemed to be waiting for them, surprised they had made it this far. Its huge waves leapt upon them like greedy, starving lions. The ship seemed frailer than a rabbit. The blizzard covering the entire sky looked like an enormous white flag billowing in the wind. Night was approaching but the storm showed no signs of abating.

Once the work ended everyone crept back into their shit-hole. Hands and feet hung from bodies like radishes, frozen and devoid of sensation. The men all crawled into their bunks like silkworms, no one uttering a single word. Throwing themselves down, they grabbed hold of the iron rails. The ship bucked and shook desperately, like a horse struggling to drive a biting horsefly off its back. The fishermen cast hopeless glances at the ceiling whose white paint had turned yellow with soot, and at the bluish-black portholes that were almost sunk underwater. Some gazed blankly into space, their mouths half open as though they had lost their minds. No one was thinking of anything. A dazed, anxious awareness made everyone sullenly silent.

They drank whisky lying on their backs, straight from the bottle. Bottle edges occasionally glimmered in the dull and turbid amber of the electric light. Empty whisky bottles, thrown from the bunks with the drinkers' whole might, hit the aisles and burst like successive bolts of lightning. Other men merely turned their heads to follow the bottles with their eyes. Someone was angrily shouting in a corner.

Broken up by the storm, the words came through as incoherent fragments.

"Guess we've left Japan," said someone wiping the porthole window with a sleeve.

The shit-hole stove merely sputtered and smoked. Barely alive human beings shivered with cold as though they'd been mistaken for salmon and trout and thrown into a refrigerator. Great waves splashed thunderously, sweeping across the canvas-covered hatchway. The reverberation of each blow within the shit-hole's iron walls was as deafening as the inside of a drum. At times heavy thuds rang out directly beside the sprawling fishermen, like mighty shoves from a powerful shoulder. Now the ship was writhing within the sea-storm's raging waves like a whale in its death agonies.

"Chowtime!" The cook stuck his torso into the doorway and shouted encircling his mouth with both hands. "No soup 'cause of the storm."

"What'd he say?"

"We're serving rotten salted fish!" The cook withdrew his face.

They struggled to their feet as best they could, like convicts seized by a voracious craving for food.

Sitting cross-legged and placing plates of salted fish across their legs, they blew against the steam, filled their cheeks with hot bits of fish, and rolled them around inside their mouths. The food was the first hot object they had been near all day, and their noses kept running, threatening to drip into the dishes. They were still eating when the manager walked in.

"Stop swilling it like pigs, damn it. You couldn't even do a decent day's work, and now you think you can stuff yourselves?" He glowered at the upper and lower bunks before strutting out of the cabin, his left shoulder swinging forward as he walked.

"What the hell gives him the right to talk to us like that," mumbled a former student, a youth gaunt with seasickness and overwork.

"That Asakawa acts like he owns the ship."

"The Emperor is up above the clouds so he can do whatever he likes, but Asakawa better not think that he can do the same."

"You stingy fucker, like you give a shit about a bowl or two of rice! Let's kick his ass!" shouted someone furiously.

"Wonderful, wonderful! Say the same thing in front of Asakawa, and it'll be even more wonderful!"

Though they were still angry, everyone laughed.

It was quite late at night when the manager, wearing a raincoat, stepped into the quarters where the fishermen were sleeping. Holding on to the bunk frames to steady himself against the ship's tossing, he walked through the aisles with a lantern. Sleepers' heads rolled from side to side like pumpkins. Rudely turning each face toward him, the manager shone the light on it. They would not wake up even if he stepped on them. Done with his inspection, the manager paused and clicked his tongue. He seemed puzzled but soon went on to the galley. With each sway of the lantern, the fan-like bluish shaft of light flickered over segments of the squalid bunks, tall waterproof boots, hanging jackets, and wicker trunks. Then the light moved on, trembled at his feet, stopped for a moment, and shifted the circle of its round projector-like beam onto the door of the galley. The next morning the men found out that one of the workers was missing.

Recalling the previous day's horrendous work, everyone concluded that the man had been swept away by the waves. It made them feel awful. They were forced to resume work before dawn and had no chance to talk about it.

"Who the hell would jump into that freezing water? He's hiding someplace, that's where he is. I'll beat the living crap out of that son of a bitch when I find him." The manager searched through the ship, twirling his club like a toy.

The storm had passed its peak. Even so, each time the ship plowed into a swelling wave, the water swept over the foredeck as effortlessly as if stepping over a threshold. Looking badly wounded by a day and night of struggle the ship made an oddly limping sound as it advanced. Clouds resembling thin smoke drifted so low they seemed within a hand's reach, struck the masts, broke into sharp angles and blew away. A chilling rain continued to fall. With each rise in the surrounding angry waves, the pouring rain could be clearly seen pelting the sea. It felt more eerie than being lost in a rainstorm in a primeval forest.

Hemp ropes were hard and cold to the touch, like iron pipes. While cautiously crossing the deck and clutching the rope to keep from slipping, the student met the cabin boy who had come bounding up the gangway ladder two steps at a time.

"Come here a minute," said the cabin boy, pulling him into a corner out of the wind. "I got something interesting to tell you."

It was around two in the morning. Waves were leaping thunderously onto the deck at regular intervals and pouring like waterfalls. At times the waves' bared teeth shone bluish-white in the darkness. No one could sleep because of the storm. That was when it happened.

The radio operator had rushed into the captain's cabin.

"Captain, sir, awful news. We have an SOS!"

"SOS? Which ship?!"

"It's the *Chichibumaru*. They were running parallel to us."

"That's a leaking old tub, that one!" Asakawa, still wearing his oilskin raincoat, sat in a corner straddling a chair with his legs wide apart. Mindlessly tapping the floor with a tip of his shoe, he chuckled. "Of course, all the other ships are just the same."

"They sound desperate, sir."

"Hmm, this is very bad." In his hurry to get up to the bridge, the captain reached for the door without bothering to put on his coat. He was about to open it when Asakawa grabbed his right shoulder.

"Who gave the order to change course and waste time?"

Who gave the order? The captain would give it, of course. For a moment the captain looked dumbfounded, yet he swiftly recovered. "I will, as captain."

"As captain? You don't say!" exclaimed the manager with rising contempt, blocking the captain's way. "Who the hell do you think owns this ship, eh? The corporation chartered it, and is paying for it. The company agent Mr. Suda and I myself are the only ones who've got anything to say here. As for you, you may act big calling yourself captain but you're worth less than the shithouse paper. You got that? If we bothered with things like that worthless ship, we'd lose a whole week. Screw that! I'm not going to be even a day behind! Plus, *Chichibumaru*'s insured for a lot more money than the damned thing's worth. If that tub sinks, it'll actually turn a profit."

"Now we're in for a terrific fight!" thought the cabin boy. No way was this going to be the end of it. But the captain stood motionless and mute as though his throat had been stuffed with cotton. Never before had the cabin boy seen him look like this. Damn, it just couldn't happen that the captain wouldn't have the last word! Yet it was happening. No matter how hard he tried, the cabin boy couldn't understand it.

"International competition is never going to be won by acting nice, and you got no business sticking your nose into this!" The manager twisted his lips hard, and spat.

In the radio room, the receiver kept on transmitting signals, sometimes giving off little bluish-white sparks. Everyone crowded into the radio room to see what was happening.

"They're really keeping it up. Signals have gotten faster," explained the radio operator to the captain and manager who were looking over his shoulder. Everyone's eyes were riveted on the radio operator's fingertips, following their nimble moves over the switches and buttons of the wireless. They all stood still, unconsciously tensing their shoulders and jaws.

With each roll of the ship, the light that was precariously affixed to the bulkhead glowed and dimmed. The thud of the waves pounding against the ship's flanks and the constant ominous hoot of the foghorn sounded through the iron doors, sometimes receding on the wind and sometimes approaching directly overhead.

Sparks scattered with a crackle, leaving long tails. Then the sound abruptly stopped. At once everyone's heart gave a jolt. The operator frantically twirled the knobs, anxiously prodding the apparatus to work. But nothing more was heard. The tapping had stopped.

The operator swiveled around in his chair.

"They've sunk . . . ," he said, taking off the headset, and quietly adding, "'Crew of four hundred and twenty five. It's all over. No chance of rescue. SOS, SOS'—they sent this message two or three times, and then the signal broke off."

At his words the captain thrust his hand under his collar, shook his head as if suffocating, and tried to stretch his neck. Casting a blank gaze all around, he turned toward the door. Then he pressed his hand against his chest, close to the knot of his necktie. The cabin boy could not bear to look at him.

"I SEE," SAID the student. The story amazed him. Yet it filled him with a dark feeling, and he averted his eyes from the sea. The sea was still heaving with great swells. Just when the horizon was about to sink underfoot, the ship would be dragged down till the sky looked as narrow as it might from the bottom of a valley.

"I guess it must have really sunk," he said to himself. It troubled him to no end. And it infuriated him that the ship they themselves were riding was not a bit more seaworthy.

Crab cannery ships were all old and battered. It didn't matter a damn to executives in some building in Tokyo's financial district that workers were dying in the northern Sea of Okhotsk. Once capitalism's quest for profits in its usual places comes to a deadlock, then interest rates drop, excess money piles up, and capital will literally do anything and go anywhere in a frenzied search for a way out. Given those circumstances it was no wonder that capital's profit-seekers fell in love with the crab cannery ships, each one able to bring in countless hundreds of thousands of yen.

Crab cannery ships were considered factories, not ships. Therefore maritime law did not apply to them. Ships that had been tied up for twenty years and were good for nothing but scrap iron, vessels as battered as tottering syphilitics, were given a shameless cosmetic makeover and brought to Hakodate. Hospital ships and military transports that had been "honorably" crippled in the Russo-Japanese War and abandoned like fish guts turned up in port looking more faded than ghosts. If steam was turned up a little, pipes whistled and burst. When they put on speed while chased by Russian patrol boats, the ships began to creak all over as though about to come apart at any moment, and shook like palsied men.

But none of that mattered in the least, for this was a time when it was everyone's duty to stand tall for the Japanese Empire. Moreover the crab cannery ships were factories pure and simple. And yet factory laws did not apply to them either. Consequently, no other site offered such an accommodating setting for management's freedom to act with total impunity.

Brilliant executives wedded such work to "the interests of the Japanese Empire." That way, fabulous sums of money rolled wholesale into executive pockets. Even so, while enjoying a drive in their automobiles these moneymen contemplated running for the Diet in order to make their bets doubly certain. And perhaps at the very same moment, in the dark northern seas thousands of miles away, the workers of the *Chichibumaru* were fighting their final struggle against the wind and the waves that were sharp as broken glass!

"This is not somebody else's problem," thought the student as he walked down the gangway toward the shit-hole. Directly at the bottom of the ladder a piece of paper had been stuck to the bulkhead with grains of boiled rice used instead of glue. The lumpy, clumsily written note read:

> To all hands: anyone who finds Miyaguchi wins two packs of *Golden Bat* smokes and a hand towel.
>
> MANAGER ASAKAWA

3

A misty rain went on drizzling for days. Obscured by the haze, the Kamchatka coastline was stretching out smoothly like an eel.

The *Hakkōmaru* dropped anchor four nautical miles offshore. Russian territorial waters extended for three nautical miles, and it was forbidden to enter them.

Nets were ready, and all preparations for crab fishing had been made. Dawn breaks around two in Kamchatka and so the fishermen, fully dressed and wearing hip-high rubber boots, were dozing in wooden boxes.

"It wasn't supposed to be like this," grumbled a student who had been tricked by an employment agency. "They told us we'd each get to sleep alone!"

"To *sleep* alone, sure. This is dozing."

There were seventeen or eighteen students. Having decided to borrow a sixty-yen advance on their pay, they had been charged train fees, lodging fees, blankets, bedding, and agency fees, so that by the time they reached the ship every one of them had ended up seven or eight yen in debt. When this first dawned on them, they felt more astonished than if the money they thought they clutched in their hands had turned into withered leaves before their very eyes. At first they clung to each other among the fishermen, like dead souls surrounded by blue and red demons.

Four days after sailing out of Hakodate, the students all grew sick from the daily diet of wretched food and unchanging soup. Suspecting beriberi, they lay in their bunks flexing their knees and pressing each other's shins with their fingers to see if excess fluid had accumulated beneath the skin. They did this over and over, their mood briefly brightening when the probing fingers did not sink in, and darkening when they did.

Two or three students felt their legs go numb, as though mildly shocked with electricity, whenever they stroked them. Letting their legs dangle from the bunks, they tested their reflexes by hitting each others' kneecaps with the edge of their hands. To make things even worse, they became constipated for four or five days at a stretch. One of the students went to the doctor to get a laxative. He came back pale with anger. "No such fancy medicine here, he says."

"That's a ship's doctor for you," said an old fisherman who was listening nearby.

"Doctors are the same everywhere. The one at my company was no different," said the fisherman who had worked in a mine.

Everyone was lying down when the manager walked in.

"Everybody taking it easy, I see. Listen up. We got a radio report that the *Chichibumaru* sank. Seems they don't know who lived or died." He twisted his lips and spat, as was his habit.

The student immediately recalled the cabin boy's words. This goddamned manager, he thought, could talk so calmly about the lives of four or five hundred workers whom he had as good as murdered with his own hands! Throwing the son of a bitch into the sea would be too good for him. Everyone raised their swollen faces. Excited talk erupted all around. Asakawa said nothing more but strode out, swinging his left shoulder forward.

The worker who had disappeared was caught while coming out of his hiding place next to the boiler. He had stayed hidden for two days but unbearable hunger finally drove him out. It was an older fisherman who nabbed him. An angry young fisherman threatened to beat the hell out of the old man.

"The annoying young fuck," said the old fisherman, blissfully smoking a cigarette from the packs he had won as a reward. "Doesn't even smoke so what's he know about the taste of tobacco."

The manager stripped the worker down to his shirt, shoved him into one of two adjacent toilets, and locked him up. At first everyone hated going to the toilet. They could not bear listening to the cries next door. On the second day the cries grew hoarse with a cold. Then they grew intermittent. At the end of that day a worried fisherman headed for the toilet directly after work but the pounding from the inside had stopped. Though he tapped on the door from the outside there was no response. Later on Miyaguchi was discovered lying prone with one hand leaning against the toilet and his head in the box of toilet paper. His lips were the dead color of blue ink.

The morning was cold. It had grown bright though it was still only three o'clock. They all got up, hunching over and thrusting numb hands into pockets. The manager went from cabin to cabin dragging out workers, fishermen, sailors, and stokers, not caring in the least whether they had a cold or were sick.

Although there was no wind, working on deck made hands and feet as bereft of sensation as wooden pestles. The foreman, cursing at the top of his voice, herded fourteen or fifteen workers into the factory. The tip of the bamboo stave he carried had strips of leather attached to it. Its length allowed him to reach out and strike an idle worker even if he was standing on the opposite side of the machines.

"When they got Miyaguchi out last night he was barely alive and couldn't say a thing, and this morning they're saying he's got to work, and they were kicking him just now," said a delicately built worker who had grown friendly with the students. He cast glances at the foreman as he spoke. "He didn't move at all so in the end they seemed to give up."

Just then the manager came up, prodding a feverishly trembling worker from behind. Having been forced to work in the cold rain, the worker had caught a cold which turned into pleurisy. He was constantly shivering, even when it wasn't cold. He looked like a sick child, his young face marred by furrows etched between his eyebrows. His thin bloodless lips were strangely twisted. He had been found pacing about the boiler room, unable to put up with the cold.

The fishermen who were lowering the boats using winches followed the two mutely with their eyes. A fisherman in his forties looked away as if unable to watch, and shook his head in disgust.

"We didn't spend all that money bringing you here just so you catch colds and stay sulking in bed. Quit gawking at what's none of your business, you sons of bitches!" The manager banged his club against the deck.

"If hell's any worse than this, better be sure never to go there!"

"When we tell people back home about this, they'll never believe us."

"Damn right, they won't. There's nothing like seeing it with your own eyes."

The steam-powered winches started to rattle and turn. The boats began simultaneously to descend, swaying in space. The sailors and stokers who had been rounded up were running about on the slippery deck, trying hard not to fall. The manager strode watchfully among them like a bristling rooster.

Taking advantage of a break in the work, the students sat down behind some cargo to get a moment of relief from the wind. Just then the fisherman who had been a miner came around a corner, blowing on his hands to warm them.

"They're trying to kill us!" His sudden, piercing words struck at the students' hearts. "Hell, this is no different than working in a mine. Seems like you can't hardly live without dying while you're at it. Sure, gas is scary but so are these damned waves."

In the afternoon, the sky subtly changed. It grew covered with an expanse of mist so thin and light as to be nearly invisible. Countless triangular waves stirred up, like raised squares of cloth. Wind suddenly began to whistle past the masts. Edges of canvas sheets that covered the cargo started to slap against the deck.

"Rabbits are flying! Hey, it's the rabbits!" someone called out loudly, running toward the starboard deck. The voice, instantly shredded by the wind, sounded like a meaningless shout.

Triangular waves topped with white spray were speeding across the entire surface of the sea, like countless rabbits flying across a great plain. This was the harbinger of a Kamchatka gale. The flow of the tide suddenly accelerated. The ship began to move sideways. Kamchatka, which had been visible off starboard, shifted unobserved to port side. Fishermen and sailors who were still working on deck began to grow alarmed.

Soon there was a blast from the overhead horn. Everyone stood still and looked up. Perhaps because they stood directly below the jutting smokestack, its massive and bucket-like form visibly trembled as it leaned aft. The horn attached to its side looked like a Tyrolean hat, and its blast sounded oddly pathetic within the raging windstorm. Its continuous call was meant to help the boats that were fishing far from the ship to find their way back through the storm.

Fishermen and seamen clustered around the dim entrance to the engine room, talking excitedly. With each sway of the ship, oblique shafts of feeble light escaped from below. The flickering light fleetingly illuminated now one agitated face, now another.

"What's going on?" asked the miner, joining the group.

"We'll beat that goddamned Asakawa to death!" exclaimed someone furiously.

Early that morning Asakawa had actually received a gale warning from a ship anchored some ten miles away. The warning added that if any boats had left the ship, they should be urgently called back. According to the radio operator, Asakawa's reply had been: "If we pissed our pants every time over this kind of nonsense, we'd have no business coming all the way out to Kamchatka."

"What the hell does he think human lives are, anyhow?" roared the first fisherman who heard this, as though the radio operator were Asakawa.

"Human lives?"

"Yes, human lives."

"But Asakawa doesn't think of you fellows as human beings."

The fisherman tried to respond but could only stutter. He turned crimson. Then he rushed back into the surrounding group.

The men stood stock still, their faces bitter but showing signs of a clear turmoil gradually rising from deep within. A worker whose father had gone out in one of the boats paced restlessly outside the assembled circle of fishermen. The horn howled without a break. Listening to it tore at the fishermen's hearts.

It was close to evening when a great shout rose from the bridge. Those below rushed up the gangway two steps at a time. Two boats were approaching. They were lashed together with ropes.

The boats were quite near now. But big waves were attacking the boats and the ship from both sides, first violently lifting them up, and then dropping them down. Large swells rose and rolled one after another. Though the boats were so very close, they could come no closer. It was maddening. A rope was thrown from the deck. But it did not reach and splashed into the sea sending up futile spray. The rope was reeled back in, twisting like a sea snake. The attempt was repeated many times. Everyone was shouting from the deck, but there was no reply from the boats. The expressions on the fishermen's faces were frozen and immobilized like masks. Their eyes too stared motionlessly. The sight, too dreadful to watch, pierced their chests.

The rope was thrown again. Coiled at first, it stretched like an eel. A fisherman raised both hands to grab it and the rope struck him on the side of the neck. Everyone screamed. The fisherman was knocked flat on his side. But he grabbed the rope! Once tightly tied, the rope stretched in a taut line dripping with water. The watching fishermen spontaneously heaved a huge sigh of relief.

The horn kept on blowing without pause, its sound made alternately shrill or distant by the shifting wind. Despite the wind, all the boats except two had managed to return by nightfall. Each returning fisherman collapsed upon stepping onto the ship's deck. One of the boats had become swamped with water so the fishermen had dropped anchor and transferred to the boat that brought them back. The whereabouts of another boat and its crew remained a complete mystery.

The manager was in a huff. He kept going down into the fishermen's cabin and coming back up. Each time he did so everyone's eyes followed him, brimming with a burning hatred.

The next day, partly to search for the missing boat, the ship moved on in pursuit of the crabs. The loss of five or six people "didn't matter," but losing the boat was painful.

THE ENGINE ROOM was filled with commotion from the early morning. The vibrations set off by hoisting the anchor made the fishermen whose cabin adjoined the anchor chamber rattle like roasting beans. The iron plates covering the ship's flanks were worn out and flaking at every tremor. The *Hakkōmaru* sailed north to the latitude of fifty-one degrees and five minutes in search of anchored Boat Number 1. Chunks of ice floated nonchalantly by like living creatures, bobbing in the troughs of gentle swells. Yet here and there those fragments of ice formed great masses that stretched as far as the eye could see. They spouted foam, and were capable of surrounding a ship in a flash. The ice was giving off a steam-like vapor. The freezing cold assailed the ship as if blown by electric fans. Crunching sounds suddenly rang out all across the ship as its wet deck and handrails grew coated with ice. The ship's sides, seemingly sprinkled with powder, glittered with frost crystals. Sailors and fishermen covered both cheeks with their hands as they ran across the deck. The ship advanced, leaving in its wake a long trail like a straight path across a plain.

The missing boat was nowhere to be found.

Close to nine o'clock a boat was spotted from the bridge, drifting far ahead. The manager agitatedly paced the deck shouting with delight: "Son of a bitch, we found the damned thing at last!" A motorboat was promptly lowered. However, what they found was not the Boat Number 1 that they had been looking for but rather a newer boat, with number 36 embossed on it. It was clear from the iron buoy attached to it that it belonged to ship X. The ship X had left it there to mark the spot to which it intended to return.

Asakawa tapped the boat's hull with his fingertips and grinned broadly. "Why'd they leave this one behind? Haul it up."

And so Number 36 was hoisted by a winch to the *Hakkōmaru*'s bridge. The boat swung in the air, dripping heavily onto the deck. Looking up at the rising boat with a magnanimous air as if to say Well done, the manager mumbled: "This is terrific, just terrific!"

Fishermen working on the nets were watching him. "Look at the thieving fucker! Wish the chain would break and the boat smash his goddamned head!"

Sweeping the workers with a murderously contemptuous stare, the manager strode past them. He called for the carpenter, his shout hoarse and impatient.

"Yes, what is it?" The carpenter's face popped out from an unexpected hatch.

Startled, the manager turned around and barked, "What is it? Idiot! Scrape off the number. Get the plane, the plane."

The carpenter looked at him blankly.

"You fool, come over here!"

The diminutive carpenter, a plane in hand and a saw handle tucked into his belt, followed the broad-shouldered manager across the deck, his steps unsteady as though he had a limp. The number 3 was planed away from the boat's side, turning it into Boat Number 6.

"This is perfect, just perfect. Ha, that'll teach them!" Twisting his mouth into a sharp grin, the manager seemed to grow taller as he roared with laughter.

Though they continued to sail north, they failed to discover the missing boat. The ship that had been standing still while hoisting up Boat Number 36 now began to move in a wide, gentle curve so as to return to its original position. The sky cleared up, turning transparent as though washed. The Kamchatka mountain range shone crisply, like Swiss hills in a picture postcard.

THE MISSING BOAT did not return. Fishermen collected the belongings left behind in the deserted bunks and looked up the family addresses so that they could act quickly if the need arose. It was not a pleasant duty. Going about it, the fishermen had the wrenching feeling that their own wounds were being peered into. Thinking to send the items once the supply ship arrived, they came across packages and letters whose return addresses bore names of the men's female relatives. One of the letters was clumsily and painstakingly written in pencil. The letter was passed from one rough hand to another. After reading it haltingly yet avidly, each fisherman shook his head as if having seen something painful, and handed it on. It was a letter from a child.

One of the men blew his nose loudly, and looking up from the letter said in a barely audible voice, "This is Asakawa's doing. If it turns out that this man's dead, I'll avenge him." The speaker was a large and burly man who had done all sorts of things in the Hokkaido interior. A young fisherman with bulging shoulders said even more quietly, "I can knock him down myself."

"Ah, this letter is too much. It brings back everything."

"Listen," said the first man. "He could easily have done us in too. This is not somebody else's problem."

A man who sat in a corner with one knee drawn up, chewing on a thumbnail and glancing up as he listened, now nodded vigorously. "When the time comes, leave everything to me! I'll fix that bastard with one blow."

Everyone was silent. All the same, they felt relieved.

THREE DAYS AFTER the *Hakkōmaru* returned to its original position, the missing boat came back with everyone alive and well.

The instant the boat's crew emerged from the captain's quarters and came into the shit-hole a veritable whirlpool of people encircled them.

The great storm had snatched away from the men any ability to steer the boat, making them more helpless than a child gripped by the scruff of its neck. They had gone out the farthest, and now the wind was blowing them even farther. All were prepared for the worst. Fishermen are trained to bid life good-bye at a moment's notice.

But something exceptional happened. The following morning their boat, half-filled with water, washed up on the Kamchatka shore, and they were all rescued by Russians who lived nearby.

The Russian family consisted of four people. The fishermen, thirsting for home and women and children, were entranced. What is more, these people were all very kind and gladly did everything they could to help them. Yet at first, as might be expected, the incomprehensible words they spoke, and the foreign, different color of their hair and eyes struck everyone as eerie.

However it soon dawned on them: "Hey, they're human beings same as us!"

As the news of the shipwreck spread, many villagers gathered. The place was quite a long way from Japan's fishing grounds.

They spent two days there recovering their strength and sailed back. "Not that we wanted to come back," one of them said. "Who'd want to come back to this kind of hell?" But there was more to their story than this. The "interesting part" had not yet been told.

It was the very day when they planned to return. They were gathered around a stove, dressing and talking, when four or five Russians came in. There was a Chinese among them too. A slightly stooped man with a big face and short red whiskers suddenly began to speak loudly and to gesture with his hands. The boat boss waved his hands in front of his eyes to let him know that they did not understand Russian. At a word from the Russian, the Chinese who had been watching him began to speak in Japanese. It was a jumbled sort of Japanese, with words out of sequence, scattering and staggering about as if drunk.

"All you, sure thing, no have money."

"That's right."

"All you, is poor."

"That's right."

"So, all you, is name *proletariat*. Understand?"

"Sure."

The Russian, laughing, began to pace about. Sometimes he stopped and looked at them.

"Rich mans do this all you." (He grabbed himself by the neck, as if in a chokehold.) "Rich mans get more, more big." (He indicated an expanding stomach.) "All you, no good, get more, more poor. Understand? Japan, no good. Working people, this." (He frowned, making a face as though he were ill.) "Rich man boss, this. Ahem. Ahem." (He strutted about.)

"That's right, that's right!" said a young fisherman, beginning to laugh with amusement.

"Working people, this. Rich man boss, this." (He repeated the previous gestures.) "That no good. Working people, this!" (Now he proudly thrust out his chest.) "Rich man boss, this." (He mimicked an old beggar.) "This good. Understand? Russia, have all working people. All working people, this." (He stands proudly.) "Russia, no have rich man boss. No tricky people. No exploit people. Understand? No terrible Russia. Terrible Russia only lies."

This, the men vaguely thought, is probably what was meant by the "terrible" phrase "turning Red." But if that's what "turning Red" was about, it seemed to make perfect sense. Most of all, they felt strongly fascinated by what they were hearing.

"We understand, we do understand!"

Two or three Russians began noisily to say something. The Chinese was listening. And then picking up the words one by one as if stammering, he translated for them. "Boss do nothing, get rich. Proletariat always this." (He showed a person being choked.) "This, no good! Proletariat, all you, one, two, three . . . hundred, thousand, fifty thousand, hundred thousand, all, all, this." (He imitated children joining hands.) "Get strong. All right!" (He slapped his arm.) "No lose, nobody. Understand?"

"Yes, yes!"

"Rich man boss, run." (He made as if to flee at top speed.) "All right, sure. Working people, proletariat, is proud." (He strode about in a dignified manner.) "Proletariat, number one great. . . . If no proletariat, all no have bread. All die. Understand?"

"Yes, yes!"

"Japan no good now. Working people, this." (He bent his back and shrank into himself.) Rich man boss, this." (Swaggering, he imitated a bully knocking people down.) "That no good! Working people, this." (With a fierce look, he stood up and lunged forward as if to knock down and trample an oppressor.) "Rich man boss, this." (He mimed fleeing.) "Japan all working people, good country. Proletariat country. Understand?"

"Yes, yes, we understand!"

The Russians cheered and stamped their feet as if dancing.

"Japan, working people, do it." (He struck a defiant pose.) "Happy! Russia, all happy. Hurrah! All you go back ship. Your ship, rich man boss, this." (He swaggered.) "All you, proletariat, do this!" (He raised his fists, joined hands, and lunged.) "All right, you win! Understand?"

"We understand!" The young fisherman, growing excited in spite of himself, suddenly grabbed the Chinese man's hands. "Yes, we will do that! We'll do it for sure!"

So this is Bolshevization, thought the boat boss. They were inciting the men to commit outrageous acts. This, he thought, was Russia's crafty way of deceiving Japan.

When the Russians had finished talking, they raised an incomprehensible shout, and shook the fishermen's hands with all their might. They embraced them, brushing the hard stubble of their cheeks against their faces. The Japanese, pulling back their necks stiff with embarrassment, hardly knew what to do.

With an occasional glance at the shit-hole door, everyone now urged the returned men to tell them more. They spoke about various things they had seen among the Russians. Their listeners absorbed every detail, like blotting paper.

"Hey, that's quite enough!"

The boat boss, noticing the strange seriousness with which everyone was listening to the story, poked an exuberantly speaking young fisherman in the shoulder.

4

The air was hazy. Contours of the sundry ventilator pipes, chimneys, winch arms, suspended boats, handrails, and so on—normally so severely mechanical—grew shaded and blurred, looking more intimate than ever. A soft, lukewarm air caressed people's cheeks and flowed on. Nights like this were rare.

The area around a nearby hatch was heavy with the smell of crab brains and flesh. Two shadows of uneven heights stood between mountains of nets.

Kept from sleeping by a pounding heartbeat, a fisherman with a sallow, swollen body and a heart ruined through overwork came up on deck. He leaned on the handrail and absentmindedly watched the sea that looked as thick as melted seaweed. With his body in such poor shape, he felt certain he would die at the manager's hands. Yet the thought of dying in far off Kamchatka, without even being able to step on land, struck him as much too lonely. Absorbed in his brooding, he suddenly noticed that there was someone between the piles of nets. He heard hushed voices and crab shells crunching underfoot.

Once the fisherman's eyes grew accustomed to the darkness, he saw them. A fisherman was speaking to a worker of fourteen or fifteen. The words were inaudible. The worker, with his back to the other, was turning this way and that like a resisting, sulking child. Each time he moved, the fisherman too moved in the same direction. This went on for a while. The fisherman inadvertently (or so it seemed) raised his voice. But he quickly lowered it again and said something rapidly. Suddenly he wrapped his arms tightly around the worker. Were they fighting? For a while only a panting voice stifled by clothing was audible. No one was moving. At that instant the worker's legs became visible through the soft haze, looking like a pair of candles. The lower half of his body was stark naked. The worker was crouching. The fisherman was covering him like a toad. The watching man saw only this much and for merely a moment, but the sight stuck in his throat. He unconsciously averted his eyes. He felt a nervous kind of excitement, as though he had been punched or drugged.

Fishermen had gradually begun to be tormented by raging surges of lust. For four or five months, these sturdy men had been unnaturally separated from women. Stories about women whose bodies they had bought in Hakodate, crude talk about women's genitals—these grew into regular nightly topics. A single erotic picture printed on frayed paper circulated endlessly from hand to hand.

Someone sang: "Lay it out, turn this way, kiss my mouth, wrap your legs, come you cunt! Oh, a whore's work is a bitch, boys!"

As though soaked up by a sponge, the song was promptly memorized by everyone. Men began to sing it at every opportunity. Once the singing was over, they shouted desperately and with glittering eyes, "Ah, damn it all to hell!"

"Fuck, this is no good! I can't get to sleep at all." Fishermen lay down in their bunks only to start tossing about. "My dick's standing up!"

"What am I supposed to do with this thing?" A fisherman finally got up, naked and clutching his testicles, his penis erect. His large body looked grim and formidable. Students, taken aback, glanced at him out of the corners of their eyes.

Many men ejaculated in their sleep. Others masturbated when no one was around. Soiled underpants and loincloths, damp and giving off a sour stench, lay balled up in shelf corners. A student who accidentally trod on one felt as though he had stepped in shit.

Night visits to boy workers' quarters began. The men would exchange cigarettes for caramels and with two or three in their pockets go out through the hatch.

If the cook opened the door to the pantry—filled with barrels of pickled vegetables that reeked like a toilet—a furious shout would suddenly ring out from the dim and stifling interior. "Shut the damned door! You come in now and I'll beat you to death!"

THE RADIO OPERATOR monitored messages being exchanged among the other ships, and reported the catch of each one to the manager. The information made it clear that the *Hakkōmaru* was lagging far behind. The manager began to lose his temper. The consequences for the fishermen and workers were immediate and overwhelming. They always bore the brunt of everything. The manager and the foreman thought up a work competition scheme that pitted the sailors against the fishermen and workers.

Whenever the fishermen and workers "lost" to the seamen by killing fewer crabs, they were made to feel that they had failed—although the work brought them no benefits at all. The manager clapped his hands with delight. Winning one day, losing the next, vowing not to lose again—days of absurdly intensive work continued, till their hands oozed blood. On the first day the amount of work they did went up by fifty or sixty percent. But by the fifth or sixth day both sides grew dispirited and the quantity of work started to decline drastically. Sometimes their heads suddenly slumped forward even as they worked. The manager struck them without warning. Jolted by the unexpected blows, the men involuntarily screamed in pain. The rest of the time they worked in total silence, as though they were enemies or had forgotten how to speak. They no longer had even the energy to talk.

The manager, however, now began to hand out "prizes" to the winning side. The smoldering firewood of competitiveness blazed up once more.

"The silly bastards," commented the manager to the captain, drinking a beer in the latter's cabin.

The backs of the captain's hands were dimpled like those of a plump woman. Deftly tapping a gold-tipped cigarette against the table, he responded with an inscrutable smile. The captain could not bear the manager's constant interference. He wondered whether the fishermen would rise up and fling the son of a bitch into the Kamchatka sea.

In addition to handing out "prizes," the manager put up a poster announcing that whoever accomplished the least amount of work would be branded with a red hot iron rod. Everybody worked on, shadowed continuously by the implacable threat of branding. The quantity of work continued to rise.

The manager knew even better than they did just how much abuse a human body could tolerate. At the end of the workday, workers dropped sideways into their bunks like logs, groaning, "Maybe this is it . . ."

One of the students recalled being taken to a Buddhist temple by his grandmother as a child, and seeing in its dim hall paintings of hell that looked just like this. Their present situation strongly reminded him of a great snakelike animal he had seen slithering through a marshland. It was the spitting image of it. The overwork perversely robbed them of their ability to sleep. After midnight, in various parts of the shit-hole there suddenly arose the eerie sounds of teeth grinding as if chewing up glass, of nonsensical words, and wild shouts.

When they could not sleep, they sometimes whispered to their own bodies: "I can't believe you're still alive . . ." I can't believe you're still alive—to their bodies!

It was the hardest on the students.

"Looking at it from our current perspective, I get the feeling those convicts in Dostoyevsky's *House of the Dead* didn't have it so tough after all," said a student who had been unable to shit for days and could not sleep unless he tied a hand towel tightly around his head.

"You're probably right." His companion had brought some whisky from Hakodate and was licking it slowly with the tip of his tongue, as though drinking medicine. "Well, that's how great exploits are carried out. We're developing rich untapped resources and that's rough work. But they say that even these cannery ships are better than they used to be. When this business first started, they hadn't yet learned about the shifts in weather and tides, and hadn't really mastered the geography, and so lots of ships sank. They got sunk by Russian ships, got captured, got killed, but they didn't give in, they kept on getting back up and fighting hard, and that's how these rich resources got to be ours. . . . Anyhow, these things can't be helped."

". . . . ."

That was how history books always told it, thought the student, and maybe it really was so. But that did nothing at all to dispel the furious feelings concealed at the bottom of his heart. He silently stroked his belly that had turned hard as plywood. His thumbs felt numb and tingled as though stimulated by a weak electric current. The feeling was extremely unpleasant. He raised a thumb to his eyes and rubbed it with his other hand.

After supper everyone gathered around a rickety stove installed in the middle of the shit-hole that was as cracked as an old map. Vapor rose from them as their bodies started warming up a little. The raw stifling stench of crabs invaded everyone's noses.

"Well, I can't make much sense out of it all but I sure don't want to get killed."

"Naturally, nobody does!"

A heavy, oppressive anxiety assailed them, an irritability and rage without a clear target. They really were being killed!

"S-shit, we may be g-good for nothing but damned if we'll let them kill us!" shouted a stuttering fisherman abruptly, his face crimson, facial muscles taut with impatience.

For a moment everyone fell silent, feeling a sudden stab to the heart.

"I don't want to die in Kamchatka . . ."

". . . . ."

"A supply ship's sailed out of Hakodate. I heard it from the radio operator."

"I want to go back."

"There's no way they'll let us go back."

"They say that lots of guys get away by supply ship."

"Really? . . . That would be good!"

"There's also some who pretend they're going fishing, run off to Kamchatka, and end up doing Red propaganda together with the Russkies."

". . . . ."

"So we're doing all this for the benefit of the Japanese Empire, eh? . . . Oh yeah, another fine phrase they've come up with." Unbuttoning his jacket the student bared a bony ribcage that resembled a ladder and, yawning, vigorously scratched it. The dried dirt coating his skin peeled off like thin mica.

"Hell, it's all about the corporate fat cats getting their mitts on every damned thing they can snatch," said an elderly fisherman. His weak cloudy eyes stared blankly from under slack lids, furrowed like empty oyster shells. He spat at the stove. The spit struck the stovetop, formed a circle, sizzled, bounced like a bean, shrank to the size of a grain of soot, and vanished. Everyone absentmindedly looked at it.

"You may be right about that."

But a boat boss, holding the red lining of his rubber-soled socks over the stove, said, "Hey, we'll have none of your traitorous talk here."

". . . . ."

"Shit, you got no business telling us what to do!" The stuttering fisherman pursed his lips like an octopus.

There was a foul stench of rubber.

"Hey, boss, watch your rubber!"

"Goddamn it, it got scorched!"

Waves were rising, and striking faintly against the ship's sides. The ship swayed as if to a lullaby. As they sat around the stove, the feeble five-candlepower light of a lamp that resembled a rotten Chinese lantern plant cast shadows behind them which tangled and joined in multiform ways. The night was quiet. Reflections of red flames in the stove's door flickered across the lower halves of their legs. Suddenly and fleetingly they were able to look back over the entire span of their unhappy lives. The night was strangely quiet.

"Got a cigarette?"

"No . . ."

"You got none too?"

"Afraid not."

"Shit."

"Hey, pass the whisky this way too, won't you?"

His companion held the square bottle upside down and shook it.

"Damn, you sure wasted it!"

"Ha, ha, ha, ha, ha, ha, ha."

"What a hell of a place to be in, yet here we are . . . even me . . ." said a fisherman who had worked in a factory in Shibaura, in Tokyo. He told them about it. To Hokkaido workers it seemed more splendid than any factory they knew. "If they did to us just one hundredth of what they do to us here," he said, "we'd have had a strike for sure."

This started them talking about the various experiences each of them had gone through. Constructing national highways, building irrigation systems, laying out railways, digging harbors and reclaiming land, excavating new mines, cultivating new land, loading ships, fishing for Pacific herring—almost everyone had done one or more of these kinds of work.

When workers on the mainland grew "arrogant" and could no longer be forced to overwork, and when markets reached an impasse and refused to expand any further, then capitalists stretched out their claws, "To Hokkaido, to Karafuto!" There they could mistreat people to their hearts' content, ride them as brutally as they did in their colonies of Korea and Taiwan. The capitalists understood quite clearly that there would be no one to complain. In workers' quarters at highway and railway construction sites laborers were being beaten to death more easily than lice. Some fled, unable to put up with the overwork and abuse. When they were caught, they were tied to stakes to be kicked by horses' hind legs, or dragged off to backyards to be mauled to death by Tosa fighting dogs. Moreover this was done in front of everyone's eyes. Hearing the ribs snap within the chest, even the "non-human" laborers spontaneously covered their faces. Each time the escapees fainted, water was poured over them to revive them. In the end they died tossed about like bundled rags by dogs' powerful jaws. Even after their limp bodies were thrown away and abandoned in a corner of some yard, their limbs continued to twitch. Savage punishments were inflicted daily: red-hot tongs were suddenly pressed against victims' buttocks; people were beaten with hexagonal rods until they could not stand up. During meals, abrupt screams rose from backyards, followed by the raw stench of burning human flesh.

"That's it, I've had it. No way can I keep on eating." Men flung away their chopsticks. But they kept on looking darkly at each other's faces.

Many died from beriberi. Savage overwork made them succumb to it. Even once they died, "no time off" meant they were left unburied for days. Their bodies remained out of sight in the darkness with only their pale grimy feet, strangely small and childlike, protruding from the edges of straw mats that had been carelessly tossed over them.

"Their faces are swarming with flies. They all flew up at once when I passed by!" said a man as he walked in, tapping his forehead with his hand.

Everybody was made to go to the work site before dawn. They were forced to work until their pickaxes glittered bluish-white in the dark and their hands could no longer be seen. Everyone envied the prisoners who worked in a nearby jail. Koreans were treated most cruelly of all, not only by the bosses and overseers but by their fellow Japanese laborers.

Sometimes a policeman stationed in a village five or six miles away came on foot to look into things, notebook in hand. He often stayed until the evening or spent the night. Yet he never even bothered to glance at the laborers. He headed back with his face flushed crimson, striding down the middle of the road, pissing in all directions like a fire hose, and muttering unintelligibly to himself.

Each railroad tie in Hokkaido was nothing but the bluish corpse of a worker. Posts driven into the soil during harbor reclamations were laborers sick with beriberi buried alive like the ancient "human pillars." The name for workers in Hokkaido was "octopus." In order to stay alive, an octopus will even devour its own limbs. It was just like that! Here a primitive exploitation could be practiced against anyone, without any scruples. It yielded loads of profit. What's more such doings were cleverly identified with "developing the national wealth," and deftly rationalized away. It was very shrewdly done. Workers were starved and beaten to death for the sake of "the nation."

"Only the gods helped me get away from there alive," said a fisherman. "I sure was thankful! But if I get killed on this ship it'll come to the same damned thing. Why, that's one hell of a joke!" The fisherman broke into a wild roar of laughter. But once his laughter subsided, his brow visibly darkened and he turned aside.

It was the same at the mines. New tunnels were dug. To find out how best to deal with whatever gases leaked from the ground and whatever momentous changes the digging would cause, the capitalists—following the methods of General Nogi, sainted hero of the Russo-Japanese War—simply used up tens of thousands of workers whom they could buy more cheaply than guinea pigs, then throw away. It was easier than discarding used tissues! The tunnel walls kept on being reinforced with multiple layers of miners' raw flesh. Horrors were perpetrated taking advantage of the mines' distance from cities. In the loaded mine cars, slabs of coal sometimes turned up with severed thumbs and little fingers adhering to them. Women and children did not even raise an eyebrow at such sights. Accustomed to them all, expressionless, they merely pushed the cars to the next station. That coal propelled a gigantic engine churning out capitalists' profits.

All the miners' faces were lusterless, yellowish, swollen, and perpetually blank, like the faces of people who had been imprisoned for many years. Insufficient sunlight, coal dust, toxic fumes, dampness, and atmospheric pressure afflicted their bodies in clearly visible ways. "When you work as a miner for seven or eight years, it's like spending four or five full years in a totally dark pit, not seeing the sun even once in four or five years!" But the capitalists, always able to obtain workers easily in plentiful replacements, did not give a damn. When winter came, they knew, workers would pour into the mines.

In Hokkaido there were "immigrant farmers" and "new cultivators." Through movies filled with enticing slogans like "Develop Hokkaido," "Solve the food problem through promoting immigration," and the childish "Strike it rich as immigrants," the powers that be encouraged the mainland's impoverished peasants who were about to be robbed of their fields to emigrate, only to abandon them on the land that—four or five inches below the surface—turned out to be nothing but clay. The fertile land was already marked with notice boards proclaiming ownership. By the following spring entire families, buried in the snow and without even potatoes to eat, had starved to death. Such things happened over and over. They first came to light when the snow melted, and "neighbors" who lived a mile away dropped by. Many of the victims had tried to survive by eating straw, and bits of it were still sticking out of their mouths.

Even in those rare cases where immigrants managed to cultivate their land for a decade without starving to death, when they finally had turned it into decent fields, they would find that the land now belonged to "outsiders." The capitalists—usurers, banks, nobles, and the super-rich—casually lent out lavish sums of money, so that once the wasteland was transformed into fields as fertile as plump cats they unfailingly fell into their own hands. Imitating such practices, other shrewd people came to Hokkaido determined to make easy money. The peasants found their possessions snatched at from every direction. In the end they were reduced to being just what they had been on the mainland: tenant farmers. For the first time they saw through the trick. "Damn!"

They had crossed the Tsugaru Strait and come to snowy Hokkaido hoping to make at least a little money before returning to their villages. Quite a few people on the crab cannery ships had been driven from their land in this way.

Dockworkers lived as hard as the cannery ships' fishermen. When out of work and idling about Otaru's closely watched lodging houses, they were dragged off by ship to Karafuto or to remote parts of Hokkaido. There, if their feet slipped even an inch, stacks of square-cut timber groaned and tumbled on top of them with an earth-shaking crash, crushing them flatter than rice wafers. When the wet and slippery lumber being loaded by rattling winches accidentally struck them, it smashed their skulls and knocked them into the sea more easily than bugs are swept away.

Workers on the mainland, who had been silently surviving for so long, united into a powerful body and stood up to the capitalists. But workers in the "colonies" were completely isolated from such movements.

Their suffering was unendurable. Yet the harder they stumbled on, the heavier grew their burden of suffering.

"I wonder what's going to happen to us . . ."

"They'll kill us, I just know it."

". . . . ."

Though they wanted to say something, the words stuck in their throats.

"Before they k-kill me, I'll kill them," exclaimed the Stuttering Fisherman gruffly.

Waves pounded gently against the side of the ship. Somewhere on the upper deck, steam seemed to be escaping from a pipe, producing a soft ceaseless hiss that sounded like a seething kettle.

BEFORE GOING TO sleep the fishermen took off their shirts and undershirts, as stiff with grime as dried cuttlefish, and spread them over the stove. Gathering around the stove, the men stretched the fabric to expose it to heat, and then slapped at it. Lice and bedbugs fell onto the stovetop making snapping sounds and began to emit a raw stench of burning flesh. As the shirts grew hot, more lice emerged from the seams, frantically moving their countless spindly legs. The insects were sickeningly greasy to touch. Some were so fat their oddly shaped heads could be made out, resembling those of praying mantises.

"Hey, hold up the end for me." Taking the loincloths' opposite edges, men spread them out and started plucking at the lice.

A fisherman crushed lice with his front teeth or squeezed them with his thumbs till his nails turned red. After wiping his hands against the hem of his jacket as a child does, he resumed his work. Even so, no one could fall asleep. Lice, fleas, and bedbugs kept on emerging from somewhere and attacking them throughout the night. It was impossible to eradicate them. As the men climbed into their damp and gloomy bunks, they instantly began to itch with dozens of fleas crawling up their shins. Finally they began to wonder whether their own flesh was starting to rot. A sinister notion assailed them that they might in fact be decomposing corpses swarming with maggots and flies.

At first they had been able to bathe every other day. It was inevitable that their bodies would grow filthy and stink. But after a week, bathing was reduced to once every four days, and after about a month, to once a week. Finally it came down to twice a month. This was done to prevent wasting water. But the captain and the manager bathed every day, and this did not amount to wasting water! With the men's bodies stained for days on end with crab juice, there was no way to keep the lice and bedbugs from breeding.

When they untied their loincloths, black beads spilled out of them. The men's bellies were circled with a red rash where the loincloths had been tied. They itched unbearably. As the men slept, sounds of desperate scratching came from everywhere. The sensation of something small crawling or springing over their legs and bellies was followed by bites. Each time this happened, fishermen's bodies twisted and turned. Yet soon the same thing happened again. It went on until the morning. Their skin grew as rough as if ravaged by scabies.

"The damned lice are going to devour us alive."

"Yeah, that'll be a wonderful way to go."

They could not help laughing.

5

Three fishermen were running frantically along the deck.

Reaching a turn, they staggered and grabbed at the handrail. The carpenter who was repairing the saloon deck stood on tiptoe looking after them. The cold wind had brought tears to his eyes and at first he could not clearly see. He turned aside and forcefully blew his nose with his fingers. The mucus flew off in an arc, carried by the wind.

The portside winch was rattling. Because everyone was out fishing it did not make sense that the winch should be moving. And something was hanging from it and swinging. The vertical line of the suspended wire swayed in a leisurely circle.

"What could that be?"

With a shock, he understood. Agitated, he turned aside and blew his nose again. The wind drove the sticky liquid against his trousers.

"They're doing it again." The carpenter focused his eyes, repeatedly wiping away tears with his sleeve.

Outlined distinctly against the sea that shone silvery gray after a recent rainfall, the black shape of a tightly bound worker hung from the jutting arm of the winch. He had been hoisted skyward all the way to the top of the winch. There he hung like a rag for some twenty minutes. Then he was partly lowered, his body twisting and writhing, his legs struggling as though caught in a spider's web.

Presently his body disappeared in the shadow of the saloon. Only the taut line of the wire occasionally moved like a swing.

The carpenter's tears seemed to be flowing into his nose, which kept running without a pause. He blew his nose once again. Then he took a hammer from his side pocket and set to work.

Alerted by a faint sound, the carpenter turned around. The wire was swaying as though shaken by someone below, and he heard dull, sinister thumps.

The face of the worker who was hanging from the winch was deathly pale. Foam dribbled from lips that were shut as tightly as those of a corpse. The carpenter, moving to a lower deck, saw the foreman standing rigid with a log of firewood under his arm, and pissing into the sea. Glancing at the wood, the carpenter wondered whether this was what he had been beating the youth with. With each gust of wind, the piss splattered the edge of the deck.

WORN OUT BY endless days of overwork, the fishermen gradually lost their ability to get up in the mornings. The manager strode through their quarters banging an empty oilcan close to the sleeping men's ears. He banged at it until they opened their eyes and got up. Those who were sick with beriberi raised their heads weakly and said something. But the manager kept banging at the can, pretending not to see them. With their voices inaudible, their mouths seemed only to be opening and closing, like those of goldfish coming up for air. After banging to his heart's content, he shouted, "Get up, damn you! You're working for the nation; this is just like fighting a war. If the work kills you, so be it! Get up, you fuckers!"

He tore away all the sick workers' bedding and drove them onto the deck. The beriberi sufferers stumbled over each step of the stairway. Gripping the handrail and leaning sideways, they climbed by pulling up their legs with their hands. At each step their hearts jolted ominously as though kicked.

The manager and the foreman dealt with the sick as cunningly as if they were stepchildren. First they made them pack meat, and then sent them up on deck to break off crabs' claws. Shortly after, they transferred them to work with rolls of paper labels. Careful not to slip as they stood motionless in the freezing air of the gloomy factory, the men felt their legs from the knees down grow as numb as artificial limbs. At any moment their knee joints might give way and their legs buckle under them.

A student stood tapping his forehead with the back of a hand stained with crushed crabs. A moment later he toppled over backwards. A hill of empty cans that stood stacked nearby tumbled on top of him with an ear-splitting crash. The cans rolled along the ship's slanted floor, flashing and disappearing under machinery and among piles of cargo. The boy's worried companions picked him up and started to carry him toward the exit. They nearly collided with the manager who was coming down into the factory and whistling. He casually took in the situation.

"Who said you could stop working?"

"Get out of the way!" growled one of the men, choking with rage.

"What did you say? Say that again, you cocksucker!" Drawing a pistol from his pocket, the manager twirled it around his finger as though it were a toy. He rocked on his feet as if to make himself taller, and suddenly burst into loud laughter. "Bring some water!"

The manager grabbed a bucketful of water and dumped it over the face of the student who lay on the floor as lifelessly as a railroad tie.

"This'll cure him. Now quit gawking and get back to work!"

Coming down into the factory the next morning, workers saw the previous day's student tied to the iron pole of a lathe. His head was slumped against his chest like that of a chicken with its neck wrung, and tips of his vertebrae stuck out prominently from his back. A cardboard sign hung from his chest, its handwriting clearly the manager's:

"This one's a treacherous faker. Untying him is forbidden."

The youth's forehead felt as cold to the touch as iron. Until coming down into the factory, the workers had been noisily chatting. Now no one said a word. At the sound of the foreman's voice behind them, they split into two lines, each passing along one side of the machine to which the student was bound, and streamed toward their respective work stations.

When crab canning reached its hectic peak, working conditions became horrendous. Workers had their front teeth broken, spat bloody saliva throughout the night, fainted from overwork, bled from the eyes, were struck about the head, and lost their hearing. Thoroughly worn out, all grew befuddled as though drunk. When the day's work ended they felt momentarily dizzy with relief.

As they were finishing up, the manager walked up and shouted, "Today you're working till nine. The only time you sons of bitches are fast is when you're getting ready to quit!"

Sluggishly, as if in slow motion, everyone got up once again. They lacked the energy to do anything beyond that. Later on the manager came down to the shit-hole to speak to them.

"Listen up. This sea is not some place we can come to any time we like. And crabs can't be caught just any old time. You can't quit working after ten or thirteen hours sharp just because that's the official workday. If you did that, we'd be in a fucking mess. This kind of work is different from any other. You got that? But when there're no crabs to catch, I'll let you lounge around as much as you damn like.

"It's only the Russkies who quit working the moment the time's up, even if there are frigging shoals of fish right under their noses. With that kind of attitude, no wonder Russia got to be such a fucked up country. Japanese men must never act like that!"

Some of the men ignored his speech, thinking: "The asshole's lying." But the majority swallowed the manager's suggestion that the Japanese were truly an outstanding people. And they felt somewhat consoled by the notion that their cruel daily sufferings seemed to have something heroic about it.

When working on deck, they often saw a destroyer sailing south along the horizon. From the warship's stern fluttered the nation's flag, glittering red and white. Their eyes brimming with tears of excitement, the fishermen clutched their hats and waved. "That destroyer," they thought, "is the only friend we've got."

"Damn, when I see that ship I can't help blubbering." The men followed the destroyer with their eyes as it gradually grew smaller until it vanished, trailing smoke.

On returning from work utterly exhausted they all shouted as if on cue, "Goddamned sons of bitches!" at no one in particular. In the darkness their hate-filled shout resembled the bellowing of a bull. They themselves did not know at whom it was directed, but as the nearly two hundred of them gathered in the same shit-hole day after day and talked bluntly among themselves, their thoughts, words, and actions imperceptibly (and as slowly as a creeping slug) began to move in a similar direction. Of course even within the same current there were some who stood still as though faltering, and middle-aged fishermen who drifted off to the side. Unawares, they soon grew sharply apart from the rest.

It was morning. Climbing slowly up the gangplank, the man from the mine said, "This just can't go on."

The previous day he had worked till almost ten at night, and now his body was twitching like a machine about to break down. He was falling asleep even as he climbed the plank. Alerted by a shout from behind, he shifted his step without thinking only to miss his footing and pitch forward.

Each morning before starting to work, everybody gathered in one corner of the factory. Their faces all looked like those of mud dolls.

"I'm going to slow down," said the miner. "I just can't keep this up."

Workers' faces came to life but no one spoke. Then someone said, "You're going to get yourself branded, you know . . ."

"I'm not trying to get out of the work. I just can't do it."

The miner rolled up his sleeve and held out a nearly transparent arm.

"It don't have long to go. I'm not trying to get out of the work, you know."

"Well, in that case go ahead."

". . . . ."

That day the manager stomped about the factory like a raging rooster. "What's going on? What the hell's going on?" he bellowed.

Because it wasn't just one or two workers who were working slowly—nearly all of them were—he could do nothing but storm about and fume. Neither fishermen nor sailors had ever before seen the manager act like this. From the upper deck they heard the rustling sound of countless crabs that had extricated themselves from the nets and were scuttling about. Like a clogged drain, the work had rapidly slowed to a near halt. Yet the manager's club was of no use at all!

After work, everyone shuffled back to the shit-hole, mopping their necks with steaming hand towels. Glancing at each others' faces, they burst out laughing despite themselves. For some reason the situation struck them as hilariously funny.

The mood spread to the sailors as well. Once they understood that they were being made fools of by being forced to work like the fishermen, they too from time to time resorted to slowdown tactics.

"Yesterday we worked way too much, so today we'll go nice and slow."

If someone said this as they started to work, everyone went along. But the slowdown only amounted to a refusal to overexert their bodies.

Everyone's body was showing signs of breaking down. "We'll work if we absolutely have to," they thought. "They'll kill us either way." But they could no longer put up with it.

"THERE'S THE SUPPLY ship! The supply ship's here!" The shouts from the upper deck carried all the way below. Still dressed in rags, everyone jumped down pell-mell from the shit-hole bunks.

Not even a woman could captivate the fishermen and sailors as much as the supply ship did. This ship did not stink of fish, and it bore the fragrance of Hakodate. It carried a fragrance of that solid earth that they had not trodden for months, for hundreds of days. Moreover, the supply ship delivered long-delayed letters, shirts, underwear, magazines, and various other necessities.

They grabbed hold of the packages with gnarled hands that reeked of crabs, and rushed down into the shit-hole. Sitting cross-legged in their bunks, they placed the packages over comfortably spread knees, and untied them. All sorts of things tumbled out: their children's letters scrawled with words mothers had dictated from the side, hand towels, toothpaste, toothpicks, tissues, clothing, and flattened in their folds, letters from their wives. From each item the men eagerly inhaled the smell of home and the land it stood on. They strove to catch the scent of their babies, still redolent of mother's milk, and a whiff of their wives' flesh.

Some sang at the top of their voices:

> Oh I'm starving to get some!
> If a three-*sen* stamp will get it to me,
> Do send me a can of it, honey!

Those sailors and fishermen who had received nothing paced back and forth with arms thrust stiffly into their trouser pockets. Everyone teased them: "Hey, somebody's snatched away your old lady while you've been gone."

One of the men was oblivious to the clamor. Lost in thought, he had turned his face toward a dark corner and was counting with his fingers over and over. From the letter that the supply ship had brought he had learned that his child had died. All this time the father had lived not knowing that his child had died a full two months ago. His wife wrote that she had had no money to send a message by radio. The man kept on brooding for so long that his companions started to wonder what was wrong.

Yet the news that reached another man was of the very opposite sort. His package contained a photo of an infant who resembled a plump baby octopus.

"This is my kid?" cried the man, bursting into wild laughter. Then he started to walk around showing the photo to his companions and saying with a grin, "Just look at this newborn critter!"

Some packages showed a special touch, with items tucked in that were nothing to speak of except that only a wife would have thought to include them. Coming upon them, the men's hearts began to pound with excitement. All they wanted was to return home.

Aboard the supply ship there was a movie projection team dispatched by the corporation. On the night when the freshly packed cans had been transferred to the supply vessel they were to show a movie on the cannery ship.

Two or three young men came aboard carrying heavy-looking trunks. With their bowties, thick trousers, and hunting caps worn flattened and slightly aslant, they all looked alike.

"What a stink, what incredible stench!" They took off their jackets and whistled as they began to put up the screen, measure the distance to the projector, and set up its stand. The fishermen were most fascinated by them, sensing that these men somehow did not belong to the sea and differed from themselves. Cheerfully, sailors and fishermen helped them with the preparations.

The most senior-looking of the visitors, a flamboyant man with gold-rimmed glasses, stood a little apart, wiping the sweat from his neck.

"Sir, if you stand there, fleas will hop on your legs."

"Whaa-at!" The man leapt up as if he had stepped onto a sheet of red-hot iron.

The watching fishermen burst out laughing.

"What an awful place this is!" exclaimed the dandy in a hoarse, puckish voice. "You probably don't know this, but how much profit do you think the corporation makes coming all the way out here? It's quite a sum. They get five million yen in six months, that's ten million yen in a year. Ten million yen may not sound like much, but it sure is. What's more, no other company in Japan pays stockholders such exorbitant dividends of 22.5 percent on the stocks. They say the company president will get to be a member of the Diet in the next election, and then their dreams will come true. I guess if they didn't operate in the awful way they do, they wouldn't be raking it in like they are."

Night fell. A celebration marking the completed packing of ten thousand crates was to accompany the movie, and so rice wine, distilled spirits, boiled vegetables, cigarettes, and caramels were handed out to everyone.

"Hey, kid, come over here." Fishermen and sailors began playfully to compete over a young factory hand. "Come sit on my lap."

"No, no, watch out for him! You come to me."

The clamor continued for a while.

Four or five men in the first row began suddenly to applaud. Everyone took up the applause without knowing why. The manager appeared in front of the white screen. Stretching his arms and folding them behind him, he began to speak using words he did not ordinarily employ, like "gentlemen" and "myself," as well as those he always used, like "Japanese men" and "the nation's wealth." Most of the men were not listening. Their temples and jawbones kept moving as they chewed cuttlefish.

"Shut up already, shut your face!" yelled men from the rear. "Get lost! We don't want to listen to *you.*"

"Go play with your stick!" someone hollered.

Everyone burst out laughing. There was a storm of whistles and applause.

Unable to outshout them, the manager flushed crimson, tried to say something (which was drowned out by the noise), and withdrew. The movie began.

First they saw footage of famous sights—the Imperial Palace, Matsushima, Enoshima, Kyoto—but the projector was rattling and at times they could see nothing. Images began suddenly to overlap, doubling and tripling in a dizzying confusion until the projector light went out and the screen abruptly turned blank.

Next they showed one foreign and one Japanese movie, but the celluloid was so badly scratched that everything seemed streaked with rain. What was worse, the film seemed to have broken in places and been spliced together, imparting jerky movements to the actors. Yet no one cared about that. Everyone was completely engrossed in the film. When a shapely foreign actress appeared, they snorted like pigs and whistled. At times the *benshi* who was narrating the movie broke off his explanations to yell at them.

The foreign movie was American and dealt with the history of "developing the West." Though relentlessly attacked by savages and struck down by merciless nature, settlers bounced back to their feet and went on extending the railroad yard by yard. Along the way towns were erected overnight, springing up like railway spikes. And as the railroad advanced, more and more towns kept cropping up. The movie showed the manifold hardships that arose from all this, weaving into the narrative a "love story" of a laborer and a corporation director's daughter. As the movie reached its final scene, the *benshi*'s voice rose to a pitch: "And so, thanks to young people's countless sacrifices, the endlessly snaking railroad succeeded at last in sprinting across the plains and piercing the mountains to transform yesterday's wilderness into today's national wealth."

The movie climaxed with an embrace between the corporation director's daughter and the laborer, who had magically mutated into a gentleman.

This was followed by a short foreign film, mindless buffoonery that made everyone laugh.

The Japanese feature told of an impoverished youth who sold fermented soybeans and evening papers before going on to shine shoes, enter a factory, become a model worker, be promoted, and end up a multimillionaire. "Truly, if hard work is not the mother of success, what is!" exclaimed the *benshi,* inserting words that did not appear in the subtitles.

Young workers greeted his comment with earnest applause. But someone among the crowd of fishermen and sailors shouted loudly, "What a crock of shit! If that were true, I'd be a company president by now!"

This brought a huge burst of laughter from everyone.

Once the laughter subsided, the *benshi* explained that the corporation had ordered him to stress the "mother of success" message strongly and repeatedly.

As a final segment they saw footage of all the corporation's factories and offices. It showed countless workers, all working industriously.

After the movies ended, everyone got drunk on the alcohol that had been provided to celebrate the packing of ten thousand crates. Not having tasted liquor in a long time and having worked past endurance, they got dead drunk. Cigarette smoke billowed in clouds under the dim electric light. The air was rotten, thick and stifling. Some stripped to their underwear, hand towels tied around their heads, others sat loosely cross-legged with kimonos tucked up above their buttocks, shouting all sorts of things at the top of their voices. Fistfights flared up from time to time.

This continued till past midnight.

A fisherman from Hakodate who suffered from beriberi and always stayed in bed got his mates to raise his pillow a little so he could watch the revelry. His friend from the same city was leaning on a nearby pillar, poking a matchstick at a bit of dried cuttlefish stuck between his teeth.

Quite late that night, a fisherman tumbled down the shit-hole stairs like a gunnysack. His clothes and right hand were covered with blood.

"A knife, a knife! Get me a knife!" he screamed as he crawled along the floor. "Where is that fucking Asakawa? Can't find him anywhere. I'll kill that motherfucker."

It was a man whom the manager had once beaten black and blue. Wild-eyed, he snatched up a poker from the stove and stumbled out again. No one stopped him.

"Well, I'll be damned!" The Hakodate fisherman looked up at his friend. "And they say that fishermen are stupid as stumps. This is going to get interesting!"

The next morning they discovered that the manager's cabin—everything from the windowpanes to the things on his table—had been smashed to pieces. Only the manager, wherever he was, had been lucky enough not to get smashed to pieces.

6

The weather WAS softly overcast. It had been raining hard till the previous day but now the rain was nearly over. Raindrops the color of cloudy sky fell into the sea of the same color, occasionally stirring up gentle circular ripples.

The destroyer appeared in the early afternoon. Those fishermen, workers, and sailors who happened to be free, ran up to the deck rail to gaze at it admiringly and talk excitedly about it. The warship aroused great curiosity among them.

A small boat was lowered from the destroyer. Bearing a group of officers, it approached the ship. The captain, factory agent, manager, and foreman of the workers waited for them below, beside the gangway that had been lowered diagonally alongside the ship. As the boat drew up, the captain and the boat commander exchanged salutes. The manager chanced to glance upward. He waved angrily at the men, his mouth and eyebrows contorting into a grimace. "What are you staring at? Go away, get lost!"

"Don't act so big, you fucker!"

The men trooped off down to the factory, those who had been closest to the railing pushing their way into line. The stench of fish hung in the air and lingered on behind them.

"It sure stinks, doesn't it," said a young officer with a handsome mustache and an elegant frown.

The manager rushed up from behind to say something to the officers and to bow over and over.

From far away men watched the officers' decorated daggers bounce against their buttocks with each step. They began discussing seriously which of the officers looked the most distinguished. In the end their debate almost led to a quarrel.

"In this company Asakawa looks pathetic," said one of the men, mimicking Asakawa's fawning attitude. His comrades laughed.

With the manager and foreman both absent, work was easy that day. Men sang and talked loudly across the machines.

"How great it would be if we could work like this every day."

After finishing work they all climbed to the upper deck. Passing in front of the saloon, they heard a clamor of drunk and chaotic shouts from within. The cabin boy came out. The interior of the saloon was dense with tobacco smoke.

The cabin boy's flushed face was beaded with sweat. His arms were wrapped around a great many empty beer bottles. He pointed to his trousers' pocket with his chin. "Wipe my face for me, would you?"

A fisherman pulled out the handkerchief and wiped the cabin boy's face. With a glance at the saloon, he asked "What're they up to?"

"Ah, it's a pretty sight in there. They're guzzling like fish, and going on and on about . . . all about women's you-know-what. They got me running back and forth hundreds of times. When functionaries from the Ministry of Agriculture and Forestry bother to show up they get so drunk they almost fall off the gangway."

"What do they come for?"

The cabin boy made a face to suggest he didn't know, and rushed off to the galley.

The fishermen ate their meal. It consisted of crumbly Nanking rice that was hard to pick up with chopsticks, and paper-thin bits of vegetables floating in salty *miso* soup.

"They've got loads of foreign foods in that saloon, foods I've never eaten or even seen."

"Fuck 'em."

A clumsily handwritten sign had been pasted to the bulkhead beside the table:

1. Anyone who complains about the food will never become a success.
2. Treasure every grain of rice. It's a gift of blood and sweat.
3. Put up with discomfort and pain.

In the lower margin someone had scribbled an obscene comment of the sort that is found in public lavatories.

After eating and before going to sleep, the men gathered briefly around the stove. Talking about the destroyer led to talk about soldiers. The topic strangely engrossed them. Many of the fishermen were peasants from Akita, Aomori, and Iwate, and many had been in the army. Although their army life had been filled with brutalities, they now recalled various incidents with nostalgia.

When they settled down to sleep, the noise from the saloon suddenly grew audible, transmitted along the ship's deck boards and sides. "Are they still at it?" thought a man who chanced to wake up. "It's nearly dawn!" Someone—perhaps the cabin boy—kept coming and going overhead, the heels of his shoes clicking against the deck. The din continued until daybreak.

The group of officers had evidently returned to the destroyer, and the gangway remained lowered in the wake of their departure. Five or six of its successive steps were covered with gobs of rice, crab meat, brown muck, and vomit. The vomit emanated a strong stench of rancid alcohol. It assaulted men's nostrils and made them gag.

The destroyer floated like a gray seabird with folded wings, imperceptibly rocking. It looked completely given over to sleep. A wisp of woolly smoke, more slender than that of a cigarette, rose from its smokestack into the windless sky.

The manager, foreman, and their fellow carousers did not get up even at noon.

"Those pricks do just as they damn like!" grumbled the men as they worked.

From the corners of the galley rose enormous mounds of beer bottles and half-eaten cans of crab. By the morning, even the cabin boy who had carried them in was astonished at the amount the revelers had managed to drink and devour.

Thanks to the nature of his work, the cabin boy knew much more about the details of the captain's, manager's, and factory agent's lives than the fishermen or sailors ever could. At the same time, he knew how sharply they contrasted with the miserable lives of the fishermen (whom the manager referred to as "swine" whenever he was drunk). He could honestly say that men at the top were arrogant characters who breezily thought up contemptible schemes in order to turn a profit. The fishermen and sailors were easy prey for those schemes. He could not endure watching that.

So long as nobody catches on, he always thought, things would stay quiet. Eventually something was bound to happen—it could not but happen—and he felt he knew what that would be.

It was around two. The captain, manager, and a few others set out by launch for the destroyer. They were wearing badly wrinkled suits that seemed to have been clumsily folded the previous night. Two sailors accompanied them, arms loaded with cans. Fishermen and workers working on deck continued to shell crabs and stared at the bigwigs as though watching a bridal procession.

"What the hell are they up to now?"

"They treat the cans we made like toilet paper!"

"Still and all," said an aging fisherman whose left hand was missing two fingers. "They came all the way here just to protect us, and that's all right . . . Ain't it?"

That evening the destroyer's smokestack suddenly began emitting billows of smoke. Sailors started to rush along its decks. Some thirty minutes later the destroyer began to move. The flag at its stern flapped loudly in the wind. From the cannery ship rose cries of "Hurrah!" led by the captain.

After supper the cabin boy came down into the shit-hole. Men were sitting around the stove and talking. Some stood under the dim light picking lice from their shirts. Each time their bodies blocked the light, the men cast great oblique shadows on the painted, sooty bulkheads.

"Let me tell you what the officers, captain, and the manager are up to. It looks like we're going to be sneaking into Russian territory to fish there. And so the destroyer's going to stick close to us all the time and guard us. They're going to be making lots and lots of this." He made a circle with his thumb and forefinger in the shape of a coin.

"They're saying that Kamchatka and northern Karafuto are rolling with money to be made, and they're making damned sure to add this whole area to Japan. They say this region is just as important to Japan as China and Manchuria. On top of that, it seems that this corporation's gotten together with Mitsubishi to nudge the government along. If the company president gets into the Diet at the next election, they'll really be stepping things up.

"And so they say the destroyer's been sent to guard the cannery ship, but it turns out that's not the main reason. They're going to carry out a detailed survey of the sea around here, northern Karafuto, and Chishima Islands, and to study the climate. That's the big objective and it has to be carried out thoroughly. I guess it must be a secret, but it seems they're quietly moving artillery and fuel oil to the northernmost of the Chishima Islands.

"It bowled me over when I first heard it, but when you come right down to it the truth is that every single one of Japan's wars to this day was fought at the orders of a few rich or super-rich men (I'm talking really rich men), with the excuses cooked up any which way. Anyhow, these crooks are itching like crazy to get their hands on every place they smell money. They're looking for trouble."

7

A fishing boat was coming down, lowered by rattling winches. Because the winches' arms were short, four men stood directly beneath the descending boat waiting to push it over the edge of the deck. Accidents or near-misses were frequent. The decrepit ship's winches creaked like the knees of a man sick with beriberi. The cogwheels that controlled the wires were worn out, causing one wire to unroll much faster than the other. Sometimes the boat ended up dangling aslant like a smoked herring. At such times a fisherman standing below could get caught by surprise and injured. That is what happened this morning. Someone shouted, "Ah, watch out!" just as a fisherman's head, struck directly from above, was hammered like a stake into his own torso.

His mates carried him to the ship's physician. Those who by now thoroughly loathed the manager decided to ask the doctor to write out a medical certificate. Because the manager was a veritable snake in human skin he could be counted on to find a way of avoiding responsibility for the accident. The men needed a medical certificate to strengthen their protest, and they knew that the doctor was fairly sympathetic toward them.

"On this ship a lot more people get hurt and sick from being punched and beaten than from work," he had once said in surprise. The doctor kept a daily diary for later use as evidence. And he treated the sick and injured fishermen and seamen rather kindly.

One of the men brought up the subject of a certificate.

The doctor looked rattled. "Well, now, a medical certificate . . ."

"Please just write what happened." His indecision was beginning to be irritating.

"They're not letting me write those on this ship. Apparently they just decided not to allow it. They're worried about the consequences . . ."

"Damn it!" The short-tempered Stuttering Fisherman irritably clicked his tongue.

"Some time ago a man came in who had been hit by Asakawa and lost his hearing. I wrote out a certificate for him and thought nothing of it. I caught hell for it. That's permanent evidence, Asakawa said . . ."

The men filed out of the doctor's cabin convinced that even he was no longer on their side.

Amazingly, the injured fisherman managed somehow to stay alive. But for many days he kept stumbling over things even in daytime, and moaning in dark corners wherever he happened to fall.

Around the time when the wounded man began to recover and no longer tormented others with his groans, the fisherman who had long been bedridden with beriberi died. He was twenty-six. He had come through an agency in the Nippori section of Tokyo together with ten or so of his friends. The manager, not wanting anything to interfere with the next day's work, allowed only those who were sick to hold a wake for him.

As they undid his clothes in order to wash him, a nauseating stench arose from the youth's body. Ghastly lice, white and flat, scattered about in panic. The body was covered with scale-like flakes of dirt, resembling the trunk of a pine. Each rib stood out sharply on his chest. Unable to walk once his illness worsened, he evidently had urinated where he lay and so his entire body stank terribly. His loincloth and shirt had both turned dark brown and tattered as if they had been sprayed with sulfuric acid. His navel was virtually invisible, its hollow completely clogged with dust and dirt. Dried shit clung to his buttocks like clay.

"I don't want to die in Kamchatka," he is supposed to have said as he died. But most likely no one had been at his side looking after him when he took leave of life. Nobody wanted to die here in Kamchatka. Thinking of how he must have felt, some of the fishermen wept aloud.

"Poor fellow," said the cook when a fisherman came to fetch the water to wash him with. "Go ahead and take a lot. His body's got to be awfully dirty."

On the way back, the fisherman met the manager.

"Where're you taking that?"

"We're washing the body."

"Don't waste it." He seemed to want to say something more, but walked on.

The fisherman got back and told his comrades, "I tell you, I wanted so bad to dump hot water over that scumbag's head!" He was trembling with rage.

The pigheaded manager kept coming around to see what they were doing. Everyone had resolved to stay up for the wake even if it meant dozing on the job the next day or doing a slowdown. The matter was settled.

By eight o'clock, the basic preparations were complete. The men lit incense and candles, and sat down with folded knees before their friend's body. This time the manager did not come, but the captain and the ship's doctor sat with them for about an hour. A fisherman who remembered some scriptural phrases was asked to chant a sutra. Although his delivery was halting and broken, everyone told him, "You're doing fine, the feeling is there." The chanting was accompanied by total silence. Someone sniffled. Toward the end, more than a few men were weeping.

Following the chanting, everyone took turns offering incense. Next they sat down less formally, gathered in small groups. The conversation moved from their dead friend to themselves who were still alive though, come to think of it, only precariously so. After the captain and the doctor had left, the Stuttering Fisherman stepped up to a table that stood close to the body. The tabletop was covered with incense and candles.

"I don't know the sutras. I can't console Yamada's spirit by chanting sutras. But I've been thinking a lot, and here's what I think. I've thought about how much Yamada didn't want to die. . . . No, to tell the truth, I've thought about how much he *didn't want to be killed.* There's no denying that Yamada was killed."

His listeners fell silent, as though held in a hard grip.

"So, who killed him? I don't need to tell you, you know who! I can't console Yamada's spirit with a sutra. But *we* can console Yamada's spirit by taking our revenge against his killer. I think that now's the time we must swear to Yamada's spirit that we'll do that . . ."

The sailors were the first to say: "You're right."

The fragrance of incense wafted like perfume through the stuffy air and fishy smell of the shit-hole. At nine o'clock, the workers went back to their quarters. Tired, dozing youths, their bodies like sacks full of rocks, found it hard to get up. After a while even a fisherman or two who stayed at the wake succumbed to sleep. Waves began to rise. Each time the ship swayed, candle flames tapered as if about to go out and then brightened again. The white cotton cloth that covered the dead face moved as though about to slide off. Watching the stirring fabric made the men shiver with an eerie sensation. The waves started to beat against the ship's sides.

After eight o'clock the next morning, four sailors and fishermen who had been chosen by the manager stopped working and went downstairs. The fisherman of the previous evening chanted another sutra, and then with the help of several sick men they placed the corpse into a hemp sack. Although there were many new hemp sacks on board, the manager had not let them have one, not wishing to waste it on something that would soon be thrown into the sea. The ship's supply of incense sticks had already run out.

"Look at the poor guy. Of course he didn't want to die."

The young man's arms were hard to fold. While trying to force his palms together in prayer, his companions shed tears onto the hemp sack.

"No, can't let your tears fall on him . . ."

"Isn't there some way to bring him back to Hakodate? . . . Just look at his face: ain't he telling us he don't want to go into these god-forsaken Kamchatka waters? Nobody wants to get dumped into the sea all alone . . ."

"This Kamchatka's a sea like no other. After September, once it gets to be winter, you can't see a single ship anywhere. The whole sea freezes over. We're at the northern edge of the north!"

"Yeah . . ." A man was quietly weeping. "And why are only six or seven of us seeing him off? There are three or four hundred of us on this ship!"

"They don't treat us right even once we're dead . . ."

They had requested at least half a day off from work, but the catch of crabs had greatly increased since the previous day and their wish was denied. "Don't mix personal affairs with business," the manager had told them.

"Are you done yet?" demanded the manager now, showing his face through the opening in the shit-hole ceiling.

"Yes . . ." they muttered reluctantly.

"Then take him away."

"But first the captain's supposed to say a few words in his memory."

"The captain? In his memory?" The voice brimmed with scorn. "You idiots! You think we got time for that?"

There was no time for that. Mountains of crabs rose high on deck, their claws rustling and scraping against the boards.

And so the dead youth was swiftly carried out and stowed unceremoniously, like a straw sack of salmon or trout, aboard a motor launch tied to the ship's stern.

"Ready?"

"Let's go."

With a put-put of its engine, the launch began to move. The water behind the boat churned up with foam.

"Well . . ."

"Well . . ."

"Farewell."

"You'll be lonely out there. . . . Try to put up with it," someone whispered.

"Take good care of him," they asked the men in the launch.

"All right, we will."

The launch moved off toward the open sea.

"Well, that's that! . . ."

"He's gone from us."

"Just looking at him you could see plain as day how much he hated it, hated to go like that. Inside that damned sack . . ."

Back from fishing, men heard how callously the manager had gotten rid of the dead boy. Even before they could flare up with rage, they shuddered with horror as though their own dead bodies had been heartlessly dumped into the dark depths of the Kamchatka sea. Speechless, they filed down the gangway. Taking off jackets soaked heavy with the brine, they muttered, "We get it, we sure get the message."

8

Outwardly they showed nothing. They kept on slowing down the pace of work invisibly. No matter how much the manager railed and lashed out at them, they remained ostensibly docile and refrained from reacting or talking back. They repeated the slowdown every other day. Though at first they were fearful and nervous, they kept it up. After their comrade's burial at sea, their actions grew more coordinated.

The output was visibly declining.

Although they were the ones who suffered most on the job, some of the older fishermen looked askance at the slowdown. Even so, amazed that their secret fears did not materialize and seeing that the slowdown was quite effective, they began to go along with the young fishermen's suggestions.

It was the boat bosses who found themselves in the worst dilemma. Squeezed between the fishermen and the manager, they bore full responsibility for the fishing boats and knew the manager would blame them for any decline in the fishing output. That made their position the hardest. Ultimately, one third grudgingly sided with the fishermen and the rest with the manager.

"Sure, it's tough. We can't have regular work hours here like in a factory. We're dealing with living creatures. Crabs won't turn up just when it suits us. It can't be helped." Their words copied the manager's like a phonograph recording.

One night, a conversation taking place in the shit-hole took an unexpected turn. A boat boss happened to make a cocky comment. Though he was not being especially arrogant, the rank-and-file men took offense. And the fisherman he had been talking to was a little drunk.

"What did you say?" the fisherman suddenly shouted. "Who the hell do you think you are? Better not act so big, you fucker. When we're fishing out there, it'll be a snap for a couple of us to toss you into the sea. That'll be that. This is Kamchatka, you know. Nobody's going to know how you croaked!"

No one had ever spoken this way. Now he roared it out in a hoarse booming voice. Nobody said anything. All other conversation abruptly broke off.

Yet such words did not spring from reckless bravado. Fishermen who till now had known only servile submission, quite unexpectedly felt a tremendous force thrusting them forward. At first they were bewildered. Gradually they realized that *their own power,* whose presence they had not suspected, was manifesting itself.

"But are *we* capable of making use of that power?" they wondered. Of course they were.

Once they understood it, a wonderful spirit of rebellion filled their hearts. The very hardships of the agonizing work that had been wrung from them turned into a splendid foundation for their defiance. Now the manager and his ilk could go to hell! They were elated. This new feeling suddenly enabled them to see their wormlike lives vividly, as though illuminated by a flashlight's beam.

The phrase "Better not act so big" grew popular with everyone. When provoked, they growled, "Better not act so big, you fucker." They were quick to say it at other times too. But among the fishermen themselves, no one acted big.

Incidents of this sort took place often. Each time they did, the fishermen's ability to "get it" went on growing. And as experiences accumulated, three or four fishermen kept consistently coming to the fore. No one chose them, nor did they choose themselves. Yet whenever something happened or something needed to be done, the opinions of those three or four coincided with those of everyone else, and so everyone started to move in the same direction. The group included two ex-students, the Stuttering Fisherman, and the Don't-act-so-big Fisherman.

One of the students spent a whole night writing something on a piece of paper as he lay on his stomach licking his pencil over and over. It was the ex-student's "Proposal (diagram of people in charge)." [See page 80.]

"How about it?" said the student proudly. No matter what happened in groups A or C, he confidently announced, they could swiftly and flawlessly focus on the overall problem. His proposal was adopted in its entirety. But putting it into practice proved not so easy. The student's proud slogan was: "Anyone who doesn't want to get killed, come and join us!"

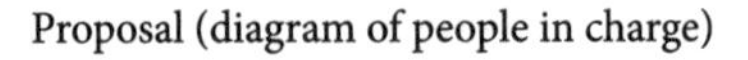
Proposal (diagram of people in charge)

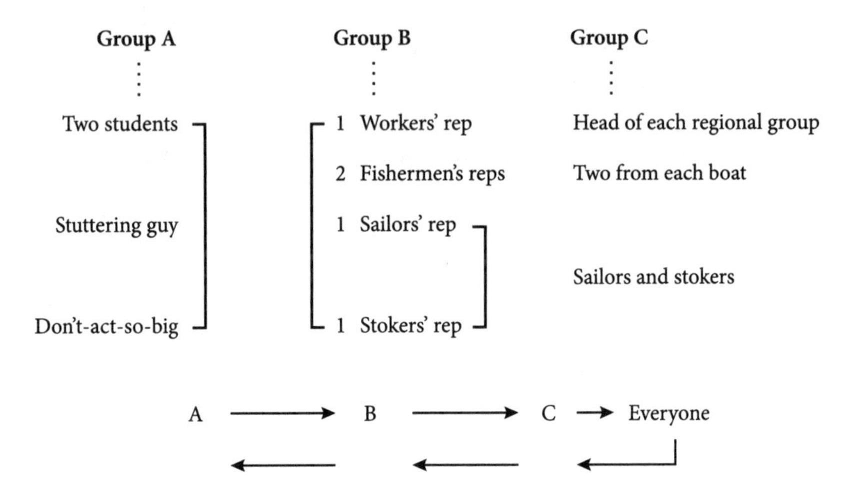

He told everyone the story of Mōri Motonari, a feudal lord who had his three sons confirm for themselves that a single arrow could easily be broken but three arrows held together could not. He described a "Tug of War" poster produced by the Home Ministry that also illustrated the importance of working together. "Given four or five of us, it's a cinch to knock a boat boss into the sea. Cheer up.

"One on one is no good. It's dangerous. But there're practically four hundred of us. If four hundred work together, we win. It's ten against four hundred! If they want to fight, just let them try it." He concluded: "Anyone who doesn't want to get killed, come and join us!"

Even the blockheads and drunkards among the men understood that the life they were being forced to lead was threatening to kill them—they had actually seen their comrades killed before their very eyes. And since the fledgling slowdown they had resorted to in desperation was turning out to be unexpectedly effective, they were quite ready to comply with the students' and the Stuttering Fisherman's suggestions.

The previous week's storm had broken the motor launch's propeller. In order to repair it, the foreman had gone ashore together with four or five fishermen. On their return, a young fisherman secretly brought along a great many "Red propaganda" pamphlets and fliers printed in Japanese. "There are Japanese out there doing a lot of this," he said. The contents dealt with their low wages, long working hours, gross corporate profits, strikes, and the like, so everyone read them to each other with great interest and questioned one another about them. Some of them recoiled against what was written in the pamphlets, doubting that their fellow Japanese could do such terrible things. But others came with fliers in hand to ask the student questions and said, "We think that this is true."

"Sure, it's true. A little overstated but true."

"Well, if we didn't do anything, would Asakawa have a change of heart?" they asked laughing. "We're getting much worse treatment, so what we're doing is only natural!"

Meantime the fishermen went on denouncing the "Red movement" as an outrage while beginning to grow curious about it.

During storms or whenever there was a thick fog, the ship continuously blew its horn calling to the fishing boats. For up to two full hours the horn's powerful siren blared like a lowing bull through the fog's liquid density. Even so, not all boats were able to return. But some crews were so worn out with the excruciating work that they deliberately pretended to be lost and drifted to Kamchatka. Sometimes they secretly planned it in advance. After entering Russian territorial waters to fish, they headed for the coast and drifted ashore with surprising ease. Many of them were ready to "turn Red."

The corporation always took utmost care in hiring fishermen. Corporate officials asked local village headmen and police chiefs to deliver them "model youths." They chose submissive workers who had no interest in labor unions or activism. They recruited "astutely," so that everything would work in their favor! However, the inhumane work aboard the crab cannery ships achieved precisely the opposite effect of uniting the workers—of organizing them. The capitalists, with all their "astuteness," had not foreseen this marvelous development. The brutal toil educated the workers—both the unorganized laborers and the hopeless "drunks" whom they had expressly and cynically brought together. It taught them to unite.

9

The manager was starting to panic.

Compared to the annual rate of catch toward the close of the fishing season, the quantity of crabs had clearly diminished. Asking other ships about it, he learned that their results seemed to be better than the previous year's. His ship was two thousand crates behind. This convinced the manager that playing the compassionate Buddha as he had up to now was a mistake.

The main ship decided to move on. The manager, constantly eavesdropping on radio communications, had even the other ships' nets coolly and swiftly hauled up. The first net was raised after they had sailed twenty nautical miles south. It was bursting with crabs, their claws squirming in its mesh. The catch unmistakably belonged to ship XX.

"Great work," said the manager with uncharacteristic warmth, patting the company agent on the shoulder.

From time to time the ship's launch was discovered raising others' nets and had to make a precipitous getaway. As a result of indiscriminate raids on other ships' nets, the amount of work rose sharply.

> Anyone neglecting his work in the slightest will be branded. Those who indulge in collective idling will be subject to the Kamchatka drill. Their wages will be cancelled as punishment, and on return to Hakodate they will be handed over to the police. Anyone showing the slightest defiance to the manager will be shot.
>
> MANAGER ASAKAWA & THE FOREMAN

This large sign was posted at the top of the stairs leading to the factory. The manager always carried a fully loaded pistol. At unexpected times he aimed it over workers' heads, at seagulls or random spots on the ship, and fired as "a show of force." As startled fishermen flinched, he flashed a broad grin. A sinister feeling struck them all that he was perfectly willing to shoot any of them dead for almost any reason.

Every sailor and stoker was mobilized and arbitrarily put to all sorts of work. The captain, long reduced to a figurehead, was unable to utter a single word of objection. He was forced to sail the ship into Soviet territorial waters in order to fish there. He had insisted that in his official capacity as a captain he could not violate international law.

"To hell with you!" retorted the manager. "Nobody's asking you for a favor!" The manager and his cohorts steered the ship into Russian territory on their own. A Russian patrol boat spotted them, however, and gave chase. Under interrogation the manager grew confused and cravenly retreated, doing his best to shift the blame onto the skipper. "Of course full responsibility for the ship lies with the captain . . ." Thus the figurehead had his uses, and that in itself was enough.

After that incident, the captain often thought of turning the ship back to Hakodate. But the power that prevented him from doing it—the power of capitalists—kept him in its grip and prevailed.

"Get it through your head: the corporation owns this whole damned ship!" sneered the manager. He stretched to his full height and roared with laughter.

Returning to the shit-hole, the Stuttering Fisherman threw himself onto his bunk and lay face up, bitterly disappointed. Other fishermen gazed at him and the students with sympathy, but felt too crushed to say anything. The organization chart drawn up by the student had been of no more use than wastepaper. Even so, the student remained rather optimistic.

"We'll spring to action when something happens," he said. "We just need to grab a good hold of that something."

"You seriously think so?" challenged the Don't-act-big Fisherman.

"Do I? Don't be stupid. We've got the numbers. There's nothing to be scared of. For now, everyone's holding back. But the worse they treat us the more discontent and frustration they jam-pack into us all, and these are more powerful than gunpowder. That's what I'm counting on."

"It'd be good if we were ready to act," grumbled Don't-act-big, looking around the shit-hole. "None of these characters are . . ."

"If *we* start to grumble, it's all over."

"Look, you're the only one who's cheerful. The next thing we start, our lives will be on the line."

The student's face darkened. "That's right . . . ," he said.

The manager patrolled the shit-hole three times a night, accompanied by a subordinate. Whenever he came across a cluster of three or four men he thundered at them to disperse. Unwilling to leave it at that, he secretly ordered one of his underlings to sleep in the shit-hole.

The workers' chains were all but visible. They weighed on everyone, making them feel as though inch-thick iron shackles dragged from their legs as they walked.

"I'll get killed for sure."

"Yeah, but when you realize you're about to get killed anyway, that's the time to do it."

"Idiot!" butted in the fisherman from Shibaura loudly. "When you realize it? And when's that going to happen, you fool? Aren't you being killed right now? They're killing you bit by bit, brother. They know what they're doing. They carry pistols like they'll shoot you any minute, but they're not likely to do something so stupid. That's just a trick. Do you get it? They know that if they kill us, they're the ones who lose out. Their goal—their real goal—is to make us work like the devil, tie us to the tree, squeeze us till we squeak, and make loads of profits from us. That's what they're putting us through every day. We're in one hell of a mess, don't you think? Our bodies are being killed just like mulberry leaves are gobbled up by silkworms."

"No way!"

"No way, my ass." A speck of cigarette flame rolled onto a thick palm. "Fucked if you don't see it for yourself soon enough!"

The ship had gone too far south where there was little to catch except many small-bodied female crabs, so it was decided to move north. The men were made to work overtime and for the first time in a long while the work finished a little earlier than usual.

Everyone tramped down into the shit-hole.

"You don't look so good," said the man from Shibaura.

"Well, look at my legs. They're so wobbly I can't even go down any stairs any more."

"Sorry to hear it. And you're still trying to work as hard as you can."

"Who, me? Can't be helped."

The man from Shibaura laughed. "So being killed can't be helped either, huh?"

". . . . ."

"Well, if you keep on like this, you've got four or five days to go."

The sick man twisted his swollen yellowish cheeks and eyelids into an indignant grimace. He mutely walked over to his bunk, sat down, and dangling his legs over the edge started to pound his knee-joints with the edge of his hand.

In a lower bunk, Shibaura talked waving his arms. The Stuttering Fisherman rocked back and forth, nodding at his words.

". . . See? Let's suppose the ship exists because the rich put up the money and had it built. If there were no sailors and stokers, could the ship move? There're hundreds of millions of crabs on the bottom of the sea. Let's suppose we all got our gear and came out here because the rich were able to put up the money. But if we didn't work, would even one solitary crab end up in the pockets of the rich? See? Now, think about how much money's coming our way after we work here all summer. Yet from this ship alone the rich will snatch four or five hundred thousand yen of pure profit. Well, *we are the source of that money.* Nothing comes out of nothing. You see? Everything's in our power. And so I'm telling you to wipe that gloomy look off your mug. Show them who you are. In their heart of hearts they're scared shitless of us, and that's no lie. So don't be timid.

"Without sailors and stokers, ships wouldn't budge. Without the workers' labor, not one lousy penny would roll into the pockets of the rich. Even the money to buy the ship, to outfit and equip it, comes out of profits wrung from the blood of other workers. It's money that's been squeezed out of us. The rich and we are masters and slaves . . ."

The manager walked in.

Everybody clammed up and began to shuffle out.

10

The air was cold as glass, transparent and clear. At two in the morning it was already daybreak. Kamchatka's mountain range, shining golden and purple, rose from the sea in a slender line that ran all along the southern horizon. Ripples icily glittered, each one catching the light of the rising sun. They kept colliding and breaking, mingling and dissolving, sparkling with each move. Cries of invisible seagulls rang through the air. The cold was invigorating. Sheets of oil-stained canvas covering the cargo fluttered and flapped from time to time. Imperceptibly it grew windy.

Poking his arms through the sleeves of his jacket like a scarecrow, a fisherman climbed up the stairway and thrust his head from the hatchway. Startled he shouted, "Hey, the rabbits are flying! A big windstorm's coming up."

Triangular waves came rushing at the ship. Fishermen accustomed to the Kamchatka sea instantly knew what that meant.

"No fishing today, way too dangerous."

An hour went by.

Men stood around in groups of seven or eight under the fishing boat winches. The boats swung in the air, each lowered only halfway. Men shrugged and argued gazing at the sea. A few minutes went by.

"I quit! I quit!"

"They can go fuck themselves!"

It was as if they had been waiting for somebody to say it.

As they jostled and milled about, someone else said, "Hey, let's pull the boats back up."

"Yes!"

"Yes, a damn good idea!"

"But . . ." A man looked up at the winch and hesitated, frowning.

"If you want to drown, go out there by yourself!" said another scornfully, turning away with a jerk of his shoulder.

The whole group began to leave. "I wonder if this is really OK," whispered someone. Two men uncertainly lagged behind.

At the next pair of winches too fishermen stood motionless. Seeing the crew of Boat Number 2 walking toward them they understood what it meant. Four or five of them waved and raised their voices:

"We're quitting! We're quitting!"

"That's right, time to quit!"

As the two groups met, their spirits rose. Two or three men who were not sure what to do looked on, baffled. The newly formed group moved on to join the crew of Boat Number 5. Seeing this, the men who had been hanging back started to walk forward, grumbling.

The Stuttering Fisherman turned around and shouted loudly, "Be tough!"

Like a rolling snowball becoming larger and larger, the group of fishermen kept on growing. The Stuttering Fisherman and the students ran constantly back and forth between the group's front and its rear. "All right, don't let yourselves get separated! That's the most important thing. Stay together and we're safe. That's it, now we're good!"

Fishermen who sat in a circle mending ropes near the smokestack straightened their backs and called out, "Hey, what happened?"

The advancing group lifted their arms toward them, and raised a great shout. Sailors watching from above saw a forest of waving arms.

"Good, that does it! We're stopping work."

They briskly began to put away the ropes. "We've been waiting for this!"

The fishermen understood. Once more they raised a great cry.

"First of all, let's get everyone out of the shit-hole. Yes, let's do it. That motherfucker knows damn well that a storm's coming up, and he still has the nerve to order the boats out! What a fucking murderer!"

"Damned if we're going to let him kill us!"

"*Now* he'll see who he's been messing with!"

Almost everyone headed for the shit-hole. A few came along reluctantly.

As they all noisily barged into the shit-hole, a sick man lying in the darkness raised his board-thin torso in surprise. At their explanation his eyes welled up with tears and he nodded his head over and over.

The Stuttering Fisherman and the students followed a stairway, flimsy as a rope ladder, down into the engine room. Hurrying and unaccustomed to the stairs, they repeatedly lost their footing and dangled precariously by their hands. The interior was dark and stifling with heat from the boiler. Their bodies soon grew covered with sweat. They crossed a flat metal footway over the boiler and went down another ramp. Loud voices rang out and echoed below them. They were assailed by a sinister feeling of descending for the first time into the deep-sunk pit of a subterranean hell.

"Damn, this is backbreaking work too."

"It sure is, but w-what are we going to do if they drag them out on deck and make *them* work killing c-crabs?"

"Not to worry, the stokers are on our side!"

"That's good!"

They were climbing down alongside the boiler.

"Damn, it's hot. I can't stand this heat. It's enough to turn a person into smoked meat."

"That's no joke. It's this hot and the fire's not even lit now. Imagine what it's like when they fire it up!"

"Goddamn, it must be bad."

"Crossing the Indian Ocean, guys work in half-hour shifts and still get totally exhausted. One time a first engineer bitched about something without thinking. First they pounded him with shovels and then threw him into the firebox. That's how ugly it can get!"

"You don't say. Yeah, I can believe it . . ."

A pile of coal ashes stood in front of the boiler. It seemed to have been doused with water, and a cloud of dust rose from it. Half-naked stokers sat nearby with arms around their knees, smoking and talking. In the semi-darkness they closely resembled crouching gorillas. The coal bunker's hatch stood half open, its chilly pitch-black interior eerily yawning.

"Hey!" shouted the Stuttering Fisherman.

"Who's there?" The stokers looked up, their cry reverberating with a triple echo: "Who's there? Who's there? Who's there?"

The new arrivals came down. Seeing them, one of the stokers bellowed, "Did you two take a wrong turn?"

"We're on strike."

"You're what?"

"We are on strike."

"You've really gone on strike!"

"No shit! How about us firing up full blast and heading back to Hakodate? That'd be interesting."

The Stuttering Fisherman thought, 'They're with us!'

"Once we're all together, we're going to take on those sons of bitches!"

"Yeah, you go give 'em hell!" exclaimed a stoker.

"Not just us, you too," pointed out the student. "Let's give 'em hell together!"

"Sure, sure, I was wrong. Let's give 'em hell together!" The stoker scratched his head, white with coal ash.

Everyone laughed.

"We'd like you all to organize yourselves."

"All right, no problem. We've always wanted to take a good punch at those fuckers."

The stokers had been won over.

All the factory workers were brought to where the fishermen had gathered. The stokers and sailors joined them within the hour. Everyone stood assembled on deck. The Stuttering Fisherman, the students, Shibaura, and Don't-act-big jointly drew up a list of demands. They decided to confront the manager and his cohorts with it, in everyone's presence.

As soon as they learned about the commotion among the fishermen, the manager and the others were nowhere to be seen.

"Hmm, that's funny."

"It *is* strange."

"That pistol of his isn't doing him a fuck of a lot of good right now."

The Stuttering Fisherman stepped up onto a small platform. Everyone clapped.

"Brothers, we're finally here! We've been waiting for a long, long time. Even while we were being worked half to death, we waited. We thought: you'll see soon enough. But now we're finally here.

"The most important thing of all, brothers, is to join forces and keep our power united. Whatever happens, we must never betray a comrade. If we just hang on tightly to that, they'll be easier to crush than worms. So, what's the second most important thing? The second most important thing, brothers, is also to keep our power united. Not to have anyone drop out. Not to have a single traitor, not a single turncoat. We must know that just one turncoat kills three hundred lives. One turncoat . . ."

"We get it, we get it." Shouts interrupted him. "It'll be all right. Don't worry, keep going."

"Whether we can beat them at negotiations, whether or not we can fulfill our task, all of that depends on *the strength of our unity*, brothers."

The stokers' delegate was the next to get up, followed by the sailors'. The stokers' delegate began to speak in words he normally never used, and grew flustered. Each time he became stuck for a word he blushed crimson, tugged at the hem of his overalls, thrust his hands into holes in its worn-out fabric, and fidgeted. Noticing it, his listeners roared with laughter and pounded the deck with their feet.

"Okay, I'll quit talking. But, brothers, give those scumbags a good beating!" With that, he stepped down from the platform. He received a mischievously overblown ovation.

"He should've just said that last part," joked someone, triggering a fresh uproar of laughter.

The stoker was drenched in more sweat than he'd work up wielding his long coal-shovel in midsummer and even his legs barely supported him. "What the hell was I talking about?" he asked his companions as he stepped down.

The student clapped him on the shoulder. "You were great, just great," he said laughing.

"It's your fault. There're so many others, it didn't have to be me . . ."

A worker of about fifteen stepped up onto the platform.

"Brothers, we've been waiting for this day. You all know how our friends have been abused and tormented inside this cannery ship. At night we wrap ourselves in those thin blankets, think about our homes, and cry. Just ask any worker that's standing here. There hasn't been a single night when we haven't all cried. All our bodies are covered with raw wounds. If things go on like this for even three more days, some of us are gonna die for sure. If our families had a little bit of money, at our age we could still be going to school and playing like kids instead of being so far from . . ."

The boy's voice grew husky and he stammered. He continued quietly, as though holding himself in check.

"But that doesn't matter now. It's all right. Thanks to the help of you grownups we'll be able to get even with those mean, rotten bastards . . ."

This brought on a storm of applause. Clapping like mad, an older fisherman furtively wiped a corner of his eye with a thick fingertip.

The students and the Stuttering Fisherman walked around collecting signatures for a written oath that bore everyone's name on it.

It was decided that two students, the Stuttering Fisherman, Don't-act-big, Shibaura, three stokers, and three seamen would take the list of demands and the oath to the captain's cabin while everyone else held a demonstration in front of it. Everything was settled with astonishing ease. Unlike on land where people live in scattered locations, here they were all concentrated in one place, and moreover, adequate groundwork had been laid. That made for smooth progress. So smooth, in fact, that it was hard to believe.

"Funny the devil's not showing his ugly mug anywhere."

"I thought he'd get so worked up he'd be firing off that fancy pistol of his."

At a signal from the Stuttering Fisherman they raised a cheer, three hundred of them thundering in unison: "Strike, hurrah! Strike, hurrah! Strike, HURRAH!"

"That ought to make the fucking manager quiver in his boots," thought the student with a smile. The delegates pushed their way into the captain's cabin.

The manager met them pistol in hand.

The captain, foreman, factory agent, and the rest of them had obviously been discussing something till that very moment. The manager was calm. As the delegates entered, he grinned. "So, you've done it."

Three hundred men stood together outside, their voices raised in a roar and their feet thunderously pounding the deck. "Noisy bastards!" said the manager quietly. The delegates, seemingly oblivious to the uproar, began to speak excitedly. The manager carelessly heard them out, cast a perfunctory glance at the list of demands and the oath, and said slowly with evident boredom, "Are you sure you won't regret this?"

"You son of a bitch!" shouted the Stuttering Fisherman suddenly, seeming about to smash the manager's face.

"All right, fine. Possibly you won't regret it," said the manager, and took on a somewhat different tone. "Listen up. Here's what I'll do. I'll give you my gracious response before tomorrow morning."

The words had scarcely left his mouth when Shibaura knocked the pistol out of his hand, and struck him in the face with his fist. As the manager gasped and clutched his face, the Stuttering Fisherman hit him across the legs with a nearby stool. The manager tumbled over grotesquely, his body snagging a table and overturning it. The table crashed on top of him, its legs pointing skyward.

"Your gracious response? Don't fuck with us, you prick! Our lives are at stake here!"

Shibaura menacingly shifted his massive shoulders. The stokers and the other delegates held him back. A window of the captain's cabin exploded with a terrific crash. The same instant shouts from the outside suddenly grew loud and all too clear: "Kill him!" "Shoot him!" "Do him in! Knock him off!"

The captain, foreman, and factory agent slipped away unnoticed to a corner of the cabin and stood there in a huddle, stiff as posts, their faces drained of color.

The cabin door smashed open, and the fishermen, sailors, and stokers surged in.

IN THE EARLY afternoon a raging storm broke out. As the evening approached, it gradually subsided.

Overthrowing the manager had seemed utterly impossible, quite out of the question. And yet they had been able to get rid of him with their own bare hands! He never even got a chance to fire that damned pistol he was always threatening them with. Everyone felt euphoric. The delegates put their heads together to confer about the various measures to take next. If the "gracious response" was not forthcoming, they planned to give their opponent something to remember them by.

It was starting to grow dark when a fisherman who had been keeping watch from the hatchway spotted the approaching destroyer. Agitated, he rushed to the shit-hole.

"Damn it to hell!" The student leapt up like a spring. His face turned deathly pale.

"Don't jump to any wrong conclusions," said the Stuttering Fisherman with a laugh. "Once we win over the officers with a full explanation of our situation, viewpoint, and demands, this strike will turn out even better. That's as plain as day."

"That's true," said others in agreement.

"That's our own imperial warship out there. It's got to be on our side, on the side of the people."

"No, no . . ." The student waved his hand. He seemed shaken by a powerful shock. His lips were trembling, and he was stammering. "On the side of the people? . . . No, no . . ."

"Look, you idiot! How the hell can a warship that belongs to the empire not be on the side of the people who belong to that same empire?!"

"The destroyer's here! The destroyer has arrived!" Excited voices drowned out the student's reply.

Everyone bounded out of the shit-hole and onto the deck. Voices suddenly joined in a great shout: "Imperial navy, hurrah!"

The manager, his face and hand bandaged, stood at the top of the gangway together with the captain and a few others. Directly opposite them stood the Stuttering Fisherman, Shibaura, Don't-act-big, students, stokers, seamen, and the rest of the men. Dimly visible in the gathering darkness, three steam launches left the destroyer. They drew up alongside the cannery ship. Each launch was packed with about sixteen uniformed sailors. All at once the sailors rushed up the gangway.

"Hey! They've got fixed bayonets! And they're wearing helmets!"

"Oh hell!" cried the Stuttering Fisherman voicelessly.

Sixteen more naval sailors poured out of the next launch. The third launch too disgorged sixteen sailors with rifles thrust in front, bayonets fixed, helmets strapped. They charged up in a horde as though boarding a pirate ship and surrounded the fishermen, seamen, and stokers.

"God damn it! They've fucked us over!" screamed Shibaura and the other delegates.

"This will show you!" growled the manager. For the first time since the strike began they understood why he had been behaving so oddly. But it was too late.

They were not allowed to say anything. Denounced as "thugs," "subversives," and "Red traitors," the nine delegates were escorted to the destroyer at the point of bayonets. It all happened with lightning speed as the others watched in a daze, uncomprehending. Not a word of objection was allowed. They saw their efforts go up in flames as absurdly as a blazing sheet of paper. Their revolt had been disposed of with the greatest ease.

"NOBODY'S ON OUR side except our own selves. For the first time, I get the picture."

"All that bullshit about the navy being on the side of the people. . . . On the side of the people, my ass! They're nothing but flunkies of the filthy rich."

Taking no chances, the naval sailors remained on board for three days. For three evenings in a row the officers got drunk in the saloon with the manager, the captain, and the rest of them.

"That's how it goes."

They may indeed have been mere ordinary fishermen, but this time they learned firsthand who their enemies were, and how (quite unexpectedly!) they were connected to each other.

Every year as the fishing season drew to an end, it was customary to manufacture some cans of crabmeat to be offered to the Emperor. Yet not the slightest effort was ever made to precede their preparation with the traditional ritual purification. The fishermen had always thought this terrible of the manager. But this time they felt differently.

"We're squeezing our very blood and flesh into these cans. Huh, I'm sure they'll taste wonderful. Hope they give him a stomachache."

Such were their feelings as they packed the cans for the Imperial table.

"Mix in some rocks! I don't give a fuck!"

"NOBODY'S ON OUR side except our own selves."

This was the feeling that now penetrated deep into everyone's heart. "We'll show you soon enough!"

But repeating the phrase "we'll show you soon enough" hundreds of times brought them no satisfaction. The strike had been miserably defeated, and the work—"Have you learned your lesson, you scum?"—had grown even harsher. The added brutality was the manager's way of revenge. It exceeded even the most extreme limits. The work had become unendurable.

"We were wrong. We shouldn't have put nine people out in front of us like that. We might as well have been saying to them, here's where our vital organs are. We should've all acted together, every one of us. That way it would've been useless for the manager to radio the destroyer. They sure as hell couldn't drag all of us away. There'd be nobody left to do the work."

"That's right."

"No doubt about it. If we keep on working like we are now, we'll really get ourselves killed this time. To make sure nobody has to be sacrificed, we all have to strike together. Let's take the same approach as before. Like the stuttering guy used to say, the most important thing of all is to join forces. By now we sure know how much we could've accomplished that time if we'd stayed united."

"And if they still call in the destroyer, let's all stay united and get handed over together without leaving anyone behind! That'll help us even more."

"You may be right. Though come to think of it, if that happens the manager will be in very hot water with the company. It'll be too late to send to Hakodate for replacements, and the output will be way down. . . . If we do this right, it might turn out even better than we expect."

"It will work out just fine. Besides, it's fantastic how nobody's scared anymore. Everybody's ready to take on the fuckers!"

"Frankly, there's no sense hoping for some future victory. It's a matter of life or death right now."

"Well, let's do it again, one more time!"

AND SO THEY rose. *One more time!*

A SUPPLEMENTARY NOTE

Let us add a few words concerning what followed:

1. The second strike was completely successful. The manager, taken aback, had rushed to the radio room only to come to a sudden stop in front of its door, with no idea what to do.
2. When the fishing season ended and the men sailed back to Hakodate, they realized that their own ship was not the only one that had engaged in slowdowns and strikes. "Red propaganda" pamphlets were found in several ships.
3. The corporation "ruthlessly" fired its faithful dogs, the manager, the foreman, and the rest, blaming them for having brought on scandalous strikes in the middle of a fishing season and causing incalculable damage. They were paid even more miserably than the fishermen—not a penny. Interestingly, the manager was overheard crying out, "God damn it to hell! Those sons of bitches were screwing me all along!"
4. The fishermen, the young workers, and all their comrades were released from police detention and went on to engage in various sectors of labor, equipped with the precious experience of organization and struggle.

THIS NARRATIVE IS a page from the history of capitalist penetration into colonial territories.

MARCH 30, 1929

YASUKO

A Day in Court

1

THE SNOW-PLOWED street crunching beneath their feet was hard to walk on. By the time they reached the Sapporo Courthouse both Okei and her mother were drenched with sweat.

Inside the gate some twenty policemen clad in overcoats stood about in clusters of two or three. Seeing the mother and daughter enter, a ruddy-faced policeman with a fearsome beard hurried over to them. "What's your business here, ma'am?"

Startled, Okei and her mother stopped in their tracks. Hurriedly removing the triangularly folded kerchiefs that covered their heads they bowed two or three times.

"Well, sir . . . it's . . ." Mother hastily thrust her hand deep into her pocket and extracted the document that the court had sent her.

The policeman grabbed it roughly and brought it close to his shortsighted eyes. He swiftly returned it to her, evidently unimpressed.

"Go to that waiting room over there."

"Yes, sir. Thank you, sir . . ."

With a sense of relief, mother and daughter bowed their heads, and went to the entrance he had indicated. After wandering in confusion up and down a long concrete-paved corridor they were finally able to find the waiting room. They were feeling thoroughly intimidated.

Spring was approaching at last, following an exhaustingly long winter. They sat down in a sunny spot by the window, and gradually their shoulders grew warm. Okei was sitting in the corner of the room, pressing herself tightly against her mother. Motionless, she looked around wide-eyed and listened intently to the continuous sound of dripping from the icicles outside the window. It was a methodical, restless, lightly splashing sound.

The only other people inside the waiting room were a woman stand-keeper clad in a white apron such as hospital attendants wear, and a clerk seated before a large desk piled with documents who occasionally stared at the grimy arrivals while pretending not to do so.

At times during the next hour or so, a gown-clad lawyer and a court clerk opened the door with a bang only to thrust their heads into the room and look around. Each time it happened, Mother and Okei flinched like convulsive children, hunched their shoulders and gazed at them.

"They sure seem to be in a tizzy," said the clerk as if to himself, and lit a cigarette. Then he walked over to a stove installed in the middle of the room. One of his legs was shorter than the other.

"It's terrible today," said the stand-keeper, evidently having overheard him. She was arranging bread and milk within her glass case.

"Hm." The lame clerk turned up the front of his serge kimono-trousers and stood before the stove with his feet planted apart.

At that moment the glass entrance door creaked sharply and a tall fierce-eyed man in boots walked in. The man paced up and down the waiting room a few times, casting watchful glances at Okei and her mother. Okei snuggled a little closer to her mother and took a light hold of her sleeve. The man, however, soon left.

The clerk turned away from the stove and began warming his

back. From time to time he chewed his drooping mustache with his lower teeth, as seemed to be his habit. It made a gritty, unpleasant sound.

"You're here for a trial?" the clerk asked in a startlingly loud, thick voice. It was the burned-out voice of a chronic drinker.

Okei glanced around before realizing he was talking to them.

"Yes, we . . ." Mother shifted somewhat uneasily in her seat and bowed.

"You're from around here?"

"No, sir, we're from the country . . ." Mother hurriedly thrust her hands deeply into both pockets and produced the court notice. "Here you are, sir . . ."

The clerk glanced at it, uttered a nasal "Hm," and was about to say something. Just at that instant a group of five or six people noisily barged into the waiting room.

2

Unceremoniously shouting, the intruders seemed to be wondering where the court's waiting room was. Okei and Mother both stared at them dumbfounded. Okei fearfully drew her starchy woolen muffler up to her cheeks to try to conceal her face.

The group consisted entirely of young men wearing greasy shapeless cloth caps, grimy crumpled fedoras, and overcoats that were torn in places. They were rather pale, and all had long hair. One of them was stocky, with a long scar across his cheek that made him look very sinister to Okei. A man in a threadbare corduroy coat took a bean-jam bun out of his pocket. Everyone reached for it. The man, grinning broadly, thrust it back into his pocket.

Although at first Okei did not notice her, there was a woman among them, small as a child, her face quite hidden by a black-hooded cloak. The woman did not say much, yet it struck Okei as extremely strange that she was part of an all-male group and speaking with them with complete familiarity. Okei gazed at her with curiosity.

The young people arrayed themselves around the stove, their voices seeming at times to rise in argument. A fierce-eyed man in a suit who had entered earlier now pushed his way into their circle. The others, who had been speaking so boisterously, suddenly fell silent.

Okei shifted her startled gaze to the man with the fierce eyes.

"What's up?" asked the fierce-eyed man.

"Nothing's up." The brusque reply came from the small woman!

Once again Okei looked at her in surprise, then pulled at her mother's sleeve. "Ma, that woman! Who are those people?"

"What happened?"

"They've got so much energy!"

"Mm . . ."

A light spring-like snow was falling outside the double windows. The snowflakes struck the glass one by one, melted and flowed. Soft sunlight cast bright patches onto the concrete pavement. Specks of dust floated in the light shining obliquely through the window. One of the youths stretched his hands into the light and, like a child, made it flutter in his palms.

Presently, a woman of about forty entered wearing a woolen shawl over her shoulders.

"Ah, it's Fukatani's mother," said the youth with the scar on his cheek, and everyone turned around. The group greeted her in unison with uncharacteristic warmth and tenderness.

The silently watching Okei could not make sense of any of this.

The diminutive woman in the hooded cloak walked over to the new arrival, sat down next to her and began to talk to her in intimate tones. The fierce-eyed man in a suit followed closely behind her. The woman in the cloak did not so much as glance at him.

Suddenly, the door was flung open, a court attendant stuck out his head and shouted, "The . . . trial is about to begin!"

The boisterous youths noisily filed out. Okei and her mother had failed to make out the court attendant's opening words. Nevertheless, they hastily rose, thinking he was referring to their case.

"That's not you," said the lame clerk.

"No?"

"Those are Reds. They're all copying Russia," said the clerk, using words unfamiliar to the mother and daughter.

3

Realizing that it wasn't their turn, Okei sat down feeling relieved.

"They all seem very energetic, don't they."

The clerk glanced at her, then resumed chewing on his mustache. "They call themselves *comrades.*"

"Comrades?"

"It means friends."

"Friends!?"

Friends doing bad things together! They came to a place like this, and so proudly too! Okei and her mother were feeling incomparably small. Whatever it was that those people did, it left Okei impressed.

"Those characters are trying to build a world where there's no rich people, only the poor. They don't think they're doing anything bad."

"No?"

In front of the stove, the clerk shifted from one foot to the other. His lameness made his shoulders wobble badly as he did so.

"The Taguchi Sango trial!" The elderly court attendant, small and frail, called out.

"Here!" cried Mother and leapt up.

"Come this way!"

Although Okei had many times braced herself for this, she felt a surge of confusion. Bundling together her muffler and shawl, she stepped out into the corridor. The long concrete corridor was still as cold as ever. After about thirty feet they turned a corner to see several dozen policemen lining both sides of the corridor searching the earlier group—going through all their pockets, opening their coats and belongings—and letting them into a courtroom one by one.

"You two are this way." The court attendant turned another corner.

Corridor windows looked onto the courtyard that faced the main entrance to the courthouse. As earlier, it was filled with policemen wearing hats with chin straps. They were shoving a group of fifteen or sixteen people out the gate. One of them, pulled violently by the edge of his coat, could be heard protesting, "You're going to tear it!"

"All right, all right, out you go. You're not getting in here," the policemen were saying.

The women arrived at the door on which was written "Courtroom No. 2." The attendant said, "Here we are, wait a moment," and went in by himself.

Along the hallway, a voice rising in argument could be heard from the other side of the walls, accompanied each time by a rattling of swords. Engrossed in their own thoughts, Okei and Mother continued standing in the cold and bare concrete corridor.

Suddenly, the corridor erupted with noise. The thickset youth with the scar across his cheek was vehemently shouting while being led toward them, his arms held by policemen.

"Quit bellyaching! You'll find out when you get there!"

"Huh, I will, will I?"

The scarred man's hat had come off and his long hair hung disheveled across his bluish face. Since both his arms were pinned, he tossed his head from time to time to sweep the hair away from his face. Even as he passed before Okei and her mother, the man wore a slight smile.

Once they were allowed into the courtroom, the two women took a seat in the very corner. A lawyer they had met and talked with in the past was sitting with his back to them and leafing through documents. The old court attendant had taken off his spectacles and was wiping them with a handkerchief. No one else was present. A stove was blazing off to the side but it seemed to have been recently lit and the room was shiveringly cold.

Mother had taken out a hand towel and was quietly wiping her tears.

The court attendant glanced at the clock, and rose.

4

At that instant Okei gave a start. She was gripped by the feeling that she could see her brother Sango standing just on the other side of the courtroom door.

The court attendant opened the door. Okei involuntarily lowered her head. Nonetheless, an ineluctable force compelled her to raise her face. The court attendant soon returned but did not close the door behind him. Okei and her mother fixed their eyes on the door.

There was a sound of footsteps.

The instant he entered, Sango glanced in their direction, slightly tilting the edge of his braided straw hat with his cuffed hands. At the same moment his somewhat swollen eyes, looking much like his mother's, flashed a weak smile. Okei pressed her hands against her chest with all her might.

A rather pale and stooped jailer was holding a rope from behind.

"Okei . . . oh, there's a rope!"

Briskly shutting the door, the jailer removed the braided hat for him. While in the village Sango had pomaded his hair and worn it long in the front, but now it had been entirely sheared off and his scalp looked blue. With his hat removed, Sango looked directly at Okei and Mother. By way of a greeting, he shook his head slightly and twisted the corners of his mouth. His expression resembled that of a child who is smiling through tears. Okei completely understood her brother's feelings. This was her peerlessly good elder brother.

Sango held out his hands toward the jailer. While doing so, he glanced again at the two women. His eyes were very eloquent. "Don't look at me just now," they were saying. The jailer rattled his sheaf of keys and removed the handcuffs.

Sango smiled then for the first time, showing his regular white teeth. He looked handsome, his face paler and slimmer than when he had been working.

The lawyer pushed back his chair, exchanged a few words with Sango from behind, stood up and approached the two women.

"Ma'am, his sentence will be handed down today. . . . He's probably looking at six months, so be ready for that." The lawyer, his face sleepy and his features blurred, mumbled only these few words.

"Oh? . . . Thank you very much, sir." Clutching the hand towel salty with her tears, Mother bowed her head over and over. The lawyer, looking as though he had missed the moment to say it, glanced at Okei and added, "All the same, it's going to be light . . . definitely on the light side."

Hearing the words "six months," Okei felt as if she had been elbowed in the solar plexus. But at least it was probably what one had to expect for cutting a person (though there were many reasons for it). Moreover, Okei and her Mother had no means to thank the lawyer. And yet, for the past three days he had been speaking quite well on Sango's behalf, thought Okei.

Silently, Okei bowed to the lawyer.

At an elevated platform in the front of the room, a judge appeared through a side door and took a seat. A prosecutor appeared through a door on the opposite side.

The trial and the sentencing went smoothly. Six months of imprisonment with hard labor. If there were any objections, the presiding judge said in conclusion, the sentence could be appealed. Okei was gazing at her brother's back and at his shoulders. Maybe she imagined it, but his shoulders seemed to move slightly. Or maybe they didn't. At that instant Okei felt a shock.

When the judge left the courtroom, Sango twisted his body and glanced back at them. A feeble smile, like a twitch, rose to one of his cheeks. It made Okei think of a cloudy day that makes the cold seem even colder.

The handcuffs were put on, the rope tied to his waist, the braided hat put on his head. . . . But as Sango was leaving, Mother was covering her face. The door opened. About to exit, Sango tilted his hat upward. His eyes were filled with tears.

"Ah, ah, ah-ah-ah-aa . . ." Mother suddenly raised her voice in a mad cry.

5

When she saw the tears in her son's eyes, Mother forgot all about restraining her pain. Hearing her cry out, Sango stopped in his tracks as though his legs had become entangled in something. The son was truly weeping now. He turned around slightly and buried his chin in his right shoulder, while his shoulders shook in little tremors.

Unawares, Okei was gripping the back of the chair in front of her with both hands and with all her might.

"Sango! S-stay strong!"

The son jerked the brim of his hat down over his face.

The door closed.

Okei and Mother stepped out into the corridor. Sango walked dragging one of his *zōri* behind him. His long underwear hung below the hem of his kimono, covering the top of his socks. He neither looked up nor turned around. As he walked, his obi grew loose and seemed about to come untied. Twisting his hands toward his back and rocking his body, he tightened the sash.

Without looking back even once, Sango turned a corner and vanished. At that moment his mother and sister suddenly felt the chill of the concrete corridor creep up their legs.

The lawyer stood behind them and waited, occasionally tapping the floor with the tip of his shoe.

"Go to the prison now, and visit him at your leisure. And by the way, it would be best not to appeal. Just let him serve his time since it's short . . ."

"Yes, sir, thank you very much."

Okei and Mother returned to the waiting room. In front of "Courtroom No. 3" stood four policemen in greatcoats, hands in pockets, feet stamping lightly against the floor. An angry voice making what sounded like a vehement speech was heard from within, but it was impossible to make out the words.

In the waiting room, the women waited for the lawyer to bring them a visiting permit.

Mother noticed the wrapped bundle she had tied to her waist. Although she was hungry, she had no appetite at all.

"Okei, aren't you hungry?"

Okei silently shook her head.

"How about you, Ma?"

Mother was staring blankly. After a while she said, "Not at all."

The clerk was sitting at his desk and writing something with a brush. He was wearing glasses now. Seeing them, he bit his mustache.

"How did it go?"

"Well . . ."

"Did he get one year?"

"Six months . . ."

The clerk placed his brush briskly behind his ear, and restlessly clamped his lower teeth over his mustache. "Hm, six months! He did very well. He did very well indeed!"

The woman stand-keeper was cutting bread into thin slices, spreading butter on them, and putting them on a metal tray atop the stove. "What did he do?" she asked, looking alternately at Mother and the clerk.

"A youthful indiscretion," said the clerk matter-of-factly.

"To do with a woman, wasn't it," said the stand-keeper smiling a little.

"He stabbed a man over a woman."

"I see."

"But the man lived, so it turned out all right . . ."

Unable to endure it, Okei stepped out into the corridor.

Just then the spectators noisily emerged out of "Courtroom No. 3." Seven or eight defendants in sedge hats came out of a different door one by one, as a rope was attached to their waists. They swaggered, shoving their hats to the back of their heads, raising their cuffed hands, and shaking them.

"Stay strong!"

"Hang in there!"

Words of encouragement were flying back and forth.

Thinking of her brother's lonesome look as he was leaving, Okei grew perplexed and remained standing still.

Concerning the Brother

1

It was twilight, four months earlier.

From a stable beside the back door came the sound of hoofs kicking repeatedly against the wooden boards. Recalling that it was time to give the horse hay, Mother pushed aside the rags she had been darning and stepped out, slapping the front of her kimono with her hands. Beyond a grove some two hundred yards directly facing the back door, Ishikari River flowed green, quiet, and sluggish along its meandering course. Although the morning snow had covered the grove, the plowed fields, and the rice paddies with a pure whiteness, after noon it began to melt, baring the trees and making the ridges in the fields stand exposed in beautiful parallel lines. Cows were mooing from across the river, as though calling out to their companions on this side. It was just then that it happened.

Someone entered through the front door.

Thinking that Okei had come home, Mother stood with the hay in her arms, her body covered with bits of straw, and merely stuck her head out.

"Is Okane-san home?"

"Yes . . . ?"

The visitor stood in the shadow of the wooden door and she could not see who it was.

"In the back?"

The visitor seemed to be moving toward the back. At that instant Mother heard the clinking sound of a sword. It was definitely a sword. Feeling inexplicably alarmed, Okane gripped the doorway. A policeman!

"Officer?"

She hurriedly opened the stable door and thrust the hay into a tub. The horse stretched his neck covered by an unevenly grown mane, drew back his lower lip revealing his gums, and tapped his jaw against the tub.

Coming out, she saw a local policeman in a coat that was too long for him standing and briskly rubbing his neck and face with a hand towel. He was a ruddy-faced, good-natured policeman, fond of drink. Not only Okane but other villagers as well took some of the first produce of each season to him.

"Ah, it's you, officer." Okane bowed deeply, bits of straw falling from her body.

"Anybody else home?"

"No, nobody, sir. My daughter and Sango aren't back from town yet."

"Hm . . ." The policeman briefly reflected, and then said, "We'd best go inside for a minute . . ."

Okane was the first to enter the dimly lit house. Two thick pieces of wood were smoldering in the large sand-filled fireplace. The smoke swirled sluggishly against a ceiling that was crossed with shining black beams sticky with soot.

Slapping the raised entryway with the apron she was wearing, Okane swept the dust from it and bade the "officer" sit down.

"Does Sango go to town often these days?" The policeman was still rubbing his face.

"Yes, sir . . ."

So that's what it is, thought Okane. A good thing too, she thought. She let all the anxiety that had been troubling her show plainly on her face.

"Yes, sir, he's been going a lot since the autumn, and he wasn't doing that before, so I'd been asking myself what's going on, yes, sir, I have."

"Hm . . . He might've got himself a woman."

"A woman?!" Mother looked at the policeman's face in surprise. Her son was still a child. And yet, lately he had been letting his hair grow long in front, coating his hands with pomade and rubbing it into his hair. . . . Maybe he really had grown into an adult.

"It's a woman, all right," said the policeman emphatically, tilting his head.

"Ah . . ."

"Have you noticed anything unusual these two or three days?" The policeman undid a button over his chest, thrust in the towel, and commenced to rub. As if talking to himself, he said, "Whenever I walk a little, I start to sweat. . . . Must be the drinking."

Okane thought briefly and said, "No sir, nothing special . . ."

"Hm . . . well, I don't want you to get alarmed but . . ." The policeman closed his eyes for a moment and clamped his mouth shut.

2

Okane tried to say something in response but although she moved her mouth, her lips grew slack and only trembled, producing no coherent words.

The policeman looked up at her with surprise. Mother's face

was visibly draining of color. The policeman silently shook his head. "What a mess," he said, as if to himself.

"You see, there was a phone call from the police station in town . . ." continued the policeman, closely watching Okane's face.

"From the police station in town . . . ," echoed Okane in a voice devoid of emotion.

"Mm, right . . . there's been trouble. It's Sango. He stabbed a man."

Okane silently stood up. She hurried over to the door. Startled, the policeman stopped wiping his face and followed her with his eyes. Mother opened the door and looked restlessly about.

"Ah, ah, what's the matter with Okei? Where has she gone?" she said. The tone of her words was strange.

"Hey, ma'am!" The policeman grew worried.

"What's Okei doing?" Mother repeated.

The policeman hastily stuck the towel into his belt, put his hands on Okane's shoulders, and shook her. "Hey, ma'am! ma'am!"

Okane abruptly sat down, fell forward onto the wooden floor with her hands covering her face, and burst into loud wailing. "Ah, ah, officer, what can I do! What should I do!"

"I've no idea. I myself haven't gotten detailed instructions about what to do. And who do you suppose Sango stabbed? That Yoshimine who was his buddy both in school and in the Young Men's Association."

"I won't be able to face anybody, ah, ah, I won't be able to face anybody! He stabbed little Yoshimine Ken! Stabbed that quiet little Ken!"

Yoshimine was the son of a town grocer and Sango's particularly good friend who sometimes came to visit him by bicycle. The two were coordinators of the Sunada Village Young Men's Association. They were the only ones in the village whom the policeman treated almost like his younger brothers. When he dropped by for tea from time to time, the policeman would declare that he was going to find a top-notch bride for Sango . . .

"Well now, ma'am . . ." The good-natured policeman faltered, now sweating only figuratively. Gazing down on the trembling old woman lying prone like a bundle of rags on the dim and damp dirt floor, the policeman wondered how to continue. "Ma'am, uh, Okane-san . . . actually, I'd like you to come with me."

Okane's body jerked up. Her hair, lustreless, grimy, and streaked with white, lay plastered over her face. Her lips moved and mumbled in a constricted voice, "I thought so! Is it . . . to the police?"

"Mm, that's right . . . the one in town."

"The police . . ."

"Don't worry too much. I'll come with you, and put in a good word for him. I'll put in a good word for you too. Anyway, Yoshimine's wound doesn't seem to amount to much."

But Mother's eyes were frantic, as though she had not heard him.

"The police! Ah, ah, I won't be able to face people!"

"A sleigh will be coming for you soon from Granny Yamadate's place. Take it. . . . Get ready, all right?"

The policeman walked along the dirt floor to the kitchen to get a drink of water. As he drank it with audible gulps, he thought of what a mess Sango had made of things. Any ideas about getting him a bride had fallen through.

At that moment, the front door opened and Okei walked in.

3

It grew cold after the sun went down. The snow that had begun to melt on the road now froze solid, forming a variety of shapes. The utterly still air penetrated the nostrils with a chill, presaging the arrival of severe cold. A starry night sky, tall and limpid, stretched above a jet-black snow-break forest and a row of bare broom–like poplars. The Yamadate sleigh, carrying Okane, Okei, and the policeman, sped along a dark road flanked by the poplars, its bells ringing. Although the sky was clear, it was dark because there was no moon.

Ishikari River flowed silently in the dark, its surface here and there glimmering deep blue from the starlight. At turns in the road and breaks in the tree line the river appeared with unexpected suddenness directly to the right of the sleigh, then soon hid behind the embankment once again.

The sleigh bells rang spiritedly through the dry and freezing night sky. Their sound carried far into the distance. At times they encountered a villager who was returning from town, carrying a lantern.

"Hullo," called out the driver, young Yamadate, from atop his seat. "Hullo . . . you're out late . . ."

The villager planted one leg in the snow bank on the edge of the road, and briefly held aloft his lantern.

That is what Okane dreaded the most. Covering her head with her shawl, she shrank behind the policeman, making herself small and hard like a clenched fist. Not only that, she was also terribly worried that the policeman's face would be seen. If word got out that the old Taguchi woman was off to town together with a local police officer...! The very thought made Mother feel as though her chest were being savagely torn.

The good-natured policeman shoved his visored hat down over his eyes and kindly pretended to see nothing.

At times the horse-drawn sleigh shook brutally, threatening to toss them overboard. A light shone from a farmhouse a hundred yards or more from the road, and a distant horse neighed at the sound of the sleigh bells. Hearing it, Yamadate's young horse vigorously stretched his neck and neighed in response.

When they had covered half the distance, the dark horizon that surrounded them grew faintly bright in a single spot. It was the town.

Okei said nothing. She did not know what to say or how to say it, nor did she know what to make of the incident. What her brother—the gentlest of men—felt when he set out intending to kill Yoshimine, what he felt now as he sat in a dark police cell. . . . Thinking of the brother who had been taken so unreachably far from his family made Okei feel that her eyes could no longer see what lay ahead.

"You know, ma'am, the only thing I regret is that now I won't be able to get him a good bride." In a subdued voice, the policeman said what he had been thinking over and over.

Mother remained silent.

"To tell you the truth, I thought that Sango was different from the young people these days who're so quick to pick up wrong ideas with one excuse or another. I thought the world of him . . . and then a thing like this. . . . It's such a shame."

"That's so true!" Mother said with a sniffle.

"A waste of a young man. I'm sure there's a worthless woman behind this. No doubt about it! If only he'd talked things over with me. What a pity. . . . There's got to be a worthless woman involved." He said the final words as if speaking to himself.

However, Okei's brother had talked with his sister, so she knew something of the truth. She knew the woman too. On reflection, she did not consider her "a worthless woman." Her brother had recently started to play around and to drink. But this too did not make Okei think that he had somehow gone bad.

Thump, thump—there was a sudden jolt. The sleigh had just crossed the railroad tracks, and was approaching the town entrance.

4

As they entered the town out of rural darkness, electric lights made their eyes prickle. Particles of vapor glittered like luminescent rings around the bare street lamps scattered here and there. The cold was closing in. Inside a general store, a young apprentice dozed curled up on top of a covered brazier.

For a while they ran again through a dark area that was not lined with stores. Then they came to a tavern fronted by an empty lot where a few horses harnessed to sleighs stood beside electric-light poles and a timber pile. As the Yamadate sleigh approached, the horses neighed from the darkness, scraping the frozen road with their forelegs. Their leather straps bent and creaked. The place was filled with peasants on their way back to the villages.

This town, like Hokkaido's other remote mountain towns, was built for the needs of the colonial peasant settlers. The town stretched in a long arc skirting a railway.

Presently the sleigh arrived at the police station. It was a small single-story building with a red lantern in front. To Mother it looked strangely ominous.

There were only two cells. They had no electric light, and were lit only by a feeble discolored lamp that cast its turbid light from the jailer's dirt-floored room. The jailer sometimes gave prisoners cigarettes, let them out to drink water, and bought them bean-jam buns or rice cakes when someone brought in money.

If even a single woman was led in, the men were all packed into a single cell. Although they knew it would get crowded, the men all eagerly waited for a woman to arrive.

Since the town was small, it rarely happened that an unfamiliar face turned up. When Sango walked in, a drunk and a burglar tilted their heads, looking bewildered.

"What! Little Taguchi Sango!" In the darkness, the wobbling drunk rubbed his eyes.

"You're not supposed to be here!" said someone from a corner so dark that at first it seemed unoccupied.

Sango sat down without a word, clasped his knees, and lowered his head. He was feeling oddly tranquil. Although a jailer was always present to prevent any suicide attempts, an additional policeman was temporarily assigned to the task. The two jailers took turns peering frequently into the cell.

"What happened?" The drunk sidled up to Sango. He was a ruffian named Gen who had always been on bad terms with Sango, the coordinator of the Young Men's Association. Gen was an impoverished tenant farmer. From time to time he came to town, got drunk, and swaggered about. In a place like this, his question struck Sango as the first friendly words he had heard. Surprised by his own feelings, Sango raised his face. He wondered what to say.

"Eh?"

Yet Sango felt terribly embarrassed to say anything in front of the drunk Gen. He sensed he would be laughed at. At the moment, Gen seemed like a formidable antagonist. This was unprecedented.

"Hm," Sango mumbled evasively.

"A coordinator, so it can't be extortion; a model Association member so it can't be a woman; it certainly can't be a fight with the landowner . . . I don't get it."

Under ordinary circumstances, Sango would have exploded with anger at such words. Now, however, he could think of nothing scathing to say.

"Not drunk either . . . I don't get it." Gen shook his head.

At that moment the jailer shouted, "Hey, hold your tongue!"
"Sure," said Gen—and stuck out his tongue.

5

For supper Sango received as a special treat a bowl of rice with toppings. However, he took only two or three mouthfuls with his chopsticks before putting them down. The other prisoners were watching his mouth with envy. Once he stopped eating, their expressions grew openly greedy, and they stared at the jailer who was peering into the cell.

"What's the matter, can't you eat it?"

"No."

"Better make an effort and eat."

Sango knew the policeman's face through his work at the Young Men's Association. He was acquainted with many others too.

"Better eat it up," said the burglar in his cell with transparently false solicitude.

"Son of a bitch, you want to eat it yourself!" said the policeman. The burglar tucked in his head and burst into giggling laughter.

Around seven o'clock, Sango was summoned by a judicial officer. A round stove was burning in the corner of a small room. The officer was short and stout, with a heavily bearded, swarthy face. Due to his closely cropped hair he had been nicknamed "Monk." Next to his desk, a secretary was rubbing an ink stick and getting ready. From time to time, he glanced up to scrutinize Sango.

"You've told us everything honestly, so the issue is extremely clear. I expected nothing less of you. It all matches up with Yoshimine's and with Sasaki Kiyo's statements. Well, then . . ." The court officer looked up toward the ceiling and briefly closed his eyes. "Lately, you've been coming to town and . . . er, it seems you've been drinking. Is there some reason for that?"

Sango thought about it while adjusting the front of his kimono, for his obi had been taken away. Did he know that things would turn out the way they did? That he didn't know.

"Well? . . . Your family is sharecropping Yoshimine's field, right?"

"That's right."

"Has the rent been getting paid?" asked the officer in a slow and thoughtful voice, his tone extremely gentle.

"The top half gets taken as rent. . . . It's been hard to keep going these days. We've been a little behind since the year before last."

"Did you ever tell Yoshimine that it's been hard to keep going?"

"I never told him."

"Telling him wouldn't have done any harm . . ."

"I thought that if I just worked as hard as I could, it would somehow work out."

"Hm . . . until Sasaki Kiyo came into the picture, you were on good terms with Yoshimine, right?"

"That's right."

"Hm. So there were no particular problems concerning the rent; for instance, you didn't feel dissatisfied over that?"

"That's right."

"Mm . . . and the reason you started drinking in town was not because you were fed up with how hard it was to make a living?"

Why is he asking about things like this, thought Sango. What does it have to do with what happened? He thought it over for a moment. The policeman who served as a secretary glanced at him, while training the tip of his brush with ink.

"Well . . ."

"You think Yoshimine took Sasaki Kiyo away from you, right?"

"He *did* take her." At the change of subject, Sango involuntarily flared up with excitement.

"Well, let me ask you: in that situation, wasn't it more than just a matter of his having taken her? Didn't your hatred of him as your landlord also play a part?"

Sango thought, "What?!"

6

Although Sango had never given it any thought, the question whether hatred for the landlord was bound up with the resentment at having his woman taken away astonished him.

When visiting Kiyo's place after finally finishing a day's work, he often found Yoshimine, who had no fixed daily occupation, in deep conversation with her. In those days, being quite certain that Kiyo thought only of him, and that he even had definite proof of it, Sango merely envied Yoshimine's leisurely life.

However, just as there are times when a single chance word instantly and easily disentangles an arithmetic problem that has defied solution for days, the officer's words made Sango look about restlessly like a man whose blindfold had been suddenly removed.

And yet Yoshimine had never acted like a landlord or a rich man either toward him or toward Kiyo. To the contrary, not a single villager spoke badly of him. But come to think of it, love affairs require leisure and maybe a man like Sango who worked covered in mud was quite unsuited for love affairs. After his relationship with Kiyo had turned to disappointment and he began coming to town to drink, he got to know a woman who worked in a cheap noodle restaurant. She was from Sango's village and since she hardly had any land of her own to till, she worked as a day laborer, helping to till others' fields, and did various other jobs. Hearing about Yoshimine and Kiyo, she'd said that love affairs demand the luxury of free time.

Sango recalled her words now.

In order to go on eating, Sango had to cultivate fields from sunup to sunset, perform hired labor whenever he was free for even a day, drive a sleigh in winter to go cut timber, and travel to Otaru in the summer to work on boats that fish for herring in the coastal seas. For Sango, having free time meant having money. When Sango first asked Kiyo to live with him, she remained silent for a long time before asking, "How are they going to eat?" Without Kiyo's help, her family would immediately start to suffer. He was aware of that. And he could not come up with any good idea of what to do about it.

Unmistakably and invisibly, thoughts about this hopeless future kept on reverberating within the bond of their emotions. And so, on reflection, even if his best and trusted friend Yoshimine had not muscled in to take her away, there was ample basis for it to happen; and even if Kiyo had not grown to dislike Sango nor wanted to break up with him, a force was working toward that end spontaneously and quite independently of everyone's will. At first he had felt that force as a mysterious, utterly irresistible, and exasperating fog. But once he tried to understand it, it struck him as the result of an unchangeable (Sango considered it absolutely unchangeable) distance separating Yoshimine from himself. Perhaps he pitied both himself and the woman who was being blindly dragged along. Gazing at her cheerless face, he had felt at times that he was entirely responsible for her misery. He wondered why their love was not as enjoyable as it was in novels and in the moving pictures they occasionally saw. Kiyo was quick to think about their future livelihood, and so she never went too far in their "flirtation" no matter how Sango treated her. For the impoverished couple, love and day-to-day existence were not entirely separate matters. But this made them both disgruntled. How wonderful it would be to let the fiery emotions welling up from within expand to the utmost with no anxiety whatsoever. Being good or bad had nothing to do with it: without being aware of it herself, Kiyo was inclining toward Yoshimine. . . . On the night of the Bon Festival, when searching for Kiyo he found her whispering intimately with Yoshimine in the deep pitch-dark grass. Sango was struck not simply by the feeling that his woman had been taken away from him, but by a different, complicated feeling that he himself had not understood. Sango was able to recall it now.

Rather than erupting in fury, he had experienced a moment of weakness, as though he were about to burst into tears. Without hating Yoshimine (whom he considered a reliable friend even now), he had felt his own arms and legs shrinking before a reality that he could do absolutely nothing about. This feeling, he understood in retrospect, arose from the fact that Yoshimine was a landlord while he himself was an insignificant pauper.

The judicial officer was silently staring at his face.

7

"What do you think?" prompted the officer, toying with a pencil.

Although the officer's earlier words were a turning point that clarified the relationship between himself, Kiyo, and Yoshimine by giving it an entirely new meaning, Sango had never before thought of Yoshimine with hostility, either as a person or as a landlord. And so he replied, "No . . ."

"Hm . . ." The judicial officer vigorously scratched his closely cropped hair, and then busily rubbed his beard. "I suppose not. I didn't think so myself but anyhow, serious problems have been cropping up lately." Once again, the officer briefly paused. "There are tenant farmers and others who harbor evil ideas . . ."

Now Sango understood the significance of the officer's question.

But the officer was fully aware that when a tenancy dispute arose in Tsukigata village adjacent to Sunada, Yoshimine and Sango had been the first to mobilize the Young Men's Association and to do all they could to end the dispute as quickly as possible with the help of wholesome ideas.

"If that's what you're worried about, please don't be. I haven't grown that depraved yet."

In fact, Sango had never entertained such ideas.

"Hm. But don't you think that Yoshimine was able to take your woman away because you're poor?"

Sango remained silent for a while. But he finally said, "Yoshimine's not the kind of guy who throws his privileges around or steals women just because he's rich."

"Hm, that's true too. He's a good young man. But if you look at the outcome, that's how it looks, doesn't it?"

Startled once again, he looked at the officer. He suddenly grew afraid of him. For this reason he said nothing else for the rest of the interview. He had the feeling that anything he said would be given an absurd interpretation.

"Anyway, it doesn't matter." Looking half at the secretary and half at him, the officer said, "If that point alone is cleared up, that'll be enough."

Then he rang a bell. The policeman appeared promptly.

"Take Taguchi back."

The judicial officer tilted his jaw slightly upward, and again audibly stroked his beard.

The village policeman, Okei, and Mother arrived just after the questioning. The dimly lit room they entered had a stove in the middle, in front of which a policeman sat leaning back and warming himself. When the village policeman handed him a slip of paper, this man who had been half dozing suddenly opened his eyes wide, looked the two women up and down, opened the door and stepped out.

The three arrivals waited for a while. A fine, dry snow was falling; in the stillness the flakes could be heard rustling against the windowpanes. Someone passed through the corridor with a short little yawn and a clicking of shoes. At each such sound, both Okei and Mother started and turned their frightened eyes toward the door.

To tell the truth, Okei had known what was happening to her brother. Being close to him she was fully aware of each incident that gradually drove her brother's feelings into an inescapable corner. With a woman's acute insight, she understood it better than he himself. She felt as keenly as if she were the one directly involved what ultimately happens to the love of people in their circumstances. What befell her brother engraved indelible traces in the deepest recesses of Okei's heart.

At that moment the policeman who had stepped out returned.

8

The policeman led only the mother into the next room. Okei's eyes silently followed her mother's thin shoulders. The village policeman and Okei were left alone. The two gazed at the stove in silence. The policeman slowly unbuttoned his greatcoat, took out a crumpled pack of "Asahi," and with shivering uncertain fingertips inserted a bent cigarette into his mouth. Touching a matchstick to the stove, he lit the cigarette. The smoke slowly rose. The two people's shadows broke at the edge of the dirt floor, crept up the wall and stayed motionless, warped by the window frame. The snow rustled against the windows.

"Hullo!" The door opened and a large ruddy-faced man walked in. His body was saturated with a penetrating scent of snow.

"Well, well . . ." The village policeman rose slightly and rubbed out the cigarette butt against the top of the stove.

The man was Yoshikuma, head of the Sunada Village Young

Men's Association and an army veteran. Okei knew him well, for he was a frequent visitor. He wore soft leather boots that reached above his knees and squeaked with every step.

"What a terrible thing to happen." As he took off his hat, vapor rose from his head. Evidently he had walked in a hurry.

"Indeed . . ." mumbled the village policeman, as was his habit.

"I knew this was going to happen. What I regret, Mr. Yamada, is the trouble this causes for the Young Men's Association. I'm thinking beyond the trouble that Taguchi himself is in. This is absolutely terrible."

"Absolutely . . ."

"In my opinion, there are two important points. The first has to do with the good name of the Young Men's Association. The second . . . when a tenant farmer raises his hand against his landlord and master, regardless of the reasons . . . it leads to unpleasant *social repercussions.*"

The Association head spoke in the tone of someone accustomed to making speeches. The village policeman who thus far had not raised his eyes from the stove, now flinched as if someone had clapped a hand on his shoulder.

". . . . . ?"

"It's true. Look at Tsukigata, our neighboring village. They've been scattering shit in front of landowners' houses. The Communist Party has been sending a pair of heinous criminals to cause incidents. Only Sunada Village is preserving our precious traditions. . . . Taguchi hadn't been showing up at the Young Men's Association lately, and he'd been going to town to drink, but it wasn't just because of a woman. . . . I see an ideological basis for it."

The Association head vigorously rubbed his face and neck with a hand towel.

"That's far-fetched, Yoshikuma," said the good-natured policeman in a low and uneasy voice.

"No, it's not. When one considers the present social chaos and the tendencies among the youth . . . it's absolutely true!"

As if to emphasize his own words, Yoshikuma made his boots squeak. Policeman Yamada glanced at Okei, and once again fixed his eyes on the stove. Okei was unconsciously tensing her shoulders while staring at the tips of her stiff shoes.

"The chief isn't here any more, is he? I'd like to have a word with the judicial officer." Yoshikuma opened the door and began to step out. At that moment there was the sound of rough heavy footsteps in the corridor as if someone new were being dragged in, and a woman's crying voice suddenly rang out. The voice of a policeman restraining her mingled with the woman's. Then a young policeman entered alone, taking off his gloves. Seeing Policeman Yamada, he smiled somewhat awkwardly.

"An amateur prostitute," he said. "In hard times, their numbers go up."

9

The door had been left slightly ajar, and a cold wind blew in. Policeman Yamada craned his neck to look down the corridor. A young woman wearing a shawl over her disheveled hair and covering her face with her hands was crying in a dark corner, her shoulders heaving with sobs.

"It's the Yamagami girl. She came to town after they lost the tenancy dispute in Tsukigata."

"Little Yamagami Yoshi?" asked Okei with a start. If so, she knew her slightly.

"Yes, she said her name is Yoshi! You could say they got punished for what they did, but when you know the circumstances you can't help feeling sorry."

"Mm . . . that's right."

"Afterwards Yamagami couldn't make any kind of a living. This is a small place, and the dispute haunted him: wherever he went asking for work, no one would hire him. Up to now he seemed to be managing somehow with the money Yoshi brought in now and then."

A policeman on duty walked in, record book in hand, to take up his shift. Having taken over, he went out and began to drag the woman who had been crying in the dark corridor toward the cells. When she grasped what was happening, the woman said a few words rapidly, then burst into violent sobbing.

"What're you crying for, stupid? You know you were having a good time of it!"

Hearing this, the face of the policeman who had arrested the woman stirred and darkened. Then he said, as if talking to himself, "Looks like she got one yen and fifty sen . . ."

Okei listened intently to the woman's cries that gradually grew weaker as they moved off toward the cells. Listening to her voice, she became aware that her own body was trembling. Although she understood the words "selling one's body," she did not yet understand what this really meant. But if her brother were now to be imprisoned for years, she herself, being the eldest, would have to find a way of providing for the family. Living was hard even with her brother working so diligently. Though they ate only the bare minimum, they could not even keep up with rent payments, and debts kept piling up. In autumn when various grains ripened, prices fell, and just when tenant farmers absolutely had to sell, they hit rock bottom. Then it would be winter, and by the time spring came, prices always began to rise. That was the time when landowners and urban wholesale merchants who had taken and stored the tenant farmers' grain would begin to sell. People like Okei stood no chance at all. To make up for the "gap," they took up day labor, piled up gravel, cut timber, and dug irrigation ditches. Now her brother would be gone. Okei felt she could see what kind of life lay ahead of her.

The Yamagami girl's cries now pierced Okei's body like shards of broken glass, one by one.

"You got your money, you had your fun—what in the world are you still bawling about?!"

Okei heard the words but could not bear to listen to them. Agitated, she stood up and then promptly sat down. In a short while, her mother returned.

The interviewer had gotten angry at Sango for becoming excited. Visiting was absolutely not permitted because, it was said, Sango would become too agitated. Okei went out to buy eggs and mandarin oranges. She asked that these be given to the prisoner.

Four months went by. Sango had been transferred to a prison in Sapporo. For Okei and Mother, that winter was dark, cold, and long.

Day after day a fine dry snow fell, piling up into snowdrifts, covering bushes, and burying stables. With nothing to obstruct the eye, the expanse of the Ishikari Plain stretched out to the horizon in all directions.

Okei, wearing a knitted muffler wrapped many times around her neck and a pair of snowshoes she had made from a straw sack, trudged every morning along a snowed-in road that led to the highway. Her cheeks, earlobes, and the tip of her nose were bright red and smarting. She then set out for the town to sew work gloves in a small factory.

In the course of a day Mother and Okei always said the same things to each other. It had become a habit.

"Sango will have eaten by now."

"Sango will be asleep by now."

On nights when she could not sleep, Mother shook Okei awake to say, "Sango's awake by now for sure."

Mother and Daughter's Journey

1

It was when Mother and Okei returned from the courtroom to the waiting room and sat down in the same corner as before that the thought first struck them: "Ah, that's right. Sango will be gone for six months."

After an hour or so, the lawyer came in. His slightly raised left shoulder and his thinness made his clothes hang loosely like a monk's surplice.

"Apparently young Taguchi himself has decided not to appeal. You have a final meeting with him, so go see him together. Though it's final, it is just for six months so don't be disheartened."

He extracted two "meeting permits" from his pocket and handed them over.

"Young Taguchi has an unusually strong character. We've talked about various things, and I can tell you that he's impressed me."

With that brief comment, the lawyer, evidently busy with some task, excused himself and left. Okei and Mother accompanied him to the door, bowing over and over.

The prison was directly across the muddy and slushy road. Its tall concrete walls, extra thick at the bottom, basked in the sunshine of approaching spring. Periodically, at the foot of the walls guards wearing swords paced back and forth. Above the walls rose just the top part of a red brick building.

Stepping out of the waiting room, mother and daughter were dazzled by the unexpectedly bright sunlight. Spring was clearly on its way. Picking the spots where the snow was hard, they crossed the road. Sewers gurgled continuously, draining the melting snow's waters.

At the prison entrance stood a large gate with iron bars. The gatehouse next to it was no bigger than a telephone booth. Okei presented the meeting permits to the gatekeeper who was standing there. After scrutinizing in turn the slips of paper and the two women, the gatekeeper opened a small side door with a loud creak. There was a dimly lit waiting room just past the entrance and off to the side. They were told to wait there. The small elderly gatekeeper, constantly sniffling and grumbling unintelligibly under his breath, walked off with crunching footsteps straight ahead toward what looked like an administration building.

Mother sat down on a bench, bending over so deeply that her forehead reached her knees, and pressed a hand towel against her face.

"Is your stomach hurting, Ma?"

But Mother remained silent.

The sun did not reach into the waiting room. It was icy cold. A young woman who had arrived earlier was incessantly pacing about, reading a book. Even when she halted, she kept on stamping loudly with her feet. She had trim eyebrows and looked intelligent.

"Your stomach's hurting?"

"No . . ."

But Mother remained doubled over.

The young woman, as if she'd suddenly remembered something, stuck her head out of the waiting room and shouted, "Mister Gatekeeper, Mister Gatekeeper!"

When the gatekeeper came up, she briskly said, "What's going on? It's taking so long. I've been waiting thirty minutes already."

"How should I know?" said the gatekeeper, somewhat rattled.

"Well, take a message to the chief then. You're treating me like a fool!"

"No, it'll be soon now," said the gatekeeper and went away.

Angrily, the woman resumed her pacing. The book she was reading contained words written in a foreign language. Okei looked up at her with surprise. Could she be a member of that "commune something" party? No doubt she was.

Okei and Mother were granted permission to go in first. But Mother suddenly said, "Okei, go see him by yourself."

2

Okei came back some ten minutes later. Her eyes were red, and her face sticky and dirty. Even after Okei rejoined her, Mother still did not raise her head.

That evening the two of them took a train from Sapporo Station to Asahikawa. There was nothing more to be done. They sat without looking out the window. After passing through the factory district on the outskirts of Sapporo, the train emerged into the snowy expanse of the Ishikari Plain. Reflections of the snow-covered fields cast flickering patterns of light on the ceiling of their carriage.

Mother began to speak for the first time.

"Okei, how was Sango?"

"In good spirits."

Okei's mind was filled with all sorts of thoughts about the recent events.

"Did he say anything?"

"Yes. He said he made Mother worry terribly. . . . He said just to tell you how sorry he was."

". . . . .!!"

Mother's lips moved as she tried to say something. But no words came out.

"He said what he did was stupid. He wouldn't do anything like that now."

"I see."

"They have exercise in there every day. Once, on his way back, he says he met someone in the hallway he recognized from the time of that trouble in Tsukigata. That's when brothers from the Association went out to tell them to quit their stupid fighting. Running into him now, he says he felt terribly embarrassed. . . . He says that man is a *com-mun-ist.*"

"You don't say!"

"And he says that working Yoshimine's fields is too hard for Ma, so we ought to go to Otaru where Yasuko is and try to make a living there. Brother says that when he gets out he'll work as hard as he can to pay you back for all your trouble."

"Uh, huh . . . maybe we gotta go to Otaru. Doesn't seem like there's anything else."

"That would be the best, he says."

"After what's happened, I don't have the nerve to face Mr. Yoshimine. . . . All right, but what'll we do in Otaru?"

"Rent a small place and we'll get by somehow."

"Ah . . ."

"Explain what happened, get Yasuko back from Kobayashi, and the two of us'll work together. We'll manage somehow."

"Ah . . . you don't want to live a long life."

Neither Mother nor Okei had ever lived feeling so small as during the four months that followed Brother's incident. Countless times they went to Yoshimine's house in town to apologize. They believed that no amount of apologizing could suffice. Nonetheless, the son who was lying in bed with his cut shoulder was friendly to them. He was truly a good person. But the Master, whose only son had been stabbed—and by his own family tenant, too—did not respond to their apologies with so much as a word. Sometimes it even happened that Okei and Mother stood for a long time outside in the cold snow with no idea what to do. Not only Yoshimine but the villagers themselves all began to give the Taguchi family strange looks. What would happen when spring came, and it was time to start tilling the fields? Okei was aware, even without Brother telling her, that she needed to do something.

With Brother's case settled, it only remained to return home and get ready to go to Otaru. Although Okei had no special feelings about leaving the village, Mother was thinking about nothing but that.

Following Brother's incident, Okei faced such a variety of thoughts that it made her head throb. As she sat still, they flashed before her eyes one by one, gnawing at her once tightly shut mind. Brother and Kiyo and Yoshimine; Yoshimine's father; the head of the Young Men's Association; Policeman Yamada; the Yamagami girl; her own work sewing work gloves these four months; Communist Party members; the woman reading a book; the strange smile on the face of the arrested man led along the courthouse corridor; the lawyer; the clerk . . . and the villagers. . . . Okei could see that in just four months, a multitude of things she had never before encountered swirled bewilderingly around her.

The train advanced through the snow-break forest with its wheels pounding monotonously. The trees on each side were entirely covered with snow.

3

It was unseasonably warm on the day Okei and Mother left the village.

Spring had truly arrived. Countless streams suddenly materialized all over the roads, fields, grasslands, and thickets; flowing as if the melting snow's waters were spilling over. Beyond the river, cows, horses, and chickens were calling out to each other. The black soil, the grass, and the thatched roofs of peasant houses dotting the landscape emitted rich clouds of vapor after half a year of being buried under the snow.

People had come out of each farmhouse and were busy unhinging winter doors, repairing sheds, and doing similar chores. As the cart bearing Okei and Mother trundled by, they stopped their work, straightened up, and waved. The Yamadate son raised his hand and shouted, "Hullo!!"

While passing by a riverside forest they suddenly heard a rustle, and the first small birds of the year flew from one branch to another and started to chirp.

Okei looked up timidly from time to time to gaze over the broad

Ishikari Plain stretching all around her, its contours blurred by spring mists. It was a familiar landscape. She had been seeing it for some ten years, ever since migrating to this village from Honshu. Yet now she felt as though she were noticing it for the first time. All the same, she would never be able to see this dear landscape again. The thought made her eyes itch as though something had grazed them. They slowly filled up with tears.

The thawing road was in poor shape. Each time the iron wheels plunged into a deep puddle, Okei and Mother seemed about to be thrown from the cart.

Mother's acquaintance who was riding with them, a woman of about forty from Tsukigata village, kept on expressing her pity and sympathy. But Mother only buried her face in her chest and said nothing in reply. Feeling obliged to say something, Okei told the woman what had happened so far.

"My, oh my!" exclaimed the woman. "So then everybody in your village just looked on silently?"

During the tenant dispute in Tsukigata Village, this woman was one of the people who had scattered manure in front of the landlord's house.

"They were telling you to get out. Without a word to you, they'd decided who'd be taking your place. . . . Unless you have a field, farmers like you can't go on eating. And still, those losers in your village just kept staring, huh . . . !"

Sometimes she sounded like a man.

"Thanks to that Young Men's Association, Sango was always hanging around with the rich—Yoshimine and whoever else—and that's bad. You see, when push comes to shove, those folks are not on the side of us tenant farmers. What happened this time is a good example. If instead of going in and out of the police station and the Yoshimine house and listening to the Association head and his sort—if instead of that you'd joined in solidly with tenant farmers, you wouldn't be getting chased out feeling ashamed like a pair of filching cats."

"Hey, madam!" The Yamadate boy sitting in the driver's seat suddenly turned around and called out loudly. "I don't care what you say when you're in your own village, but while you're here in Sunada cut out that propaganda of yours!"

"He, he, he . . ." The woman from Tsukigata Village burst out laughing. "All right, all right! You too have grown into a splendid young man! Take Sango's place in the Young Men's Association now, and work hard!"

The woman continued to laugh, revealing grimy teeth that had once been dyed black with *ohaguro.* Somewhat later the Tsukigata woman said, as if talking to herself, "Well, when you get to town and taste the hard life, you'll understand . . ."

Yasuko

1

"Welcome! Welcome!"

"Thank you very much! Please come again!"

"Welcome!"

As customers poured in and others poured out, Yasuko, carrying trays of *miso* soup, boiled rice, and pickled vegetables, bustled between kitchen and tables, shouting out greetings.

She rushed to the sink, both hands filled with stacks of empty trays. Next she nimbly wiped off the soiled tabletops, for new customers already stood waiting beside them.

The clock showed it was not yet six. Outside, the morning air as chilly as fog flowed onto the deserted streets and the still sleeping rows of houses. This was just the time when laborers on their way to the port and workers going to the factories came in one after another to eat a ten-sen breakfast. Since most of them came every morning, their faces were all familiar to Yasuko.

"Yasuko gal, the miso soup doesn't taste good this morning! Did ya do something bad last night?" a longshoreman wearing a short coat asked with a laugh, his unshaven face clouded by steam from the miso soup.

"Idiot! I'm not talking to you!" Yasuko hit the longshoreman's shoulder with all her might.

Everyone burst out laughing.

Unlike her elder sister Okei, Yasuko was a cheerful woman with white skin, long soft eyebrows and big eyes. She was bigger than Okei. The customers all liked her and affectionately called her "Yasuko gal," Yatchan, and the like.

BY AROUND EIGHT o'clock the crowd of customers was gone, replaced by solitary individuals who dropped in from time to time as though recalling some errand. Yasuko went over to the kitchen to help wash the dishes. Once that was done, she was free until about eleven so she hitched up her kimono a little and sat on a chair to read tattered magazines and books that customers had lent her. Having gotten up early, she sometimes dozed off and dropped her book onto the earthen floor. But because she liked to read, she ignored the owner's grumbling and always kept a book close at hand. At first she read at random: so long as it was a book she would read it, even when she was lying in bed. Gradually, however, she stopped reading that way. She became interested in books that a man who came to eat almost every day a little before noon brought her one after another.

To tell the truth, Yasuko had had no clear idea of who this customer was. Judging by his oversize muddy shoes and worn-out corduroy clothes that shone in places, he certainly seemed to be a worker yet the words he spoke differed from those of any other factory hand, port worker, or day laborer who came into this place. At first she thought he was an impoverished scholar. Shortly afterward she realized he was not that, but rather a "union man." He spoke a great deal, and each time he came talked with Yasuko about a variety of subjects. It became clear to her that he belonged to a "labor union" that was starting up in Otaru just around that time. Since the union was located nearby, other men from it also often came to eat.

Although the customer talked with Yasuko most enthusiastically about what it was that a labor union did, she was unable to grasp it thoroughly. Yet she felt an odd charm in the intensity of the man's feelings that lit up his face with passion as he spoke.

Her morning work done, Yasuko sat on the chair turning the pages of a dog-eared book, and—without being clearly aware of it herself—waited for that customer to arrive . . .

2

The hillside eatery where Yasuko worked was situated in the working-class section of Otaru. It faced a street leading to the harbor that was lined with various factories, warehouses, and shipping agencies.

A corner of the page she was reading flashed with light—someone had shoved the shop curtain aside and come in.

"Welcome!" The greeting had already become a reflex action for Yasuko, requiring not the least effort. She put the book down, pushed it into a corner, and stood up.

It was the union man.

"Welcome!" Now she said it in a more lively voice. It was not her automatic greeting, but a "Welcome!" that she used for no one else.

The man sat down where he always did, in a corner chair to the right.

"What's today's treat?"

"Something very delicious!" Flashing an even row of white teeth, she mischievously tilted her head.

"Can there be something delicious for ten sen?" asked the man with a laugh.

A slim man, he looked good in corduroy. A shock of hair hung across his forehead, below a hat he wore pushed back on his head. His face was slender and well defined.

Yasuko turned toward the kitchen as she always did and called out, "One daily special!"

Then she picked up the book she had been reading till now, put it in front of the man, and asked him about the words she did not understand, which she had marked with her fingernail.

There were many such words: "organizer," "factory council," "industrial union," "agitating point," "cell," "chapter," "thesis." . . . With no other customers present, Yasuko sat beside the man while he ate and explained.

When reading the daily papers, she confronted such odd lines as: "planted a cell within a factory . . ."; and "having been detected by the authorities, their agitating points (mobile headquarters) were simultaneously raided at dawn . . ."; and "the man was a district organizer. . . ."

Once she understood what this meant, Yasuko became interested, especially since there were times when a phrase she had just heard appeared in print the very next day. At first it was for the sake of novelty, disregarding the meaning of words and passages, that Yasuko read books in which such things were written. She did not advance beyond this limited scope. Gradually, however, this changed and she herself was conscious of the change.

After her father died, she had served as a nursemaid at the Yoshimine house; together with her sister Okei she had carried loads of radishes and red beans to town to sell; she worked in Otaru to help keep her family alive—all the memories of her life were as cold as the drenching rains that fall as winter approaches. Although, of course, she was unaware of it, this formed the groundwork for everything Yasuko understood.

"Do you understand?" asked Yasuko, showing rows of even white teeth. "From spring to autumn the whole family works together plowing the fields, sowing the seeds, and pulling up weeds. And then, once we've finally harvested the crop, a full half of it gets taken away and we get nothing for it. Unless you're a tenant farmer yourself, you really can't understand how it feels when that happens."

Diffidently yet mischievously as always, she flicked her thumb toward the owner at his counter. "It's the same thing here with the boss! I know just how much he makes with me working like this. And all I get is ten yen a month! He's exploiting me! No wonder he gets fat!"

Yasuko had recently learned the word "exploit," and liked to use it often.

As he ate, the union man sometimes seemed absorbed in thought. Glancing around, he said in a low voice, "Yatchan, there's something I'd like to talk with you about."

3

"Talk? About what?" Yasuko dramatically opened her lovely dark eyes, and pulled her chair closer. There were no other customers. The late morning sunlight shone through the glass door casting a checkerboard pattern onto the earthen floor.

"Well," again the man paused briefly to think. "You said that your family's been renting a room since coming to Otaru, right?"

"Right."

"Our work's gotten extremely difficult lately. And we badly need a place somewhere . . ."

"It's about that?"

"That's right."

"There are two people in a six-tatami room, my sister and my mother. Would that be all right?"

"That would be all right, but . . . please tell your mother and sister everything. About the work that we're doing. Otherwise it would be a problem." He lowered his voice again. "It will be a secret place."

"I understand. I'll talk it over with them."

"Thank you."

"I'll do it. But they've just come from the country and don't know anything, so it may be hard for them to understand."

"I don't think so. Tsukigata Village is famous for its tenant disputes, and your village is right next to it."

Yasuko chuckled at hearing that. "But my big brother is a coordinator of the Young Men's Association, you know. He's a goodhearted guy, though . . ."

"Is that the brother who stabbed the landlord's son over a woman?"

"Yes."

A wry smile faintly lit up the union man's face. "He's quite brave."

"When it comes to women, yes. You can expect as much from an Association coordinator."

"It's amazing how far you've come, Yatchan!"

"But, you know, there's something more embarrassing. . . . When there was that strike in Tsukigata, my brother went over there and went around telling people that such disputes were bad and that they'd better quit! What do you think? A fine brother, eh?"

"That's how it is. We can't expect everyone to understand us, and to think the way we do. That's exactly why we must work with all our might. Even with the workers in Otaru, it's the same thing. There's heaps of them who are more incorrigible than your brother." A faint, cutting smile flashed across his face. "Hasn't it been that way even with you, Yatchan? It's taken you a year to get to where you're now! A whole year!"

Yasuko's shoulders rose in a spontaneous and impish shrug, but she soon thoughtfully lowered her eyes. "It's true!"

Amiably and gently, he gazed at Yasuko's beautiful face with its long eyelashes.

"There are so many women who don't understand, aren't there . . . ?"

"That's right."

"These days when I think about it, I somehow feel like I just can't keep still."

"What do you mean?" The man looked at her intently as if he had discovered something rare.

"When I think of myself repeating all through the day words like 'welcome,' 'thank you,' 'one daily special,' 'one chicken and egg on rice' . . ." Yasuko spoke with her eyes still lowered, rubbing a stain on the tabletop with her fingertip. "Maybe I'm being cocky, but I feel like there's something else I should be doing . . ."

4

"You might laugh, but I do have some idea of what you're all doing." She continued to look down and rub at the stain.

Yasuko had received good grades at the village elementary school, even better than her elder sister Okei. While Okei studied aloud with all her might, Yasuko went cheekily to catch carp, or painted her mouth bright red chomping loudly on winter cherries. Mother had often scolded her for it. She memorized sentences as she listened to her big sister read, and teased her by repeating them. Only in arithmetic could she not keep up with her.

In school too, Yasuko was a favorite of her friends, older pupils, and teachers. She was vivacious and amiable. She was also pretty. Okei, by comparison, was quiet, shy, and withdrawn; at times she was referred to merely as "Yasuko's sister." Because Okei's body and face were smaller, when the sisters walked together Yasuko was often mistaken for the older of the two.

When Yasuko learned something new, she was in the habit of

showing it off wherever she went. One day, returning from school, she suddenly announced that the food they had been eating at home up to that time was bad. She brought up the subject of "vitamins," unfamiliar to both Mother and Okei, because the teacher had said there was no nutritional value in eating only vegetable soup and sesame paste as they did almost daily, or potato cakes (boiled dumplings made of mashed potato starch) that they ate for three or four days when there was no rice. And she fretfully insisted that they should eat meat, eels, and tomatoes.

"There's no need for the schoolteacher to teach you that," said Mother. "If he taught you instead how to make money, I'd feed you both meat and fish right away!"

Okei had burst out laughing, but Yasuko pouted angrily for two or three days. From then on whenever she teased her younger sister, Okei always said: "Vitamins." That certainly had an effect on Yasuko.

But there was a different aspect to Yasuko. Because they came from a family of impoverished tenant farmers, the sisters sometimes had to take to school boxed lunches of baked potato starch instead of rice. The elementary school had been built at the edge of the village and, typically for Hokkaido, was attended by a fair number of pupils from relatively prosperous tenant-farmer families cultivating a dozen or two dozen acres. The children all made fun of the sisters and their "potato starch" lunch. When Yasuko was eating her lunch they would at times chase her, take it away from her, and as a prank either eat it or juggle with it. Okei hated that so she sometimes brought her lunch home without eating it, or quietly hid herself and ate it. Occasionally she was discovered, and when that happened she would burst into tears. Yasuko, however, looking as fierce as if she were not a child, would at such times go get the teacher and explain clearly what was happening. The pranksters were soon made to stand in the corridor. The next day Yasuko ate her "potato starch" as though nothing had happened. While the other children liked to conceal their lunches with a lid as they ate, Yasuko ate hers in full view.

At the time of the tenant dispute in Tsukigata Village, the sisters were walking along the highway on their way back from an errand when they saw an unfamiliar man (i.e., not from their village) coming toward them by bicycle. The man stopped his bicycle, lowered one foot to the ground, and asked, "Are you from Sunada?"

When Yasuko answered that they were, the man pulled out a sheaf of flyers from his pocket and asked the girls to distribute them in their neighborhood. Okei drew back, but Yasuko asked, "Just distribute them?" and took the flyers.

When they returned home they were scolded by Mother and Brother, and the flyers were taken away.

5

One incident from Yasuko's days in the village elementary school was indelibly etched in her memory.

She was the head of her class for two or three years in a row, including the time when it happened. Just before graduation the principal asked the pupils how many would go on to attend middle school. Of the twenty pupils from Sunada and Tsukigata only three were able to do so. Those three raised their hands.

The other pupils—children of poor tenant farmers, small-time candy store owners, and barkeepers—turned around to look at them, their faces vivid with envy. With everyone's eyes focused on them the three blushed a little but, as might be expected, they looked proud. Not only was each of the three inferior to Yasuko in grades, they—except for the assistant class leader—were from the bottom half of the class. At that moment Yasuko was assailed by a strange and incomprehensible feeling. She felt she could not bear to explain it away convincingly even within her own heart. Pupils who were much, much worse than she were going on to a higher school! She understood of course that it was because their families had "money," but understanding alone was not enough to make Yasuko accept it.

Similar things had happened a number of times. For instance, when a Hokkaido government director came to inspect their school it was really Yasuko who as head of the class should have delivered the congratulatory address. However, since she did not even have a different kimono to change into, a rich child took her place. The lack of clothes and money also led to her being absent from athletic meets and excursions. But at such times Yasuko, unlike Okei, assumed a scornful expression. She smiled faintly while listening to the rich child read the congratulatory address; and said that only those with nothing better to do wanted to take part in excursions and athletic meets. Unlike Yasuko, Okei often cried at such times, saying it was a terribly cruel and unfair way to treat fellow schoolmates.

Nevertheless, Yasuko felt intensely insulted, as if the higher school incident were a blow against her entire existence. The pupils going on to middle school began to stay after classes daily in order to study. Seeing them walk about displaying books like *How to Study for Tests* and *Arithmetic Solutions* caused Yasuko acute suffering. Moreover, these pupils did not raise their hands in class even half as often as Yasuko. It was about this time that Yasuko started to grow irritable and sullen. From time to time she fretfully insisted "Let me go to higher school."

It pained Okei to see her younger sister's personality change so completely. Since her grades were so good, Okei wanted to send her on to school if only she herself could find some work. When Okei said so to Mother, her only response was, "A farmer knows how to smack a horse's butt without any studying." Brother kept silent. Of course the prospect of Yasuko's continued education grew hopeless. Yasuko stopped playing with winter cherries and began to brood.

On the way back from her errands one day, Yasuko met the three pupils who were returning from studying for their examinations. Yasuko stopped and glared at them. The three drew close to each other and said, "What're you staring at? You're just sore 'cause you can't go to middle school!"

Without saying a word, Yasuko picked up a stone from the roadside and threw it at them. In a daze, she did it again. One of the pupils fell, bleeding from the nose.

Yasuko turned deathly pale and ran all the way home. The moment her foot touched the earthen floor of her house, she began suddenly and loudly to cry.

6

One of the girls going on to middle school was the daughter of a landlord who had had night soil strewn in front of his house during the Tsukigata dispute. In scholarly ability she ranked just below the assistant class leader. Yasuko had never been so happy.

"If you dream that you picked up shit, it means that you'll come into money!"

During recess, Yasuko went to the spot where everyone had gathered and spoke loudly enough for that pupil to hear. She was feeling thoroughly mean. The moment everyone grasped what she meant, an uproar broke out. They had all been waiting for someone to broach the subject.

"Does shit stink even in a dream?" asked another girl even more loudly, evidently supporting Yasuko. She had reddish hair and came from a Tsukigata tenant family that had joined the strike. "It probably stinks bad enough to bend your nose!"

Everyone burst into uproarious laughter.

"Money and shit are connected!"

"And sex too!"

Unable to take any more of it, the landlord's daughter walked off toward the gymnasium.

"Serves you right, little bitch," thought Yasuko.

Although Tsukigata was the nearest village to Sunada, its soil was not very fertile. Many of Tsukigata's fields were stony, and the black soil was thin. Though the yield per field was considerably less than in Sunada, there was no difference in the rent paid by the tenant farmers. The landlords had agreed on this. As a result, the Tsukigata tenants frequently went on strike. Once a dispute began, Sango would go out to the village every day as a representative of the Young Men's Association. Given the strong influence of Yoshimine and the other landlords, the Association made every effort to terminate the strikes as swiftly as possible and prevent their bad influence from reaching Sunada. That was the goal of the "arbitration" pursued by Sango. Yasuko knew nothing about this, but wanted the strikes to continue as long as possible to give those bastards a hard time.

It was just around then that a startled Yasuko was shaken awake one night by Mother who was sleeping beside her. Evidently Yasuko had uttered a loud scream. She had been dreaming.

She is running along a road as fast as she can. One of her hands is gripping a clump of shit. The landlord's daughter is fleeing from her, her hair disheveled. In the dream, she is just about to seize the girl and yet she cannot quite reach her. Damn it, damn it! Yasuko grits her teeth and keeps chasing her. Wind whizzes against her earlobes and howls past her cheeks. Yasuko is running with her right hand raised high overhead. At last she draws so close her left hand can reach the nape of the girl's neck. She suddenly grabs her. At that very instant the girl spins around and with all her might sinks her teeth into Yasuko's wrist. "Aaah!" Yasuko unwittingly cries out. That was when Mother shook her awake. . . . Yet Yasuko was disappointed with her dream-self. Why had she been unable to smear the girl's face with it?

Her eyes wide open within the darkness, Yasuko kept on winding various childish fantasies into her dream. The girl is thrown into a ditch by tenant farmers. It would be pretty amusing if she got thrown in head first. And what if she were no longer able to go to "higher school!" . . . Yasuko's fantasies all ended the same way, with the girl getting crippled and unable to go on to school. When her fantasy reached this point, Yasuko felt relieved and at peace.

This was why Yasuko grew disgusted with her brother once she understood that Sango went to the neighboring village in order to put a quick end to the strike.

7

Around the time when her school-bound classmates left for the boardinghouses of Sapporo and Otaru, Yasuko came to Otaru to work at the restaurant. She and her former classmates, however, were headed in completely different directions.

Yasuko wrapped up and brought with her old magazines with missing covers, and books, some of which Okei had given her. That constituted all of her luggage. Even if she could not attend school, she was determined not to be outdone in reading books.

Various people came to the eatery. Most of them were workers, who hurriedly ate their meals and left. There were also others, and not just the union man, who joked and chatted with the charming and sociable Yasuko. Some invited her to the movies, or left her magazines like *New Youth* and *King*. Yasuko avidly read every single copy. There were men who smoked and talked about novels, about Nevlyudov and the like, and groups of young ruffians who often barged into this working-class suburban eatery. Yasuko, without being aware of it herself, especially enjoyed talking with union people and drew ever closer to them.

At the union man's invitation, Yasuko attended one of the union's meetings held on the third Sunday of each month. She had agreed to go half in fun, but when the time came did not know what to do. She went reluctantly and somewhat fearfully, and saw only four or five other women present. Yasuko sat stiffly, surrounded entirely by men.

Each speaker was greeted by applause. She noticed that the women too were enthusiastically clapping their hands. Most of the speakers were familiar to her: she had heard them talk any number of times when they came to eat their meals. "Workers, peasants . . . !" "Workers and peasants!"—the words were spoken as though they were some sort of a code. Though the words were quite unremarkable, they mysteriously went straight to Yasuko's heart.

The people who were sitting near her, unlike those she saw in places like movie theaters, were all impoverished workers just like those in her own village. None of them had the proud air of someone who was able to afford higher education. Yasuko felt as thoroughly at ease as if she had returned home for the first time in years and stretched her arms and legs to her heart's content. To Yasuko who had been spending every single day from dawn to dusk with the restaurant owner, this was a feeling she had not experienced in a very long time.

After a while, "her" union man went up to the rostrum. (Yasuko did not know his name, but thought it was either Yamada or Sasaki.) Stepping up to the table, he took a sip of water and swept back his long hair. Everyone clapped, so Yasuko did too. After clapping, she suddenly blushed.

His distinct features illuminated from the left by a strong overhead light, the man stood before sheets of text and slogans, making a deep impression on Yasuko. His way of speaking was not gruff like that of the others but he sometimes made people laugh, and his delicate reasoning felt like a hand soothing an itch. Yasuko too found it quite comprehensible. But although she thought that he was more skillful than the others, Yasuko worried that there was something lacking in a speech that did not cause its listeners to clench their fists. The man stepped down from the rostrum before being told to stop. The applause was even more passionate than what had followed earlier speakers. Yasuko joined in, feeling a little calmer.

There were many policemen in the meeting hall. All wore hats with chin straps and swords strapped close to their sides. A gold-striped police superintendent sat on guard beneath the rostrum, a sword planted between his thighs.

"Stop!" bellowed Gold Stripes in an astonishingly loud voice.

As the meeting drew to a close, each speaker was ordered to stop within two or three minutes. Each time, the audience rose to its feet in unison. Those who protested the most loudly were abruptly dragged from their seats, grabbed by the arms from both sides, and arrested.

Speakers who went on speaking even after being ordered to stop were rushed by policemen who ran up onto the stage and dragged them down. Such scenes could be glimpsed through gaps among the mass of shoulders that swayed and stirred as if seething.

Excited, clenching her teeth, and hemmed in on all sides, Yasuko was borne toward the exit by a human avalanche. The meeting had been "dispersed."

8

After the police brought the meeting to a halt, the crowd poured out of the assembly hall and surged in a great torrent toward the main street. Carried along by the wave of humanity, Yasuko wondered what had become of her union man. He had not been arrested, had he? The way things were going, she feared that he might have been.

A police wagon filled with those who had been arrested blew its horn incessantly, but no one made way for it. The wagon gunned its engine till it rattled, yet it could not budge.

"Who the hell would let you pass!"

"Sons of bitches, if you want to run us over, try and do it!"

Men who seemed to be factory workers and others wearing artisans' short jackets stood flexing their burly shoulders. A closer look showed many students also mingling with the crowd.

The restaurant owner was entering his profits into the account book when Yasuko returned. He asked if she had enjoyed her outing. Yasuko had said she was going to see a movie at the park cinema, so she gave a haphazard reply and went up to the second floor. Her room, an attic with no ceiling boards, became stuffy whenever the setting sun shone in. Agitated by her new experiences, Yasuko could not fall asleep for a long time. She imagined and fantasized about various things, recalled scenes from the meeting one by one, thought of how the man had looked as he drank water from his glass and swept back his long hair.

At the time of the tenant strike in Tsukigata, a speech meeting had been held in Sunada seeking to "impeach the evil landlords." There was no farmers' union in Sunada. The unions from Tsukigata and Asahikawa struggled to use the Tsukigata strike to plant the shoots of unionization in Sunada. On that occasion the "Sunada Village Young Men's Association" obstructed the meeting and even came to blows with the union people. When Yasuko and her friends, able to see only one or two grainy movies per year, had innocently said that they wanted to go to the meeting they were scolded by Sango. Come to think of it, thought Yasuko, that meeting had no doubt gone much like the one tonight. Now that she had gotten to know the union man, heard him talk about various things, and actually gone to a meeting herself, Yasuko felt that she was beginning to understand for the first time the "true" nature of their life in the village. The clarity with which she realized this startled even herself.

In the past too—as evidenced by such small incidents as that of the "vitamins"—once Yasuko was convinced of something, she wanted to act on it by whatever means. She could not bear to keep still. In fact, although she had no idea where to go or what kind of work to do, she felt compelled even before considering such matters to throw herself into action. Telling the union man Yamada (or Sasaki) that she wanted to work and had to do it came from an idea that surprised even Yasuko.

"I'd been waiting for you to say that," said the man, his eyes shining.

"But I don't know anything. Besides I'm a woman, so I feel like I'm being forward . . ."

"Far from it. Asada's wife in the organizing section makes rapid rounds of back-street tenements carrying one child on her back and pulling another by the hand."

"Really?! . . ." Yasuko remained absorbed in thought and kept rubbing the tabletop stain with her finger.

"You'll be working with us, but since you have a family it won't be possible for you to get in completely right away. It might be good if you started in a small way, helping with our work . . ."

"Yes, that's just what I want to do!" Yasuko raised her flushed face and looked at the man.

"Well, as we discussed earlier, I'd like you to persuade your sister and mother to let us use their room . . ."

Okei's Burden

1

After the shop closed, Yasuko set out for the place where her mother and elder sister were renting a room. Okei usually got home late so the timing seemed just right.

Soon after Okei came to Otaru with the restaurant owner's help, she was able to get work at a factory that sorted green peas for export. The working day was from six thirty in the morning until five in the evening, or until nine at night. In order to obtain as much work as possible the factory owner used the "piecework" system, and some of the employees worked as long as fourteen or fifteen hours a day. By working until five o'clock, you got an average of about seventy sen. By working until nine, you could sometimes get as much as one yen. However, it was impossible to keep on working till nine every night. Forcing yourself to do it was counterproductive: you were too tired the next day and your output would fall off drastically.

The work was simple. A worker received a fixed amount of green peas from the supervisor, spread them across a flat tabletop, picked out the shriveled peas with quick practiced fingers, put the rest into a separate box, and submitted it for the supervisor's inspection. If the peas passed inspection, the worker received the next batch. Although the work appeared simple, failing the inspection or having an ill-tempered supervisor meant being unable to earn even half the wages of an ordinary day.

At first Mother too had worked at the pea-sorting factory but she had gotten sick and taken to her bed. Although Okei had wanted to work twice as hard as anyone else, she was badly hampered by the fact that her fingertips had grown hard and thick from all the farmwork and she could not use them as nimbly as the others. It took her three months to catch up with them. With Mother no longer able to work, the women had to manage by mostly relying on Okei's wages. Yasuko was at best able to earn only five or six yen a month. Okei felt the weight on her shoulders.

Quietly and tirelessly, Okei kept on working at the "factory." It occupied a second-floor corner in one of the warehouses (used mainly for grain storage) that lined the harbor canal. Although large enough for two or three hundred people, it usually held one hundred, and at times only twenty or thirty. Women workers numbered from about fifteen to forty-five. Groups of fishermen carrying gaffs on their shoulder-pads passed beneath the windows, calling out to the second floor. During lunch the women stood side by side at the windows calling out in turn to the passing men.

"Hey, hey, you dropped something!"

Although realizing that they were being teased, the men stopped to look around.

"Dropped what?"

The women burst into peals of laughter.

"The most important thing you have!" said an old woman nonchalantly.

Her words amused the other seventeen or eighteen women all the more. Okei was surprised.

Since the factory contained only tables and no dangerous

machinery, many of the women who had children brought them along and let them play near the tables or in the corridor. The factory's low ceiling echoed with the clamor of children running around, fighting, and shouting, intermingled with the incessant rustle of the peas in the women's hands. While sorting out the peas, the workers moved in rhythm and sang.

> Better not look down on the factory girl
> When she goes back home she's a beautiful bride
> Just look at her then, and you'll love her at once

At noon, the women with the youngest children bared big breasts within the swirling dust, casually perched the children under an arm, and fed them.

By the time Okei returned home after working all day, she was utterly exhausted. Even climbing up the dark staircase was laborious for her. Once she sat down in the room with her legs out to one side she did not move. She did not feel like thinking about anything, or reading a book, or moving about, or even saying anything to her bedridden mother . . .

Mother, looking strangely small, was lying under a thin quilt with her legs drawn up. On the mat near her pillow two or three bowls remained scattered about, evidently from her lunch.

Okei was sitting absentmindedly at Mother's bedside just when Yasuko, having greeted the owner of the house on the first floor, climbed up the creaking stairs.

2

The house where Okei and Mother were renting a room stood two blocks away from the main street, in an alley that stayed soggy even in prolonged good weather. The house was reached by stepping carefully along a planked pathway. In addition to Okei and her mother, three other families rented rooms and cooked their meals in the same house. As Yasuko passed the shared kitchen, wives who were preparing supper looked her up and down. Children too abruptly stopped chattering, clutched the hems of their mothers' kimonos, and stared at Yasuko. Each of the families lodging in the house had many children.

"Good evening," said Yasuko and lightly patted a child on the head.

Seeing that Yasuko had come to visit, Okei, to her surprise, suddenly felt invigorated. Her physical exhaustion was not only due to arduous work. Having lived all her life in a village, she was unable to adapt easily to the city life of Otaru. This affected her body in ways not visible to the eye.

"How are you, Mother?" Yasuko pushed the *natsumikan* she had bought along the way toward Mother's pillow.

"Ma's much better."

Okei gazed at Yasuko. Since she had seen her last, Yasuko had grown beautiful just like a city woman. She looks beautiful even to her big sister, thought Okei. Yasuko's words were also different from the time when she lived in the village.

"Have you been busy?"

"Not so busy, but I'm not used to it."

"You'll like it when you find a better place and go there."

"There's a better place?"

Yasuko laughed. "In a big city like Otaru, I'm sure there is."

"But can I do it? . . ." Okei brought her fingertips up to her eyes and looked at them, then thrust them toward her younger sister. "Look at these! See, I just can't pick out the peas with these thick fingers."

"Peasants have the thickest fingers in the world," said Yasuko, filling the entire room with her bright laughter. She was the same old Yasuko after all. "I too have been trotting around, scrubbing and washing in the kitchen and all that. Even so, look, I've gotten this elegant."

Yasuko too thrust her fingertips toward her elder sister. They were dark red and swollen, their skin chapped and rough. Still it was possible they were more "elegant" than Okei's.

Mother raised her head at the sound of Yasuko's voice. The three women opened the package of *natsumikan* and ate them. With practiced fingers Yasuko peeled the *natsumikan* one by one so that Mother could eat them right away.

"Oh! Sour!"

With every *natsumikan* they ate, Okei and Yasuko grimaced fiercely by turns. Then they looked at each other and giggled.

"What's so funny, you silly child?"

Mother's question made Okei giggle even more. "It's Yasuko. She bought 'em without picking 'em out."

"I couldn't tell 'em apart, Ma!" With the three of them together, Yasuko reverted unawares to the way she used to speak in the village.

"You two are so hard to please!" said Mother in exasperation. But her face continued to beam with happiness. Okei was silently laughing.

Mother's face suddenly clouded over. "If only Sango were here . . . then we'd all be together!"

That was the subject none of them had touched on.

3

After they had spent an hour or so together, Yasuko said, "Shall I treat you to some noodles, Big Sister?"

Thinking she had better discuss her reason for today's visit elsewhere, Yasuko was trying to entice her sister out of the house.

"I myself made eighty sen today, you know. . . . Shall *I* treat *you*, Yatchan?" Okei was being unusually talkative.

"You worked so hard for that money, it'd be a shame . . ."

"What are you talking about, silly? It's the same thing with you."

The sisters went on talking like this until Okei said, "All right, shall I let you treat me then?"

Okei retied her obi, and the two went out. After making their way through an alley so dark they could not see their feet, they emerged onto a bright riverside street. But because this was a working-class district and it was slightly late, only a few people were still walking about.

A block or two downstream, along the river that flowed through the middle of the street, they found a small noodle shop.

"Shall we try this place?" Yasuko bent down and peered in. There were no customers. It looked suitable.

But Okei who hardly ever entered a restaurant to eat noodles felt ill at ease. Yasuko, however, briskly and casually brushed the shop curtain aside and stepped in. Okei, hunching her shoulders, followed. With her body halfway into the shop, she looked around anxiously.

"It's all right," said Yasuko, showing her white teeth in a smile.

Okei walked in but took a seat close to a corner.

"Since we've come all the way here, let's have it with tempura instead of plain," said Yasuko. Okei looked at the price list. Searching through the list item by item, she found it: *Tempura noodles 15 sen.*

"It's double, isn't it."

"That's all right, it's my treat." Yasuko ordered for them both. So now, how to broach the topic? It was still extremely difficult for Yasuko to bring it up.

"Sister . . . I wanted to talk with you about something today . . ."

The difference in Yasuko's tone made Okei look questioningly at her face.

"Well, I'd like to borrow your room from time to time . . ."

"The room?"

"Yes, there's someone who'd very much like to use it . . ."

"Huh? Not you?"

"Someone who comes to the shop . . ."

". . . . . ?!"

Thoroughly familiar with her younger sister's character, Okei had the premonition that she was engaging in something outrageous.

"It's someone who's involved in the movement."

"Huh?"

"The movement . . . someone working for the union."

"Union . . . ?"

"Well . . . there was a farmers' union in Tsukigata, right? In Otaru, there's a workers' union . . ."

"And they asked you to do this?"

Unsure how Okei meant this, Yasuko paused for a moment.

"They asked me, yes . . ." Yasuko's face expressed uncertainty.

"If they only asked you, that's good but . . . that union . . . er . . . aren't they *com-mun-ists?*"

4

"Communists!" Yasuko stared at her sister in surprise. Where had she learned the word? "Certainly not! . . . They're working for the union!"

"So why does that person want to borrow the room?"

"Work is work, right? And he needs to talk with people about various things in a place that nobody else knows. He's worried because he doesn't have such a place."

At this point it occurred to Yasuko that she would have to persuade her sister by telling her in detail about the work the union people were doing. She thought about it, and told her. Okei listened attentively, gazing at Yasuko's face. Even so, there were things she did not fully understand. In just two or three years since coming to Otaru, her younger sister had changed beyond recognition. This was a tremendous surprise for Okei.

"So you've joined them too, Yatchan . . . ?" said Okei sadly.

Yasuko looked at her sister's face. "Not really . . . but . . ."

"I understand it, and I don't understand it. . . . But they found two of those *com-mun-ists* in the Tsukigata Farmers' Union, you know . . . I'm kind of worried about you, Yatchan."

Okei vividly recalled the people she had seen at Sango's trial, like the man in the sedge hat with his arms tied up. According to the clerk in the waiting room, they were working to build a world where the only people were the poor. And now her little sister was saying the same thing! Okei felt panic-stricken, as if she had discovered her sister among the friends of the man in the sedge hat. It did not matter to Okei whether they were right or wrong, but that this should be happening to her sister after what had already befallen her brother alarmed her.

Most of all, Okei had unwittingly begun to feel that she bore the responsibility for her whole family. And this was becoming an invisible burden weighing on her shoulders. Feeling half reproachful and half envious, Okei gazed at her younger sister. Was her little sister giving any thought to the family?

Of course, various things that Okei had not previously understood had become clear to her, especially since the incident with Sango. She had also come to understand that the suffering and poverty they had been enduring came ultimately—if their roots be sought—from the ties between landlords and tenant farmers. If she considered it in connection with this, she could also understand the "work" that those people were doing. Whether or not it would go as they hoped was another matter. But what should she do about her immediate hand-to-mouth existence from which she could not extricate herself no matter how hard she worked? And what about this burden that she had to bear alone? Things were not as simple as Yasuko thought. At present Okei was the crucial "pillar" to her family. Although she was barely twenty, she had to be as watchful about every crumb and coin as a grandmother of sixty. Peasants, workers, and others who suffered while barely making a living might desire to live differently and call their desire just, but they could not leap effortlessly into a new life. They were shackled by their day-to-day existence.

But Yasuko, her cheeks flushed, spoke passionately of the things she had been thinking about. In the end she said, "I can't remember her name, but there's a woman who devoted her life to workers and peasants and who's famous throughout the world. Here's what she says." Yasuko closed her eyes for a moment to recall the phrase. Her lowered long lashes were beautiful. "She says, 'We must not live like trampled frogs'!"

Okei unwittingly raised her eyebrows.

"Ah, I remember now!" exclaimed Yasuko. "She's the great woman revolutionary, Rosa Luxemburg."

5

They were served two bowls of tempura noodles. Sprinkling the noodles with chili pepper and blowing at the steam, they began to ply their chopsticks.

"You know, Sunada villagers really live like trampled frogs, don't they!"

". . . . ."

Without being aware of it herself, Okei was starting to feel irritated with her younger sister. It seemed as though Yasuko was saying that Okei herself lived like a trampled frog. Noticing that Okei had said nothing in a while, Yasuko stopped talking. Okei was not talkative to begin with. She only spoke after thinking something through. Although Yasuko always addressed her elder sister insistently (in part as a typically indulged baby sister), she had always had a certain fear of her sister in her heart. It seemed to her that she had now accidentally collided with that fear.

"You know," said Yasuko slowly, "I'd really like you to let him use the room. Even just out of our sense of duty . . ."

Okei finished her noodles, slurping up the soup to the last drop. Rubbing the edge of the empty bowl with her finger, she said, "Yatchan, are you thinking about our family a little? . . ."

Unsure what her elder sister was trying to say, Yasuko watched her lips.

"Yatchan, I understand what you're saying. But if we lend the room to such a person and things happen to go wrong . . . what then? I don't know much about what they do, but aren't the police watching them like hawks?" Looking down into her bowl, Okei slowly added, "If something happens that can't be undone . . . !"

Why, my big sister thinks like any run-of the-mill person, thought Yasuko. In a clear voice, she said, "If that were to happen . . . and I don't think it's likely to, but if it did . . . then I'd live with it."

Okei raised her face and stared at her in amazement. "I wish that for a moment I could be like you!"

Wondering what she meant by that, Yasuko stole a glance at her face. Okei looked back at her, her expression cold and hard. Yasuko had lost her foothold.

The sisters fell silent. It was a strained, unpleasant silence in which each tried to sound out the other's feelings. After a while they rose and left.

As she walked along the street, Yasuko felt perplexed. She herself had spoken bravely, yet come to think of it, perhaps she was being as rash as her sister suggested. If something did go wrong, it really would bring disaster to Sister, and Mother, and herself. . . . What was to be done?

Looking at it from a different perspective, this work was extremely difficult and required a great many sacrifices, as the union man had said countless times and as was written in the books she had borrowed. Rosa Luxemburg, the woman who had spoken about trampled frogs, had been thrown into prison dozens of times for her work and was finally beaten to death with rifle butts. It was a noble sacrifice for the sake of the exploited and hungry working people of the whole world. Her life was unforgettable, especially for the women of the working class.

The letters that Rosa Luxemburg had sent from prison to her comrades on the outside were collected and published as a book in Japan too. The union man had brought her a copy and urged her to read it. Each evening after her work ended, Yasuko climbed up to her attic room to read it, and she had finished it within three days. It astounded her most of all that Rosa was a *woman*, just as she was. Yasuko remembered feeling too ashamed of herself to sit still . . .

"That's right," thought Yasuko as she walked: "I must convince my sister, no matter what."

6

Yasuko decided to talk to her once more. If that didn't work, she would speak with her again, and yet again.

"They're working for our sake, you see, so they're sure to be extremely careful. . . . Since you come home late anyway, you wouldn't even get in each other's way . . ."

It was not that Okei did not understand what her younger sister was saying, far from it. She herself had been struck by various things since her brother's incident, and she even felt somehow that what had been stagnating within her heart had become clear. (Indeed it was Yasuko's words that made her notice that something had been stagnating there.) But did that mean she could take on the matter of "the room" so easily? Okei's way of doing things had always been different from her sister's. She did not wholeheartedly commit herself to something unless she was thoroughly convinced of it, and unless she took some time to examine its possible consequences. Although she felt she understood the present situation, the truth was that Okei had only a rough idea of it based on what Yasuko had told her. Even such limited information alarmed her because, as she had seen while they lived in the village, the police hated those who did that kind of work most of all. During the Tsukigata strike, even the *saké*-loving and good-natured Patrolman Yamada had kicked a Farmers' Union youth with his boot. More than anything else, Okei's strongest and conclusive brake was her awareness that with Brother gone they had to make a living by themselves, and that she was bearing the entire weight of it on her own shoulders.

Whenever Yasuko said something, Okei took in the various ideas readily but in the end everything returned to "the weight on her shoulders." If she stopped working for just a day or two, Mother and she could not so much as eat. Although they had relatives, they had all drawn away blaming them for having produced a criminal. Under such circumstances even asking for sick leave was no trivial matter. How much more so if she lent the room to someone and the room was raided, or if it eventually came to light that secret meetings had been held there! Even though Okei would certainly have no idea what the meetings had been about, the consequences would be unthinkable! . . . Yet despite all this, Yasuko threw herself into it with such purity, unconcerned about how it might affect her. Okei truly envied her. Yasuko had always been like that. It was partly due to the fact that Yasuko was the younger sister. No doubt that Rosa what's-her-name Yasuko spoke about was also the same, and she surely must have had some way or other of feeding herself no matter what she did. Because her sister was speaking with such enthusiasm, she felt awkward about bringing that up. And yet, come to think of it, if the work those people were doing was truly for the sake of workers and peasants as Yasuko said, then it was kind of strange that she herself who was one of the poorest of them could not join in their work.

Okei remained silent for a long time. Could she leave this enthusiastic sister of hers to her own devices? She thought about it while walking. She contemplated the weight of her family's livelihood that weighed on her shoulders, and the fact that a person has to eat at any cost. Though she could not possibly leave her present job at the pea-sorting factory, shouldn't she at least free Yasuko from having to worry about her daily life since she was getting so enthusiastically involved in her work? It had angered her at first that Yasuko had so matter-of-factly entrusted her with something without giving a thought to the painful circumstances in which Mother and she were forced to live. However, the reason for her anger had nothing to do with the kind of work that Yasuko was becoming interested in. Okei did not yet understand this work well, but she understood that her sister and her friends were trying to do what was right.

"I'll let you use the room. Just be careful."

Yasuko raised her face in surprise and looked at her sister.

7

One evening around seven when Okei returned home exhausted, Mother called out to her from the top of the stairs, "The people you said would come are here . . ."

Although Okei was tired to the point of collapse, she suddenly stiffened upon hearing this. Her heart pounded as she climbed the stairs, and she hesitated to go in. Sitting down briefly near the entrance, she quietly asked, "Is Yasuko here?"

"She just brought them and left right away."

"She did? . . ."

At that moment deep quiet voices stopped talking, and tatami mats creaked. Soon the paper door slid open and a broad shaft of light flooded the staircase.

"Forgive us for intruding . . ."

"Please come in."

Okei grew flustered and blushed. She could not see the man's face because the light was behind him, but her own face was in plain view. The man's way of speaking was quiet and polite, different from what Okei expected of people who did that kind of work.

Since she could not go on standing outside, Okei stepped in along with Mother. There were three men. They all wore similarly threadbare corduroy suits and sat cross-legged, their hands thrust aslant into a pile of printed matter they had been examining. As Okei entered, they raised their haunches slightly and greeted her.

Okei uneasily sat down in a corner with her back pressed against the wall.

One of the three, a man with a slender face and clear-cut features who had been the first to greet her, said, “I believe you have heard about us from your sister . . . Thank you so much for your kindness.”

Okei mumbled “Yes,” and bowed. She remained motionless for a while until it occurred to her to go to the public bath so as not to be in the way. Asking Mother to accompany her, she left.

“Sorry to be in your way!” called out the man from behind her.

The two took a leisurely bath. Okei moved behind Mother and scrubbed her back. Mother’s dark, slack skin was hard to scrub. Her shoulder blades jutted out, shifting eerily each time she took a breath. It occurred to Okei that Mother might not live long. But her arms and legs were surprisingly big and bony. They were the only prominent part of her.

On their return, they noticed that only two pairs of shoes remained in the earthen-floor entryway. One of the men had evidently left. The other two lay inside the room, smoking Golden Bat cigarettes. The room was stifling with tobacco smoke.

“Ah, welcome back.”

Wiping her face with a hand cloth, Mother asked, “Did one of you leave?”

“Yes. If we left together we’d stand out, so we’re leaving one by one, with a few minutes in between.”

Okei listened quietly, thinking: “That’s an interesting way of doing it.”

But Mother looked puzzled. “What . . . ?”

One of the men rose to his feet. While pinching his knees and stretching his legs, he said, “Well, I’m off . . .”

“All right, so it’s the fifth, seven in the evening, at the place we said, right?”

“On the fifth at seven . . . right.”

The man climbed down the squeaking stairs and left. Only the man with the slender face who had been the first to address Okei remained behind.

“Where do you work?” asked the man.

“At the pea-sorting factory.”

"It's terrible, isn't it?"

Okei silently nodded.

"How about going on strike!" said the man with a laugh.

8

At the sudden mention of going on strike, Okei grew bewildered and blushed crimson.

Smiling, the man watched her. Then he began to ask her various things about the factory: what time the work began, how many rest periods there were, how much she received in wages. . . . Okei told him about leaving the house before daybreak and working continuously till after sunset, about eight, coming home too tired even to go to the bath, then dozing off only to wake up to go to work again, and repeating the same thing day after day. Hearing this, the man lightly shook his head a few times.

"And yet most people consider this kind of life only natural, or they're convinced that nothing can ever be done about it. The boss who makes you work like that and doesn't do a lick of work himself grabs profits dozens of times bigger than what you get. All the same, there's still a lot of folks in Japan who accept all this as a matter of course because he's got money and they don't. Many women tend to think like that . . ."

Listening to him talk, it occurred to Okei that he was probably the man who spoke with Yasuko about these things.

"It's especially women who've been trained to submit unquestioningly to everything. Even if she has a family, the woman must not raise her head because it's the man who brings in the money. A man gets away with doing wrong, a woman gets blamed even when she's right. That's why women ought to work on their own, so as to become fully self-reliant. For instance . . ."

While exhaling the smoke, the man glanced mischievously at Mother who was dozing.

"It's a little cruel to say it, but the case of your mother and you is a good example, don't you think?"

Okei unwittingly raised her eyebrows.

"You are providing for your mother, and so you have absolute power over her," said the man with a laugh.

"How could that be? . . ."

"Because you are the head of the family. . . . Well, it's merely an example. Since the economy is so bad nowadays, capitalists can't profit enough unless they lower workers' wages as much as possible. That's why women will be employed more and more in various kinds of work.

"Women's work has long been limited to sewing, cooking, and taking care of children, but now they'll find themselves in the wider society, occupying the same workplaces as men. As a result women's way of thinking will also change, and anyway they'll earn money, enabling them to gain economic independence. Therefore they'll be able to break free from slavish ways of thought that have taught them till now to depend on men. Right? . . . First of all, since you've got a boss then you don't just cook and clean, you go out to work every single day, and with the money you get working for that boss you provide for your family and you handle various household matters all with your own strength. Without realizing it, you've become different from a woman who does needlework . . ."

Okei had never before heard such talk. Although this was her first time, she felt she understood its meaning as accurately as if it had struck some measuring instrument within her heart.

"In the old days, women's only profession was prostitution. Look at you now: tens of thousands of factory workers, café and bar waitresses, office workers, typists, bus conductors. Not only are your numbers growing, but your sphere of work is rapidly expanding too. This sort of thing will have an extremely socializing and elevating effect on women's way of thinking about things."

Having smoked his cigarette till the flame reached his fingers, the man rubbed it out against the top of the ashtray. Okei felt downright amused at how immensely this talk fascinated her.

9

"You understand what I've been saying, right? . . ."

The man smiled amiably. Okei silently nodded.

"I've said that this can happen once women become economically independent . . . but actually, the way things are now—in a capitalist world where idle people with money make immense profits—a great many people, far from being independent, are painfully struggling just to get by, as you yourself are first to know. That's why this capitalist world that's founded on exploitation offers no hope at all for women to live truly unfettered lives."

The man swiftly finished smoking a cigarette he had just lit.

"You understand, right? . . . That's the truth, you see. Working-class women are bound by double chains: on the one hand they must be liberated from men, and on the other hand they must be liberated from capital. To be liberated from men, women must first of all be economically independent, but to solve that basic economic problem it's essential that women be liberated as workers. So, enabling women to exist truly as women is only conceivable through a liberation of the working class. It may sound like a self-serving argument, but to join our work on a mass scale is the best way to break both these chains at once."

The man looked at Okei inquiringly, as if to make sure that she understood.

Though unable to follow every argument, Okei understood the feeling clearly. By now she was glad she had listened to her sister. Yasuko's way of thinking originated entirely from this kind of man. If she herself had been exposed to it first, thought Okei, she might have been convinced even sooner than her sister. The arguments the man used might not have been easily comprehensible to an ordinary person, but to Okei who came home each night having had to work to the point of collapse, they felt like a hand taking hold of hers in the darkness.

A double chain! It was troubling to think of it that way, but in her heart Okei felt it was true.

"I got awfully carried away, didn't I . . ." said the man with a laugh, and left.

Meetings were held about twice a week. Sometimes they were over before Okei came home, and sometimes they were still going on. When they were still on, the man with the slender face stayed behind for a while and talked with her about various things. Without even realizing it, Okei began to look forward to hearing him talk.

Whenever Yasuko came to visit, Okei brought up one topic after another, or asked her to explain things she did not understand. “What’s happened to you?” asked Yasuko with surprise. “Never mind . . .” answered Okei with a teasing laugh.

Yasuko suddenly turned serious. “Has Mr. Yamada been talking with you?”

“Mr. Yamada? Who is that? I don’t know him.”

Yasuko’s face clouded over and she said nothing more.

Could it be true? thought Okei. It occurred to her that her younger sister might be in love with the slender-faced man.

10

Around six o’clock in the evening a few days later, a woman who worked at an adjacent table told Okei, “Your sister is downstairs.”

Something must have happened, Okei thought. Ever since lending out the room, a suppressed fear that something might go wrong had never left her consciousness. Okei hurried downstairs. Yasuko was standing with her face turned sideways; her expression struck Okei as somewhat agitated. At the sound of Okei’s footsteps, Yasuko turned toward her and their eyes met. Okei looked at her questioningly.

“Are you still working?” asked Yasuko.

“What is it?”

Okei was feeling unwell that day due to her period, and had been trying to decide whether or not to work until eight.

“If you can quit for today . . . there’s something else that I’d like to talk to you about . . .”

“All right.”

Okei returned upstairs. Picking up a box she had just filled, she walked over to the supervisor.

According to rumor, the supervisor was almost certainly the factory manager’s mistress. Originally a worker, her swift promotion had given rise to much talk that was partly motivated by envy. A brisk and beautiful woman, she was friendly and generous toward the countrified and inefficient Okei.

"Going home already?" Looking fresh in her becoming white apron, the supervisor inspected the peas perfunctorily, and approved them.

Okei went to the bathroom, quickly washed her face and hands, and left. Stepping outside, she felt a sense of relief as though her chest had spontaneously expanded. Instead of the dusty air that quickly made her throat itch, a faint mint-like fragrance smooth as water permeated deeply into her lungs.

The sisters emerged into a street that was lined with warehouses. In a vacant lot at the corner, a crowd of laborers was waiting to be paid. Catching sight of the women, they all began to shout banteringly.

"Check out these beauties!"

"Hey, hey . . . !!"

Okei hated having always to pass along this road. But Yasuko shouted back as though she were a man.

"What is it?"

"You're beautiful!"

"Of course we are!" replied Yasuko in a loud, nonchalant voice.

"Wow! These girls are incredible!"

Glancing at Okei, who walked looking as though she were trying to hide, Yasuko laughed.

They left the beachfront road and entered a street that led uphill into the city. Yasuko still said nothing about why she had come. Worried that something bad might have happened, Okei asked, "What did you want to tell me?"

"Well, it's something big . . . ," said Yasuko hesitantly.

To put her at ease, Okei said, "Maybe you'll laugh at me, Yatchan, but thanks to you I've lately gotten to understand things a little . . ."

Yasuko laughed, drawn out by Okei's words. "But if I tell you, I'm sure you'll be speechless!"

Okei wondered if this might not be about Yasuko's feelings for that union man Yamada she had chanced to notice earlier. She found it hard to believe that her "baby sister" had already reached the age to think about such things.

Once again, she urged her lightly, "Stop making such a big deal out of it, and tell me!"

"All right, I'll tell you! Well . . ."

11

"I'll tell you . . ."

Yasuko suddenly shut her mouth tightly and dropped her gaze to the ground.

"Well, it's that I'm thinking I'll start working for the union," she said at last.

Once again she clamped her mouth shut.

"What I mean is that, unlike what I've been doing, I'm going to concentrate on it completely. Recently the boss also noticed that there's something going on between the union man and me. Whenever I do anything, he interferes, makes sarcastic comments, and gives me a hard time. I don't know why, but it's been showing up in everything he does and says ever since I started talking with the union man. There's no doubt about it. And he has the nerve to say that lately I've become insolent. . . . So, it doesn't look like I'll be able to stay there much longer, and besides Yamada . . . Mr. Yamada says I ought to make the best of this by resolving to join the movement all the way . . ."

Join it all the way? Okei glanced up unawares at her sister's face. What did it mean to join all the way?

"He says that the union is hurting from not having enough people, and in particular that there's almost no women working in it. But if women only devoted all their energies to it, there's a good chance the work would progress rapidly."

"But . . . ," Okei began to say. Her sister appeared earnestly focused on her own words, however, and did not seem to hear her. Gazing at the ground, she continued to speak.

"You know, if I seriously think about it, I feel like it would be cowardly of me not to join the movement when I understand so well that the work it's doing is right."

"But . . . ," Okei ventured again. "But if you do that work all the time, then . . . you'll quit your job and . . . what will you do then?"

"What will I do?" Yasuko looked at her sister for the first time. For some reason Okei found herself bewildered and stammering.

"About the family . . . ," said Okei.

"Ah, that's what I wanted to talk with you about. I think that what

I'm doing to you is truly unforgivable, because if I quit that job and completely dedicate myself to union work I won't be making any more money and won't even have any idea how to go on eating . . . What's more, I won't be able to help you out any longer, though you're already working so hard without even knowing if you'll get anything to eat or not. . . . I feel really sorry about this . . ."

Her sister's words alarmed Okei so much that she felt her blood draining from her face.

"So then . . . ," Okei said, and could not go on. But then she added in a voice as quiet as a whisper, "All right!"

"I am truly so sorry!" Yasuko's eyes were filled with tears. The slowly welling teardrops clung to her long lovely eyelashes, glittering beautifully. "Only please understand that I'm not doing this out of selfishness . . ."

Feeling overwhelmed, Okei lowered her chin into the collar of her kimono.

"Please take care of Mother . . ."

Okei remained silent, absentmindedly staring at her soiled white socks moving forward one after the other.

For some time, the sisters walked in silence. Twilight was approaching, and the street was bustling with a ceaseless movement of people returning from the harbor and the factories, laborers whose work was done for the day, bicycles, automobiles, and carts. The two women walked on indifferent to their surroundings as though they were not a part of humanity.

After a while Yasuko said, "And then, after I quit that job I'm thinking of moving in with Mr. Yamada . . . !"

"What?" Okei raised her face abruptly as if someone had suddenly grabbed her by the shoulders.

12

Okei felt her footsteps grow unsteady with a sort of light dizziness.

If Yasuko was moving in with Mr. Yamada it meant that the two of them would marry. It should have come as no surprise to Okei that her sister had become intimate with the union man. That possibility had already occurred to her. So why this strange, dizzying sensation that she felt at her sister's words?

Come to think of it, Okei had lately been feeling so light and cheerful that she herself found it odd. She had become uncharacteristically talkative. There seemed to be a reason for the way she felt. Whenever she returned home from the factory and discovered that the people who came to the meeting had left, her disappointment was like a sudden onrush of exhaustion. On her way home she had unwittingly been looking forward to hearing Yamada speak.

What Yasuko had now so clearly said made Okei realize that she had developed an affection for Yamada that went beyond simply liking to hear him talk about various subjects. It was an affection that she herself had been unaware of. . . . And it was a feeling that she had to erase at the very moment that she had become aware of it!

Nor was that all, for at the same time the great burden of making a living lay heavily once again on Okei's shoulders. She felt as if she had been born merely to go on bearing such a weight, forbidden from stretching her hands in any direction or turning aside for even a moment.

Yasuko blushed as she started to speak again.

"I think that you can understand, but . . . Mother would not understand no matter how much I talked with her. Also, she knows about the Tsukigata strike so . . . if I told her I was going to live with a union man, she would never agree. Please try to explain it to her as best you can . . ."

Even this did the younger sister try to press on the older.

Yasuko had taken time off from work, so when they reached a corner adjacent to a sunken road, she repeated her appeal and headed back to the restaurant. Okei stood still for a moment and followed her retreating figure with her eyes. While the sisters were walking together, Yasuko had been stammering and hanging her head but now she walked like a different person, swinging her shoulders and flicking the front of her kimono upward as boldly and vigorously as ever. Her sister was pursuing a worthy goal, thought Okei and remained standing for some time.

But what about herself? What was her goal? Okei recalled her gloomy room in the depths of a winding alley. Mother lay there like a poor bundle of rags. With all this to carry, would Okei too get a chance to swing her shoulders and flick up her kimono like her sister? While listening to Yamada, she'd had the barest feeling that she might—but that feeling had been nipped in the bud. She would have to go on working for "a living," and for nothing but that, even harder than ever. She was just like a snail that pokes its head out of its shell only to withdraw it swiftly when anything touches it. Compared with Yasuko, how slow she was in everything. In that respect too, Okei had the feeling that she resembled a snail.

Okei did not even feel like walking.

"I'm really like a snail . . . ," muttered Okei as if persuading herself. A snail! But in fact the similarity went even further. A snail forced to go on dragging a heavy shell on its back—that's what she was!

Okei began to walk slowly.

In the Union

1

Crossing a sunken road that separates the city center from the working-class suburbs and climbing up a riverside road, one reaches a jumbled mass of houses, the entire zone emitting an odd stench. Yamada and Yasuko were entering one of its back alleys.

Yamada was walking with his legs bent outward, carrying a large bundle wrapped in cloth. Yasuko had been walking by his side, but once they entered the alley she moved behind him. She was carrying a small cloth-wrapped bundle.

"Well, here we are . . ."

At Yamada's words, Yasuko suddenly blushed. She had been here a few times before and knew the people who lived downstairs, yet the thought of working here from now on, and moreover of living here with Yamada, made her feel strangely queasy and weak.

"If you can get the moving done as easily as this, Yatchan, you too are a proletarian," said the man with a laugh as he rattled the rear door.

Yasuko swept up with her little finger a strand of hair that had fallen across her face. "Wasn't it heavy?"

"Nah."

"Really? . . . But watching you from behind, it looked like you were going to drop it any second!"

The man burst out laughing uproariously.

"Oh, you clobber me like this when I least expect it . . ."

"I seem to be the stronger of us two, you know . . . because I used to do this in the village."

Talking with him later, Yasuko learned that Yamada had studied for a time at a university in Sapporo.

The householder's child opened the rear door in response to the rattling.

"Ah, Mr. Yamada, a spy was here earlier so I locked the back door."

"Is that right? Did he say anything?"

Yamada sat down on the doorstep and looked up while taking off his shoes.

"Yeah. He said he heard you got yourself a real beauty for a wife and asked if she'd already come . . ."

The boy rattled on, chuckling with delight.

"That son of a bitch! What a thing to say."

"And he said you sure tricked her good . . ."

Yasuko turned crimson. The cheeky child did not seem about to stop chattering any time soon. He stood rooted to the spot, opening wide his big eyes.

Paying no attention, the two climbed to the second floor.

"That kid's a bit odd!" said Yamada, tapping his head with his finger.

The room was a mess. The desk was covered with books, newspapers, a small mirror, a dusty teacup, an empty pack of Golden Bats, and the like. A teakettle, a tin of Lipton tea, and other odds and ends stood abandoned in a corner. On her earlier visits Yasuko had put these things in order any number of times. Although Yasuko was not good at such chores and tended to be lazy, tidying up Yamada's place had struck her as extremely enjoyable.

"My, my, not again!" exclaimed Yasuko stopping in the doorway with an exaggerated show of surprise.

"Here it goes," said Yamada, throwing the bundle down in the middle of the room. He added with a smile, "From now on, it's going to be beautiful!"

Charmed by his gentle smile, Yasuko reddened all the same and began to laugh. Seeing this, Yamada too started to laugh wildly.

"You're hopeless!" Yasuko turned away from him.

Yamada had been sitting on top of the bundle; now he stood up and drew close to Yasuko.

Yasuko stood still.

2

Yasuko began assisting in Yamada's work with an entirely fresh feeling.

It was some time later that she realized the true nature of the work that Yamada and his friends were doing. They were active in a group they had secretly formed within the union.

After Ōyama Ikuo proposed the formation of a new political party in August of that year, a great deal of turmoil had arisen within the union. Repressive actions—such as those of March 15 and April 16—had already dealt unions heavy blows from which they seemed unlikely to recover. Whenever such incidents took place in Otaru, two hundred or more workers, students, and others were dragged away and brutalized. As a result, many of the waterfront workers who joined the union were dissatisfied with its present course of action. Some could not understand why the union was always treated so badly, while others who had long been active in the union blamed young inexperienced workers for wrecking the union with their communist connections just when they themselves were starting to enlarge it. . . . It was at precisely such a time that the proposal for the formation of a new political party appeared.

Its basic point was that in Japan the movement to organize workers could never grow large in the present manner. Until the organization grew in size, it made sense to form a "legal" proletarian party. It would provide a steady grip for those who, hesitant and perplexed, vacillated between the right and the left. As they fumbled in their search, they would come in contact with it and grab hold of it. Many people clung eagerly to the proposal.

At the head of the union stood the committee chair. A former miner, he was rather advanced in years, ruddy-faced, and fat. A good-natured man, he gained widespread popularity through lending a noncommittal ear to various people's complaints. The committee chair agreed with the proposal for a "new party" not from any theoretical reasons but because after so many years of working discreetly in the labor movement he felt, just as though he were an employee of the government or a corporation, that it was time his work took a concrete shape. He wanted to use his workers' constituency to run in the election for the city assembly, and yearned to be addressed for once in his life as "city councilor." The "left wing," with its close links to dangerous elements, was inconvenient to his quest.

But if he opposed the "proposal," he might be outmaneuvered by the young people within the union who supported the left wing, and such a split within the union would spell the end to the sole purpose of his work, his bid to become a city councilor. Therefore the committee chair convened numerous meetings to "criticize" the new "proposal," and began to publicize it. The number of people increased swiftly.

After the proposal came out, many people who had earlier been reluctant to visit the union office for fear of being arrested began to arrive in droves. Such people soon became the committee chair's allies. It was rumored that a man named Kusumi who served directly below the general secretary as his theoretical support had been an early participant in Ōyama's plan. After a clandestine look into whether the nation was receptive toward the publication of his pamphlet, Ōyama apparently entrusted various people with the important role of publicizing it once it was printed. Kusumi was the man behind the scenes who utilized the committee chair for his own benefit.

Yamada and his friends were starting a campaign within the union to oppose this tendency.

3

Ōyama's proposal was clearly a retreat when the movement was at its low point. Although badly battered by repression and nearly crushed, a working-class party already existed and was trying to recover from its wounds. At the same time, though frightened and made hesitant by repeated repression, people continued to seek a way out of the steadily worsening poverty that constricted their lives. The formation at just such a juncture of a legal—officially licensed—party functioned as a destructive and reactionary move against the only party the working class had. It also served to contain the upsurge in popular consciousness within its officially licensed, legal bounds, and to take advantage of people's fears to divert them into a blind alley.

Yamada and his friends were determined to fight resolutely against the legalism, defeatism, and threat to the party that had surfaced at this most difficult time. But they could not openly conduct such a campaign within the union. If they tried to do so, they feared that the authorities would soon realize they had some connection to the party—just like those who were caught on March 15 and April 16.

Therefore they had to go on working "underground" and pretend to be ordinary union activists while winning over dependable fellow members, and bring genuine left-wing leadership to people wherever they worked, in factories or at the waterfront.

But to tell the truth, Yasuko did not actually understand why Yamada and his comrades were rushing about so much and speaking so heatedly. Though she knew the meaning of such words as "legal," "illegal," "dissolutionists," and the like, it was not quite clear to her why Ōyama's proposal to form a legal political party had to be fought against so relentlessly.

However, the basic reason why workers all led such distressed lives within the current system was that the system was structured to benefit the bourgeoisie, and because the bourgeoisie controlled it. Therefore in order to construct a system where workers would not be exploited and where no one would be unemployed and hungry (in Soviet Russia there was a shortage of workers!) it was necessary to get rid of the bourgeois system and this could only be achieved by going beyond the bounds permitted by law. Working within those bounds ultimately meant leaving the bourgeoisie in power and attaining nothing but a limited degree of "reform." The life of exploitation would continue as before but would merely be carried out even more ingeniously, concealed under the name of reform. The best illustration of this could be seen in England where the formation of a "Labor Party" cabinet not only did not make people's lives any easier but on the contrary led to a rapid succession of strikes.

The so-called "lawful" way of seeking change was clearly a deception. Thinking about it in her own way based on what she was familiar with, Yasuko wondered if this was the reason why at some of the recent left-wing speech meetings the police outnumbered even the audience.

Nonetheless, in the depths of her own mind Yasuko was not yet clearly and thoroughly convinced. Instead, she merely took Yamada's word for it that Ōyama Ikuo was a detestable traitor, a backtracking legalist afraid of repression, and a dissolutionist who sought to sidetrack a fully extant working-class party by pitting against it a party of his own.

4

At first, Yasuko only did what Yamada asked her to do. Her work, which she did not understand, consisted of delivering envelopes to various people who lived in tenements.

"What exactly is a dissolutionist, and what's a dissolutionist faction?" asked Yasuko on her return. She had heard the words at all the places to which she had brought the envelopes.

"Something very serious."

"I guess so, but this movement uses awfully complicated words, wouldn't you say?"

"It can't be helped. It's a new movement, with no ties to the bourgeoisie, and even the words carry a completely different content than before, so they've got to be new words."

". . . . ."

But for Yasuko who had not had much education, it was extremely hard to learn the words used by the left wing.

"What we mean by a dissolutionist faction," said Yamada, putting on a professorial air, "is just what the words suggest: a group that wants to dissolve a party. To put it more precisely, it's a tendency that seeks to liquidate the party's existence as an independent unit. . . . This really is complicated. . . . Roughly speaking, a political party is the head of a class. It takes the lead in representing the interests of that class. It's a unit that fights for the class as a whole. So this means that—essentially, a single class can only have a single political party. Therefore there can only be one party that thoroughly represents the interests of the working class."

"Really?" said Yasuko looking clever and batting her lovely eyelashes. "But what about the Seiyūkai and the Minseitō?"

"So, you've noticed that too, Yatchan?" said Yamada with a laugh. "Well, they look like two, but in fact they are one. What I mean is, their essence is the same. They're just a bourgeois party. It's divided in two merely to perform various sly bourgeois tricks, nothing more. They're badgers out of the same hole. For instance, the system of "cabinet resignations and reshuffles" is partly a skillful way of evading responsibility . . ."

Yasuko listened grimacing, scratching her cheek, and impishly poking her fingers up her nose.

"It's awfully complicated!"

"Is it? Maybe so . . ." Yamada looked crestfallen. "Anyway, you do understand that a single class only has a single party, right?"

"Right."

"But Ōyama says he wants to make it two."

"Right."

"And if you compare the two, Ōyama makes his own sound very similar but ultimately his will only pursue reforms within that permitted sphere. Therefore, this will weaken the sole, actually existing working-class party, and divert its strength in a reformist direction. . . . In other words, it will perform the reactionary role of a dissolutionist factional act."

". . . . . ?"

Yamada peered at Yasuko's face and burst out laughing. "What do you say? You look like you don't understand."

But Yasuko, refusing to yield, said, "I'm a peasant, you know. I haven't had much schooling, so arguments go over my head. I'll get to understand things as I rush around doing my work. That will be the way."

"That's right. In our situation, that's the very best teacher!"

5

Due to the nature of their meetings, Yamada and his comrades could not hold them at the house where he and Yasuko were lodging. A spy stopped by every other day or so. They had therefore come up with the idea of borrowing the room that Okei was renting. This was the reason for the negotiations that took place while Yasuko was still working at the eatery.

Yamada worked in the union's vitally important "organizing section." This was convenient in every respect, but because the section chief was an ally of the committee chair, Yamada's work demanded utmost secrecy. Yasuko became a member of the organizing section staff, and decided to continue helping him in his work.

The work did not progress commensurately with their efforts, and they also had to be careful about every word they said. It was just as imperative not to arouse the authorities' suspicions as it was not to be seen through by union officials. They found themselves, so to speak, between two fires.

One sunny day, with two or three hours still left before going to work, Yasuko washed Yamada's clothes and her own, and was hanging them up to dry near the back door.

"Hi!"

The tone was familiar but the voice was not. Someone suddenly ducked beneath the laundry and stood before her.

"You work with such . . . charming innocence."

Although it was Yasuko's first time to see the man, she knew immediately that it was the spy. She frowned and raised her chin.

"Ha, ha . . . that's Yamada's, I suppose . . . and this must be yours."

"Do you have some business here?" said Yasuko curtly.

"Awfully fierce, aren't we? . . ." Acting a trifle shy, the man asked, "So how goes it?"

"How goes what?"

"Really . . ."

"Who the hell are you? Turning up casually without even apologizing, and then spouting all sorts of nonsense . . ."

The man chuckled. "I guess you know who I am . . ."

"No I don't." Yasuko rattled the laundry pole vehemently.

"I'm from the police."

"Yamada isn't at home," she said without so much as a glance at him.

"No need to be so unfriendly. . . . How are things with Yamada? Has he been busy lately?"

Busy? The nonchalant question gave Yasuko a start. Unwittingly she looked at him. She wasn't about to take the bait.

"Not particularly."

"Of course. Still enjoying the newlywed dreams . . . !"

"Right."

"That surprises me," said the spy in an exaggerated tone. "I would've guessed differently."

"It's the truth."

"Aren't you doing some sort of work in the union, madam?"

"Work?"

"As a woman warrior. Anyway, there's been a lot of talk about a distinguished woman warrior, you see."

"Woman warrior? Me, I'm a 'good wife and wise . . .'" She had started to say "wise mother" but broke into a laugh despite herself.

"Ha, ha, ha, ha, ha, it's too soon to be a 'wise mother.' But perhaps you're in the family way already."

The spy kept tapping his stick against the ground, and glancing up at the second-floor window from time to time. Yasuko had noticed it. Although Yamada was out, it irritated her intensely.

"Yamada really isn't here?" The spy abruptly changed his tone.

"He isn't."

Her first experience of dealing with a spy was starting to make Yasuko unexpectedly frightened. She found it difficult to speak.

"Hmm. There's something suspicious about Yamada lately . . . ," said the spy as if talking to himself, and glanced at Yasuko.

6

"What's suspicious?"

The instant she retorted, Yasuko's heart began to pound.

"I can't say what, but something is definitely suspicious."

". . . . ."

"Is Yamada going to the union every day?"

"He is."

Distracted by the spy's words, Yasuko kept putting the laundry onto the drying pole and taking it off again unawares.

"Does he come back early?"

"Sometimes he's early, sometimes late, and sometimes in between."

"Hmm." The detective from the Special Higher Police flashed a thin smile. "What kind of union people stop by here?"

Yasuko briefly knitted her brows in thought. It would be dangerous if the names of the people who came to the house enabled him to guess the nature of the work that was secretly being done inside the union.

"No one goes to the trouble to come here. . . . They see each other at the office every day . . ."

Yasuko sensed the agitation in her own voice.

"This missus is shrewder than I expected . . . looks like Yamada has trained her well."

The blunt familiarity with which the Special Police detective referred to Yamada made Yasuko shiver with dread. Poking at the ground sporadically with his thick-handled stick, the detective glanced by turns at Yasuko's face and at the second floor.

"Have the two of you talked about the formation of the new party?"

"I don't understand that kind of talk. Do you?"

"Really . . . !" The policeman scratched the side of his ear lightly and laughed. "You are one tough customer."

At that moment a clattering of boards that covered the ditch announced someone's arrival into the alley. It was either Yamada or a friend of his, thought Yasuko, and whoever it was the timing was bad. The footsteps soon told her that it was Yamada. Absorbed in his own thoughts, Yamada turned the corner and unexpectedly found himself before the Special Higher Police officer. Yamada's confusion showed plainly on his face.

". . . . . !"

He stood bolt upright, his eyes darting between the spy and Yasuko.

"Hello there!" said the detective, the lip below his clipped moustache twisting into a smile.

But Yamada soon recovered his usual voice. "What are you doing here? When I'm not around, beat it."

"So your good lady is a woman warrior—in the *organizing section*," said the Special Police detective, and turned toward Yasuko as if seeking confirmation.

Yasuko felt disconcerted. Why was it already known that she was working in the union's organizing section? But Yamada appeared even more startled.

"How could a woman like her work in the organizing section?"

"Ha, ha, ha, ha, ha! What do you say to that, madam? Will you keep silent even in the face of this?"

Yasuko squatted down before the laundry, thinking it best to stop talking to him now that Yamada was back.

To avoid the annoyance of having him come up to their room, Yamada attempted to send the policeman on his way.

"Better cut out the stupid talk and get packing. You're making us get in the way of each other's work."

"It's good that it's mutual. By the way, what's the latest with your campaign to oppose the formation of the new party!?"

Hearing this, Yasuko gave a start in spite of herself and stood up.

7

"What are you talking about? This union has decided to support the new party. Just take a look at the committee chair," said Yamada rapidly, and averted his eyes.

"Nice try." The detective flashed a thin smile and said it lightly, as though not listening to him.

"Well, think what you like."

"Ha, ha, ha, ha. Anyway, from now on I'll be coming a little more often."

The man from the Special Police finally showed signs of being about to leave. Yasuko wondered what would happen next. Although he was turning to go, his words lingered on and worried her. Watching the spy walk away in his dusty Western-style suit, Yasuko felt she could see the difficult road facing them from now on.

That night, for the first time in a while, Yamada ate dinner together with her. Busy with his tasks, he had long been eating all his meals away from home. Moreover, tonight he did not need to go out after dinner.

Yasuko slowly raised her eyes with their long lashes, and gazing at Yamada's face asked, "It's nothing to worry about, right?"

"Right. I wonder how they guessed it so soon. . . . If they're really sure of it, it'll make the work hard."

"It'll do more than just make the work hard. . . . If the police know about it, it's not going to just end there, is it?"

"Right. That's true too . . . but if that's so, we'll stick to it. One expects such things in doing this kind of work. Still, it'll be too bad to get hit again before we've had a chance to grow big . . ."

Yasuko suddenly felt vaguely forlorn.

". . . . . ?"

"Today I stopped by Yamamura's flat; he's a comrade who's in prison. When his wife talks about what the union's been doing lately, her eyes fill with tears and she asks if we don't feel ashamed toward our comrades who are in prison. She's a strong woman. She's working at the pea-sorting factory and supporting two children, yet she never complains. Far from it, she's angry, and says that the people who're presently running the union have betrayed her husband and his comrades. . . . Sure enough, reality is the greatest teacher."

"It certainly is."

"'If that's what the union is up to,' she says crying, 'all the work my husband and others have done will come to nothing.' . . . And it's true."

"She's right! What in the world did they work for, sacrificing three or four years in prison? It becomes meaningless, doesn't it?"

"If the comrades in prison heard what's up with the union, shedding tears wouldn't be enough. That's why the responsibility that's been handed to us is very serious. . . . No matter what happens, we'll keep going!"

Yamada's eyes shone as he spoke still holding his bowl and chopsticks but forgetting to eat. Yasuko felt she was once again hearing the passionate voice that had fascinated her when she was still working at the eatery. It had exerted an unforgettable charm on her.

"Anyway, Ōyama probably thought the whole country would be shaken up by his new-party proclamation, but that doesn't seem to be happening. Statements opposing the new party are pouring into the union daily one after another, from Tokyo of course and also from various provinces. The opposition has roots! Interestingly, even the All Japan Federation of Proletarian Arts—the artists' organization—is opposing it. And so is the *Proletarian Newspaper,* though that's only to be expected. Thanks to all this, I can keep working and feel completely confident once more."

"Certainly!"

At that moment a voice from below called out "Yatchan!"

8

"Ah, it's my sister."

Yasuko rose from the table. Whenever Okei came to visit, she always called out from below like this and waited for her to come downstairs.

She had stopped by two or three times since Yasuko and Yamada started living together. On coming downstairs, Yasuko would find her standing patiently at the side of the dark stairway and saying, "You know, I think I worked a little too much today." Then she would press twenty, thirty, or at times fifty sen into Yasuko's palm, and leave. Yamada from the outset did not have a single sen of income. At times he received a tiny amount from the union, but only enough for one meal a day. Once Yasuko began to work full time in the organizing section, their living expenses doubled. Livelihood became a severe problem. During a visit to Okei's place, Yasuko told her of walking around the city of Otaru till about twelve at night having eaten nothing since breakfast. What surprised Okei was the extremely happy tone, seemingly free from any anxiety, with which her sister spoke of such misery.

"Even in the humblest cottage . . ." Okei suddenly recalled the phrase the village policeman had used long ago when he came to talk about finding Brother a bride. Living together with a man whom one truly loved, moreover a good man, one could doubtless be happy despite such hardship, thought Okei. "Even in the humblest cottage . . ."

But Okei soon realized that her sister's situation was different. Viewed from another angle, what Yasuko and Yamada were doing amounted to voluntary poverty; they seemed to be bustling about engaged in work that failed to bring in a single sen—a grave matter to the poor. Yet the great force motivating them originated not in such a simple cliché as "even in the humblest cottage," but rather in their devotion to the liberation of the working class.

To tell the truth, Okei had felt forlorn at first, lonely at having been abandoned. However, Okei could never have watched silently while her own sister risked hunger by persisting in her work. Okei remembered how wonderfully light and cheerful she had felt when she first began to understand various aspects of the direction in which her sister was moving. Those feelings had since been erased, but—come to think of it—if they had continued to expand, they might have been able to move her in her sister's direction. That being so, Okei wanted at least to extend some help to her sister who was now doing such work. She also felt it only natural that she should do so.

At present she was too heavily fettered to find a way out from the conditions she was bound to. Nonetheless, she thought she had to do something within the given situation. That was why instead of quitting work at six she worked until seven or eight and took the extra money to Yasuko from time to time.

But even when visiting Yasuko, she never went up to the second floor. It made no difference whether or not Yamada was present. Impervious to Yasuko's urging, "Don't be ridiculous, Sister!" Okei would stand at the foot of the dark stairway making no move to come up.

At those times when Okei pressed what little money she had into her palm, Yasuko could feel directly the depth of her reticent sister's emotions.

To Yasuko's question, "Aren't you pushing yourself too hard?" she would answer, "Oh no, it's nothing much," and promptly leave.

9

As expected, Yasuko came downstairs to find Okei standing beside the dark stairs.

"Won't you come up?" she asked as always.

"No." Okei was holding a heap of laundry in her arms. "I guess you forgot this. It wouldn't be good for the night dew to get on it."

"That's right, that's right! I completely forgot. Thank you so much."

"You know . . ." Okei seemed to find it hard to say the words. "You must be quite busy. So, you don't have to do the laundry . . . I'll come to pick it up . . ."

"Oh, I can do that much, it's nothing!"

Yasuko sensed she had touched on her sister's unfathomable emotions once again.

"It's nothing for me, Yatchan," said Okei laughing, "but for you . . ."

Okei knew better than anyone that Yasuko was poor at cleaning and disliked cooking.

"If you did that, it would make you responsible for absolutely everything, wouldn't it?" said Yasuko with a laugh, took the laundry from her sister, and went upstairs with rapid steps.

Yamada was eating dinner when Yasuko walked in, her arms filled with laundry. Looking puzzled, he asked, "Your sister?"

"Yes."

"She still won't come up?" he said laughing.

"Right. And now she says she'll even do our laundry for us."

"At any rate, you're pretty lazy!"

Yasuko put on a slightly offended look. "Naturally. But she is really thinking about us. She's concerned that if I do it it'll interfere with our work."

"She is?" exclaimed Yamada with surprise. "You have a wonderful sister, Yatchan!"

"I certainly do!"

"Can you ask her to come up for a minute? There's a favor I'd like to ask of her."

"You think she'd come?"

"I see. All right, I'll come down with you."

Yamada followed Yasuko downstairs.

"Hello there!" Yamada called out, craning his neck over Yasuko's shoulder.

Okei turned around automatically but realizing it was Yamada, grew suddenly flustered and began searching for her *zōri* in the dark entryway.

"Sister, wait!"

"I'd like to ask you for a favor."

Half in jest and half in earnest, Yasuko held the back door shut. Okei had tucked her feet into someone's *zōri* and was trying to brush away her sister's hands. Someone watching on the side might have found her seriousness comical.

"It's all right, Sister, don't be so silly!"

At last Okei stood still, facing the doorway and looking small.

"What's the matter? Come on up!" urged Yamada, feeling a bit awkward, and led the way to the second floor. The younger sister finally dragged her elder sister upstairs.

Okei reached the top of the stairs, but would not step into the room. She stood outside the sliding door, and then crouched beside it. Okei simply could not bring herself to enter "the couple's room." She was still giving out the room that she and Mother rented, and she spoke with Yamada calmly when they were alone. During Yasuko's occasional visits, she spoke serenely with her too. But she found it strangely unbearable to see Yamada and her sister together.

"Come, Sister. I'll bring you in at least this once!" shouted Yasuko cheerfully, and dragged Okei into the room.

10

"Why won't you ever come up?" asked Yamada. "I can't figure it out."

Yasuko had at length forced her sister to sit down inside the room. Okei was blushing crimson all the way to her neck, and covering her face with both hands.

"Yatchan, you're terrible; Yatchan, you're terrible!" Okei's body was shaking.

In terms of the work they were engaged in, Yamada in a sense found Okei even more promising than Yasuko. But what worried him most about Okei was that the relentless burden of making a living could, on the contrary, make her servile. It happened sometimes that workers who were forced into extreme poverty fell into a so-called "servility of the poor" before they had a chance to grow resilient.

Yamada now detected the tiniest shoots of such servility had begun to grow within Okei's heart. To break free and stand up would be a hundred times more difficult for Okei than it had been for Yasuko, but unless she were helped to rise, unless she could be helped to rise—not Okei alone but millions of women like her—this movement would not truly take root.

"How are things at the factory?" Yamada rubbed off the ashes from the tip of a half-smoked Golden Bat and relit it. "Listen, there's something I'd like to ask you. Are people complaining about the wages, or about the work?"

Okei was still holding her face in her hands, and now she herself found this funny. Laughing, she asked in turn, "Why are you asking me that?"

"As you know, since Ōyama Ikuo got frightened by repression and tried to form a legal working-class party, practically the whole union has been wavering. I've been doing my best to steer the movement in the right direction with an opposition group within the union, but to tell you the truth, a movement that's limited to union leaders is quite ineffective and there's almost no possibility that it will grow. What must be done, of course, is to promote this opposition movement from within the 'masses' who make up the union's substance, and to isolate the defeatist and corrupt labor leaders from below."

Yasuko took over the story from Yamada.

"The committee chair has been saying lately that we must reelect various union agencies because they've been operating on a makeshift basis since the repression. But his real intention seems to be to try to kick out the opposition group!"

"That's right. It's becoming more and more necessary to resist this with real power from below. We'll turn the legalist faction into a rootless floating weed. They can play their tune, but we'll make sure the people don't dance to it. Our work can never be accomplished by one or two individuals. We must carry it out with the united power of the people. Besides . . ."

Yamada paused in thought, and then quietly continued.

"What we have been doing inside the union has already surfaced, and even the police have gotten wind of it. So, if they eliminate us, our work will be crushed. However, if the pressure and the objectives of people who work in factories and other places are moving our way, then solid roots will remain even if we are eliminated, and our opposition work will no longer stand out. That's the principle of our movement, you see. It's as Marx or Lenin said: 'The factory is the proletarian fortress.' In order for a union to become truly strong, it must be rooted in the workers who are actually laboring in the factories. . . . And so there's something I would especially like to ask of you who are working in a factory . . ."

With Yamada engrossed in his words, flakes of ash from his cigarette dropped onto the tatami.

11

Okei was feeling happy.

She could do this work without quitting the factory! It meant there was no need to throw irresponsibly away the life she was bearing on her shoulders. She had earlier thought it strange that this movement for the sake of the impoverished workers and peasants could hardly be carried out by the impoverished workers and peasants who were its very aim. But of course that was not so. Above all, she understood from what Yamada had said that the work done in factories was essential to constructing the union's true foundation. Okei at last felt the happiness of being able to cast off her shell.

Although her task would certainly differ from the open and specialized work that her sister was doing, Okei sensed that the feelings that had long been wavering within her heart had finally taken a clear and satisfactory shape.

Okei's task would seemingly consist of nothing more than finding friends, one by one, in the factory where she worked. But the prospect of being able to do even that much beyond slaving away for her living at that harsh factory cheered her up so greatly she herself was surprised at it.

Most of the husbands, siblings, and parents of the women who worked in the pea-sorting factory earned their living at the port, the warehouses, or the open sea. Since much of the real power of the city's labor union came from the workers engaged in waterfront transport, quite a few of Okei's women coworkers had direct links with the union through their close relatives. Therefore her work at the factory was of great importance.

"But I'm not like Yasuko. . . . Can I really do it?"

Yamada laughed. "This is work that everyone has to be able to do, so long as you're being exploited!"

Yamada was quite aware that the quiet work of factory organizing was not something that Yasuko would be good at.

Okei looked puzzled. "Besides, the women who work there are all like me, you know!"

"If that's so, then the prospects are very good!" said Yasuko, laughing as loudly as a man and showing her even white teeth. Okei and Yamada joined in her laughter.

It was early morning, so Okei could not stay long. Yasuko saw her off to the corner where the dark alley emerges into a bright street.

Once she was alone, Okei began to feel a different form of quiet excitement welling up from the depths of her being. She thought she had never before walked through the city so lightheartedly. The streets were bright and still flowing with people. Vendors were shouting loudly from night stalls that lined both sides of the street. But Okei felt as if she were walking through it all by herself. Till now she had seldom had friendly conversation with the people at the factory, and that was not good. From now on she must join them and start to talk. While talking, she would look for people to win over. Many people were angry with the supervisors for turning them down during inspections—if things continued like this, something was bound to happen. These people presented a good opportunity! . . . There were various other complaints too. . . . Turning as serious as a child, Okei kept on thinking about such matters as she walked.

It was wonderful—could so little make a person so happy and buoyant?

When future meetings were held in her room, Okei decided to listen from the side as best she could even if she could not understand everything. Although earlier she truly could not understand, once she began to think about it hard she came to feel that little by little she was starting to grasp what those people were talking about.

At Yasuko's suggestion, Okei also decided to go to strikes and union speech meetings. Few women came to them. Sometimes Yasuko spoke at the meetings. But as soon as Okei saw her younger sister standing on the platform, the tears came and covered her face, and she could hardly understand what she was hearing.

12

When Yamada came to one of those secret meetings, he kept reiterating that speaking from platforms was growing relatively less important, while extensive and tireless organizing within factories was becoming essential. But as Okei watched her sister mingle with so many men, and heard her speak before hundreds with her hand raised, she felt an excitement that made her tremble to the core. Even if what Yamada said about speaking from the platform was true, it was not something that anyone could do.

"Hey, that's Yamada's missus!" A nearby waterfront laborer stopping by on his way from work clutched his empty lunch box as he gossiped. "That's the woman who used to work at the sunken-road eatery. She's somethin' else."

When Yasuko occasionally stammered in search for words, Okei felt as much pain as if she herself were struggling to speak at that platform, which looked out over so many people.

As she spoke from the platform, Yasuko revealed in a white-hot form the strongest aspects of her temperament, as well as a liking for flamboyance that distinguished her from Okei. Her talk concentrated only those elements of her character. Evidently when a person ascended the platform, her sundry traits all merged into a single daring spirit.

While listening to Yasuko's speech, Okei was unwittingly clutching the crosspieces of adjacent chairs. When the speech was over, all her strength ebbed away from her shoulders. And then, startled, she would look at the people all around her as if she had dozed off.

After the meeting, Okei, jostled by the crowd, could hear everyone talking about Yasuko.

Once, at a speech meeting in a small factory during a strike against a cut in wages, the union had decided as one of its tactics to have the workers' wives speak. They were supposed to get up with their babies on their backs and talk about how much hardship they would suffer if their husbands were fired or got their wages cut.

When the wives climbed up to the platform, they could say nothing at all. The babies on their backs had suddenly started bawling. Nonetheless, the very sight of the women appearing on the platform one by one threw the audience into an uproar. The last one to come out was Yasuko. She tried to express the heavy emotions that the wives who preceded her had wanted to express but couldn't. However, less than two minutes after she began to speak the police superintendent rattled his sword.

"Stop!!"

The very next instant all the policemen in white uniforms who had been positioned in every row waded into the crowd.

"Tyrants!"

"Give it to them!!" The gold-striped superintendent stood up and waved his arms.

"Disperse! Disperse!"

The words reached Okei from the front of the crowd. She saw policemen rush up to the platform, their shoes stomping across the polished floor. Okei gasped. Her sister, standing bolt upright at the platform, was suddenly grabbed by her arms and dragged off to the edge of the stage. There, Yasuko said something and managed to free one of her arms. At that instant a policeman's hand tore off Yasuko's left sleeve from her shoulder.

"What are you doing? I said I was coming!" screamed Yasuko. Only her white cotton undershirt remained hanging and fluttering from her arm.

The audience, shoved by policemen in their chin-strapped hats, surged toward the exit. Those who were shouting loudly were swiftly dragged out and arrested.

Okei suddenly felt a powerful thrust against her shoulders.

"Keep moving!"

She saw her sister dragged away through a side exit next to a deserted backstage room. Okei was petrified with worry. Pushed by the crowd, her face contorted, she was half crying.

"My sister! My sister!"

What had happened to Yamada?

13

Her sister was being dragged away, but Okei could not stop. The audience poured toward the exit, yet unable to leave all at once, expanded and contracted as the policemen shoved it from behind. Okei had no idea what to do. Pushed from all sides, not only could she not move but feared she might get crushed. In a daze, she craned her neck in search of a familiar face.

A man wearing a jacket that smelled of paint glanced over his shoulder. "Hey Miss, please don't fidget so much!"

But she was indifferent to his plea. There were only unfamiliar faces wherever she looked. She wanted to get out as quickly as possible. If she could only get there before Yasuko was dragged away, they might let her go. She would fall on her knees and say, "I'm her older sister," and refuse to budge no matter how much they trampled or kicked her. Yasuko hadn't done anything bad. How dare they get violent and tear off a person's sleeve just for standing up and speaking!

She pushed people aside in her hurry to get out, got stepped on, and finally came out to find the front of her kimono wide open. But there was no time to fix it. Once the audience emerged from the building, it stood around in groups and showed no intention of leaving.

"Hey, no stopping!"

Each time they were shoved by the police, the people stepped back a little but soon halted again. Okei looked restlessly around, searching for someone. Sure enough, there was no one. What had happened to everybody? She tried to go round to the rear exit.

"Miss, Miss!"

A sword rattled. The side of the building was hidden in darkness, and Okei had run toward it thinking that no one was there. She stopped, paralyzed with terror.

"Where do you think you're going! You can't go in there. Get back, get back!"

A large hand grabbed her by the shoulder and pushed her toward the bright front of the building. The sound of a car engine made Okei turn around, and she saw a truck packed full of policemen in chin-strapped hats moving toward the back exit. The truck's tailgate fell open with a bang, and the policemen jumped down one after another.

"They're violent bastards, so don't hold back but let 'em have it!"

People were dragged out by their arms, all of them shouting. Okei could not see well because of the darkness, but quite a number seemed to have been arrested. She thought she saw her sister among them.

"Quit dragging your feet. Step lively!"

With a thud, she was thrust into the crowd that was coming out of the building.

"Sister, oh, oh!" Someone called out from the crowd. Despite her frenzied state of mind, Okei heard the voice.

"What?"

The policeman suddenly let go of Okei and pushing his way through a cluster of men stretched his big hand over their heads. "Was that you who spoke just now!?"

But the men he was trying to push past pressed their bodies together and prevented the policeman from wading into the crowd. They seemed to be waterfront workers and had big burly shoulders.

"Hey! Hey!" said the policeman impatiently, leaning forward against them. Before long the men pulled back into the crowd and disappeared from sight.

Okei was utterly at a loss what to do. Now truly ready to cry, she was pushed by the crowd toward the bustling street. Policemen stood lined up some six feet apart and violently shoved anyone who so much as paused or slowed down.

The "arrest truck" was ceaselessly blaring its horn from behind. As Okei halted, trying to see it, someone said "Oh!" and grabbed her shoulder.

14

Okei started and turned around. She freed her shoulder.

"Ah, Mr. Sasaki!"

Like a lost child worn out with searching who catches sight of her mother's face, Okei suddenly felt like bursting into tears. Sasaki was a union man who came with Yamada to the meetings held in her room.

"I've been searching too," the man said.

Okei had never felt such relief. Wonderful, she thought, wonderful! Her throat felt so constricted that for a moment she could not say a word.

"My sister!!" she managed to say at last.

"Right! Let's go get her from the police!"

"Get her?"

"We'll all go to the police and demand to have them back."

"Hey!"

The man was suddenly shoved from behind by a policeman. The push propelled him into Okei's arms. Her face struck against Sasaki's thick chest.

"No stopping!"

The male scent emanating from Sasaki's chest threw Okei into momentary confusion. Sasaki himself hastily pushed back against the crowd. It lasted only an instant. They hurriedly began to walk, dodging others.

But they were in danger of becoming separated, for Okei couldn't keep up. Sasaki sometimes turned around and waited for her.

"This won't do," he said, and held out his hand to Okei. She took hold of it. "That's better."

Even so, people occasionally came between them and seemed about to separate them. Each time this happened, one of the two tightened the grip on the other's hand. Unlike Yamada, Sasaki had originally worked at a canning factory and had big hands. Although

Okei too had thick fingers from her farm work, her hand looked tiny within Sasaki's grip.

The arrest truck was moving at less than a walking pace. It blared its horn without a pause but could not advance because of the crowd. When Okei and Sasaki had walked about one block, the truck finally spurted ahead. The arrested people had been packed in like baggage and were guarded by the police. There was no one who looked like Yasuko! However, as the truck went by they caught a glimpse of a woman's kimono, but it swiftly vanished from sight.

"Oh! That's her!" they both shouted at once.

As they reached the intersection, the crowd grew sparse. They turned a corner. At that moment they suddenly noticed they were still holding hands, and grew embarrassed. They let go of each other's hand at the same time. Their palms were moist with sweat. Sasaki blushed like a child and rubbed his palm against his corduroy trousers.

"Looks like we've taken quite a beating," he said awkwardly, feeling he had to say something.

"Will they let them go soon? . . ." asked Okei without looking at him.

"Sure they will. Why, they haven't done a thing."

". . . . . ?"

Okei tightened her obi as she walked, and kept pushing her hair up with her fingers.

A few moments later they were overtaken by a youth in a raincoat, evidently a student, his arms gripped by policemen. The student's face, deadly pale with excitement, lit up with a shaky smile when he saw them. Okei felt she had seen something similar somewhere. Of course, in the corridor of the Sapporo courthouse! Come to think of it, each of them seemed to have invisible links connecting them with the others.

15

As they approached the police station, Okei suddenly began to feel uneasy. It was a breathless, wavering sensation.

"Ah . . ."

"Yes?"

Sasaki turned around. But Okei, not knowing how to put it, merely blushed.

"Ha, ha, lost your spirit?" The man laughed. In a tone that was neither joking nor serious, he said, "You need a good drink of water."

"No I don't!"

The man laughed even louder.

When they reached the police station, Sasaki walked in with a practiced air. Since it was bright inside, Okei fixed the front of her kimono and her obi. Sasaki held the door ajar and waited for her.

The Special Higher Police office was on the second floor. The policeman seated behind the front desk stifled a slight yawn while staring rudely at Okei. Loud voices were heard from the second floor.

Okei wondered: Was her sister up there?

As she climbed the stairs following the broad-shouldered Sasaki, Okei's heart suddenly began to beat fast.

The Special Higher Police office was filled with seven or eight union men and two women with babies on their backs who had earlier been up on the platform. They too had come to get their people back. Seeing the new arrivals, all were delighted. However, the unionists who were present all belonged to the group opposed to the new party; there was no one from the committee chair's legalist faction.

Yamada was not there. Had he too been arrested? Yasuko had been dragged down from the platform, so her arrest was presumably known to everyone. If Yamada had not come here, it doubtless meant that he too had been arrested.

Catching sight of Sasaki with Okei, two or three Special Police officers wearing dress shirts clicked their tongues.

"You here again? We're telling you, it's out of the question!"

"Go home, all right? We'll let them go tomorrow."

"Ha, same trick every time, isn't it?" said one of Yamada and Sasaki's comrades clutching a hat in his hand.

"It's no trick. Orders from the Special Higher Police section of the Hokkaido Government Office. It's out of our hands."

"It's always 'government office, government office.' You're trying to shirk responsibility!"

Suddenly a tall police officer with narrow eyes shouted angrily, "If you think it's a lie, then telephone the Government Office yourself! . . . You can stay here till morning comes, but out of the question means out of the question!"

"What's it got to do with the Government Office anyway?" Sasaki put in. "Arrested for speaking from the podium, arrested for talking loudly, arrested for brushing somebody's arm away—what's that got to do with the Special Higher Police of the Government Office? Don't the Special Police here have any authority at all?"

"Hey! You're Sasaki, aren't you?"

"That's right."

Okei, feeling terrified, tugged at the back of Sasaki's jacket. He, without realizing it in his excitement, reached around, touched Okei's hand, and removed it.

"Huh, you'd better not come around here too often!"

A thin scornful smile twisting a corner of his lips, the Special Police officer walked up to Sasaki. Okei unwittingly pulled at Sasaki's hand.

"Thanks for your concern, but that's up to me!"

Evidently unaware that he was holding Okei's hand, Sasaki squeezed it so hard she wanted to scream.

"Oh well, have it your way then . . ." The policeman broke into a broad scornful grin.

16

"If you're all just going on strike and holding speech meetings for workers' benefits, then it's nothing serious. But if you're trying to use that—"

"Enough!" Sasaki waved his hand with annoyance.

"I'm telling you, Sasaki, you'd better not come to this place so casually. I think you yourself get the idea . . ."

Sasaki gave a start. Maybe, he thought. He gathered from the policeman's words that Special Higher Police agents from the Government Office were on their way here. It occurred to him that despite being routine, the arrests of Yamada, Yasuko, and the others were not being taken lightly.

"Never mind about that," he said. "Who exactly has been arrested?"

"Dunno about that. We haven't checked yet. Anyway, there's lots more still coming."

People started to grumble with impatience.

"Just tell us about the ones you've thrown into detention so far," said another unionist.

"Don't know that either."

"We've come all this way, so can't you look into it a bit for us?"

"Nobody asked you to come!" retorted the policeman, rolling up his sleeves and grinning.

"We're not joking."

"I'm not joking either."

"Damn it!" The young unionist slapped his hat against the desk.

There was one policeman, seated behind the others, who often came to the union headquarters. Sasaki took a different approach and addressed him.

"Listen, Mr. Inoue. You're holding a woman, right? Her name is Taguchi."

The policeman named Inoue looked flustered, and glanced at his colleagues.

"What about it?"

"What about it? Arresting her for just being up on stage when the speeches ended—that's terrible. This is her elder sister who's come for her. We want you to let her go."

The policeman shifted his chair and sized up Okei who was standing in Sasaki's shadow.

"She's quite a looker, isn't she."

"It doesn't matter if she's a looker or not, just let her go. Her mother's terribly worried. First of all, she's a woman—"

Suddenly the policeman who had spoken earlier smiled coldly.

"That's Yamada's precious little missus, isn't it? She may be a woman, but she's one tough customer!"

"What's that got to do with her getting arrested?"

"Listen, you!" The policeman's tone of voice changed somewhat. "Let me put it in a way that'll convince you. Even supposing Taguchi and the others have been arrested for no special reason, if their arrest helps our investigation to uncover a *legitimate reason*, what then?"

Sasaki suddenly felt his face change color.

"Only there is no legitimate reason, is there?"

"Huh! Oh well, never mind." The policeman's tone of voice had changed again, as if he were abandoning a wasted effort. That in itself got to Sasaki.

From time to time a sound of heavy and chaotic footsteps rang out from the downstairs corridor. Evidently, those who had been arrested were being brought in one after another.

"Let us speak to the police chief," demanded the union man clutching his hat.

"We regret to say, but the Chief has already gone for the day!"

"Sure he has!"

One of the policemen began to laugh loudly.

"Like you say, the police are the agents of capitalists and landlords after all . . ."

17

The union folk kept on negotiating for more than two hours, but the police placed the responsibility for everything on the Government Office and refused to release anyone. Since nothing could be done, everyone decided to leave and come back the following day.

As they came outside, Okei suddenly felt exhausted. It was an unpleasant weariness that emanated from her head and made her dizzy. Although it had been only two or three hours, everything that happened during that time was new to Okei and overwhelming.

Moreover, her knees were not at all steady. Though they were her very own knees, they would suddenly get wobbly and drained of strength. She pressed one hand against her forehead and gripped the edge of Sasaki's jacket with the other.

As they were taking leave of other people, one of them, a woman rocking a baby on her back, tried to cheer up Okei.

"And to think that we've caused you so much trouble . . . ," she said apologetically.

Okei and Sasaki walked on alone. Any number of times along the way, Sasaki said to her, "Steady now!"

But Okei was so strangely exhausted that even such heartening words now struck her as painful.

"I wonder if Sister will come home tomorrow . . . ," she said weakly, her words trailing off as if she were talking to herself.

"Sure she will!"

". . . . .!"

Somehow, Okei could not help feeling that she would not be back.

"Besides, this will be good for your sister, you know. It's her first time in detention, right? It's this kind of ordeal that turns you into a full-fledged fighter!"

Maybe so. Okei felt she understood that. But when she thought of it actually happening to her sister right now, she was seized by an unspeakable terror.

The dark sunken road led to the working-class district. At this hour all the doors were locked for the night and everyone was asleep. The only sound reaching Sasaki and Okei's ears was that of their own footsteps. For a while the two walked in silence. Their excitement was gradually subsiding. Having been dragged into an incident so overwhelming that she didn't know what to do, Okei found the sight of Sasaki's thick shoulders in front of her immensely dependable.

"Can you go to the police tomorrow?"

"Well, only at night."

"After the factory, right?"

"Right."

"I'll come too. Please bring some paper tissues and a towel. If they don't let her out tomorrow, she'll need them . . . And I wouldn't tell your mother about your sister."

"No, I couldn't possibly! Just letting her know that Sister had moved in with Mr. Yamada made her take to her bed and stop eating for three or four days . . ."

"Yeah, I suppose so."

They were approaching Okei's second-floor room, but many dark alleys still stretched ahead.

"I'll go with you as far as your house."

Sasaki turned up the worn collar of his jacket and hunched his shoulders. It was late autumn, and nights were especially chilly. On reaching the plank-covered gutter, Sasaki said, "This is dangerous," stopped, and extended his hand.

"It's all right, I'm used to it."

Okei turned crimson within the darkness, but after saying the words was startled by the cheerfulness of her own voice.

"I wonder . . ."

Sasaki took Okei's hand and started saying gallantly, "There's a hole here," and "There's a puddle here." But there was something so funny, and so unlike Sasaki about this, that a strange mixture of embarrassment and happiness welled up within Okei.

18

At the police station the next day, they found that several of the arrested had been released but that several more still remained in detention. Yasuko was among those still detained. Okei left tissues and a towel for her at the station, and went to Yasuko's lodging house. She thought that Yamada might possibly be there.

Opening the back door, she saw the eyes of the owner's precocious son peering at her from the interior.

"Ah, it's Yatchan's big sister!" he said and came out. "I thought it was the spy again."

"Surely not!" said Okei and laughed.

"Oh yeah, four or five spies came yesterday. They tore up the whole room upstairs looking for stuff, and left."

Okei glanced up at the second floor and frowned uneasily.

The boy lowered his voice a little: "You know, Mr. Yamada and Yatchan didn't come back yesterday. I'm sure they both got busted."

He tilted his head knowingly.

She went upstairs and found the room in shambles. They had come to search the premises, ransacked everything, and left. Books taken from the bookshelves lay scattered over the tatami mats. The closet was crammed with crumpled bedding, and a wicker trunk lay half open with its contents jutting out. Standing amid the clutter, Okei thought it looked just like the aftermath of a devastating storm. This was no trivial matter. She felt more and more certain that Yasuko would not be coming back soon.

She returned home to find Sasaki waiting for her. Since Mother was in the room they could not talk there, so she made some excuse and stepped outside.

"How did it go?"

"I'm worried. Just as I thought, they haven't let her out yet. Also, I stopped by Yatchan's place on the way back, and the room is a complete wreck!"

"Hmm. They came to search it?"

"That's right!"

"I see. A routine arrest, and then a search. That's gotta mean . . ." Sasaki paused before musingly adding, "I too may be in danger."

"Really?" Okei looked up through the darkness at the man's face with its big jaw. "I don't have any idea what's going on, you see? I keep feeling afraid because I don't understand at all . . ."

"I started getting worried when we went to the police and the Special Police guy dropped those heavy hints. . . . If that's so, I've gotta be prepared. When you see the police letting go ordinary members of the audience and the so-called union moderates, while keeping in jail the ones they suspect of opposing the new party, it tells you they're desperate to learn how the opposition operates . . ."

They were about to emerge into the brightness of the main street, so they retraced their steps.

"Anyway, they're saying that the opposition group is the Communist Party!"

Unlike the previous day, Sasaki seemed strangely awkward and solemn. Okei realized that a part of her was disappointed by this, and blushed at the thought.

"We must immediately work out a plan of response, so let us use your room tomorrow evening," said Sasaki as they reached Okei's house. Looking preoccupied, he left hurriedly.

Okei paused, feeling let down, and followed the man with her eyes as he walked off, gutter planks rattling under his tread. She let out a sigh, then slowly climbed the dark staircase.

19

Mother was already asleep.

Feeling tired, Okei thought she might take a bath. She stepped around the foot of Mother's bed to take money for the bath from the desk. What was this?

"To Keichan"

What first caught her eye were the big, uneven, forcefully written characters. Okei felt a sudden tightening in her chest.

"I can't say it so I'll write it. I've always loved you. What about you?

"I'll be embarrassed if you tell me, so please write me a short answer.

"This isn't like me but I screwed up my courage and wrote it."

Although Okei did not know what the mark at the end of the letter represented, she instantly realized that it was written by Sasaki. Now she understood for the first time why he had been so strangely solemn and awkward when they parted. Holding the piece of paper in her hand, Okei glanced around nervously. She felt as if she had been caught in an embarrassing moment. Still holding the paper, she walked—she herself didn't know why—over to a small mirror-stand in the corner of the room (if the humble object could be called a mirror-stand), sat down with her back to it, and reread the letter. Slowly, character by character.

But feeling restless again, she walked to the desk and sat down in front of it. Until she went to sleep that night, Okei remained sitting motionless in front of the desk.

When Okei returned from the factory the next evening and quietly opened the front door, the first place she looked was the earthen floor of the entranceway. She saw rickety geta and shoes! Everyone was here. Okei stopped and held her breath. Then she looked up toward the dark second-floor landing. What was the matter with her? She could clearly hear her heart pounding in the darkness.

This had never before happened to her. Although Yamada had once brought a sort of hope into her lightless existence, that feeling had been entirely different. Okei had not slept well the night before, and at the factory too she had been absentminded all day. Every so often she realized she was thinking about Sasaki.

While wondering what to do, Okei took off her geta and lined them up next to Sasaki's ungainly shoes.

"I think . . . I must love him too?"

Okei climbed the stairs soundlessly, as though walking into something supremely frightening. Sasaki would surely look at her as soon as she opened the sliding door! That's why Okei made up her mind to enter without raising her eyes.

She lifted her hand to the door any number of times, then drew it back feeling short of breath.

"I'm home . . ." As she resolutely entered at last, the light inside the room struck her as brighter than ever before. From the corners of her lowered eyelids, she fleetingly sensed Sasaki looking at her.

Okei sat stiffly at her desk with her back to everyone throughout the meeting. But as Sasaki spoke ardently, Okei could feel his every gesture, down to the last detail, even more clearly than if she had actually been facing him. As if aware of her presence, Sasaki shifted his tone of voice more often than usual, and brought out words that he had seldom used before.

The meeting ended. The people in attendance went away one by one, and only Sasaki remained.

20

As she listened to people leave one after another, Okei felt something that resembled both dread and anticipation. And when at length Sasaki was the last one to remain, Okei's back that was still turned toward him felt as hard and stiff as a board. She had long since stopped turning the pages of the book that lay open on the desktop before her. As she stared at the print, the lines multiplied and slid away or converged and lay on top of one another.

Okei had turned crimson even to the back of her ears.

He was putting his hands into his pockets or somewhere. His legs scraped against the tatami; evidently he had shifted to a new sitting position. Then he scratched his head—that she could hear distinctly.

The mats creaked as he stood up! His knees cracked. He was patting his trousers.

"Ah . . . ," he said and cleared his throat. "Did you write me an answer?"

At last Sasaki stepped up to Okei. She sat even more stiffly and remained silent.

"Did you?" he pressed, squatting beside her and peeking at the book she was reading. His manner was shy and hesitant. Okei's entire face flushed, and her heart began to thump. She barely managed to shake her head.

"You didn't write it?"

The man remained silent for a while.

Seized by the feeling that she had behaved abominably, Okei grew flustered and said, "I couldn't write it . . ."

"Couldn't write it? . . . Why? . . ."

". . . . ."

"If you don't feel it, Keichan, don't go against your feelings. You can answer any way you like."

"I know . . . but I've never written something like this!"

As he gazed at her, Okei's face struck him as even more beautiful than Yasuko's. It was the kind of face whose beauty could only be grasped by a steady gaze. Quite unlike Yasuko, the beauty of Okei's eyes, lips, and earlobes was hidden beneath a layer of dusky skin. Sasaki was startled by his own belated discovery.

"So you just didn't write it, that's all!" His voice suddenly cheerful, he put his hand on Okei's shoulder and drew her close. Okei drew her shoulder back and slid to the side.

"Oh!" With a chuckle, Sasaki again drew her close. Okei slid away from him as before. At last she approached the edge of the desk. While repeating his own action, Sasaki admired the beauty of the crimson earlobes directly before his eyes.

When they reached the edge of the desk with no further place to go, they both burst out laughing. At that instant, Sasaki lightly embraced her and rose.

"Don't!" Okei squirmed in his embrace. Embarrassed, she buried her face in the man's chest as if clinging to it.

"Ha, ha, ha, ha, ha, ha, ha." Laughing, yet breathless with excitement, Sasaki walked up and down the room two or three times. Then, twice, he lifted her higher and buried his face against the nape of her neck. The man's stubbly cheek hurt her. Okei twisted away each time.

"Mother will be back soon," Okei whispered.

21

At the rear entrance of the police station, Yasuko and the others were taken down from the truck one after another.

"Hey, is this your sleeve?" a policeman waved it from atop the truck.

"That's right."

"It's terrible they did that!" exclaimed the other detainees, wiping mud off their clothes. It was Yasuko's first experience of being brought to a police station, yet contrary to her worries the presence of so many comrades put her in high spirits.

They were taken into the police station one by one.

"Open up, please," said her guard through a small opening in a glass door. A bunch of keys rattled within, and the heavy door opened with a creak.

"Get in."

Yasuko was pushed inside. She glanced around. There were four cells in a row with thick doors and heavy locks. There was a gap at the bottom of each door with an eight-inch-square hole next to it. That must be where the food was pushed through. In front of each cell there were four or five pairs of frayed *zōri*.

The people inside the cells were invisible. A stifling stench pervaded the entire area.

As Yasuko walked in, voices rose from one of the cells.

"Hey, shut up over there! Want to get smacked again?" shouted a policeman seated at the desk. "As soon as a woman walks in, they start up! Horny bastards!"

"Sir, please let me out. My stomach's hurting and I gotta go," called out someone from a corner cell labeled "Cell No 1."

"You can't! Outside the scheduled time, you can't! If you gotta go, go in there."

The voice from the cell called out two or three more times, but the policeman made no reply.

"Come here, Miss." Drawing the register toward him, the policeman motioned Yasuko to stand before the desk. "Take off your obi."

Yasuko stood silent and motionless.

Looking up, the policeman asked, "Is this your first time?"

"Yeah."

"I see. You're here because you're mixing with a rotten bunch. Take off your obi, take out all your personal possessions, and put them here."

Yasuko had not known about this. Being told to take off her obi struck her as utterly insulting.

"I don't have anything."

"Idiot, even if you don't, take off your obi and put it here. Can't take an obi into the cell."

Blushing somewhat, Yasuko reluctantly untied her obi, took out her purse and tissues, and shook her only sleeve to show it is empty.

"Take off the underwear obi too."

"Underwear?" exclaimed Yasuko angrily.

"Huh, don't act so shy. I bet you bitches let those men activists take turns banging you. That's communism, I guess."

"What're you talking about?"

"You insolent slut."

The policeman roughly jerked Yasuko's body forward, and yanked at the obi of her under-robe. Yasuko gasped and instinctively clasped her hands over her exposed breasts. At that instant she suddenly felt a violent ringing in one of her ears.

22

The moment Yasuko was hit, prisoners who had been arrested at the meeting and packed into each cell began banging on the walls all together. Yamada too was among them.

"Tyranny! Tyranny!!"

Since all were shouting at once, there was nothing the policeman could do. An off-duty policeman, wondering what was going on, ran up noisily and peered through a small door.

"Those bastards from the meeting?"

"Yeah, and they don't know that something a lot bigger's gonna hit 'em!"

Without even asking about Yasuko's address, permanent or current, the policeman put her into what was labeled a "Protective Cell." As she walked in holding the front of her kimono closed, three women looked up at her at once. One was in her forties and neatly dressed, another was about eighteen with disheveled hair and a swollen face, and yet another—although Yasuko did not see her at first—was in her sixties and lay face down and with her back arched in a corner, resembling a cloth-wrapped parcel. Yasuko lowered her gaze slightly, and sat down close by the door.

"There'll be no stupid chitchat!" said the jailer as he slammed the door shut and locked it with deliberate noise. Yasuko's cheek was bright red and kept burning.

"Who was it, huh? Who's the big man who was talking just now? Want me to drag you out one by one and smack you?" Toying with his bunch of keys, the jailer peered into one cell after another.

"Sir, please let me go to the toilet! I really have to go!"

"Ah, go where you are! Outside the scheduled time, absolutely nobody gets out!"

Yasuko sat motionlessly, gazing at the cheap pattern that covered the knees of the woman who crouched with downcast eyes across from her. The pattern suddenly grew blurred, and great bitter tears welled up in Yasuko's eyes. One after another, the tears slid down her cheeks, turned slightly as they passed her nose, and entered the corners of her mouth bearing a salty taste. The strong-spirited Yasuko had not cried like this for as long as she could remember. Being hit by that wormlike cop was mortifying.

"Were you hit just now?" asked the neatly dressed woman in her forties. Her quiet and elegant voice sounded surprising in a detention cell.

"Yes, by that son of a bitch!" said Yasuko.

The woman had seemed about to say more, but startled by Yasuko's vehemence, she refrained and gazed at Yasuko sympathetically.

As bedtime approached, the prisoners were allowed to go to the toilet one by one, starting with cell number one. Yasuko stood on tiptoe and tried to see who was held in which cell, though it was hard to make it out from that angle. Unshaved men with sharp eyes, and men wearing headbands passed by one after another. There were two comrades in cell number one. If there were two of you in one cell, thought Yasuko, you wouldn't be a bit lonesome. She was envious.

Cell number two was next. She caught sight of Yamada. His face looked harder than usual. He was constantly looking in her direction. Yasuko spontaneously raised her hand to the mesh-covered opening. But he could not see well.

Women were the last. As she passed the other cells, Yasuko cleared her throat in a distinctive way. Those inside the cells responded in the same way.

"Stay strong!"

It was cell number two! The voice was quiet, but it was Yamada's. It struck Yasuko with electrifying force.

"Hey! What are you doing! Move it!"

Yasuko shrugged with contempt, nonchalantly entered the toilet, and squatted unhurriedly.

23

Not surprisingly, she could not sleep that night. The blanket she was given was damp, stained, and smelly. After a while the lower half of her body began to feel restless. In less than an hour, Yasuko sat up on the blanket, her body bitten by fleas. But the bites hurt more than flea bites.

"What's the matter? You've been bitten, haven't you?" The woman with the air of an elegant wife raised her head slightly from her pillow. Evidently she too had been unable to fall asleep.

"Yes, it's really awful!"

"They're bedbugs, you know!"

"Bedbugs!? Ah, that's a first for me! No wonder!"

"Otaru is a port town, you see, and it also has a lot of Koreans. This place is crawling with bedbugs!"

Yasuko stood up and began to slap at the front of her kimono.

"That won't do any good, you know."

The jailer peered into the cell from the outside. "What are you doing? Get to sleep, get to sleep!"

Catching sight of the eighteen-year-old woman's sleeping posture, he added, "Look at the way that woman's sleeping! Guess a whore can't help it. Number Six, cover her with a blanket."

Silently, the elegant wife drew the woman's bared legs together and covered them with a blanket.

Huh! thought Yasuko. He knows damn well that this was just the kind of woman who appeals to him. No doubt the woman was a daughter of a peasant family, like Yasuko and others. She must've been working to feed her hungry family and ended up here.

As she lay staring at the high ceiling, various thoughts came to Yasuko. Much had happened to her, but this night spent in jail would surely leave a long-lasting impression throughout her life. Electric lights stayed switched on inside the cells in order to make them easy to monitor. But the lights were dimmer than moonlight. The moon shone through the metal bars of the window, projecting diamond shapes obliquely onto the left-hand wall. Those distorted projections of the metal bars struck her as a symbol of what would be awaiting her at every turn from now on.

Had Yamada been able to fall asleep? Having already experienced a night in jail countless times, maybe he'd fallen asleep and was even dreaming of something. Or maybe he was too worried about her, who was here for the first time, to be able to sleep.

How worried her sister must be. She had certainly been present at the meeting, so she must know of Yasuko's arrest up on the platform. A vivid image of her sister wandering about arose in Yasuko's mind.

As she thought of such things, Yasuko drifted off unawares into a shallow sleep. But each time a drunk or a burglar was dragged in, she was awakened by the creaking of the heavy door, the jailer's violent shouts, and the screams of a beaten detainee. Since her sleep was shallow, she had many dreams. The dreams were such that she could remember none of them, even if she awoke and immediately tried to think back on them. A strange fatigue brought on by extreme stress made her head throb with pain.

She had no idea what time it was when she was awakened by a woman's convulsive sobbing. Yasuko raised her head. A woman had been brought in and was standing before the jailer.

"You didn't do anything? Nonsense! Do we drag in somebody who didn't do anything? You were doing it in the park, back of the library, weren't you? What? You didn't do anything? Ah, never mind. You got till tomorrow morning to give some serious thought to what you did. What're you looking surprised for? You're somethin' else. You must've been so caught up in it that you didn't even know what you were doing."

The jailer's tone had turned lewd.

Before long the woman was put into the cell. She looked like an office worker at some bank or corporation. She sat motionless until morning, crying.

THE NEXT DAY, shortly after breakfast, Yasuko was taken away for interrogation.

24

Breakfast came in a wooden box with peeling lacquer. The contents under the lid were pitch-black. Most of it was barley. A small section of the box held a few scraps of thinly cut pickled eggplant. That and a cup of hot water was all.

Yasuko raised the lid, but did not feel the slightest desire to eat. The elegant woman did not even open it but simply pushed it to the side. The woman who came in late during the night did not so much as glance at it. This woman was released before Yasuko was taken to be interrogated.

The custodian quietly said, "Let me have any leftovers. There's lots of folks here who can never get enough." Before leaving with the women's food-boxes, he whispered, "Message from Yamada for a woman called Taguchi. Tell them you know nothing, and stay strong."

Yasuko thought of those words countless times as she was taken out of the cell and led to the second floor by a Special Higher Police officer in a dress shirt. The place she was brought to had tatami on the floor, and seemed to be the room for whomever was on duty. There was a small desk, and a man with a clipped moustache was sitting behind it. He too was wearing a dress shirt. As she entered, he flashed her a broad grin. The man did not have the cruel expression peculiarly common to those in this line of work. In fact he was startlingly handsome, with regular and pleasing features.

"So, how's detention?" He raised his eyebrows slightly while lighting a cigarette. "It's your first time, so it must be tough."

"No."

"No? Aren't you impressive. By the way, you wouldn't like to be released soon, would you?"

"Of course I would."

"Looks like the splendid woman warrior would like to be released soon!" The handsome policeman laughed, showing his even white teeth. "But since Yamada is still in detention, you won't be too lonely even if you stay here. I wonder if you people use words like 'loving wife' and 'loving husband.'"

". . . . ."

Yasuko was inwardly angry. What was this man after?

"Yes, I'd like to be released soon. It's unfair to be detained just for making a speech."

She said the words quickly and with rising fury.

"I hear that you two never come to the union office these days. What's the matter? Do you have an office of your own someplace?" Then he ambiguously added, "A love office perhaps?"

"So that's it!" thought Yasuko. The police were eager to find out the location of their "agitating point," their secret base of operations! Since Yamada and his comrades opposed the formation of the new party, while the union leaned toward supporting it, obviously they had set up a secret office and were carrying out "underground" activities. The police seemed determined to take advantage of the arrests to find it, and so get hold of definite proof that they were working under the direction of the Communist Party.

"We live in a boardinghouse," said Yasuko at random. "We don't need any other place."

The policeman sniggered.

"And I've only been in the union for a short time, and being a woman I hardly understand any of the details."

"Sure you don't."

The Special Higher Police officer glanced at Yasuko out of the corner of his eye, while picking at his ear with a matchstick.

25

"Listen. If you were an ordinary wife, you might not know what your husband was doing. But we already have all kinds of evidence. First of all, you've been going around visiting union members who are wavering, and telling them that the new party's no good. That's enough to let us know that you're working with your husband."

Yasuko suddenly felt her heart constrict, but tried not to show it.

"I don't know what you mean. I've been going around trying to make the union bigger, that's all. I don't know anything about such complicated things." She glanced at the policeman and added, "What is this new party?"

"This woman is surprisingly impudent!" Laughing, the handsome policeman looked up at a colleague who was standing nearby. "We go easy on her thinking she's a woman, so she says whatever comes into her head. Shall we . . . do it a bit?"

His colleague picked up one of the bamboo swords leaning against the wooden wall, and swung it about for a few seconds.

Grinning, the handsome policeman toyed with a pencil on his desk.

"We'd like to hear a lecture about the new party. If you absolutely refuse to tell us where the actual meetings are held, then there's nothing we can do but keep holding you for ten days, twenty days, a month, or more. We know exactly where the place is and who the members are. If you won't tell us, we won't ask. There's no need to ask because we know. Well . . ."

The policeman stood up briskly, and thrust his arms into a jacket that had been hanging nearby. "Could you take this woman back?"

"Get up, you idiot! You're going back. To the cell."

Yasuko clutched the front of her untied kimono and stood up, but she felt oddly uneasy. It was a lingering unpleasantness, worse than if she had been hit. As she bent down to put on her shoes, the policeman sent her off with a parting message. "So, think about it over the next ten or twenty days. You can tell us whenever you decide to. Once you do, we'll let you go right away."

But why had he bothered to bring her from her cell for such a pointless interrogation? Just to make fun of her? Or to see the face of the woman he would be keeping under surveillance from now on? Did they really mean to keep her here for so long? Yasuko had no idea about any of it, and that made her uneasy.

The accompanying policeman handed her over when they reached the lockup. "Here she is."

Passing his hands over her sleeves and hips, the jailer asked, "What happened? Get beaten?"

Without answering, Yasuko said "Please let me use the toilet." Although he didn't reply, she went in. After coming out she paused briefly in front of cell number two to show Yamada that she was fine. Listening carefully she heard a quiet voice say something quickly, but could not make it out.

Yasuko spent the next four days in detention. During that time, Yamada was taken out countless times for interrogation.

On the morning of the fifth day the jailer told her, "Get out." Yasuko shuddered, fearing that this time the interrogation would be no trifling matter. Surprisingly, however, she was being released.

Moreover, Yamada and the others were also released at the same time.

The Storm

1

The year passed with extraordinary speed. Both Okei and Yasuko underwent a succession of various experiences, all of a kind they would never have expected to befall them.

No sooner were Yamada and Yasuko released by the police than the union started openly keeping an eye on them. However, one day the good-natured committee chairman invited Yamada out for a meal. Yamada felt somewhat awkward, but left the office together with the chairman.

With a broad grin, the chairman proposed that they go to the restaurant where Yasuko used to work. Yamada had not been there for some time.

"Ah, Mr. Yamada!" The owner who had been sitting at the counter, abacus in hand, slipped into his geta and came out, his face expressing exaggerated welcome. "It's been a while!"

Yamada reddened slightly.

"Ah, you're a selfish man, Mr. Yamada!" said the chairman, his heavily bearded face beaming. "Ha, ha, ha, ha, ha, ha."

"No, he probably just doesn't like what's on the menu at this eatery anymore. Anyway . . ."

"All right, all right!" Yamada took a chair in the corner where he always used to sit.

The chairman ordered a bottle of sake. It was a prerequisite to broaching a difficult topic. Yamada tasted the sake tentatively, as though it were medicine, before swallowing it.

After speaking of various things, the chairman suddenly closed his eyes and said, "What I wanted to talk about is this . . . I've been doing this union work for many years so I know it well, and it's absolutely clear to me that you folks are once again starting to repeat the fiascos of March 15 and April 16. I'm not saying this for my own benefit, but under the present conditions, your work will again be crushed before it has any chance to catch on. Just like March 15 and April 16, I can't just stand by and look on knowing what I know."

Keeping his eyes closed, the chairman spoke very slowly.

"Whatever anyone may think, I am a genuine working man. Even so, to you I may seem an old-fashioned, feudalistic union boss. But I think I'm extremely realistic. The reason why March 15 and April 16 were such failures is because they disregarded the real situation of the working man."

It was the committee chairman's habit to refer proudly to his working-class origins as his sole source of authority.

"Listen," the chairman continued, "the police are keeping an eye on all of you now because they say they found a copy of a new *Proletarian Newspaper* inside the union. They say that a report was sent to Tokyo from Otaru, and they're looking into it on the assumption that you people were responsible. Things have gotten to the point where you're followed even when only two or three of you go someplace! Any time now you'll be arrested before you can get anything accomplished, and sent away for years. When I think of it, I feel more sorry than I can say . . ."

Yamada was silent. His own views and those of his comrades meant nothing to this man who, though good-natured and likeable, was an old-style boss and a legalist to the core. Yamada knew that what mattered were the countless thousands who stood in the background—the people. Moreover, he had recently managed at last to establish contact with the center, which would enable him to carry out the work in a truly organized manner from now on.

Realizing that Yamada was not about to say anything, the chairman lapsed into a forlorn silence.

2

Because the chairman intended to run for city assemblyman in the fall of the following year, he utilized even the smallest "dispute" and strike toward that end. Consequently, when strikes grew large and strikers became militant, the union that led and assisted them only sought, ironically enough, to restrain their spirit and work out an amicable solution. The communist organizer sent secretly from the center said it was crucial to seize the opportunity provided by such disputes and strikes to stage opposition to the new party on a mass scale. They had to expose the legalists' true colors and their treacherous dealings with capitalists and show that those who opposed the new party were the ones who represented the workers' real interests, who would struggle to the end. Yamada and his comrades were trying to work in a new and systematic way toward that objective.

The pressing issue was to oppose absolutely sending representatives to the "Convention to form a New Labor Farmer Party." At the approaching general meeting of the union it would be essential to assert the correct theory openly, and to mobilize the power of the people to oppose the dispatch of representatives. They were preparing for this now.

The committee chairman understood Yamada's real intention from his silence, and said nothing more. After this day, the chairman's attitude suddenly changed. Until this time he had not shown outright hostility toward Yamada and his comrades, but now he began to exhibit clear and aggressive malice. He seized various opportunities to slander the characters of Yamada and his comrades. Yamada was a student, he said, a starry-eyed Marxist boy who knew nothing about the movement, a womanizer wrapped up in Yasuko. Alternatively, he began to accuse Yamada and his comrades of being plotters who, if caught, would end up as convicts.

It was a cold day shortly after, drenched with a rain that heralded winter's approach. Yasuko was returning home. She had made a round of opposition unionists and given them the date and time of a meeting to be held at her sister's room to discuss what measures to take at the general meeting of the union. She arrived at the corner nearest her lodging house and saw the owner's precocious child standing in front of the house and looking her way. Catching sight of Yasuko, the boy ran over to her as fast as he could.

"A terrible thing's happened! A terrible thing!" he exclaimed breathlessly.

Yasuko flinched.

"Ten spies came just now and tied up Mr. Yamada and put him in a car and drove off. And they were asking about you, and looking for you all over the place. There's two spies in the room right now, waiting for you to come back. You can't go there now. I've been waiting for you here to tell you!"

Ten policemen! A car! And two policemen waiting for her! This was highly unusual and looked serious! The storm that Yamada had often said might come had finally hit, thought Yasuko. Perhaps it had arrived not only in Otaru but the entire country.

So this was it! She couldn't just stand there. There were many friends she must warn. And she mustn't lose her head and allow herself to be arrested.

"Thank you!"

Normally she didn't much like this child, but now she spontaneously stroked his head.

She thought she would go to Sasaki's place right away. If he too had been arrested, or if they were lying in wait for him, she would know the real situation. But come to think of it, she could not casually go to Sasaki's place. It was much too dangerous. Where should she go?

She thought about it for a moment. But standing here was extremely dangerous too.

Yasuko decided to go to her sister's. For the time being it was the only safe place there was.

3

Approaching her sister's house cautiously, Yasuko looked up at the second floor, swept her eyes over the entire building, and opened the door. The entrance looked the same as always.

"Anyone home?" Still careful, she called out from below.

The second-floor door slid open and Sasaki peered down from the top of the stairs.

"Yatchan?" said Sasaki quietly.

"Yes. Is everything all right?"

"Yes." As soon as Yasuko climbed up the stairs, Sasaki asked, "What happened to Yamada?"

"Arrested!"

"Arrested . . . !"

"So I came here for safety. This time they're doing it in a big way, and I'm worried . . ."

"Looks like a mass roundup . . ." Sasaki carefully slid the door shut, and led Yasuko to a corner of the room. "Just like March 15 and April 16! Do you know what I mean? Anyone who gets caught is in for a long time."

Of course! Yasuko suddenly grew anxious. It meant that Yamada too, like his comrades arrested on March 15 and April 16, was not likely to come home for a long time. Those who were left must do everything they could not to get caught.

"I see. It isn't very safe here either, so we have to hurry and come up with a backup plan."

"That's right. Our friends are getting arrested on a big scale. Maybe the two of us are the only ones left."

"Can you think of a plan?"

"Yes, there's one fellow whom the police don't know. We'll hide at his house, and have him check if it's safe outside and get in touch with others. It's impossible to do underground work in a small provincial town like Otaru. We can come up with an alternative at his place once we have a general idea of what's going on. What do you think?"

"I can't think of anything better, so it'll have to do. And it does seem the best."

From time to time Sasaki discreetly glanced out the window. "We can't leave here before the sun goes down. We should disguise ourselves a little."

"That's right. If we get pinched, it's two or three years."

Sasaki laughed.

"My sister's not back yet?"

"She doesn't seem to be. And Mother is off to the bath or somewhere. I took the liberty of coming up. I wonder if Keichan will get back before we leave . . ."

"Yes, this might end up a long separation from Sister . . ."

Each for a different reason eagerly awaited Okei's return from the factory.

"I hope she won't choose tonight of all nights to work overtime and come back at nine or ten . . ."

"She might. To leave here very late would be dangerous too."

The two discussed in detail the best ways of promoting the work from now on.

The sun set. Taking care not to cast a shadow against the window, Sasaki drew the curtain and switched on the light.

It was eight o'clock, and Okei was not back yet. Yasuko's face looked understandably gloomy.

"Well, I'll leave her a note." Yasuko sat down in front of the desk. While writing her message, Yasuko—who seldom cried—secretly wiped away tears.

Sasaki gazed at her from behind. The emotions he was feeling were even more painful.

4

In the end, Okei did not come back. She had been working overtime almost every night lately. The end of the year was approaching and money was needed for various things. Aware that Brother would be coming home from prison, and wanting also to do something for her little sister who had no income at all, she was pushing herself to the limit.

"My sister is reading so many books these days. . . . And working so hard at the same time," observed Yasuko glancing at the books piled up beside her as she wrote. Picking them up one by one, she exclaimed, "They're all your books!"

Sasaki was eagerly awaiting the sound of footsteps from below. Somehow he could not escape the feeling that if he did not see Okei now, he would never see her again.

They waited until nine, but she did not come. Unable to wait any longer, the two cautiously stepped out.

The house in question was far from Okei's place, but it was convenient for that very reason (being outside the working-class district). The two started walking separately. It was one of the nights when the cold gradually penetrates to the body's core. Before leaving the working-class district they saw many people on their way back from working overtime. Both kept searching for Okei, but could not find her among them. Sasaki felt the strength that supported his entire body suddenly falling away from him.

Trying their best to avoid the brightly lit main streets, they chose streets they had not taken before. They were going to a house in which a mother lived with her only son Yoshizō, who worked in town at a small factory. The son respected Sasaki, occasionally treated him to meals, and gave him a little help on paydays. Although Yoshizō was sympathetic when Sasaki told him of their predicament, he looked slightly embarrassed.

"There's no place to sleep except together with us . . . ," he said hesitantly.

Sasaki felt bad for Yasuko when he heard this, but of course they were in no position to choose. After looking about to make sure it was safe, Yoshizō led them into the house. His mother was already in bed but raised her head from the pillow to say, "If you don't mind sleeping all jumbled up like this, stay as long as you like."

They discussed what to do from now on.

"See how it looks outside every day, and get in touch with any of our friends who might've escaped arrest. I want to rebuild the movement," said Sasaki.

Yoshizō nodded in agreement.

"Getting in touch with them sounds good," said Yasuko, "but in this town there's a danger that they'll catch you doing it. If you aren't careful, you could end up leading them here."

"That's true. Well, let's do it this way . . . ," said Sasaki musingly. "If you're not back in two days, we'll assume you've been arrested, and we'll clear out of here. So, let's decide that if you're arrested you'll stick it out for three days without giving away your address."

"No objection."

Gazing at Yoshizō's face, Yasuko said, "Because if we get arrested now, this movement will be ruined for another half a year . . ."

Yoshizō nodded. "I'll do my best!"

It was getting late. Yasuko lay down next to Yoshizō's mother. Sasaki and Yoshizō lay down slightly away from them.

Unaccustomed to the new place and anxious over Yamada's arrest, Yasuko found it difficult to fall asleep. She dozed off only to dream of being pursued by spies whom she could not escape no matter how hard she ran. She kept waking up out of breath.

Sasaki too seemed to be constantly tossing and turning in his sleep.

5

Yoshizō's mother worked as a cleaner at the Colonial Bank, and got up early in the morning. Before leaving, she showed Yasuko where everything was in the kitchen so that they could manage without her.

Yoshizō decided that on his way back from the factory he would visit a unionist he knew and, if possible, would also stop by the secret union.

While Yasuko was busy putting away the kimono, nightclothes, and underwear, Sasaki hurriedly asked Yoshizō to drop by Okei's place too. What he really wanted was to see Okei one more time. He wanted her to visit him secretly. But because this was dangerous, it was essential to take some stock of the situation first.

"Just let her know that we're fine."

Perhaps thinking Sasaki's behavior odd, Yoshizō glanced at his face and asked, "Nothing else?"

"Right. Yamada's wife who's here now is her younger sister, you see. She's really worried . . . ," said Sasaki with a touch of confusion, ascribing his own feelings to Yasuko.

The day that followed the departure of mother and son was long, irritating, and unsettling. In the course of discussing repeatedly what to do, they found themselves saying the same things over and over.

Neither Yasuko nor Sasaki had brought a single book. At Yoshizō's place there was nothing except a few magazines: an old copy of *King* and four or five very old copies of *Marxism.* Although they picked them up and tried to read them, they simply could not concentrate. They had a feeling of being constantly pressured by something invisible. They were not aware of it but the unfamiliar sensation of being by themselves in a stranger's house clung to them.

At noon Yasuko went to the kitchen and began to prepare lunch. She worked awkwardly and noisily. Sasaki, who had been reading *King,* stood up.

"How goes it?"

"It's strange, isn't it, to be meddling in someone else's kitchen!"

Yasuko peeked into the cupboard, and under a floorboard.

"Let's just have some pickles with our lunch! It'd be embarrassing if it got out that we ate a lot!"

"Not to worry, there's nothing but pickles!"

Nonetheless, a short while later they placed their rice bowls on a small table, sat across from each other and ate.

"It's strange somehow . . . !" said Sasaki with embarrassment, handing his bowl to Yasuko. "When it gets to be mealtime like this, it makes me think of Yamada and the others."

Yasuko blushed slightly but feigning composure said, "I can't be bothered with something like that when we're up against the wall like this!"

As the evening drew near they eagerly awaited Yoshizō's return, wondering what sort of news he would bring.

Around five, Yoshizō's mother came home. Yasuko helped her to prepare dinner.

"Why didn't you grill some fish for lunch?" the mother chided Yasuko. "Didn't I tell you to?"

They decided to postpone dinner until Yoshizō came home. However, Yoshizō was slow to arrive. Six o'clock came, then seven, then eight, yet he did not return. It got to be past nine. The three of them waited, their hearts consumed with anxious thoughts.

6

Once it passed nine o'clock, both Sasaki and Yasuko fell silent. It seemed that thrusting Yoshizō into a raging storm of arrests had been extremely dangerous.

"I wonder what happened . . . ," said his mother, suspecting nothing. His being so late meant that he would eat dinner out, she suggested, so there was no need to wait for him. But Yasuko and Sasaki had no appetite. Sounds of footsteps passing in front of the house deceived them countless times.

After some time, Yoshizō's mother suddenly looked up. "Ah, he's coming!"

"Really?"

Sasaki and Yasuko could not tell. The mother, however, had been able to identify her son's footsteps from among the sounds of many distant feet. A single pair of footsteps approached, entered the alley, and arrived in front of the house. The door rattled open. As though he had been holding his breath all this time, Sasaki exhaled a big lungful of air and shifted for the first time to a comfortable sitting position.

"I'm so glad! I'm so glad!" he exclaimed with childlike delight.

Yoshizō's clothes were torn in several places, and he was agitated. "That was close," he said, repeatedly wiping the sweat from his face with his sleeve.

On the way back from the factory Yoshizō had visited an old friend who was working for the union. As soon as the friend saw Yoshizō, he told him there had been a mass arrest at the union. He said that spies were lying in wait in front of the union and pouncing on anyone who walked in, whether a tradesman's apprentice or one of the chairman's (legalist) followers.

"It seems the old chairman himself was arrested at his house," the friend said. "I don't know why, maybe because the Communist Party had infiltrated the union like before. But they haven't caught Sasaki or Yamada's wife so I hear they're desperately looking for them. If you're thinking of going to the union, you'd better not . . ."

Yoshizō took care to leave the friend's place in a casual manner. He had it in mind to visit next a fairly conspicuous oppositionist who had once or twice come with Sasaki to his house. Seeing that fellow, he thought, should give him a good sense of the whole situation. Since it was dangerous to go to his place directly, he was about to step into a neighborhood bar about two houses away when he suddenly noticed a man in a suit standing in front of him. He was alarmed, but he knew that turning back would make him look even more suspicious.

"Hey, just a minute!"

Sure enough, it had been a bad idea not to change out of his factory clothes! All the same, determined not to get caught, he spun around and dashed into an alley. He knew the area well.

The man in the suit shouted loudly "Thief!! Thief!!" and rushed after him. Glancing back as he rounded a corner of the alley, Yoshizō saw that passersby and people running out of their houses were joining the chase. At the same instant he suddenly felt himself seized from the side with a powerful grip. Damn it! he thought. He struggled with all his might but the other man was stronger.

At his wits' end, Yoshizō gasped, "Please! I'm in the union!"

"Union? Labor union?"

"Yes, the joint labor union!"

The man released his hold on Yoshizō.

"Thanks!"

He ran off through a narrow passageway and into the main street. He had never before felt so grateful. Once he emerged into the main street he was safe since it was already dark. Thanks to this experience, he knew now how things stood. There was no further need to go around and ask other unionists. He thought he had better follow Sasaki's directions and go to Okei's place.

"Being called a thief and getting chased threw me off," he said, rubbing his arms and his trousers.

7

Okei looked very thin and pale when Yoshizō made his secret visit. The night she read Yasuko's letter she remained wide awake till dawn. Though she did get up in the morning, she did not feel like going to the factory at all. She felt unsteady and strangely weak, as if she were running a high fever.

Although Yoshizō delivered the message that Yasuko and Sasaki were both safe and not to worry, she felt more envious than glad at the news that the two of them who shared the same goal were able to be together, even if they were in danger of arrest. Once again, the hope that had enabled her to endure the staggering burden of making a living had been taken away. She was alone, and she had no idea what to do about it.

Okei wanted to see them once more. If she parted with them now, she would forever be holding feelings that were unbearable, especially her feelings toward Sasaki. Besides, there were many questions she wanted to ask about what she ought to do from now on. Left alone as she was, she would surely end up a worm "creeping sluggishly along the ground its entire life . . ."—what had she called it once?—yes, a snail dragging its shell. She would be turned into a snail spending its lifetime squirming under a heavy load, groping forward through darkness inch by inch without seeing a glimmer of light ahead.

Although Okei had led such a life till now, she had always received a sense of will and purpose from her sister. And being embraced in Sasaki's powerful arms had given direction to her life. But now they were both being snatched away from her.

"Please tell them I would very much like to see them once," she said again to Yoshizō.

IN ORDER TO hunt down Sasaki and Yasuko, the police had set up a veritable cordon that covered the entire city. They kept detaining one person after another for being even remotely connected to the union, or just for being friends with a unionist. Yoshizō's house was in constant danger.

The reports that Yoshizō brought in daily made it clear to Sasaki what they needed to do at once.

"Hey, Yatchan," said Sasaki. Cooped up in the same house day after day without being able to take a step outside, they had unawares switched to such familiar terms. "It's impossible for people who're being pursued like us to do any work at all in this small town. I think the most important thing we can do is to travel secretly to Tokyo and to make sure a new organizer is sent here."

"To *Tokyo?*"

"Yes. And for us to work there. I think there's no other choice. What do you think?"

". . . . ." Yasuko remained silent for a moment. "Of course. There's nothing else we can do. Even so, we can't just go tomorrow . . ." She suddenly averted her eyes and said, as if to herself, "Yamada . . . should I ask my sister to take care of the daily things Yamada needs . . . ?"

ON THE DAY when with firm resolve Sasaki and Yasuko set out for Tokyo, Okei was on a train bound for Sapporo.

They were going in exactly opposite directions. Okei was on her way to meet the brother who was being released, terribly sick, from the Sapporo penitentiary.

In the end, Okei was not able to see Sasaki . . .

(NOTE: THIS IS only the first part of the novel. For the time being I will stop here.)

[IN HIS NOTES for the second part of the novel—which he never got the opportunity to write—the author indicates that Okei too will go to Tokyo, and work in a factory.]

SERIALIZED FROM AUGUST 23 TO OCTOBER 31, 1931

LIFE OF A PARTY MEMBER

1

I WAS WASHING my hands in the bathroom when groups of guys from Factory Number 2 who were starting to come back from work passed just under the window, talking loudly and making a racket with their shoes and wooden *zōri*.

"Not ready yet?" asked Suyama, bringing up the rear. He worked at Factory Number 2. My face covered with soapsuds, I turned around and frowned slightly. Suyama and I had agreed some time ago to avoid returning from the factory together. If we did, it would make us more noticeable and might even lead to a lot of people getting into trouble. Yet from time to time Suyama violated our agreement. Then he'd say, "Come on, don't get so angry," and laugh amiably. Suyama was a lighthearted and charming fellow whom it was impossible to dislike, so I'd smile wryly whenever he did that. But the times being what they were, I gave him a stern look. On top of that, today we were about to invite a new member to drop by an eatery someplace for a bowl of *shiruko*. . . .

I suddenly noticed that Suyama's face was not wearing its usual joking expression. Instantly a premonition unique to people doing our kind of work came to me, and I said, "I'll be there right away," and doused my face with water.

Seeing that I understood, Suyama abruptly changed his tone and added, "How about a Kirin?" Although this resembled Suyama's customary tone, I immediately noticed that it sounded forced and different from usual.

Sure enough, when we stepped outside, Suyama walked at least thirty feet ahead of me. The road from the factory to the train line was narrow, squeezed between the National Railway embankment on one side and a row of shops on the other. A plainclothesman was standing by the second electric pole, looking in our direction. It was eerie how he both seemed to be watching us and not watching us. Observing him from the corner of my left eye, I promptly joined shoulders with five or six men coming up from behind and talked with them, never letting "the suit" out of my sight. Bored by the daily routine of his assignment, the suit seemed apathetic and lazy. He had recently been keeping a lookout every day at the factory's opening and closing time. Suyama sauntered directly past him, pointedly flinging out his legs as if mocking the suit. It was funny that I could see him doing it.

I caught up with Suyama after we emerged from the crowds near the train line. He was gazing about nonchalantly and rubbing his nose. Then he said, "It's odd." I watched his face. "Ueda lost track of Whiskers! . . ."

"When?" I asked.

"Yesterday."

Though I knew that contingency plans were unnecessary with a man like Whiskers, I asked, "Was there a backup plan?"

"It seems there was."

According to Suyama, yesterday's contact involved an extremely important task to which a day's delay would be fatal. Consequently, a day earlier Honda and Whiskers had taken a walk down the street that links the three train stops at river S, town M, and bridge A, and decided on which stretch to meet. Acting with utmost caution, Whiskers had taken the rare step of choosing a safe-looking coffee shop to meet twenty minutes later if they could not meet in the street. Moreover, they coordinated their watches before parting. The comrade called Whiskers was an important leader from our highest ranks. Among some thousand contacts to date (all made in the streets), this comrade had only been late twice. Occasional mishaps are to be expected among people doing our kind of work, yet this man was unusually reliable. Besides, one of the two times he was late had been due to a mutual misunderstanding, and he had set out punctually. The other time it happened because he had not realized that his watch was not working properly. With other people, a single missed contact was no cause for worry but Whiskers not showing up at the appointed place or even at the backup spot struck us as downright incredible.

"What about today?"

"It's supposed to be the same place as yesterday."

"What time?"

"Seven. And the coffee shop at seven twenty. Anyway, I've been worried about it so I've arranged to meet Ueda at eight thirty."

I thought about my schedule for tonight and said, "All right, meet me at nine."

We decided on a place and parted. As he was leaving, Suyama said, "If Whiskers is done for, I'm turning myself in!" Of course he was joking yet he sounded strangely convincing. "Idiot," I said, but I fully understood how he felt. That is how much we all relied on Whiskers and drew our strength from him. It was no exaggeration to say that he was like a beacon for us. If Whiskers were truly gone, we would instantly feel quite discouraged about carrying on our work. Of course we would find a way to carry it on. Yet as I walked, I hoped with all my heart that Whiskers had not been arrested.

ALONG THE WAY I stopped by a small confectionery and bought a box of Morinaga caramels. Approaching the lodging house, I saw the owner's son standing in front of a candy machine together with some children from the neighborhood. If you inserted a one-sen coin and pushed a handle, a baseball would fly toward a base. The base where the ball landed determined what kind of candy came out of the hole below. Such machines were becoming popular lately, and crowds of children surrounded each machine in town. Eyes fixed and lips tense, the kids pressed the handles. A single sen might just get them something worth more than a sen.

I jangled the coins in my pocket and gave the lodging house owner's child two one-sen copper coins. At first the boy drew back his hand just a little, but suddenly his face flushed with joy. Apparently he had up to now only been watching from behind what the other children were doing. I also stuck the recently bought caramels into the child's pocket, and went home.

By eight o'clock that evening, I needed to write up what had happened at the factory today and have the report ready for use in the fliers to be distributed tomorrow. I was to meet S at eight and hand him the copy. Taking a trunk filled with various papers out of the closet, I unlocked it.

Kurata Industries is a metalworking factory that used to employ only two hundred people, but after the war began it recruited six hundred temporary workers. It was at this time that Suyama, Itō (a woman comrade), I, and others got into the workforce using other people's résumés. Adding six hundred temporaries to the two hundred regular workers shows the size of the upsurge in the work. Once the war began, Kurata Industries stopped manufacturing the electric wires it had been making, and began to manufacture gas masks, parachutes, and airship fuselages. But recently there had been a pause in the work, and it seemed that as many as four hundred of the six hundred temporary workers would be fired. This was the main topic of conversation at the factory these days. Everyone was saying, "We'll be fired, we'll be fired!" The company responded with: "There is no such thing as firing temporary workers. Moreover, we have been employing you more than half a month longer than originally agreed upon." It was true that people had been working more than half a month longer than the original agreement called for, but the work during that period was brutal to the extreme. Women and men worked continuously from eight in the morning till nine at night for only one yen and eight sen. Not only was the pay between six and nine in the evening just eight sen per hour, but the company went so far as to withhold two or three sen from the night work wages for the twenty or thirty minutes (they expressly calculated this) that it took to eat supper. One time while eating I said, "I guess the company thinks that workers can work without eating." To that, one of my fellow temporary workers said, "Yeah, that's right." His tone was so convincing that it made everyone laugh. When paying out the daily wages, the company always handed out a five-sen note and three one-sen copper coins to each of the nearly four hundred women workers. This took a great deal of time. One might start waiting at six and wait until seven. "Shit, this is so annoying! We'd save so much time if they just gave us ten sen instead of eight. Maybe we should lower our price and make do with a five." Everyone in the line was irritated and grumbling. "Looks like the rich are greedier than we can even imagine!"

The rumor was spreading that the company would pay ten yen to each temporary worker whom it fired. It was not obligated to pay them a single sen since they were temporaries, yet the company wished to show everyone that it appreciated their hard work. Although it was unclear how reliable the rumor was, everybody knew that if they quit this job they would not be able to find another one for a while, and so they unconsciously counted on the rumor being true. But why would a company that docked two or three sen from wages for suppertime, which casually made hundreds of workers wait for more than an hour, which lined up one-sen coins three apiece—why would such a company give six hundred people ten yen each, the princely sum of ten yen! By circulating the rumor about paying them ten yen, the company was clearly playing a trick. The rumor served as a means of preventing unrest by the workers in the face of the firings, and of getting rid of them smoothly.

Because this had been a major conversation topic at the factory today, I decided to write about it in the flier to be distributed in the factory tomorrow. The fliers that were brought in the day before yesterday contained a detailed report on the previous day's loud demands for speeding up the payment process. Though they dealt with an insignificant matter, the fliers were greeted with much enthusiasm. I seated myself before the desk, and comfortably crossed my legs.

A short time later, the lady from below came upstairs. "Thank you for being so kind to my son!" she said, offering me a rare smile. People who do our kind of work must be as sensitive as anyone to even the smallest events. Having our fellow lodgers think "There's something strange about the guy upstairs," or "Wonder what he does," must be avoided at all costs. Comrade H (presently active in prison) once took his lodging-house mates to the Imperial Theater in order to continue his work even while the police were searching for him so intensively that they circulated his photograph in restaurants, coffee shops, barbershops, and public bathhouses. We too need to be able to talk like other people about everyday things, to exchange civilities, and the like. But I'm incredibly clumsy in such situations and get all embarrassed. These days I'm getting somewhat accustomed to it . . . I said to the lady, "Oh, it's nothing," and flushed red. I'm really not good at this.

I NEEDED TO write two or two-and-a-half pages at most, but doing it after completing the daytime work was not easy. When I finally finished the piece exposing the truth of the ten-yen bonus, it was already past seven. All along I had been rubbing my face with a hand towel. I sweat when I write. I put the pages into an envelope, addressed it randomly with a woman's name as though it were a love letter, and left the house at seven-forty. "I'm going out for a walk," I said, and the lady who was usually silent turned to me and said, "Enjoy your walk." The effect of the candy was clearly miraculous. Stepping out into the darkness, I smiled wryly. One time earlier when I was about to go out, the lady had said, "You go out a lot, don't you?" Her words had startled me. I really was going out every evening, and so she had good reason to be suspicious. Though my heart was thumping, I laughed and started to say, "Oh, it's just . . ." when the lady brought the matter to a close with a laugh of her own, saying "You're still young, aren't you?" Realizing that she did not mean to say what I had feared, I was relieved.

The meeting place for eight o'clock was a road lined with many factories that stretched in back of the railroad tracks. The street was crowded with shop clerks and factory workers; the workers wore their hair long in front. I always made an effort to wear the kind of clothes that were suitable to the place where I was going. Although I could not completely succeed, it was quite important to do my best. At any rate, we had to be dressed neatly in order to avoid being questioned for appearing suspicious, yet in a place like this at eight in the evening a western suit and a walking stick would attract attention. With this in mind I went out wearing a kimono with a casually tied obi, and without a hat.

At the opposite end of the ruler-straight street, I spotted S coming toward me, swinging his right shoulder as was his habit. Once he noticed me, he briefly paused by a display window and then nonchalantly turned into an alley. I followed him, and after turning into yet another street began walking side by side with him. S asked about the response to the fliers that had been distributed at the factory the day before yesterday. After various questions, he said, "It's good that you're always raising the issues through conversations at the factory. However, what still needs to be done is to move the discussion to a *political* level."

I looked at S's face with surprise. What he was saying made sense. Delighted with the popularity of the fliers, I had forgotten to view things from a higher plane.

"In other words, we are swayed by everyone's spontaneous feelings. In order to clarify the substance of imperialist war through everyday dissatisfactions, a special, systematic and rather professional effort will be necessary. This is what we need to make the comrades understand."

In trying to make up for the flaws of the many earlier antiwar fliers that had been formal and abstract, we were now making the mistake of limiting the problem to economic demands. Such a right-wing tendency is popular for a time because it appeals to the masses. Consequently, popularity too needs to be carefully examined. Such were the things we talked about as we walked.

"We need to be cautious, because grafting trees and bamboos comes to nothing. It's a regression! Up to now we've been like blinkered horses, looking only at isolated aspects of everything."

After walking a while, we entered a coffee shop.

"Here's the love letter." I placed the manuscript on a shelf under the table. Humming a tune while keeping an eye on the waiter, S stuffed it in his pocket.

"Do you want to contact Whiskers?" he asked, pressing the skin beneath his nose.

I told him what I had heard from Suyama on the way back from the factory. S deliberately hummed on, but listened with attentive eyes. This was his habit.

"I was supposed to see him at six yesterday, too, but couldn't make contact."

I felt uneasy when I heard that. "I wonder if they got him . . . ," I said, though I actually wanted to be reassured.

"Hmm," S thought it over. "He was very careful."

After deciding that someone should get hold of Whiskers, and making arrangements for bringing in the fliers the following morning, we parted.

When I met Suyama at nine, the pallor of his face told me everything. Nonetheless, all was not yet lost. Suyama and I decided to do everything we could to find out what had happened to Whiskers. Then we promptly parted.

As a rule we do not carry out any tasks after nine-thirty in the evening, unless the contact is made in the vicinity of our hideout. Moving over longer distances is dangerous. Returning home alone after leaving S, I realized that I was profoundly worried about Whiskers. Even as I walked, I had an odd sense of disquiet. My knees felt weak, and I even seemed to be short of breath. People who lead their lives in ordinary circumstances may think that my description is somewhat exaggerated and false. Yet a person who is totally isolated, who has cut off all contact with old intimate friends, who cannot even enjoy a casual stroll to a public bathhouse, and who on top of everything will get at least six or seven years if arrested—such a person can only rely on comrades. If even one of those comrades is snatched away, the feelings that link us together suffer a deep and powerful blow. This is all the more so in the case of a comrade who has always guided us. Earlier when I was working legally in an opposition group within a reactionary union, a similar event did not affect me with such intensity. At that time various facets of daily life undoubtedly played a distracting role.

ŌTA WAS WAITING for me at the lodging house. I had resolved not to reveal my hideout to anyone, but Ōta knew it with the consent of the leaders. In order to carry on work at Kurata Industries it was necessary to appoint someone full time and to meet them frequently. Meeting people outdoors was likely to cause delays, and did not allow sufficient time to work things out to a satisfactory extent.

Ōta had come about tomorrow's fliers. I told him I had just made arrangements with S to have him come to the National Railway platform of the T Station at seven the next morning. S would hand over the fliers to me there.

Having taken care of the urgent business, we chatted for a while. When I had smilingly proposed, "Shall we chat?" Ōta had laughed: "You're launching into your specialty!" Once a task has been completed I almost invariably and with great pleasure say "Shall we chat?" and so chatting has come to be known as my specialty. Lately however I've realized the reason for my longing to chat. In the course of work we meet our comrades almost every day. But at such times, keeping our voices low in coffee shops, we discuss only business and omit idle talk. When that's over, we promptly leave the place and part as soon as possible. This is repeated three hundred and sixty-five days in a year. Of course I have adjusted my ways to that kind of everyday life, and am now accustomed to it. However, just as a person who has been locked up for a long time may develop an unbearable and sometimes feverishly intense craving for sweets, my own reaction to the one-sidedness of such a life seemed to take the form of wanting to chat whenever I saw a companion's face. But to Ōta, who led a normal life that included occasional beer-hall rowdiness, this feeling reflected merely a different, extremely carefree character. He could not share my feelings and at times (cruelly!) went away without chatting.

Agreeing now to a chat before leaving, Ōta presented an evaluation of various women workers at the factory. I was surprised by the number of women he had managed to become familiar with. He said, "Factory women don't fall in love in the sticky and ceremonious way of young bourgeois ladies. They're quite direct and concrete, so it's tough to know what to do!"

"Direct and concrete"—the words amused us, and we laughed.

2

Once the fliers that clearly bore the *party*'s signature had been distributed, Kurata Industries suddenly began keeping a close watch mornings and evenings over everyone coming in and going out. The times being what they were, and the products it manufactured being what they were, the company began to panic. One morning a woman who works beside me rushed in with a scream. At the factory entrance there is a gloomy storehouse whose door is always open. The woman was casually walking past it when from a far corner a figure covered entirely in black began to lurch forward. Later she learned it was a security guard. From this and other signs it was clear how shaken the management was.

After the war started, masses of young factory workers were sent off to the front. At the same time, the number of jobs in the manufacture of munitions rose astronomically. To make up for the gap, factories were forced to recruit huge numbers of new workers. Up until then no worker could be hired without undergoing a stringent background check and providing a guarantor, but once the war started this became impossible. We watched for this opportunity. Of course getting hired in such circumstances meant becoming a "temporary worker," and the harsh exploitation of temporary workers under the pretext of a "national emergency" ultimately served to lower the wages of all workers. Nonetheless companies felt torn by conflicting interests, and were forced to resort to such absurd and shameless measures as hiring black-clad masked security guards.

I didn't care about the figures in black; the ones who lay in wait for me wore suits. My photograph was making the rounds of all the police stations. Of course I had altered my features, but I could not afford to be careless. A comrade had been arrested by a police spy who had never met him, on the basis of a photograph taken thirteen years earlier. One of my friends has recommended that I go entirely "underground." Of course that would be best, but experience has taught me that organizing a factory from the outside is a hundred times more difficult and a hundred times less effective. This is even true when one is very closely connected to members inside the factory. Needless to say, "going underground" for us signifies neither retirement nor simply hiding or running from place to place. People who don't know may think that it does, but if that were so it would truly be a hundred times more comfortable to let ourselves be quietly arrested and keep still in a prison cell. To the contrary, we "go underground" in order to insulate ourselves from enemy attacks and to carry on the struggle with utmost boldness and resolve. Needless to say, it is easier to work legally. That is why I tell Ōta and others to stay legally active as long as they can. In that sense, "going underground" is not the correct term: we never go underground because we want to, we are simply forced underground.

And so I have been exposing myself to danger in front of the enemy, and am really worn out by the suits' constant attention. I'm somewhat relieved to know that lately the suit that stands there is always the same, but when I see a different face in the distance I slow my pace, adjust my hat, and ascertain before approaching whether or not I know him. After this first barrier comes the inspection by the gatekeeper. The task there is to make sure not to get caught bringing in the fliers. Ōta uses women members for this. According to Ōta, "It tends to be the safest from the woman's navel on down." Evidently they have not yet gotten sufficiently shameless to search there.

The next morning I opened my locker to discover a flier! A sudden wave-like emotion surged fleetingly through my body. When I entered the workshop, the woman who works next to me was reading the flier. She was picking out the words one by one like a schoolchild, scratching her head with her little finger whenever she came across a word she did not know. "Is this true?" she asked when she saw me. She was talking about the matter of ten yen. "It's true," I said, "it's very true." "Shit," she exclaimed, "that's disgusting!"

The workers at the factory had a fairly clear idea of my political identity. Whether or not fliers were around, whenever people talked about the company, I always put in a word, trying to steer the discussion in a correct and clear direction. It is important in quiet times to gain people's trust as someone who can be relied upon to lead in a crisis. In that sense we need to stand at the head of the masses and win the workers over "massively" to our side. A sectarian approach formerly practiced in factories recruited workers secretly one by one, but it became clear that such a method could never create a mass movement.

Since a few minutes still remained before work, I began to walk toward the shop floor where the workers were all standing in groups and talking. Just then a supervisor came up: "Anyone who's got a flier, give it to me!"

Everybody automatically hid their fliers.

"It won't do you any good to hide it!" The supervisor turned to the woman next to me. "You, give it here."

The woman obediently took out the flier from behind her obi.

"Treating a dangerous thing like that with such care!" said the supervisor with a bitter smile.

"But sir, the company's doing very rotten things to us!"

"That—that's why I say you cannot trust fliers!"

"Really? So will they really give us ten yen when we quit?"

The supervisor hesitated. "How should I know? Ask the company!"

"But you too were telling us that they would! Ah, it's just as I thought: the fliers are telling the truth!"

At the woman's words, everyone began to laugh. "Yeah, you tell him!" someone said.

The supervisor suddenly flushed crimson, nervously rubbed his nose, sputtered and stormed off. All of us in the third annex raised a loud cheer. It had been a minor incident, but as its result the supervisor had left, forgetting to confiscate everyone else's fliers.

That day, less than an hour after the work began, I heard that Ōta had been taken away from the factory. Evidently they realized that he had entered carrying the fliers.

ŌTA CAUGHT—and he knows my hideout!

He had once said that if it came to this he would do his best to hold out for just three days. When I asked him how he had come up with three days, he replied that everyone said so. For some reason, "three days" had become somewhat of a rule. We had kept up our joking at the time, but I remember suddenly sensing a weakness in Ōta.

That was the first thing that came to my mind when I heard that Ōta had been arrested.

A comrade whom I know went on living calmly in his hideout although his roommate had been arrested. I and others urged him to move out right away. The comrade's face took on an odd expression. Not surprisingly, on the fifth day the hideout was raided. The comrade jumped out of the window. That might have worked, but he sprained his ankle. He was brought in stripped stark naked to keep him from running away. In the police cell, as soon as he caught sight of his companion who had been arrested earlier, he angrily shouted, "You idiot! You're so damned spineless!" But his companion thought to the contrary that it was the accuser who had been "sloppily careless" in his rash failure to make the least effort to escape in the face of danger, and tried to tell him so. When the comrade eventually came out, we told him, "It isn't that we didn't warn you. To know and still get arrested is downright undisciplined." To which he retorted, "It was because he talked. Saying a single thing to those jerks is what's downright undisciplined!" Indeed, this comrade had not uttered a single word during his own interrogation. Since he himself considered talking unthinkable, it never occurred to him that anyone else might talk, and so he had "sloppily" stayed on in his hideout. At the time I felt struck in my most vulnerable spot. Advising him to flee the hideout was a defeatist admission that if I myself were arrested I would reveal the hideout on the third or fourth day. Yet such an attitude is utterly foreign to Bolsheviks. This is quite elementary. We later decided to make that comrade's attitude the standard for our own conduct. But now, confronted with Ōta's unreliability, I could hardly stay "sloppily" on. I had to move out of the lodging house at once.

I should never have told anyone about my hideout. Formerly, one of our outstanding comrades had told seven people about his residence. These included not only other comrades but even mere sympathizers. As a result, the outstanding comrade's hideout was raided. Such cases abound. We must always keep in mind that we are carrying out our work while being pursued by the world's most thorough police network.

The only good thing was that Ōta did not know Suyama and Itō

Yoshi. In order to carry out the work more smoothly, I had thought of letting him know that they were companions whom we could trust. But then I thought of possible consequences and changed my mind. For one thing I wished to minimize repression's reach, and I also realized there is dangerous opportunism in attempting to carry out work on the basis of established networking.

After work, I joined Suyama and Itō and had an urgent talk with them at the Shirukoya sweetshop. As a result, it was decided that I would move out of the lodging house immediately (tonight), stay away from the factory until things cleared up and, keeping very close to the other comrades, prepare two or three alternative courses of action. In the past, many comrades had come to grief thinking, "Today is still safe," or "Nothing will happen." I agreed definitely to carry out the above three tasks as resolutions of the *factory cell.* Itō and Suyama then gave me a part of the day's wages they had just received, Suyama eighty sen and Itō fifty sen.

Suyama, as was his habit, asked me if I knew what Kanda Hakuzan, the famous storyteller, used to say. Here you go again, I said with a laugh. According to his story, Kanda Hakuzan throughout his life kept a hundred yen bill tucked away in a band that was wrapped around his belly. It seems he thought that there was no telling when or where a person might meet with a catastrophe and that to be caught without money at such a time would put his manhood at intolerable risk.

"It's the same thing: if you got arrested because you didn't have enough money to maneuver, you would be committing class betrayal!" said Suyama. "We must learn to draw a lesson from *their* experience too."

Itō and I began to laugh, convinced that Suyama's head was as filled with random information as a scrapbook.

WITHOUT THINKING, I turned a corner into the alley that leads to my lodging house. But it wasn't really carelessness. It had just never occurred to me that Ōta might reveal my address so quickly. In my second-floor room the light was on! And I sensed the presence of at least two people in the room. There was no doubt that they were lying in wait for me. But there were many things I wanted to take out of the room. There were even things I would badly need the very next day. Yet I promptly realized that this attachment to things was dangerous.

There was no place that I could go to right away. In the course of my wandering life so far I had just about run out of acquaintances' houses and could no longer rely on those. Knowing that I had to leave this area urgently, I walked toward the railroad tracks and after looking all around hailed a taxi. At random I said, "To S town."

It suddenly occurred to me that the factory clothes I was still wearing clashed with taking a taxi. I tried to think of a place to go but could not come up with anything. I grew impatient and irritable. Then I recalled a woman who had several times helped me find a place to hide. Whenever I asked her, she came through without fail. The woman rented a room on the third floor of a certain shop, and worked for a small company. Although sympathetic toward the left-wing movement, she herself was not actively participating in it. I knew her address, but it would be strange to visit a woman who lived alone; until now I had always phoned her at the company when I needed to contact her. But this woman was the only person left to me now, and I could not worry about such things. Getting out of the taxi in S town, I made up my mind and got on a streetcar.

I sat as close to the corner as possible and placed my hands on my knees. Quickly and unobtrusively I looked around. Luckily, no *odd types* were in sight. A western suit beside me, seemingly a bank employee, was reading the *Tokyo Asahi.* Glancing at it, I noticed a headline above the middle column on page two: *Red Elements Arrested at Kurata Industries.* I looked at the column repeatedly, but could not make out the contents. Anyhow, the slowness of the streetcar struck me as it never had before. I was really impatient.

To be on the safe side I got off two stops earlier, entered an alley and turned a few corners in the direction of the woman's house. Because it was my first time and I had taken the alley, I briefly got lost. An old man stood in the storefront, pounding his fist against a plaster pasted to his bare shoulder. When I asked him whether Miss Kasahara who lives upstairs was at home, he gazed at my face in silence. I asked again, somewhat more loudly. He turned toward the sliding doors of the living room and said something incomprehensible. Someone peeked through a glass inset. A suspicious voice said, "She is out."

I was at a complete loss. I asked when she might return, but they didn't know. They seemed to be looking at my clothes. I stood there not knowing what to do. There was no help for it. I said I'd try again around nine and left. Once I got outside, I looked up at the third floor. The light was out. Suddenly I felt disheartened.

I went out into a street lined with night stalls and tried reading a book, watched hustlers play *go,* spent two hours in a coffee shop, and went back. Turning the corner, I saw that the third-floor window was now lit.

I briefly explained the situation to Kasahara and asked her if she knew of a house somewhere. However, she had already used up nearly all the houses she knew to help me. There were two or three women friends from her company, but they did not understand the movement at all, "and they are all still single." Kasahara tilted her head and thought hard, but there really was nothing. I glanced at my watch: it was nearly ten. To wander outside after ten was extremely dangerous. The factory overalls I was still wearing made it even more dangerous. If I were her female friend I could ask her to help me in various ways but, as she said with a laugh, "Your being a man is a problem." I thought so too. Yet if I didn't want to get arrested, there was only one thing left. I needed to say it in a cheerful way.

"How about here? . . ."

Though I said it resolutely, I blushed and stammered. The suggestion might strike anyone as brazen, but I had no choice.

". . . . . !"

With a little catch in her breath, Kasahara gazed at me with eyes grown suddenly wide. Then she blushed, and looking confused straightened up so that she was no longer sitting with her legs off to the side.

After a while she made up her mind and went downstairs. She informed the owners that her elder brother from S town had come to stay with her. Being called her elder brother was funny no matter how one looked at it. She always dressed simply but properly and in Western style, with her hair cut rather short. No brother of hers wore overalls. When she made her announcement, the woman from downstairs evidently surveyed her childlike figure from head to foot without saying a word. Kasahara's face looked hard and tense. To have a man spend a night at her place was no trivial matter for a self-respecting woman.

Having decided what to do, we suddenly grew awkward and tongue-tied. I borrowed a pencil and paper and stretched out on my stomach to draft a plan for the next day. I wrote a memo about the need to find an immediate replacement for Ōta and distribute fliers about Ōta's arrest among the Kurata employees. Licking the pencil, I kept on writing. Suddenly I noticed that the woman could not bring herself to say "let's go to sleep."

"What time do you go to sleep?" I asked.

"Usually around this time . . . ," she said.

"Let's go to sleep then. I'm done with my work for now, too." I got up and yawned.

There was only a single futon. I declined her offer of a quilt, and lay down just on a padded kimono. After switching off the light, the woman went into a corner of the room, and there apparently changed into a nightgown.

I had wandered in a variety of places since running away from home, so I was accustomed to sleeping like this, and soon fell asleep. But it was my first time to stay with a woman. Sure enough, I did not sleep well. Dozing off, I would start to dream and promptly wake up. This happened countless times. In every dream I was being chased. As often happens in dreams, I had trouble running away. Chafing with impatience, I panted and gasped—and woke up. I remained still while one side of my head throbbed with a dull pain. I felt as though I had hardly slept at all. And I kept tossing and turning. But Kasahara did not turn even once all night, and never made a sound. It was clear to me that she had resigned herself to spending a sleepless night.

I had slept a little at least. When I woke up her futon had already been put away and she was not to be seen, probably cooking downstairs. After a while she came up the stairs, making them squeak. "Could you sleep?" she asked. "Yeah," I replied, a little dazzled.

We left the lodging house together when it was Kasahara's time to go to the office. The old woman downstairs in the kitchen stopped whatever she was doing and followed me with her eyes.

No sooner were we outside than Kasahara shouted "Ah—ah!" as if expelling in a single breath all the troubles that had been weighing on her since yesterday. Then she quietly added, "The old bitch!"

3

When I met S that evening and told him about last night, he said "that's bad" and arranged to rent a room. I found a house, got Suyama and Itō to gather some furniture, and decided to move right away. At first I was quite at a loss whether or not I should live in the same district where Kurata Industries was located. The same district would be rather dangerous, but a different district would be expensive to commute from. Of course in a situation like this a different district made more sense, but perhaps the police also thought that I had taken refuge in another district. Therefore it would not be bad to outwit them and remain in the same district. There is a precedent for this. A comrade presently living in Russia, on hearing that a comrade active in Kōtō had started a tactical rumor that he was often seen around the diametrically opposite Jōsai, objected that if he himself were active in Kōtō he would instead encourage a rumor that he was often seen around Kōtō. Since the spies around here did not yet know my face well, and since I had quit working at the factory, I decided for economic reasons to stay on in the same district.

Lodging on the second floor of a small trader's store was good. It was especially good if the owners were an old couple. Such people had little connection with our work, and limited understanding of their second-floor tenants' activities. Intellectual landlords would instantly sense that their tenants were not ordinary people just from a single glance at them or their belongings. But shopkeepers' homes were not subjected to frequent census taking or rude inquiries; the police came to their gates half as often and merely asked "Is there anything new?" The present lodging house belonged to an intermediate category. The lady of the house said that she once ran a geisha teahouse, and seemed to be someone's mistress.

Suyama and Itō soon brought in my things and I finally settled in, with a feeling of relief. However, one drawback was that there was another lodger in the room below. I needed to learn immediately what kind of a person this was. I went downstairs, to the toilet. The sliding door to my fellow lodger's room was open, and no one was there. Above all else I focused on the bookcase. This was the first thing I did whenever moving into a house where I was not the only lodger. A glance at the bookcase quickly gave me an idea of the kind of person who lived there. The bookcase was lined with extremely ordinary books. There were many books on geography and history, suggesting that the owner was a teacher someplace. On top of the desk was a volume of the *Complete Works of Japanese Literature.* I noticed that it was opened to the first page, which bore the photographs of left-wing writers like Kataoka Teppei and Hayama Yoshiki. However, it was the only book of that type; there seemed to be no others.

Among our friends, there are many cases of finding a place to live after much trouble only to discover that the owner worked for the police. To find out the owner's occupation early on was a stroke of luck, sometimes a full month went by before it became clear. In view of our own work, even a simple question like "What do you do, sir?" was not something we could ask lightly.

Asking the lady where the public bathhouse was located, I stepped out. This was the second stage of my investigation. Soap and towel in hand, I leisurely strolled down the street through which I would pass every day, surveying the nameplates of the houses that lined it. At the corner six or seven houses away, a nameplate read "Officer ——, National Police Agency." However, as it was affixed to the back gate of a large residence it did not call for very much concern. On the way back from the bath, I examined the local alleys and byways. Strangely, much of the factory zone in this city coexisted in tight proximity with an area of millionaires' mansions. Although my new place too was in the same district as Kurata Industries, it was in a silent neighborhood sequestered from the squalid street. Another good thing was that the long quiet street merged abruptly into a busy one so that if I returned home with additional errands to do I could leave the house and, followed or not, quickly melt into the crowd bustling along this street.

The window of my second-floor room opened onto a small balcony lined with poles for drying laundry. I saw that I could easily step over to my neighbor's balcony and from there cross a wall to a different house. I decided to buy a pair of *zōri* and put them on the balcony right outside the window. The only problem was that the houses in this area were closely packed together, like "under Parisian roofs," so that if I opened the window even a crack I risked becoming visible to the residents and second-floor tenants of five or six neighboring houses. Until I learned the occupations of all those people, I had to stay put and not show myself to anyone. I went downstairs for a chat. I thought I would try to acquaint myself with the neighborhood that way.

I learned that my neighbors included an office worker at a law firm, a *shamisen* teacher, a clerk at a second-floor stock brokerage, a domestic servants agency, seven or eight company employees, and some rich people whose houses all had pianos. To be able to learn so much about the neighborhood on my first evening here was a great success. With the possible exception of the gossipy agency, I had to admit that it was a rather pleasant environment.

Nonetheless, I knew from past experience that the possibility of a raid or other trouble necessitated finding an alternative place that I could quickly move to. No matter how safe a house looked, it by no means signified permanent safety. In fact, at the lodging before the most recent, coming back from a bath only a day after moving in I spotted a man in a suit standing in front of the house. There was only one street, and by the time I discovered him I was too close to back away. There was nothing to do but stroll swaying by with my towel shading my eyes, whistling the vaguely remembered tune of "Longing for the shadow of a dream, far, far away . . ." and keep on walking past the lodgings. The man in the suit seemed to look at me, and his watchful expression made me think he suspected something. After a while I glanced back, but the man was still standing there and looking my way. I stayed at a comrade's place that night. That comrade was experienced and concluded, first, that that was no stakeout, and, second, that it was impossible they would show up less than two days after my moving in without making a preliminary investigation. He sent someone to take a look the next day, and it turned out to be nothing. At any rate, it is always necessary to have a backup plan that enables a swift response to a sudden calamity. That is the favor I asked of Kasahara the next time I contacted her.

SOON I WAS working again. Itō Yoshi, who had taken Ōta's place, had lately grown outstandingly active, and I decided to support her. Only a few stay so intensely active when the storm of repression is raging. She had graduated from junior high school, but had worked at so many factories for so long that there was nothing of the schoolgirl about her. Since going underground she had always found her way into factories, and was arrested countless times. That made her strong. She was the exact opposite of those who, once they go underground, become absorbed with making organizational contacts on the streets, thereby becoming removed from the ambiance of actual workers' lives. Whenever Itō was arrested, her mother was summoned and she was handed over to her, but within half a day she would flee her home and resume her underground work. Her mother always begged her, "Don't go away anymore." When the daughter was arrested and the mother received a written order to come to the police station, she was delighted. Before returning home, she thanked the police countless times. The third or fourth time that Itō came home, she went to the public bath together with her mother, something she had not done in quite a while. She knew that her work would gradually grow more important, and that the police would no longer release her as easily as before. She was discreetly saying farewell. But at the bathhouse, the mother saw her daughter's naked body for the first time and her legs gave way under her. Itō's body was covered with black and blue bruises inflicted by repeated torture. According to Itō, after seeing her body the mother suddenly began to sympathize with her daughter, and to understand her. "I'm never going to bow my head again to the police who did this to my daughter!" she angrily exclaimed. Up until then, if Itō ran short of funds for transportation or living expenses and in desperation sent someone to ask her for money, the mother refused saying, "I'll give her no money until she comes home." From then on, however, if she asked for two yen she got four, if she asked for five she got seven or eight, along with a message, "Everything's fine at home." To everyone she met, the mother now said, "Beating an innocent girl like that just because she is working for the poor—I'm sure it's the police who are in the wrong."

How can someone be expected to organize massively all sorts of people in a factory, if one cannot convince even one's own mother? There was much truth to that, and Itō seemed to prove it. I greatly admired her ability to attract unorganized workers. Whenever she was free, she attended revues in Asakusa, went to Japanese movies, and read proletarian novels. She then promptly and skillfully used her experiences as conversation topics in talking with the unorganized. (Incidentally, she was outstandingly pretty and even when she said nothing, male workers on the way home from the factory invited her to Shirokiya, Matsuzakaya, or other department stores, and bought her various things. She used such opportunities too with composure and great skill.)

She was a gentle woman and listened attentively to people's opinions, but when it came to the views she herself had acquired after sifting them through many layers of experience, she was obstinate as a rock. We needed women comrades like her now. They were especially vital because seventy percent of the eight hundred workers at Kurata Industries were women.

In addition to Kurata Industries, I was also working with the regional committee, and now that Whiskers was almost certainly out of action, I needed once again to take up that part of the work. Suddenly I grew busy. However, having a settled hideout and being no longer engaged at the factory, I had plenty of time to plan my daily life and was able to set to work more energetically than ever.

While I was at the factory, I understood the everyday "movements" taking place within it, and was able to reflect them promptly in the next day's fliers. Now Suyama and Itō had taken charge of carrying out such work. At first I had worried about the consequences of being away from the factory. But interestingly, far from feeling cut off, I felt just the opposite by maintaining a close and systematic contact with them. Watching from a distance, I realized that Suyama and Itō had all their attention snatched away by immediate events (just like what happened to me) and were not seeing the gradual developments that diverged from routine. Indeed, their way of observation was extremely detailed as if they were watching a framed area through a magnifying glass. Of course I saw this partly because I enjoyed a good view from my post on the regional committee. As a result, I learned that I didn't need to fear becoming isolated.

The first thing I noticed was that in a factory of as many as eight hundred workers, a cell of only four or five members was struggling with all its might to conduct its activities. Of course without the mighty efforts of those four or five it would be impossible to mobilize the factory as a whole, but in order for them to do this it was essential to focus concretely on organizing and uniting the workers en masse. If a practical plan to that end were not carefully thought out, all the efforts of the cell members would amount to tilting at windmills, and go nowhere. In fact, female temporary workers had been trying to set up social gatherings, concerned that despite having gotten to know each other they might scatter and break up. "Just our sleeves brushing against each other is a sign of a tie from a previous life," they said to each other. Although the company deliberately incited quarrels between temporary and full-time workers over wages and conditions, some of them nonetheless formed mutual assistance groups. These were just two examples. However, if the cell made a great endeavor to enlarge and organize such spontaneous groups and if it learned to work *inside them* (and not just among its own four or five members), it would be quite possible to mobilize the entire factory on that approaching day when the company was to fire *six hundred* workers.

Because Kurata Industries produced war supplies such as gas masks, parachutes, and airship fuselages, the importance of organizing it now that war had started was particularly obvious. Once the war broke out we started putting special emphasis on organizing war-oriented factories, mainly metal and chemical industries, and the transportation industry that moved troops and weapons. That was why Suyama, Ōta, Itō, I, and others infiltrated Kurata Industries. However, as we were all temporary workers we would be fired in less than half a month. Within that time we needed to build at least a basic foundation for organizing. To do that, we needed to win over the full-time workers. That way even if we were fired, we would be able to continue our work unhindered, through maintaining close links from the outside with the remaining organizers. I therefore decided to promote ties between full-time and temporary workers by bringing them in touch with each other using even the most trivial conversation topics. But at the same time organizing the temporary workers was important as well, because they would seek out and enter other factories after getting fired, and thus constituted a sort of seed. Consequently we had to stay in prolonged contact with every single one of them. ——We needed to accomplish all this work in the very short time that remained.

TWO OR THREE days later I saw Suyama in the street, and he came toward me waving his hand in an odd way. He often did that when something had happened. His impatience always manifested itself in his gestures. Something is up, I thought. I turned into an alley and was going to turn into another, as was our custom, before falling into step beside him, but he came trotting up and greeted me from behind.

"We received information from Ōta!" he said. No wonder he's excited, I thought.

The message came from the inside, and had been brought by a gangster. The entire area around the railway tracks near Kurata Industries is a red-light district. Brothels with round windows line the alleys that stretch on both sides of the tracks. In the evenings night stalls open for business, and the place grows crowded. Gangsters belonging to a certain crime family infest the whole district. When "Crazy Goro" was taken away to a police station on charges of extortion, he happened to be put in the same cell as Ōta. And when Crazy Goro was about to be released, Ōta asked him to take a message to our acquaintance T.

According to the message, I was being pursued very closely; they even knew the sort of round-rimmed glasses I wore. He also wanted me to be very careful because they were saying that a guy like that could be caught easily by putting a minimal price on his head.

On hearing this, I said, "It's because Ōta told them everything that I'm being pursued."

"That's right," Suyama said with a laugh. "Unless a spy saw you face to face and recognized you, how would he know what sort of glasses you wear?"

We concluded that Ōta had written the message in order to rationalize what he had done. What we really wanted to know was just what Ōta had said to the police, and in how much detail. That would determine the kind of measures we urgently needed to take. I told myself that as things stood Ōta would no doubt be out soon, but that a person with his attitude called for maximum caution.

But at the factory, the sight of Ōta dragged away from his workplace gave people a considerable shock. So *he* was the person who had been bringing in the fliers, thought everyone, feeling sympathetic and moved. Moreover, the terrible *Communist Party* that the supervisor was constantly denouncing as "extremist" and "treasonous" turned out to be Ōta. They had always thought of its existence as invisible and distant from them, so the realization that it could mean Ōta, who worked together with them every day ironing parachute cloth, struck them all as quite astonishing. "Ōta was always looking out for us and that's why they took him away, so let's take up a collection for him and send a few things to the police station." Itō Yoshi promptly took this approach to the Ōta incident and began to gather money and goods. Seven people contributed money, including a few women who especially liked Ōta. Yoshi moved from talking about Ōta to talking about the fliers, about factory work, and so on, and finally succeeded in making eight friends. Thanks to her long life at factories, she knew what topics attracted people's attention. Because nearly all the parachute workers were women, Ōta was rather popular. She deftly grasped that, too. Choosing the most assertive among the eight, she formed "Kurata Industries Women Volunteers," and they took the collected items to the police station. The package contained underpants, an undershirt, a lined kimono, an obi, a towel, toilet paper, and one yen in cash. After making the women wait the police told them to take it back, saying that Ōta was grateful for the gift but felt unable to accept it. Unaccustomed to such treatment, the women did as they were told. Itō, familiar with police tricks, took the package to the station again and forced them to accept it. —— But later, when she heard about Ōta from Suyama, she flared up with anger.

In his inconstancy and servility, Ōta was quite likely thinking *only of himself.* But he did not understand that this would cast a large dark shadow over many workers. He was an individualist, a defeatist, and a traitor. He told the police both about my position, of which they were not yet aware, and about my recent activities. As a result, my work with my companions at Kurata Industries would be ten times more difficult from now on. —— We were thus caught in a crossfire, hurt not only by enemy spies but by our own "rotten elements." Today I didn't have enough money for transportation, so I returned home on foot. As I walked, my nerves felt on edge. Every man I passed looked to me like a spy. I looked over my shoulder any number of times. According to Ōta's "information," they were watching this district very closely in an effort to arrest me. Whiskers had earlier told me that they could receive fifty yen for arresting one of us. Attracted by such bait, they must be working like mad. ——But being edgy like this was apt to be all the more dangerous, I thought. I had to keep out of their clutches. I stopped by the Shirukoya sweetshop for a leisurely rest, and then continued on home.

We have no path of retreat. Our entire lives are immersed in nothing but work. That sets us apart from people who lead their lives legally. A treasonous act causes us to feel anger and hatred with our entire being. Because at present we have no private life, our emotions dominate our entire existence.

I must have been in a bad mood. Though I usually make a point of greeting my landlady when I enter or leave the house, this time I went up to the second floor without a word.

"Damn!" I said as I sat down in front of my desk.

NOT LONG AFTER that, I suddenly became very close to Kasahara. Even I thought it was strange. In various ways she promptly accomplished everything I asked her to do. Following Ōta's betrayal I decided to move to a different district but since I could hardly walk around in search of a suitable house, I asked Kasahara to do it for me. At the same time I thought about living together with Kasahara. It was convenient for the sake of carrying out illegal work securely over a long period.

An unemployed man living alone in a lodging house and going out every night as soon as it got dark—this was a perfect set of factors for arousing suspicion. Particularly so because I averaged three or four contacts per night and, as I could not loiter outside when there was an hour's interval between them, I briefly came home only to go out again later. At such times my landlady looked at me very strangely indeed. "How is he managing to feed himself?" her face seemed to say. As things stood, I was afraid that when patrolmen came by on a register-checking round they would soon guess what I was up to.

Because Kasahara was working for a company, she left the house each morning at a fixed hour. Consequently even if I appeared to be idle it would be assumed that I was living on my wife's salary. The world trusts only those who have a fixed job. —— And so I asked Kasahara whether or not she would live with me. Once again she suddenly looked at me with those big eyes of hers—they grew larger as she gazed at my face. But she did not say anything. After a while I urged her to reply. She kept silent. That day she returned home without saying a word.

The next time we met she seemed to be sitting before me more tensely than ever before. She had drawn in her shoulders, placed her hands on her knees, and kept her body stiff. There was no trace of the woman of that first morning, after I had stayed at her place, when she had stepped out and shouted "Ah—ah, what a bitch!" with a male cheerfulness. I gazed at her in wonder.

We talked about various tasks. She fidgeted at every pause in our conversation. We both avoided the earlier topic and kept on postponing it. After we had finished discussing the things to do, I finally brought it up. —— She had made up her mind.

Shortly after that, Kasahara and I moved together into a new lodging house. It was at some distance from Kurata Industries, but since Suyama and Itō were of a "rank" that allowed them to take a train I had them come out here for meetings. That way I was able to save on transportation, and to reduce the risks of travel.

4

When Suyama had something to do in the area where my mother lived, he sometimes visited her. At such times he told her I was well, and brought me news about her.

When I left my home I was forced to go underground so suddenly that I had no time to explain to my mother what was going on. Around six o'clock that evening I had gone out to meet my usual contact. Although I was doing illegal work, I was active within the broad legal setting as a member of an opposition group in a corruptly led union. But the comrade whom I met at six told me that F who worked together with me had suddenly been arrested. Though the reason for his arrest was still unclear, I as his close associate should go underground right away. I felt rather stunned. If they learned about me through F, it would do more than affect the revolutionary opposition within the corrupt union. It would involve the top-dog level. I said I'd return home to pack a few things and get ready to leave. I thought I had enough time for that. But the comrade (it was Whiskers) said, "Be careful how you joke." His tone was light yet he firmly forbade me to return, saying that someone else would be sent to get my things and that there was nothing to do but leave with only the clothes I happened to be wearing. "It isn't a school trip, you know," he said with a laugh. Whiskers was one of those rare people who can say the toughest things in an affable manner. He told me of a comrade who having finally run out of places to go underground returned home thinking, "Surely tonight will be safe," only to be arrested the next morning. He also told me of another comrade who went out to take care of some important matters despite plentiful reasons to fear the risk of surveillance, and was arrested. Whiskers seldom spelled out what one shouldn't do. He simply narrated relevant examples. Having evidently lived through a variety of experiences, he possessed a wealth of stories.

I borrowed the five yen that Whiskers had with him, and moved to the house of a married couple I knew. —— Sure enough, the next morning four spies from the central government office and from the S police station turned up at my house to arrest me. Startled, my mother who knew nothing told them that I had gone out the previous evening and had not yet returned. Thereupon the most "distinguished"-looking among them commented that I must have fled with the speed of wind.

I have never been back. That is why when Suyama visited her bearing my news, she welcomed him into the house as though her own son had returned, offered him tea, and gazed intently at his face. Suyama scratched his head in embarrassment. Whenever he paused in telling her of the things that had happened since I left, she urged him on with "And then? And then?" Since my mother had hardly been able so sleep nights, the skin under her eyes was swollen and slack, her cheeks hollow, and her neck so thin and wilted it seemed barely able to support her head.

In the end mother asked, "How many more days before Yasuji comes back?" Suyama had no idea how to reply to this. How many *days*? Yet gazing at her slender and unsteady neck, he found himself quite unable to tell her the truth, and said, "Well, it probably won't be very long . . ."

Of course my mother had already had to get used to my being taken away by the police countless times and to my twenty-nine-day detention stretches. The year before last was particularly hard: I was imprisoned for a full eight months. During that time mother often brought me things in jail. But she couldn't understand why this time I hadn't meekly allowed the police to arrest me. She worried that running would only make things worse later.

I may have been too heartless toward my mother up to that time, but I hope that ultimately the nature of my unbreakable commitment will have made things clear to her. Nonetheless, as I see my sixty-year-old mother draw near to understanding my own feelings, I think I can discern a struggle within her heart that is a hundred times more painful than the hardships we suffer in carrying out our movement. My mother is a poor peasant who never even went to elementary school. Yet while I was still at home she was starting to learn how to read and write. Putting on her glasses, she would slide her legs under the quilt-covered heater, place a small board on top of it, hunch her shoulders and begin to practice using a pencil and the reverse sides of my scribbled manuscript pages that she had collected. "What are you starting up now?" I asked with a laugh. When I was in prison the year before last, mother had been unable to send me a single letter because she could not write at all. "That was my only regret," she told me. Mother understood that after coming out I had become even more deeply involved in the movement. No doubt I would be arrested again. Even if I remained free for a time, I was out on bail and would be imprisoned again once a penalty was decided on. Mother was learning to write in order to be ready when the time came. Just before I vanished, her handwriting was large and uneven but I noticed with surprise that it was quite legible. Yet when she asked Suyama "Can't I meet him?" and he replied that it would be better not to, she responded, "I probably can't write to him either, can I?" When I heard this from Suyama my mother's emotions struck me with a painful directness.

When Suyama was leaving mother handed him a lined kimono, an undershirt, some underpants, socks, and similar articles. Then she asked him to wait a little and went to the kitchen. She bustled about for a while, making Suyama wonder what she was up to, and then brought out about five boiled eggs. She asked him to tell me that since one could buy three or four eggs for ten sen, I should choose fresh ones and make sure to eat them. I shared the boiled eggs with Suyama and Itō. "Hey, Itō, let's have just one," Suyama said with a laugh. "We don't want his mom to get mad at us later." Itō was dabbing at her eyes, hoping we wouldn't notice.

I decided that the next time Suyama dropped by my house I would have him say clearly that I would not be able to return for four or five years. What was keeping me from returning was not my work in the movement but the agents of the rich—the police. I decided to have him tell her to bear no grudges against me but rather against this upside-down society. If instead of being vague I could make her understand things clearly, it might strengthen her resistance all the more. When my companions were arrested by the police, and their families were told that they were involved with the Communist Party, some of the wives and mothers denied that their husbands and sons had anything to do with such "dark" or "criminal" activities. But if they really *were* involved with the Party, then their own family members were in effect denouncing their work as "dark" and "criminal." My sixty-year-old mother must not think or speak like that, I thought. My mother has been living in the depths of hardship for more than fifty years. If I spoke clearly, I thought she would be able to understand.

According to Suyama, my mother listened to my message in silence. Then switching the topic, she put a question to him. Being sixty and all, if she were to become sick and have only a short time to live would I be able to return even for just a bit? Suyama had not expected such a question, and didn't know how to answer. Later I told him that I would not be able to return even at such a time.

"I can't tell her that!" Suyama said with a troubled face.

I knew that this was cruel toward my mother, but it could not be helped. I also thought it was necessary to tell her all this in order to awaken within her heart a lifelong hatred of the ruling class—her entire life truly called for it. Therefore I emphatically asked him to reiterate that it was the ruling class that would prevent me even from being present at my mother's deathbed. —— Nonetheless, my heart was beating hard when I met Suyama that day.

"How did it go?" I asked him.

"I'll tell you."

My mother had recently been losing weight, and her face had grown pale. She asked him whether or not it would be possible to meet me once.

I suddenly recalled Watanabe Masanosuke's mother. "Watamasa," as we called him for short, was, as you'll remember, the party's young general secretary who chose to die rather than surrender. When Watamasa first went underground, his mother (now the mother of the entire proletariat) asked his comrades, "Won't I be able to see Masa any more?" The comrades replied, "You won't." I told Suyama about it.

"I understand that," he said, "but meet her somewhere at least once, without revealing your whereabouts."

Suyama had been deeply affected by my mother's appearance.

"They're looking for me as it is. What if something goes wrong?"

Yet in the end I was persuaded by Suyama. Resolving to be very careful, I chose a place in a district that we never use, and decided to have Suyama bring me there by car. When the time came, I went out to a small restaurant we had agreed upon. Mother was sitting at the far side of the table, slightly away from the edge. Her face looked sad. I noticed that she was wearing her best kimono. Somehow that touched me deeply.

We didn't talk very much. Mother took a cloth-wrapped package from under the table and extracted from it bananas, beef, and boiled eggs. Suyama soon went away. Before he did, Mother pressed him to accept some bananas and eggs.

After a while Mother gradually began to talk more. "I'm so happy to see that your face looks a little rounder than when you were at home," she told me. Lately she had been dreaming almost every night that I had become emaciated, or that I had been arrested and was being punished (her word for tortured) by the police. Such dreams woke her up all the time, she said.

My brother-in-law who lives in Ibaraki had said he would look after her, Mother said, so I shouldn't worry about her. Our conversation having taken this turn, I repeated in person the things that up till now I had been communicating through Suyama. "I understand," Mother said with a little laugh.

At some point I realized that Mother was somehow ill at ease. She seemed too jittery to pursue any topic quietly to its conclusion. ——In the end she told me the reason: though she could barely wait to meet me, now that she had seen me she was terribly worried that I might get arrested while we were together, and so she wanted to go back. No wonder that when customers came in and sat at other tables she sometimes commented, "That customer looks all right," or "I don't like the looks of that one." When she unintentionally spoke in the same voice she used at home, I cautioned her to speak a little more quietly. Rather than meet me and suffer such anxiety, she said, it would have been better had she contented herself with knowing that I was safely doing my work.

As she was about to leave, Mother told me that though she intended to live another twenty years until she was eighty, given her age there was no guarantee that the next day wouldn't be her last. If I learned that she had died, I might be tempted to come home, and since that would be dangerous she had decided that I would not be notified. There may be nothing more important to an ordinary person than the matter of a loved one's presence or absence at the moment of death. This holds even truer for a sixty-year-old mother. The enormity of my mother's resolution gave me a powerful shock. I kept silent. That was all I could do.

As we stepped outside, Mother assured me from behind that she could return by herself and urged me to be careful on the way back. And she suddenly said in a worried voice, "You're still doing that with your shoulders. Anyone who knows you can recognize you right away, even from behind. You must learn to walk without swinging your shoulders."

"Ah, everybody tells me that."

"It's true. Anyone can tell right away!"

As if talking to herself, Mother kept repeating "Anyone can tell right away" until we parted.

THIS WAS HOW I severed the ties of flesh and blood—the last remaining path of retreat to private life. Unless a new world were to come into being one of these years (and this is what we were struggling for), I would not live with Mother again.

AROUND THIS TIME we received a message from Whiskers.

First Whiskers had spent just five days at the T station before being taken to K station where he was detained for twenty-nine days. A Korean worker who had shared a cell with him brought the message to T's place where Suyama and Itō were frequent visitors, and that is how we first learned about him. In the message he wrote that he had been arrested at his hideout though he had no idea how they found him, and advised us to rebuild our group without ever becoming impatient, or overworking like packhorses, or being opportunistic. He had underlined the words "impatient," "like packhorses," and "opportunistic."

Reading his message, Suyama, Itō, I, and others felt ashamed that we were hardly so diligent as to deserve being cautioned against impatience or working like packhorses.

Whiskers had parents and siblings at home, and a message came from them, too. It was addressed to me, using a name I am called only among ourselves. —— "Intending to create a blank record, I kept on saying 'I don't know' to everything." When we all saw this we said, "This clears away the bad aftertaste of the Ōta case!"

Undisturbed by traitors or opportunists, we firmly believed that a correct course of action drew a bold red line through any obstacles.

As Whiskers was always so fond of pointing out, uttering a single word during interrogation meant violating our own iron rule to say nothing and submitting to the enemy's rule to make us say everything. A communist and a party member, he said, must of course follow our own iron rule and not that of the enemy. Now he was demonstrating this in actuality.

"Yoshi, have you heard of Shavarov?" asked Suyama.

"He's a Marxist."

"Your scrapbook again?" I said with a laugh.

"After Shavarov was arrested, he held out for seven months without saying anything. Then he said, 'For an ordinary person, there is no better tactic than to make no statement at all, the way I stuck it out for those seven months.'"

Hearing this, Itō said, "But our woman comrade who was recently featured in a proletarian play stuck it out till the end without even telling them her name and address, which they already knew. She outdid Shavarov!"

She said it as though she were talking about herself. Suyama scratched his head, looking as if he were vexed.

As a resolution of our cell's meeting we decided to implement the "ordinary person" policy of not replying to enemy interrogation with even a single word. We also decided to write a report to a higher level, proposing that the resolution be adopted by the entire party.

According to a message that T received later, Whiskers was shunted off from K station to O station where he was tortured by seven or eight men who beat him continuously from morning till evening for three days. Tying his hands from behind, they suspended him from the ceiling of the interrogation chamber and beat him from below with bamboo swords. Whenever he lost consciousness they forced some water into his mouth, and repeated the process dozens of times. But he never said a word.

"How hateful!" said Itō when she saw the note. She herself had twice been stripped stark naked by the police, and then beaten and jabbed with the tip of a bamboo sword.

Our comrades' heroic struggles brace us up. At times when I'm too sleepy to do the work that must be done by tomorrow and want to go to bed, I think of the people on the inside and I persevere. Mere sleepiness turns to nothing when I remember them. What is happening to them now? Are they being beaten? I go on to finish my absurdly easy work. Our daily lives are linked in various ways with the lives of our comrades on the inside. Although the inside and the outside are different, from the standpoint of our struggle against the ruling class there is no difference between them at all.

5

Itō made eight or nine friends among the temporary workers. ——At Kurata Industries, the firing of six hundred temporary workers became more and more certain, and it became clear to everyone (after the Communist Party fliers had been distributed) that the ten-yen bonus was unlikely to be paid. The sense of anxiety dovetailed with our own objectives, and a group that resembled a circle of friends came into being more easily than we had thought.

On the way home from the factory, the women were feeling very hungry. Itō, Tsuji, and Sasaki (Tsuji and Sasaki were the ablest among the group of friends) invited everyone to stop for *shiruko* and soba. Worn out from having to work standing all day, they all ate nothing but sweets. In loud voices, free for the first time from the din of machinery, they talked over the day's events.

Itō's method worked as follows. Everyone recognized her as "one of those." Consequently even if she talked about "those things" at a restaurant, it did not strike anyone as particularly awkward. Tsuji and Sasaki were her "secret assistants." When everyone got together, they asked her various questions, at times from a reactionary standpoint, thus giving her a chance to discuss them. At first it did not go well:

they could not coordinate the rhythm, they faltered, or went round and round the same topic. One time the assistants' disguise nearly came off, and it scared them. After stepping out of the restaurant that time, they noticed that all three were soaked with sweat. Nonetheless, after a few tries they grew noticeably skillful. Giving no thought to their increased skill, the assistants could effortlessly attract other women workers simply through their role as friends. It was essential for the assistants to understand clearly the ideas and prejudices that ordinary women workers of low consciousness were likely to hold.

When women workers gathered, they tended to bring up only such topics as who was odd, who paired off with whom, and who did not. Itō told me this once when we met. The fact that Kinu who worked making parachutes had received a love letter from Yoshimura, a regular worker who made masks, a letter that said "Let's enjoy a long talk someplace quiet" became a subject of excited commentary as soon as everyone left the factory. It was the only conversation topic at the soba restaurant, too. Since receiving that letter, Kinu had suddenly started powdering her face more heavily, had hung a round mirror on a string from the front of her obi, and was taking a peek at it throughout the workday—the talk of this was endless. However, a rather bright woman worker named Shige said that Kinu had complained to her bitterly, saying, "He says he wants us to have a long talk somewhere quiet, but there's always this clanging noise in the factory, and when I finish the night work at nine or ten I'm totally worn out. And he gets done around seven so there's no time for us to meet at all." "That's such a pity," someone said. At this, the assistant Sasaki observed, "So, the way things are, we can't even whisper words of love!" Everyone began commenting, "That's right" and "That's true!"

"First of all, you can't even whisper about love if they make you work as long as this. And wouldn't it also be nice if you were able to go out to a movie once in a while with that special someone?"

"Yes, it sure would!" everybody said, laughing.

"Not that we can do much with the kind of daily wage we're getting!"

"That's right. If we don't get them to shorten the time and to raise the wages, we won't even be able to whisper about love!"

"This company is heartless, and that's the truth!"

"Our supervisor was yelling at us today, saying things like: 'You know what time it is right now? It's wartime! You have to think of yourselves as a part of the army, and keep your noses to the grindstone! If the war gets any worse, we'll have to have you work your butts off at the same pay rate as the troops! That's what you'll do for your country.' That's what Baldy was saying!"

Even Itō was surprised by this. Before she herself had noticed it, the talk of "whispering about love" had transformed itself into a discussion of the workers' treatment by the company. The "assistant," too, was astonished. Without any prodding, the conversation had turned into an attack on their maltreatment by the company.

I heard about this from Itō, and it made sense. The outbreak of war had a terrible impact on workers' strength everywhere, and the exploitation of women workers—though they do the same work as men, or more—drastically intensified. At present, even "whispering about love" was quite impossible without an economic solution. Everyone felt this whether they put it into words or not.

These days Itō often invited people to go to see an interesting play. When everyone was trying to decide between an Asakusa revue and a movie that starred Kataoka Chiezō, Itō and her assistants rooted for the Leftwing Theater.

After hearing Itō's report I suggested adding a male worker to her group. If I contacted Suyama, it would not be very difficult to arrange. Even a single male worker would change the group's enthusiasm by joining, and it was also most important to bring a full-time worker into a circle that only had temporary workers. Itō agreed with the idea.

In order to prepare for the firing of six hundred workers, we decided that instead of putting out newspaper-style fliers, we would set up a separate and independent production of fliers and of a factory newspaper.

When I asked Suyama to come up with a title for the factory newspaper, he said with a twitch of his nose, "How about *The Love Parachute?*"

It was decided to call the factory newspaper *The Mask.* Since

I was now free from factory work, I took over the editing from S, collected reports from Itō and Suyama, wrote manuscripts based on them, and forwarded them to the printer. Early in the mornings, notified by the printer, Itō would pick up the copies. I kept in daily contact with Suyama and Itō, studied the paper's effectiveness, and promptly incorporated the lessons learned in the next issue of *The Mask*.

Listening to Itō and Suyama's reports, I realized that the company too was refining its countermeasures moment by moment. At present they were eerily silent about the ten-yen bonus and the dismissals. Clearly, they were entering some sort of second stage in their planning. Of course we understood that they were devising a stratagem to dispense with the ten-yen bonus and to dispose deftly of the dismissals. But we had to gain a clear grasp of what their stratagem actually entailed, and disclose it in front of everyone. If we just kept on repeating the same things, everyone would break away from us. Our own tactics had to adapt accurately to the zigzagging tactics of the bourgeoisie. A look at our earlier failures showed that although at first we were always a threat to the enemy, once they caught on to our method they looked for a way to subvert it. We, however, would stick to the same course, oblivious to what the enemy was trying to do. Seizing the opportunity, the enemy would rout us at the last moment.

Indeed, Itō noticed that and said, "Something is strange lately." But she couldn't pinpoint what was wrong.

The next day Suyama brought a small slip of paper.

> Notice
> Thanks to everyone's great diligence, the company's work is progressing extremely well, and I wish to celebrate this with you. I think you will all agree that a war can never be fought by soldiers alone. If all of you were not working with your whole might making masks, parachutes, and airship fuselages, our country could never win. Therefore, even if the work is a little hard at times, I want us to be as resolute as the soldiers who are fighting the war under the hail of enemy bullets. I urge you all to be resolute.
>
> FACTORY MANAGER

"Our work has entered its second stage!" said Suyama.

In accordance with the initial agreement, the factory was going to dismiss some six hundred workers at a certain juncture in the work. Now, however, it changed course and said that it would transfer some two hundred workers who had excellent track records into the full-time workforce. It wanted everyone to work as hard as they could. It began to spread rumors to that effect throughout the factory.

Suyama and I groaned. The rumors clearly aimed to disrupt the organizing of resistance until the very moment of the firings. On the other hand, the "Notice" with its bait of possibly offering full-time work was designed to make people work their hardest and to exploit them more intensively.

Suyama had copied the notice to help us expose the true nature of the scheme. In this way we learned the second stage of the company's tactics.

SUYAMA, ITŌ, AND I kept in daily contact with each other. But since detailed countermeasures could not be planned through brief contact alone, we decided that the three of us should sit down together once a week. Itō took care of providing a house. Luckily, Suyama and Itō were living a legal existence, but for me it was rather dangerous to stay seated in a fixed place for two or three hours, and so I needed to be very careful. Itō would tell me the place when we met in the street, and after checking out the area to make sure it was safe, I would have her and Suyama go there first, and then go there myself by a different route. I would not enter the place directly on arrival but watch it and wait. If there was nothing wrong, Itō would signal me.

One evening as a lukewarm breeze was wafting from the asphalt that had been steaming all day, I left the house carrying a bulletin and pamphlets to hand over to Suyama and Itō. That night we were going to sit down and talk. As I walked, I saw two policemen standing at a street corner. At the next corner, there were three policemen. This is not good, I thought. I was carrying *things*, and didn't know what to do about tonight's meeting. Walking on still undecided, I passed a police box and here too stood two or three policemen. Surprisingly, they had fastened their hats with chinstraps. I didn't want to turn back, but there was no help for it. My pace faltered a little. One of the patrolmen at the police box looked my way, and seemed about to head toward me. I immediately tried to look lost, touched a hand to my hat, and asked, "Is S town this way? Or . . ."

The policeman gave me a disagreeable glance. "S town is this way."

"Ah, thank you very much."

I began to walk in that direction. Having gone a little way, I casually turned my head and saw the same policeman following me with his eyes and discussing something with two others. "Damn!" I thought, slapping my hands against the pockets that held the bulletin and the pamphlets. "He must be annoyed to lose a fifty-yen reward!"

Still anxious, I finally returned home. The next morning I saw in the newspaper that a murder had been committed. We often suffered by-blows from unrelated incidents. But they tended to turn such incidents into pretexts for "hunting Reds." That they growled "We got a byproduct!" each time this happened proved it. According to S, foreign magazines wrote that in Japan there was neither freedom to walk outside late at night, nor freedom to chat leisurely in a coffee shop without being forced to undergo a bureaucratic inspection—and it was true. Such inspections were especially intended as an attack against us.

I always paid attention to newspapers, and before going out morning or evening checked to see whether anything had happened in the area where I wanted to go. I read with particular thoroughness articles on the arrests of murderers or criminals who had been on the run. At such times I read not only the paper I was subscribing to, but also had Kasahara buy various others, and carefully read them too. One time I read an article about a criminal who had been hiding for seven years, and I found it full of good information. Every morning I read such articles first.

Currently I was engaged in a socialist competition with S, N, and other underground companions. We called it the "Arrest-free five-year plan." The longer it took to carry out the plan (six years, seven years) the higher our grades got, and so our slogan was "Six years with the five-year plan!" Consequently we could not leave our everyday conduct to chance, but had to base it on scientific reasoning.

Kasahara sometimes bought a copy of *New Youth* at a secondhand bookshop and told me to read it. At times I even found myself seriously reading detective stories.

The next day I went to our regularly scheduled meeting, and when Suyama saw me he exclaimed, "I'm so glad, I'm so glad!" All he had been able to think of, he said, was that I had been arrested (because I never missed meetings), and until actually seeing my face he had been imagining the worst. I told him about the by-blow received the previous day.

"You've made it: Six years with the five-year plan!" he said with a laugh.

"Just barely . . ."

Because I had been unable to come the previous day, Suyama had made the arrangements for today's meeting. The place was Itō's lodging house. She was about to move out in a day or two so she decided to put it to use. There were as many as seven or eight lodgers, making the conditions less than ideal. If I needed to pee, I had decided not to go downstairs to the toilet but to use a chamber pot Itō kept for use in case she were ill. It would be disastrous if I were to meet in the toilet one of her housemates who might know me.

Telling the other two to look away, I went to the corner of the room and relieved myself. Itō's shoulders were shaking with laughter.

"It stinks!" Suyama made a show of holding his nose.

"It's Kirin Draft!" I said, pushing the chamber pot further into the corner and making them laugh.

We knew that Kurata Industries had at last launched its final offensive. This was evident, for example, from Itō's report. A woman working together with Itō in the parachute section had been reading the third issue of *The Mask* this morning, when a male worker who had joined the section just four or five days earlier suddenly snatched the paper out of her hands and struck her. Whenever *The Mask* or the fliers appeared, everyone watched out for the supervisor and not for their fellow workers, and so the woman had let down her guard. Witnessing the incident, Itō found it rather strange and decided to check up on the man. She later learned from a cleaning woman that he was a member of the local Young Men's Association and an army veteran who had been expressly hired after the war began. It became evident through observing him that he had colleagues in Factory Number 1 and Factory Number 3. There were times even during working hours when he left his machine and went out to the other factories. The supervisor clearly saw him yet said nothing. We also learned that followers of Kiyokawa and Atsuta (leaders of the Masses Party–affiliated "Workmates' Club") were lately becoming increasingly visible within Kurata Industries. They had long been present but had not been active until now.

These days, oddly enough, the Workmates' Club was starting to move a little. Also, since it was a time of national emergency "when the grave responsibility of our work demanded that we work harder and more intensively than workers in other industries," they were trying, it was rumored, to form a chapter of the Military Veterans Association within Kurata Industries. They seemed to have the approval of the factory management, and it was certain that the veterans had been specially hired and were being assisted by one or two members of the Workmates' Club. However, it was also clear that because the company's open support for such a policy would render it rather ineffective, they were scheming to make it appear as though it had emerged spontaneously from among the workers.

"What do you think?" I asked Suyama.

He replied that he wasn't sure yet, but after a moment's thought added that he had recently seen men who walked around during lunchtime talking enthusiastically about the war. "I thought of it just now, thanks to Itō's report," he said. The times being what they were, everyone had been talking about the war—whether relating what they had heard, proudly and volubly expressing their own artless thoughts, or speaking of it with utter dejection. But now it was different: there seemed to be those who wandered about discussing the war in a deliberate and inflammatory fashion. —— A closer look made it unquestionably clear that the other side was launching an all-out campaign.

In order to win, we had to have an accurate and objective understanding of the enemy's strength. They knew now that merely pressuring the employees from above and subjecting their comings and goings to surveillance by police agents was insufficient, and thought that as a third line of defense they needed to obstruct our organizing inroads by attacking us from within the workforce itself. That is why the Workmates' Club was becoming active, and aggressively trying to organize chapters of the Young Men's Association and the Military Veterans Association inside the factory. Precisely because this was a factory (and a war supplies factory at that) the conditions for organizing such chapters were dangerously favorable. We had to conclude that we were presently confronting a three-pronged concentration of enemy power.

According to Suyama, the method used by those who roamed around the factory talking about the war had gone beyond simple appeals to "loyalty and patriotism" or exhortations to kill Chinks because they were doing evil things. Unlike earlier wars, they claimed, the present war was not being fought so that Mitsui, Mitsubishi, and other corporations could erect gigantic factories in the occupied territories; it was being fought *to create a way out for the dispossessed.* Once we took Manchuria, we would exclude the big capitalists and set up a monarchy of our own. The nation's unemployed would rush off to Manchuria, and some day not a single unemployed person would remain in Japan. *There was not a single unemployed person in Russia, and we too must become the same.* Therefore, they said, the present war was a war for the good of the proletariat, and we too had to work as industriously as we possibly could at the jobs that we had been given.

At lunch, Kiyokawa and Atsuta of the Workers' Club argued with the workers from the Young Men's Association and the Military Veterans Association, insisting that the current war ultimately aimed to let big capitalists carry out new exploitation in the colonies. Nevertheless, Kiyokawa said, this war was bringing profits to the proletariat in other ways. For instance, factories producing metal and chemical war supplies were enjoying such prosperity that no matter how many workers they hired it was never enough—and this boom was also obvious from the skyrocketing prices of the so-called "war stocks." A share of Imperial Gunpowder stock, originally valued at four yen, had more than doubled to nine yen; Ishikawajima Shipbuilding's stock had gone from five yen to twenty-five yen; and the market price of antimony used in the production of shells and bullets had shot up from some twenty yen to one hundred yen. Furthermore, though Germany had lost the World War and was ruined, the Krupp steel factories were making a clear profit ten times higher than in peacetime. Since our lives too were bound to benefit as much, it was no use to oppose war indiscriminately, a war must instead be utilized to the limit. Such was the opinion held by Kiyokawa and Atsuta. Although they had started out by arguing with the members of the Young Men's Association and the Military Veterans Association, they had come unawares to agree with their views.

The temporary workers had seemed skeptical about the Young Men's Association's "Manchurian monarchy," considering it desirable but somewhat unrealistic, but they found themselves in agreement with Kiyokawa and Atsuta. Going off to war to die or become disabled did not appeal to them, nor could they be sure that the "Manchurian monarchy" would ever favor them very much. Thanks to the war, however, they had been able to find jobs after a long stretch of unemployment. It is true that they had many complaints: as temporary workers they received no bonuses; were forced to work overtime; and were paid less than the full-time workers despite doing the same amount of work. Apart from that, they thought they were benefiting from war.

Forgetting even that he belonged to the Masses Party, which was supposedly "for the workers," Kiyokawa worried about stock prices as though he had become a capitalist, while his musings on the benefits of war showed how skilled he was at grasping only the short-term interests of the workers (especially the temporary workers).

When it came to lambasting such ways of thinking in front of everyone and fully convincing the women workers that they were false, Itō and her companions were awkward and unable to refute them well. "It's so irritating, I can't bear it," she said. I knew exactly what she meant. We understood clearly the true nature of this war. But we still had a long way to go in learning to persuade people humbly, to explain in the words that made sense in their daily lives. Lenin says that sometimes even revolutionary workers' unions are wrong about war. With Kiyokawa and Atsuta doing their best to muddy everything further, things became more and more difficult.

Lately the company had started asking people to work past five o'clock to six or seven, though it did not pay any extra wages. This was becoming nearly a daily occurrence. Temporary workers complained about it but stayed, fearing they would not be made full time if they refused. However, they were not permitted to work until six without eating a box supper—which the company declined to pay for. This meant that working until six they actually earned less. It was in fact an indirect way of lowering wages. "They're making fools of us," everyone said, becoming indignant. Whenever Itō's parachute section stayed on until six, they grumbled, "They really have to give us dinner money."

Not only that, hours of work had recently increased to ten, quite different from what they had been. Hopes of becoming full time spurred everyone to work with unprecedented intensity. Earlier one could talk with one's neighbor while working, or peer into a hand mirror from time to time as Kinu had been doing, but now there was no time even to wipe the dripping sweat with one's sleeve. Pressing the parachutes using electric irons, workers grew drenched with sweat. Drops of perspiration kept falling onto the parachute cloth spread out before them. In terms of output, the company was exceeding its earlier profits by more than 40 percent. Yet, it was paying just the same wages as before. The workers were actually quite aware of this. But when it came to their own lives, each of them split reality into two, thinking that war is war and work is work. They did not know that the cruelty weighing more and more heavily upon them at work all came from the war. If they could only be shown that connection, they would instinctively see straight through Kiyokawa's and the Young Men's Associations' arguments.

In view of all this, it became clear what our cell's new focus of struggle ought to be. In order to cut off the influence that Kiyokawa, Atsuta, and the rest wielded among temporary workers, we would jointly introduce into the Workmates' Club such messages as "No to speedup," "Raise wages," and "Improve labor conditions." They would then bring up various counterarguments, and far from leading the struggle, would end up enticing everyone away from it. Promptly seizing on this, we would make it clear in front of everyone that these people were not on their side. We also decided, as a resolution of the cell meeting, to take up in the forthcoming issues of *The Mask* a new and persistent exposure of fascists within the factory and the society.

Burning the scribbled sheets of paper one by one with a match, Suyama said, "Looks like a decisive battle is approaching!"

"That's right," I said. "To win it, we must have a scientifically correct course of action, and be resolved to carry it through to the end no matter what. Once the fascists start to move, our lives will be at stake!"

Suyama laughed. "For us the factory is not a fortress, it's a battlefield!"

"Who are you quoting this time?"

"Myself!"

Later, when I attended a "regional organizer" (a meeting of the organizing section of the party's regional committee), there was a report that the state-run N military factory, considering it insufficient to guard the facilities using only military policemen armed with pistols and swords, now infiltrated the key departments of the workplace with military police in workmen's clothing. The local cell had recently been arrested thanks to undercover police. What made such "workers" supremely dangerous was that they deliberately pretended to be politically conscious.

Since Kurata Industries was not a state-run military factory it had no military police yet, but it was quite possible that as the situation progressed they too would arrive.

6

I glanced at my watch: it was only nine. We decided to chat a little and stretched out on the mats. Looking at Itō's mirror stand I noticed it was more elegant than Kasahara's and complete with yellow, red, and green boxes of face powder. "Well, well!" I said.

Itō saw what I was gazing at. "You're a pain!" she said and rose.

"Itō transforms herself red, blue, and yellow, and displays her wonderful powers night after night," said Suyama, laughing. "Look, there's all that wrapping paper from Mitsukoshi and Matsuzakaya. What a fortunate lady!"

At the factory, an attractive woman worker was likely to draw the attention of the supervisor, clerks, or male coworkers who would buy her things, take her to Matsuzakaya, or treat her to meals at Shirukoya. Itō accepted invitations from promising rank-and-file workers, and she of course also asked them out herself. That is why she always went to the factory with her face prettily made up. It was the same with male workers who were neat in appearance and passably handsome—they were followed about by women workers "directly and concretely," as Suyama would put it.

"How is it going these days?" I asked him.

Suyama stroked his chin and flashed a broad grin: "Very hard times!"

"And you, Yoshi—not yet?" Resting my cheek against my hand and keeping my head still, I inquiringly pointed only with my eyes.

"What?" Itō asked in return. Once she understood, her expression changed a little (only for a moment), but soon she was calm again. "No, no, not yet!" she said.

"I hear she's planning to wait till after the revolution," said Suyama laughing. "When our comrades marry, even though they're Marxists, a three-thousand-year-old consciousness still latent makes them try to turn Yoshi into a slave."

"You're just making a confession about yourself!" said Itō, with a chilly expression.

"It's hard to find a good comrade," said I looking at Itō.

"What about me?" Suyama asked, raising his torso off the mat.

"Too late, too late!" I said.

"For whom? For me?" asked Suyama, grinning.

"Look at him! He's shamelessly conceited!" The three of us burst out laughing.

Doing a quick mental survey, I could not think of very many comrades who measured up to Itō. If she actually found a mate, he would certainly be an outstanding comrade and their lives would wonderfully sustain their mutual life as party members. —— Although I had worked with her for so long, I had never before considered Itō in these terms. This was a proof of Itō's strength, which had subtly affected our own feelings.

"Let's be responsible and introduce her to a good guy," I said lightly, yet meaning it. But Itō turned to me with a frown . . .

ON THE WAY back, I went out to the main street and picked up a taxi. Evidently taking a shortcut, the car turned repeatedly through dark streets but suddenly emerged into a bright and bustling road. I tilted my hat forward as though I were tipsy. "Where are we?" I asked. "Ginza," the driver replied. This was a problem. I am bad at handling entertainment districts. Saying nothing, as though I did not understand, I tilted my hat further forward. It had been months since I had last seen Ginza. I counted on my fingers—four months. From time to time I looked out the windows on both sides. Much had changed since I had last walked around here. Before I knew it, I was greedily gazing around. I had felt this way before. It was the year before last, when I was being driven to prison. I was on the way to court for a preliminary hearing, riding handcuffed in a prison van, and looking through the iron-barred windows at the crowds of Shinjuku for the first time in six months. I looked at each building, each signboard, each car, and tried to look at each person in the bustling crowd. Thinking that a comrade I knew might be walking amid the throng of people, I strained my sight as hard as I could. I remember that a flickering and prickling sensation in my eyes lasted a day or two after I returned to the prison cell.

When the car reached the Yon-chōme intersection, a bell jangled and a light on a pole on the opposite side turned red. The car stopped at a designated line. Scores of people of all sorts trooped directly past the car window. I felt uneasy. Some of the people even peered into the car. Lowering my chin to my chest, I placed my hand on the opposite door handle in order to be able to flee if needed. Shortly the bell began to jangle. With a feeling of relief, I loosened my hold on the handle.

Watching countless people walk along, I realized that in my life there was no such thing at all as taking a walk. I could neither go out for a stroll, nor could I even carelessly open a window in my room and allow my face to be seen from the outside. In that respect, I did not differ in the least from comrades held in detention centers and prison cells. What made it in a sense even more painful, was that I was free to go out and yet forced to refrain from it.

Fortunately I was fully aware that this was what I must do, but Kasahara who was living with me seemed to find the situation very trying. Not surprisingly, she occasionally wanted to go out for a walk with me. Not being able to do so seemed to irritate her. Moreover, I always went out just around the time when she came back from work. During the day I stayed at home, using only evenings for my errands. The times when we could sit in the room together became few. After a month or two of such an existence, Kasahara grew visibly discontented. Not wanting to give in to her feelings, she did her best to control herself but at long last she lost her patience and confronted me. When a person who can lead no private life at all lives together with a person who does have a sphere of private life, it presents a problem.

"Ever since we got together, you haven't even once been at home in the evening, and haven't even once gone for a walk with me!" At last, Kasahara foolishly pointed out the obvious.

In order to close the gap between us, I tried several times to draw Kasahara into the same sort of work. However, after we started to live together I realized that Kasahara was not suited for it. Her feelings were superficial, and she lacked perseverance. "You're like a meteorological observatory," I told Kasahara. Trivial things made her exuberant one moment and sulky the next. A person of such nature cannot possibly do our kind of work.

Of course it was a pity that she led a life of heavy burdens and very little free time, spending most of the day at a typist's job that was removed from ordinary workers' lives, returning home to cook, and doing our laundry on Sundays, but she didn't have the energy or even the consciousness to break away from it. I tried to get her to do it, but she didn't go along with it.

I got out of the taxi, walked along the railway for two station stops, entered an alley, and returned home. Kasahara was sitting on the mat with her legs off to one side, looking pale and depressed. Seeing my face, she said, "I got fired . . ."

It was so sudden it left me standing speechless and staring at her.

Kasahara had done nothing, but a rumor that she was a Red had spread at her company. Because of that, a company official had paid a visit to her old landlord, who was her guarantor, only to learn that she was no longer living there. Since she could not reveal my hideout to anyone, she had kept her former address. The discrepancy made the company even more suspicious and they fired her at once.

Until now I had been paying the room rent and miscellaneous daily expenses with Kasahara's salary, and just managing to make ends meet so as to carry out my activities without a hindrance, so her getting fired was quite a blow. This might have been a good time to demand a lot of money from the company but I could not suggest that to her strongly, being "illegal" myself. In fact, the company official discreetly pointed out to her that she was lucky they were keeping the police out of it and asked her to leave quietly.

We were presented with an immediate problem. Unfortunately, the landlady downstairs would soon realize what had happened. Unless we won her confidence by punctually paying the rent, she would become suspicious. That would not only be bad, but downright dangerous. For that reason we decided to pay the rent no matter what. However, we only had two or three yen left. Such a small sum would soon run out. Kasahara would go out every day to search for work, and I too would have to go out an average of four times a day. I decided to walk to places I had gone to till now by train or car. As a result, making a contact required extra time: depending on the place, thirty or forty minutes there and back might now take as much as two hours, and the efficiency of my work markedly decreased. Saying that I was conducting a "fund-raising campaign," I squeezed five or ten sen from every comrade I met. I'd never catch up with Suyama's "Uncle Kanda" this way, I said with a wry smile. Suyama and Itō were concerned about me. Saying that a lack of money was not a matter of life or death for them because they lived legally and could borrow money from anyone, they gave me a yen and fifty sen from their daily pay. I could not spend such money carelessly so I used it for work-related transportation expenses, and economized on meals. Since eggplants were inexpensive—some two dozen for five sen—I had the landlady pickle them in her salted rice-bran paste and ate them for breakfast, lunch, and dinner. Three days of that took a heavy toll. Each time I climbed the stairs, I panted and sweated.

Although I was feeling hungry and looking haggard, I had no appetite at all for always eating the same thing. In the end I poured hot water over rice, shut my eyes tightly, and bolted it down. Still, I was lucky to have a meal at all. On nights when I had three contacts yet had to walk all the way for lack of money, and had eaten only a single meal since the morning, I felt miserable. One time I went out hoping to get some bread when I met a comrade, but was completely disappointed. The comrade, looking sympathetic, said that the next comrade he was going to meet was M, who was likely to have some money to give me, and suggested I come along with him. Being acquainted with M, and desperate, I agreed to do so. I was able to get bread and butter from him. "Can you imagine if a man got arrested coming all the way here to eat a loaf of bread!" said M with a laugh. "Just give me the bread first!" I replied laughing—but aware that the present situation must not continue. If I hoped to settle down to long and steady work without risk of arrest, my present strained and anxious way of living had to change.

I decided I had no choice but to ask for the ultimate. Returning home that day, I mustered my courage and said to Kasahara, "How about becoming a café waitress?" Going out every day to look for work had exhausted and upset her. Hearing my words, she suddenly turned around and her face grew dark and angry. I averted my eyes from her. She remained stubbornly silent. Disconcerted, I kept silent too.

"You mean, for the sake of your work, don't you? . . . ," she said not looking at me, her voice surprisingly calm and low. And then, without listening to my reply, she suddenly screamed, "I'll do anything, I'll become a prostitute!"

Since she was not interested in allying herself with my commitments, Kasahara always thought that everything she did was a sacrifice for my sake. When it came to that, I, too, was sacrificing nearly my entire life. At times, on the way back from a meeting with Suyama and Itō, I brooded over the fact that whereas they were returning to ordinary free lives in an ordinary world, I had to return to a life of constant watchfulness and tension. If I were arrested, four or five years of imprisonment awaited me. Nevertheless, such sacrifices were trifling when compared with the sacrifices endured by millions of workers and poor farmers in their daily lives. I had learned this intimately through the lives of my father and mother who had been suffering as destitute peasants for more than twenty years. Therefore I considered my sacrifice to be vital in emancipating those millions from their own enormous sacrifices.

But Kasahara had no deep understanding of this, and unfortunately thought of everything as "my sacrifice." "You're a great and important person, so it's only natural to sacrifice a fool like me!" —— But I had no personal life at all. What my sacrifice meant was clear. I was a member of an organization, and it was my duty to protect that organization, and to persevere in carrying out our task—the emancipation of the entire proletariat. In that sense, I had to value myself most highly, but not because I was great or heroic. ——Kasahara, who only knew personal life, could only understand someone through a personal standard.

I talked to Kasahara earnestly about this. She listened in silence. That day she did not say another word, and went to sleep early.

7

That night I stayed up late writing an article for *The Mask*, sorting out reports to be sent to the regional organizing meeting, and reading the pamphlets and data that had piled up a bit since being distributed and sent to me, and so I slept until about ten the next morning. —— Even I was surprised at how sensitive I was to the presence of a visitor downstairs. I awoke with a start and raised my head. Sure enough, it was a policeman on a census-taking round. In order not to be dragged out at a time like this, I had written out beforehand my name and original address and handed it over to the landlady. The policeman's questions were detailed and persistent. It was as if he had come to conduct a criminal investigation of the entire household. I had a premonition that something was wrong. Pricking up my ears, I locked the trunk containing the documents, and began noiselessly to change. ——“Are there tenants?” he was asking. “Yes, there are . . .” The landlady seemed to be returning to the living room and handing him the slip of paper I had written. “This doesn’t say where he was living last. . . . A married couple?” he asked. “It isn’t clear when he was registered, or if he’s registered.” The landlady was saying something. “Isn’t the husband working? . . . Is he here now?” Here it comes, I thought. “He’s out at the moment,” I heard the landlady say. Along with a feeling of relief came the thought how good it was I had used up all the money I had to pay the rent. “Well, ask him later for some more details,” said the policeman, seeming about to leave. As I relaxed and sat down on the bedding, the policeman slid the front door open and said, “These days Reds are renting rooms a lot, so be careful . . .” I gave a start. The landlady asked, “Who is?” The policeman seemed to add a few words more. The landlady had not known the meaning of “Reds.”

I felt that this inquiry was no trivial matter. That day, on the way back from a meeting, I saw policemen carrying census records and name registers visiting a small family-run shop in a neighboring town. Before I had walked a single block in the same town, I saw two policemen emerge from an alley carrying similar documents. When I met S and told him about this morning’s visit, he told me the police were conducting a thorough search of lodging houses in the whole city and advised me to be careful. I had sensed as much from the overblown intensity of the investigations.

Those bastards had said countless times that the party had been uprooted and annihilated. They publicized this prominently in the big newspapers they owned, and worked frenziedly to brainwash workers who didn’t know any better into believing it, and to cut off the party’s influence from the masses. But soon after they had so prominently publicized its destruction, the party was active everywhere. No matter how they tried to misrepresent this, their deception was ineffective. In this time of war, they focused especially on the great campaigns like the International Workers’ Day on May 1, and the International Antiwar Day on August 1, determined to eradicate the party’s strength in every way possible. To achieve this they were mobilizing all their might, all the forms of state power that they held. They reviled the party with their words, spread rumors about it and ridiculed it, but this very fact betrayed them, demonstrating clearly that the party was their greatest enemy. A certain foreign article described us as "a small but combative party." However, S (who unlike Suyama's "Uncle Kanda" was well versed in these things) said: "This small but combative party is a mighty force confronting on equal terms, no, on more than equal terms, the full power of the state." They, who were millions of times bigger, were desperately trying to eradicate this "small but combative party," he said, and therefore every one of us, small as we were, must proudly keep on working. "We ought to be wonderfully proud!" he exclaimed, and we felt extremely happy. In order to carry through that pride till the end, it was imperative not to let them arrest us.

The way things were, living in a lodging house had become highly dangerous. Suyama, Itō, and I were thinking of mobilizing Kurata Industries for May Day. The dismissal of the six hundred temporary workers was approaching, and there was abundant possibility of success if we only poured our energies into it. If we were arrested now, we would truly be committing an act of class betrayal. It was said that S lately slept with a thick stick and a pair of *zōri* by his pillow. Hearing that, I stopped on the way home and bought a pair of my own to put next to the laundry-drying pole which I had not yet put to use. I met Suyama to discover that "Red hunting" was by no means limited to the outdoors. —— Walking to meet him, I saw him coming my way, his entire face bandaged, dragging one leg. I was stunned. "I got my butt kicked!" he said. From time to time, he pressed his hand against his bandaged face. Though the wound was hurting and he hadn't known what to do, the times were such that he felt he could not miss our meeting, and barely made it. We decided not to walk outside and entered a restaurant.

Becoming convinced that the external police presence alone was rather ineffective, the factory had introduced Kiyokawa and Atsuta's Workmates' Club and the army veterans' Young Men's Association in its effort to "hunt Reds" from the inside. When *The Mask* and the fliers brought the scheme to light, however, the management evidently began to panic. Two or three days earlier they had started collecting money for comfort packages to be sent to the troops. Kurata Industries began belatedly to do this with the objective of creating an atmosphere of unity within the factory, and eliminating the space that the so-called Reds were carving out. Be it "loyalty and patriotism" or anything else, if it didn't further their profits, they took no notice of it at all. It was the Young Men's Association that recommended this policy to the factory. One of its members was the veteran in worker's clothing who had struck the woman worker in the parachute factory for having a copy of *The Mask*.

Grasping the problem, Suyama thought we should try to cut off Kiyokawa and Atsuta of the Workmates' Club from the masses. Itō agreed. It was necessary to make everyone aware of the fact that the Labor Farmer Masses Party, though supposedly a workers' party and opposed to imperialist war, was in fact not a workers' party at all and merely pretended to oppose the imperialist war. Suyama and Itō were rank-and-file members of the Workmates' Club. In order for the proletariat to uncover the true nature of each of the bourgeoisie's deceptive policies and keep up the difficult work of opposing the war, it had to struggle most of all against the right-wing opportunism of such false friends as the Workmates' Club. Suyama went to Kiyokawa with a proposal that a general meeting of the Workmates' Club be held to discuss the matter of money for soldiers' comfort packages. At the same time, he decided to extend the general awareness of the issue of collecting the "comfort money," using Itō and her friends and his own friends.

Surprisingly, the Young Men's Association workers also came to the general meeting. The reason we paid attention to the Workmates' Club was that it numbered only a few temporary workers and a great many full-time workers. Among Itō and Suyama's friends there were only one or two full-time workers. Although we repeatedly stressed the importance of winning over the full-time workers, this was quite difficult to do and the results were meager. Since the Workmates' Club, with two or three exceptions, consisted of people who had joined with vague ideas, the chances of attracting them to our side were excellent once we clearly demonstrated in front of them who was right, Kiyokawa or Suyama.

Although the war had been going on for half a year already, the Workmates' Club had met only once or twice. Even many of its members were grumbling about this. Suyama began by saying in front of everyone that for the Workmates' Club not to hold a single serious meeting at a time when so many workers and peasants had been dragged off to the battlefront, and when even daily life had been turned into a forced march, constituted class betrayal. Five or six of those present said, "No objection . . ." Yet they squirmed after they said it. But Suyama and I were familiar with counterrevolutionary thought of reactionary unions, and well understood why they squirmed after saying it. I laughed, and so did Suyama. Exclaiming "Ouch, ouch!" he pressed his hand against his bandaged face. He was good at capturing and mimicking people's quirks.

When the issue of money for the comfort packages came up, Kiyokawa said that since the soldiers who had gone to Manchuria were workers and peasants, they were our friends and sending them comfort money as an expression of proletarian solidarity was permissible. Everyone listened in silence, scrubbing their fingernails. On the factory floor, he said, our comrades were exploited by capitalists, but once on the battlefield, they are being sacrificed to enemy bullets. *No one but we* protected our comrades, and so collecting money for the comfort packages was a legitimate response. —— Everyone nodded gravely at Kiyokawa's argument.

Itō was frowning. "Is that really true?" she said.

The Workmates' Club had some fifteen female members but only about two came to meetings. This time Itō had managed to persuade six women to attend. But since no woman had ever said anything at a Workmates' Club meeting until now, everyone suddenly looked at Itō's face.

"As I listen to you talk, Mr. Kiyokawa, it all sounds plausible and yet I have a feeling that I'm listening to an address by the Army Minister . . ."

Everyone burst out laughing.

"Kiyokawa understands as well as anyone that this war is being waged not for our benefit but for the benefit of the capitalists. If it really were being waged for us workers, for the unemployed, and for the poor farmers, then of course we would collect and send all the money we had even if we had to strip ourselves naked. But it is not."

As Itō said this, a worker from the Young Men's Association suddenly began to shout her down. Suyama intervened. Quoting Kiyokawa himself, he said, "'In factories, we workers are exploited, when the capitalists no longer need us we are thrown out into the streets at will, and when a war breaks out we are the first to get dragged off. In every single situation, we are sacrificed for the benefit of the capitalists.' ——Precisely so! Therefore, if money is to be sent, *they're* the ones who ought to send it!"

People's faces expressed agreement with his words.

"Making us give out money is a trick to make us think that the war is being fought not for them alone, but for the whole nation."

Itō took the floor after Suyama and spoke of "Red comfort packages," and of the fact that our lives haven't gotten the least bit comfortable since the war broke out. Kiyokawa and his friends were no match for either her or Suyama. Kiyokawa's prestige as the chief of the Workmates' Club declined visibly. Even the Young Men's Association workers found nothing to say. However, such social fascists do not play their real tricks in front of the people but behind the scenes, and it would have been a big mistake to think that all was now well.

On the way back from the meeting, three members of the Young Men's Association called out to Suyama, "Hey, you radical! Come here for a moment!" As soon as they entered an alley, they fell upon him and gave him a beating.

"Three on one, no wonder they beat me to a pulp!" said Suyama laughing.

Suyama decided to have Itō tell the members of the Workmates' Club about their friends' cowardly behavior. This would best demonstrate which side was right.

An hour after meeting Suyama, I met Itō who told me that everyone was eager to know why the question of comfort money had led to a fistfight. She was happy because talking about the fight gave her a good opportunity to discuss the real meaning of comfort money. It had worried her that she had not been sufficiently able to clarify the matter. Even without the arguments, however, people said that being asked for money on top of being worked so hard would make them "just drop dead of exhaustion," and so the money collection ended in unexpected failure. After the beating, Suyama's credibility in the factory suddenly rose. Such an event impressed the workers immediately and deeply. On the other hand, the supervisor began to keep an eye on Suyama. That might be dangerous, Itō said.

"Did the company deliberately start collecting money to measure the strength of Reds among the workers?"

I replied I was sure of it.

"I guess we fell for it . . . ," Itō said.

I thought she looked uncharacteristically dismayed. "Not at all!" I said. "Instead, we were able to demonstrate, in front of dozens of workers, who is right. At the same time we made ourselves influential within the Workmates' Club, and if we don't leave it at that but secure our gains through organizing we'll get wonderful results. We can't work making no sacrifices at all. I'm sure this will be helpful to us at the last, decisive moment."

Itō suddenly blushed. "I see! Of course . . . I see!" She nodded repeatedly, with the thoughtful look that was so typical of her.

Jokingly, I said, "They say that those who laugh last laugh best, so we'll have Suyama keep a sullen face for now!"

We both laughed.

She then told me about taking her group to see a play at the Tsukiji Little Theater. All the women knew only kabuki (which I myself had never seen) or Mizutani Yaeko, and were evidently astonished to see male and female workers come out on stage and "raise hell." After it was over, they all said that that was not a play. When Itō asked them what it was if not a play, they replied, "It's reality." She asked them if it had been interesting, and they said, "Well . . . !" Yet it seemed to have greatly surprised them, and they often brought up Tsukiji even in later conversations. Kimi, a petite woman habitually attached to Itō, said, "I'm awfully embarrassed to be called a factory girl. But in that play they're proud of being factory girls, so I thought that's a lie." She thought about it some more. "If we went on strike I'd be really proud, but when neighbors call me a factory girl I still feel embarrassed!"

When Itō asked everyone if they would like to go to the theater again sometime, many said they would. They had especially enjoyed seeing a supervisor who closely resembled their own get mercilessly teased.

Itō casually suggested that since they would all get fired anyway, without even getting a bonus if they kept quiet, why didn't they all get together like in the play to stage a strike and give the supervisor a hard time? They all grinned, and said, "Yes . . ." Then, looking at each other and saying, "If we did that, it would be interesting!" they excitedly discussed how to take the supervisor to task. Unawares they were proposing a method identical to that in the Tsukiji play.

Thanks to Itō's influence three women from the Workmates' Club had joined her circle. Being somewhat familiar with the atmosphere of a legal labor union, they often casually used words that Itō and the others seldom did. This created a bit of a gap between them. They were also "sophisticated" in some respects, and displayed an attitude of understanding "the movement." Itō was now creating a variety of opportunities to make the two sides get along. "It isn't going as smoothly as in novels," she said with a laugh.

We fixed the day for our next meeting, and Itō offered to find us a place. It was time at last to plan our final countermoves.

"Are you still eating *eggplants?*" asked Itō, rising to her feet.

"Yes," I said laughing, startled by her unexpected question. "Thanks to the eggplant diet, my knee joints have just given out!"

Itō's hand moved to her obi and she pulled out a piece of paper folded into a square. Thinking that it was a report, I looked up at her and put it into my pocket.

When I returned to the lodging house I took it out. Wrapped in thin tissue paper was a five-yen bill.

8

Kasahara found work at a small coffee shop. Deciding on this had been sad. It is truly terrible that people in the movement work in places of that sort in order to secure a livelihood. No matter how strong they seem to be, such comrades degenerated visibly. To us, "atmosphere" is just as vital as water is to fish. It is the same when a woman comrade starts working at a coffee shop, whether on her own account or in order to avert ruin for herself and the man she is working with. It was obvious that Kasahara, having had no preparation for our work to begin with, would go steadily downhill. —— However, given that she had never had the spirit to participate in the movement, and I on the other hand had to protect the organizing work with all my might, I could not be sentimental.

At first Kasahara commuted to work from our lodging house. She returned late at night, worn out by anxieties of the unaccustomed work, her face looking sullen. Tossing aside her handbag, she sat down with her legs to one side, her shoulders sagging limply. Even speaking seemed to require too much trouble. After a while, she wordlessly stretched her legs toward me.

"............?"

I looked at Kasahara's face—and touched her legs. Her knees and ankles were swollen beyond recognition. She tried folding her legs on top of the mat. Her knees faintly cracked. It was an unpleasant sound.

"Standing all day is hard," she said.

I told her about a cotton mill that Itō had described to me. Legs grew so swollen and sore from standing that the workers couldn't keep still beside the machines. They worked while getting kicked from behind by supervisors' shoes. I told Kasahara to think of the pain of her work not as just her own pain that can be fled through individual escape, but as the pain of the entire proletariat in chains.

"True!" she said.

Sitting cross-legged on the floor, I drew Kasahara's small frame into my arms for the first time in a while. She closed her eyes, and remained that way . . .

After that, it was decided that Kasahara would live in the coffee shop. The proprietor was a woman, evidently someone's mistress. Thinking it unsafe to live alone, she asked Kasahara to move in with her, assuring her that she would pay her the same and not charge for the meals. Kasahara moved out from our place, telling the landlady that she was going back to her hometown for a while. The coffee shop owner was a graduate of a higher teachers' school or a women's college, and was fluent in English. She had not just one lover but three, spending nights with them in turn, and coming back in the mornings.

They were a university professor, a famous novelist, and a movie actor. When she returned, the woman spoke about each of them in suggestive detail, comparing them, and embarrassing Kasahara. Then she slept until two or three in the afternoon. On mornings when I got up to find no food, I went to the coffee shop. Since there were hardly any customers in the morning, I had Kasahara dish up some of the food she ate and boil some rice, and stuffed myself. At first Kasahara didn't like it, but in the end she said, "You deserve this much!" The coffee shop kitchen was cramped, cluttered and damp. I crouched there, gulping down the food.

"How good you look!" Kasahara laughed watching me. She was keeping her voice low and focusing her attention on the second floor.

Kasahara's circumstances were extremely bad. There was the proprietor's lifestyle, and there were also the customers many of whom did not merely come to drink tea but to engage the women who worked there in silly chatter. Every one of them had to be humored. I knew that these things affected Kasahara deeply. I had not yet entirely abandoned Kasahara, and brought her various books at every opportunity, and talked with her about various topics as much as I could. She was burdened more than ever with all sorts of troubles, and no longer inclined to think persistently about things.

I was not able to devote much time to Kasahara. The busy nature of my work was dragging me along. With the situation at Kurata Industries growing increasingly tense, it reached a point where I started going to Kasahara's place only to get transportation money or to eat, and hardly ever to talk with her. I noticed that sometimes Kasahara looked lonely. It was thanks to Kasahara that I was able to carry out my daily activities successfully, and in that sense she played an important part in our work. I talked with Kasahara about this, telling her that she needed to be clearly aware of her role and keep an unbroken attitude.

Gradually I lost even the time to go for money or food, and my visits to the coffee shop grew ever fewer: once in three days, once a week, once in ten days. "Regional," "district," and "factory cell" work was piling up, and at times I even had to make a dozen or more contacts in a single day. On such days I went out around nine in the morning and did not return until about ten at night. I would come back to the lodging house with the back of my neck stiff as a rod and my head pounding with pain. Barely managing to climb the stairs, I'd collapse onto the mat. These days I was simply no longer able to stretch out and sleep on my back. Evidently I had damaged some part of my body through extreme fatigue, and like a weak child would quickly roll over on my stomach in order to fall asleep. I recalled that when my father was farming in Akita, he would often return from the fields and, still wearing his muddy straw sandals, fall face down to take a nap the moment he walked in. Father could not work without punishing his body. Because the rent he paid as a tenant farmer was harsh, he took on extra work cultivating rocky "wild" fields that no one in the village would touch. He was trying to supplement our livelihood with whatever few crops he could raise there. As a result, he badly damaged his heart. —— Now that I was only able to sleep face down, it occurred to me that I was gradually coming to resemble my father. It was more than twenty years ago since father, without protesting to the landlord and getting him to lower the rent, had sought to escape from his situation through work, even if it meant destroying his body. But I was different. I had cut connections with my mother, become a missing person to my younger sister and brother, and had now sacrificed a life with Kasahara as well. It looked as though I too was beginning to destroy my body. —— However, unlike my father I was not doing this to render more service to a landlord or a capitalist, but for a purpose that was diametrically opposite!

All traces of my private life had vanished. Even the seasons became no more than components of life in the party. Seasonal flowers, blue skies, and rain did not strike me as having an independent existence of their own. I was delighted when it rained. It meant I had to carry an open umbrella when going out, which made it harder for my face to be seen. I wanted summer to end quickly. It wasn't that I disliked summer, but summer clothes were thin making the distinctive features of my body (devil take them!) recognizable. If winter arrived quickly, I thought, "Well, I can live on and stay active for another year!" But Tokyo winters were too bright, which made them inconvenient. —— Far from growing indifferent to the seasons since entering this life, I had become extremely sensitive in an entirely unexpected way. And this was clearly different from the exceptional keenness to the seasons I had developed during my imprisonment the year before last.

It had happened without my being aware of it. The life I had been placed into had in itself transformed me. Earlier, before the police began to pursue me, I still had retained much of my own life even while devoting myself entirely to the emancipation of the proletariat. At times, I even strolled around Shinjuku or Asakusa chatting with fellow members of the factory union (it was a reactionary union affiliated with Shamintō, the Social Democratic Party, within which I worked in an opposition group). Although the political life in the factory cell was strictly controlled, such activities as socializing, going to the movies, and frequenting bars and restaurants—natural aspects of a legal existence—occupied a significant portion of my life. (Come to think of it, these days I've completely forgotten that movies even exist!) Living the way I was, I sometimes put off my cell work for a day or two. My desire for prestige was operating unbeknownst to me, so that if work likely to heighten my prestige conflicted with my cell work, I unconsciously and repeatedly first took up the work that centered on me. This of course changed in my subsequent work, and yet I could not say that I was living "twenty-four hours a day of political life" as a party member. Yet the fault was not entirely my own. There is a limit to the conscious efforts of a person who is not leading a disciplined life. Placed into a life where all private social ties have been cut off, where all personal desires unrelated to life in the party are kept in check, I learned to my surprise that things I had formerly found so difficult to carry out were done very naturally and easily. I became able to do in two or three short months what had earlier taken a year or two of effort. At the beginning of this new life, I felt that unbearable and indescribable tightness in the chest that children feel when they compete to see who can stay underwater the longest. But of course I had not yet been tempered by real hardship. Concerning "twenty-four hours a day of political life," S, who likes different scrapbooks from Suyama, told me that I must forge myself into a "type who doesn't grow fatigued even working twenty-eight hours a day."

At first I didn't know what was meant by working twenty-eight hours a day, but once I began to make a dozen or more contacts in a single day, I got to understand just what it meant. If I can come even a little closer to an existence in which my personal life is simultaneously a class-oriented life, I shall feel thoroughly satisfied.

At Kurata Industries, the rumor that the company would make a few of the temporary workers into full-time workers was reaching its final pitch. In preparation for the approaching events, we decided to reorganize our cell. We recommended three new members: a young full-time worker from Suyama's group of friends and two workers from Itō's group, one full time and one temporary. I took their personal histories to the organizing meeting and obtained approval. Then we clearly divided up workplace responsibilities putting each cell member in charge of one section, and drew up a plan so that even if something were to happen to Suyama or Itō the others could quickly take up their prearranged posts and there would not be even a day's interruption of work. If anything befell Suyama or Itō this would soon become known at the factory, in which case the new cell members were to come to the place where Suyama and I normally met. Since our meetings were the headquarters of struggle, any loss of contact that might prevent the announcement of urgent countermeasures and objectives would amount to class betrayal. Our earlier approach—to say that something did not go well because someone was arrested and contact cut off—was defeatist in pretending that we were not already under pressure and that such incidents were entirely unpredictable. It was obvious that someone might be arrested. Therefore we needed to promote the struggle by making double and triple preparations from the outset.

Actually, ever since the fray at the Workmates' Club, Suyama had been in great danger. He came to the factory daily quite aware that he might be arrested any time. A simple "Come here a minute" was all it took. Yet he continued to come because the possibilities for organizing were rising. Although his position had grown dangerous, he simultaneously gained freedom to say some things openly at the workplace, and won everyone's confidence.

The end of the month drew near. It seemed that the company

would be firing people on the thirtieth or the thirty-first. Despite promises to make some workers full time, nothing concrete was being done and everyone was finally growing suspicious. *The Mask* wrote that the company was operating through deception, aiming on the one hand to boost efficiency, and on the other hand to block resistance. The meaning of the newspaper articles was starting to be unequivocally understood. Since most workers were temporary, the power to organize would decline once the dismissals were announced. It was essential to reach a decision within the next two or three days.

Through fliers and news bulletins, we had been advocating the urgency of opposing the war, yet once the workers themselves rose up against the dismissals, it would show them "with a speed matched only in fairy tales," as Lenin might have put it, why the war must be opposed. That the factory was making war supplies made it especially possible to wage a clearly conscious struggle. ——First it was necessary to raise some hell.

I made up my mind.

We would have Suyama and Itō's new cell members who were assigned to every work station hold simultaneous workplace meetings demanding "No dismissals." To ensure their success, Suyama would openly scatter fliers through the factory. ——A woman in Itō's "Shirukoya group" had an elder brother who worked in an office at Kurata Industries. Through her we learned that the company was making a preemptive move to convince everyone that the thirty-first was the key day when in fact it intended to carry out all the dismissals on the twenty-ninth. It seemed that on that day not only would the police turn out but the army as well. Consequently it was vital to take the initiative and strike on the *twenty-eighth* no matter what.

The danger of Suyama getting arrested, however, was increasing. According to Itō's report, plainclothes police had been observed leaving the office once or twice, and frequently talked with the supervisor at the entrance of Factory Number 2 where Suyama worked. This had happened within the last two days. The party fliers and *The Mask* had each been distributed twice inside the factory even after Ōta's arrest. It was no longer possible to doubt that they were keeping an eye on Suyama. People think, or are made to think, that "the Communist

Party" exists somewhere on high or else consists of gods and goblins who dwell in the depths of the earth, popping up often to the surface. It was necessary to demonstrate clearly that in reality it comprises people like Suyama, trusted by all and working side by side with the rest of us, and to awaken a sense of friendship and confidence. ——This is what prompted my decision to have Suyama scatter the party fliers openly.

Carrying on the struggle even if Suyama were temporarily absent was a task that someone else would have to take up. People cannot be mobilized through conspiratorial methods alone. An invisible organization must be stretched like a cobweb, and open agitation brought into play.

We held a meeting to plan these final measures. Although the proposal was put forward and accepted, thinking about Suyama made my heart ache. Scattering fliers would enhance his record of struggle but also compel him to resign himself to between two and five years of penal servitude. Normally whenever I took even a single step outdoors I put a stop to all daydreaming and contemplating in order to pay full attention to my surroundings (I had gotten rather accustomed to this), but on this day I suddenly noticed that I was brooding about Suyama. However, it was not good to come to pause so long over Suyama. He himself, taking a clear look at our situation, was surely able to understand the inevitable and indispensable nature of the action. So long as there was no other path and no bypass, and assuming besides that it was essential to take that road for the emancipation of the proletariat, we could hardly draw a conclusion that transcended our work and say, for instance, that to do such a thing was "cruel" or "pitiless."

And yet, the image of Suyama who made us laugh with his crazy scrapbook stayed with me all the way to the meeting, continuing to trouble me.

The place, which we had used some three times earlier, was a house belonging to Suyama's old friend (and drinking partner). Removing my geta in the dark dirt-floored vestibule and tucking them into a fold of my kimono, I climbed to the second floor where amid slanted rays of light Suyama's face peeked out.

Itō sat leaning against the wall, stretching her legs off to the side and massaging them with her hands. As I walked in, she combed back a strand of loose hair and glanced up at me. "Wow!" I exclaimed. She made no particular response. When she was organizing at the factory, Itō wore a lot of face powder but she had never before come to a cell meeting with her face powdered, nor had there ever been any need to. Her face looked lovelier than I had ever seen it.

"Comrade Itō just came back from recruiting a full-time male worker into the organization," Suyama said playfully, pointing at Itō's face.

Itō kept quiet, as she always did under such circumstances. For some reason, however, she looked at my face just then.

As the meeting began I paid special attention to Suyama's report, as usual. In accordance with the resolution of the earlier cell meeting, he had arranged to hold assemblies at all the work stations. A look at how things stood in the factory, he said, suggested that the coming two or three days would be the decisive moment when we urgently needed to do *something.*

Itō added that the volume of parachutes and masks accepted for production indicated that the report I had received earlier was indeed correct: the firings supposedly scheduled for the thirty-first would in fact take place on the twenty-ninth. For that reason, she said, we must put up a decisive fight by the twenty-eighth at the latest, which was only two days away.

We were all in agreement. Therefore the question was: what was to be the form of that decisive fight? —— Suyama thought for a moment and said, "Preparations have been made and everyone's morale is high, so once the people become incensed we can strike a blow." He paused briefly. "Whether or not a single blow will suffice may determine whether we win or lose . . ."

"That's right. All that's still needed is a spark . . . For the eight hundred!" Itō's face colored uncharacteristically with excitement.

"Lately—well, these two or three days—I've been feeling a little nervous," said Suyama looking at my face. "We've used various methods to eliminate sects from the era of Fukumotoism, but they're still around. If we can't win the fight at this factory with a single effort now, it may be due to that . . .

"I think that unless someone openly does something in front of people, there won't be a fight. There has to be a turn from quantity to quality. I don't consider that ultra-left, do you?"

Suyama said this forcefully, as though someone had argued that it was ultra-left.

I think we must conduct our struggle not through dogma, but through consent. Therefore I kept quiet, merely wanting everyone to pay attention to advancing the question in the right direction. That was happening, as expected. In particular, Itō and Suyama were starting out not with quibbling over methods but rather from the point of a solution to the hourly developments at the factory; moreover they were in agreement on the right point. In not diverging from workers' lives, our situation presented a delicate unity of theory and practice.

I told Suyama that "ultra-left" was in this case nothing but a word hurled by cowardly right-wing opportunists in order to misrepresent their own practical defeatism. "That's right!" said Suyama.

At this point, I put forward my proposal. There was a moment of restrained tension but it passed very quickly.

"I think so too . . ."

Suyama, his voice understandably taut, was the first to break the silence.

I looked at Suyama, and he said, "Naturally, I'm the one who must do it."

I nodded.

Itō's body stiffened, her eyes flitted from Suyama to me and from me to Suyama. When I turned in her direction, she muttered in a low voice, "No . . . objection."

Suyama, sitting cross-legged, was unconsciously cutting up an empty pack of "Golden Bat" cigarettes into ever smaller fragments.

The decision was followed by an abrupt and brief stillness. The sounds of many footsteps passing through the main street, and the persistent loud shouts of night-stall keepers—all of which we had not noticed until now—suddenly flooded our ears.

Next we took up the concrete problems. Guessing that women workers were bringing fliers and the newspaper *The Mask* into the factory thanks to the loose manner of the body searches, the company suddenly began searching the women rigorously. For that reason, on the appointed day Itō would take on all responsibility. She would wear a pair of bloomers with tight elastic closings on the thighs. When she received the fliers from S in the morning, she would step into a public toilet and insert them next to her skin. Once inside the factory, she would at a prearranged time use the toilet and hand over the fliers to Suyama. It was decided to scatter the fliers from the rooftop during lunch break.

As the meeting ended, the emotions we had been suppressing till now suddenly welled up.

"We won't be seeing each other for a long time . . . !" I said to Suyama.

"Let me tell you about two of my friends," he said. "They are very close, but one of them was caught in the mass arrests of March 15th and given three years. The other was arrested on April 16th of the following year and given three years. The one arrested on March 15th came out, was arrested again in December of last year and got three years. *He* had been looking forward to seeing his April 16th friend come out. When he entered prison he said, 'Looks like he and I will be playing *hide and seek* forever like this and never be able to meet, but that's all right!'"

Then he himself said, "I wonder if this is my final scrapbook anecdote?"

In spite of ourselves Itō and I—burst out laughing. Yet my face felt stiff, as it does when something makes me cry.

"No matter what happens, so long as a solidly built organization remains *here,* the struggle will have its roots and can continue, so just make sure you don't get arrested," Suyama said. "If you do get arrested, my work too will be as useless as a dead dog!"

Deciding to proceed with preparations in accordance with today's resolution, and to meet once more on the evening of the twenty-sixth, we rose saying, "Well, then . . ." Though we had not in the least planned it, Suyama and I stood up in the middle of the room and vigorously shook hands. Suyama, growing suddenly as awkward as a child, said to me, "Why, Sasaki, your hands are tiny!"

ON THE WAY out, Suyama told me that he had paid another visit to my house, thinking he would have no opportunity to do it from now on. "Every time I see your mother, she somehow seems to be gradually getting smaller," he said.

". . . . . ?"

I wondered what he would say next. But suddenly Suyama's words "gradually getting smaller" struck at my heart. In those words I felt I could vividly see Mother's small figure growing worn out with worry. ——Yet this was no time for such talk. Feigning indifference I said, "I suppose that's true . . ." and put an end to the matter.

After parting with Suyama, I took a short walk with Itō, who had some thirty minutes to herself before her next contact. We talked about giving a small party for Suyama on the twenty-sixth. Itō decided to buy sweets and fruit for the occasion.

Itō usually walked with long strides like a man, swinging her shoulders a little, but at my side she seemed feminine and took short steps. As we were about to part she said, "Please wait a moment," and entered a small shop. Presently coming out with her purchase wrapped, she handed it to me saying, "This is for you." Although I objected "No, you shouldn't!" she insisted that I keep it.

"Lately your shirts have been getting dirty. . . . They notice such things, you know!"

Opening the parcel back at the lodging house, I unexpectedly found myself comparing Itō and Kasahara. Though both were women, I had never before thought of Itō in comparison with Kasahara. But doing it now, I felt for the first time how very far away from me Kasahara was.

——I hadn't been to see Kasahara for some ten days already . . .

9

Factory Number 3 at Kurata Industries was still under construction and had a flat rooftop where everyone went during lunch break. Some sprawled at full length to expose their bodies to the first sunlight of the day, others talked or joked around, and still others played volleyball. On that day the early summer sunshine reflected off the concrete floor with a dazzling intensity. Suyama positioned several friends around him to obstruct any attempt to arrest him.

At exactly quarter to one, he suddenly raised a great shout and began scattering the fliers with all his might. "Down with mass firings!" "Strike against the firings!" . . . The rest of his words were drowned out by everyone's voices. The red and yellow fliers glittered in the sunlight. As the fliers began to scatter, everybody at first jumped up with surprise and then, crying out, rushed to the area where they were falling. Dozens of workers picked up clusters of them and heatedly flung them high into the air. In the twinkling of an eye, the fliers originally scattered in one area were spreading out above the heads of six hundred workers. —— The guards posted here and there in anticipation of just such an event waded into the crowd yelling at the top of their voices "Hey, hey! You're not to pick them up!" but in doing so lost sight of who had scattered the fliers. By now, everyone was scattering them.

Not knowing what to do, the guards blocked off the rooftop's narrow exit and tried to identify the culprit by letting people past them one by one, though this would prevent the work from resuming for over an hour. When the sirens announcing the start of work began to howl from the thick concrete chimneys, everyone linked arms and raising a roar rushed the narrow exit. The guards could no longer do anything. —— As Itō watched, a perfectly composed Suyama surrounded by the crowd calmly descended the stairs.

Afterward the supervisor went around asking workers one by one "Do you know who did this?" and although some of them surely knew that it was Suyama no one said so. The fools from the Young Men's Association were fuming with rage. That day, spirits were very high at Suyama's Factory Number 2 and Itō's parachute section. Electing representatives, they negotiated with the other factories and decided to issue a protest to the company.

When Suyama and Itō found themselves on the way back, Suyama said, "At a time like this, even we can allow ourselves to cry a few tears!" Tilting his hat wildly, he was vigorously rubbing his face.

As they walked he kept repeating over and over again, "I didn't think it would go this well! I didn't think it would go this well! Support from the masses is an awesome thing!"

I had arranged a meeting late in that day to ask Itō how it had gone with the fliers. It had never even occurred to me that Suyama would come together with her. As he walked in behind Itō, I looked at him two or three times. Realizing this was unmistakably Suyama, I involuntarily rose to my feet.

I asked them for all the details. Growing excited myself I said emulating Suyama's words to Itō, "At a time like this, even we can allow ourselves to drink a few beers!" and the three of us decided to share a bottle of Kirin.

Growing merry, Suyama playfully said to Itō, "You know, there was a touch of fragrance to those fliers!"

"Watch it!" I grabbed his shoulder and laughed.

But since the decisive struggle would be fought out tomorrow, we went over the preparations for it once more.

AS THE WORKERS arrived at the factory the next morning, the company dismissed four hundred out of the six hundred temporary workers directly at the gate, handing them two days' pay. Some sixteen policemen had turned out, and as the stunned women wandered aimlessly about even after getting their pay, the police kept chasing them away: "Off you go now, off you go!"

A large notice had been posted next to the cashier's window: "The work scheduled to end on the twenty-ninth has been brought to conclusion today. However, please be assured that the company, determined not to cause you any inconvenience, will pay the remaining two days' wages in advance. Moreover, please understand that at such time as new work becomes available, the company will grant you preferential treatment." Their intentions were apparent from the fact that they had retained two hundred temporary workers. Our unity had been broken.

Both Suyama and Itō were among those who had been fired. ——We had been forestalled at the last moment. ——Suyama and Itō were so dejected it was painful to look at them. It was the same with me too. The enemy was no fool. We had to recover our footing quickly, learn from the experience of this failure, and make the reversal in the situation serve us in our next struggle.

Although we had been badly beaten, two of our members remained among the full-time workers. Also, even though those who had been fired scattered in search of work, they included Itō and Suyama's group of nearly ten, so that by maintaining strong links with them the field of our struggle was in fact suddenly expanded.

Our enemies believed they had "beaten us to the punch" and were able to throw our work into disarray, yet they didn't know that with their own hands they had blown the seeds of our organization far and wide!

At present, Suyama, Itō, and I are doing new work, more energetically than ever . . .

AUTHOR'S NOTE: I dedicate this piece to Comrade Kurahara Korehito.

[END OF PART One]

AUGUST 25, 1932

Glossary

Akita, Aomori, and Iwate: Prefectures (i.e., administrative units) of northern Honshū, the main Japanese island. Like most of Japan's north, each of these three regions is predominantly agricultural.

Asakusa, Ginza, Shinjuku: Tokyo's popular entertainment districts

benshi: Screen-side narrator who accompanied showings of Japanese silent cinema; film commentator and interpreter

Bon Festival (Obon): Three-day summertime celebration honoring the spirits of one's ancestors; Buddhist in origin

Chishima Islands: Better known as the Kuril Islands, a volcanic archipelago that stretches for more than eight hundred miles from northeast Hokkaidō to southern **Kamchatka** Peninsula. First inhabited by the indigenous Ainu, the archipelago became a bone of territorial contention between Russia and Japan. In the prewar period, the islands were under Japanese control. The northernmost island is Shumshu.

Colonial Bank (Takushoku Ginkō): Bank engaged in financing the colonial development of Hokkaidō and Karafuto (southern Sakhalin Island), founded in 1900

Fukumotoism: Theories of Marxist intellectual Fukumoto Kazuo (1894–1983), highly influential from 1925 to 1927, but then rejected for overemphasizing theoretical struggle and ideological purity of the revolutionary party

geta: Wooden clogs, a form of traditional footwear

go: Ancient board game whose objective is to capture opponent's territory; originated in China and popular throughout East Asia

"good wife and wise mother" (ryōsai kenbo): A patriarchal idiom coined by samurai scholar Nakamura Masanao in 1875, epitomizing an idealized traditional role for women

Hayama Yoshiki (1894–1945): Japanese proletarian writer, probably best known as author of the novel *Umi ni ikuru hitobito* (Those Who Live on the Sea, 1926)

Ishikari Plain (Ishikari heiya): An extensive cultivated region in west Hokkaidō, it stretches along the coast north of Sapporo and is drained by the Ishikari River for which it is named

Japanese Communist Party (Nihon Kyōsantō): Founded in 1922 and immediately outlawed, the JCP was subjected to intense persecution and repression by the police and military in prewar Japan. It was the only Japanese party to oppose the country's overseas expansionism and its resort to war.

Kamchatka: One of the world's largest peninsulas, rich in wildlife and natural resources such as coal, gold, and natural gas. Part of the Russian Far East, it is populated by Russians and the indigenous Koryaks. Covered in snow from October to late May.

Kanda Hakuzan (1872–1932): A highly popular professional oral storyteller

Karafuto: Japanese name for Sakhalin Island. At the beginning of the twentieth century, its population comprised Russians and the indigenous Nivkhs, Oroks, and Ainu. From 1905 to 1945, the island's southern portion was administered by Japan as Karafuto Prefecture. Sakhalin and its surroundings abound in timber, coal, fish, petroleum, and natural gas.

Kataoka Chiezō (1903–1983): One of the stars of Japanese cinema, originally a Kabuki actor. In the early period of a long career, he often appeared in the role of a handsome samurai.

Kataoka Teppei (1894–1944): Journalist and popular novelist, writer (for a time) of proletarian literature

King (*Kingu*): A hugely popular mass-entertainment monthly magazine founded in 1925, which reached a circulation of over a million by 1927

Kurahara Korehito (1902–1991): Literary critic and historian, translator of Russian literature, foremost Marxist theoretician of the late 1920s and early '30s and staunch proponent of the proletarian literary movement

Labor Farmer Masses Party (Rōnō Taishūtō): Reformist party formed in

July of 1931 through a merger of the Masses Party and the New Labor Farmer Party. Its full name is National Labor Farmer Masses Party (Zenkoku Rōnō Taishūtō).

Left-wing Theater (Sayoku Gekijō): Tokyo theatrical company producing working-class plays, active between 1928 and 1934

Luxemburg, Rosa (1871–1919): Polish-German Marxist theorist, philosopher, economist, and activist. Opposed German participation in World War I and spent much of the war in prison; in the turmoil of a postwar uprising was assassinated by right-wing military officers

Marxism (Marukusushugi): Monthly journal published by the **Japanese Communist Party** between 1924 and 1929

Masses Party (Taishūtō): Reformist party formed in December 1928, growing out of the Japan Labor Farmer Party. Its full name is Japan Masses Party (Nihon Taishūtō).

Military Veterans Association (Zaigō Gunjinkai): One of the most important officially sponsored patriotic organizations in 1920s and '30s Japan, with branches throughout the country. Counterrevolutionary in intent and practice, it engaged in community service while promoting conservatism, nationalism, and militarism. Strongly connected with local chapters of the **Young Men's Association**.

Minseitō: A leading liberal party in prewar Japan, traditionally identified with Mitsubishi financial interests. It alternated in power with the more conservative **Seiyūkai**. Big business tended to give campaign contributions to both parties.

miso: Bean paste, typically produced mostly from soy; a traditional Japanese seasoning

Mizutani Yaeko (1905–1979): Stage and screen actress, appeared in *Taii no musume* (The Captain's Daughter, 1923) and numerous other films

natsumikan, "summer tangerine" (Citrus natsudaidai): Type of citrus fruit also known as Chinese citron

New Labor Farmer Party (Shin Rōnōtō): Legal successor to the dissolved Labor Farmer Party. Though Ōyama Ikuo's proposal in August of 1929 to form the new party met with a great deal of opposition on the Left—for being divisive and opportunistic— Ōyama (whom see) went on to found it in November of the same year.

New Youth (Shin seinen): Popular magazine first published in 1920 and aimed largely at a young audience. Lighthearted in tone, its contents included Japanese and foreign modernist prose, detective fiction, comic banter, stories about sports, comics, etc. Its monthly readership was around forty thousand.

obi: A sash wound as a belt around the waist of a kimono; those worn by women tend to be broader

ohaguro: An ancient aristocratic custom of dying the teeth black. Concealing the teeth—the only exposed part of the human skeleton—was considered aesthetically desirable. Over time the custom spread to other social classes but gradually died out in the early twentieth century.

Okhotsk, Sea of: Northwest arm of the Pacific Ocean, mostly ice-bound from November to June and prone to heavy fogs. Named after the first Russian settlement in the region, the sea is rich in fish and crabs and used to be a major whaling center in the mid-nineteenth century—North American whalers began hunting its whales in the 1840s.

Ōyama Ikuo (1880–1955): Reformist politician and writer. In 1926 elected president of the Labor Farmer Party; in 1929 founded the **New Labor Farmer Party**; in 1930 elected to the Diet.

Peace Preservation Law (Chian Iji Hō, 1925): One of a series of laws enacted to suppress dissent, it was especially directed against socialists, communists, and anarchists. The law prohibited anti-capitalist agitation, making political offenses punishable by up to ten years of imprisonment with hard labor or—following a 1928 emergency imperial decree—by death.

Proletarian Newspaper (Musansha shinbun): Published by a front for the Japanese Communist Party from September 1925 to August 1929 when it was banned by court order. At first a fortnightly; from January 1926 a weekly; later appearing six times a month and even daily. Its successor, *Dai-ni musansha shinbun (Second Proletarian Newspaper)*, with a circulation of about ten thousand, continued to publish until 1932.

Russo-Japanese War (Nichi-Ro sensō): 1904–1905 armed conflict between Imperial Russia and Imperial Japan for control over Korea and Manchuria, won by Japan. As the first victory in modern history of an Asian nation over a European power, the war emboldened anticolonial liberation movements across the globe—while consolidating Japan's colonial hegemony over Korea.

Seiyūkai: A leading conservative party in prewar Japan, traditionally identified with Mitsui financial interests. It alternated in power with the more liberal **Minseitō**. Big business tended to give campaign contributions to both parties.

sen: Old unit of currency, equivalent to one hundredth of a yen; small change

Shamintō (abbreviation for Shakaiminshūtō): Social Democratic Party, founded in December 1926 by members of the Labor Farmer Party; it was anticommunist and advocated a parliamentary system

shamisen: A three-stringed musical instrument played with a plectrum called *bachi*. Its precursor was introduced to Japan from Okinawa in the sixteenth century; it in turn originated in China.

shiruko: a sweet porridge of *azuki* beans, served with *mochi* (glutinous rice cake)

Shukutsu lighthouse (Shukutsu no tōdai): Located on a promontory cliff-top north of Otaru, Hokkaidō, originally built in 1883; also known as Hiyoriyama *tōdai*

soba: Buckwheat noodles, a popular inexpensive dish throughout Japan

Special Higher Police (Tokubetsu Kōtō Keisatsu, often shortened to Tokkō): Political police, established in 1911 to investigate and control movements considered dangerous to established order, especially anarchists, socialists, and communists

tatami: Straw mats, about three feet by six feet, traditionally used as floor coverings

Tsukiji Little Theater (Tsukiji Shōgekijō): A prestigious theater founded in Tokyo in 1924 and dedicated to the production of modern drama. After 1928 its repertory included numerous left-wing plays.

Watanabe Masanosuke (1899–1928): Labor organizer who joined the Japanese Communist Party in 1922; jailed from 1923 to 1924; elected general secretary of the JCP central committee in 1927. On his way back from a meeting in Shanghai, Watanabe was surrounded by police at a seaport terminal in Chilung, Taiwan (at the time a Japanese colony); he turned his pistol on himself rather than give up.

Workmates' Club (Ryōyūkai): A company-based labor union associated with a reformist political party

Young Men's Association (Seinendan): One of the most important officially sponsored patriotic organizations in 1920s and '30s Japan, with branches throughout the country. Counterrevolutionary in intent and practice, it engaged in community service while promoting conservatism, nationalism, and militarism. Strongly connected with local chapters of the **Military Veterans Association**.

zōri: Flat Japanese sandals with thongs, generally made of rice straw or other plant fibers, wood, leather, or rubber. Comparable to flip-flops, which originated from *zōri*.

Works by Kobayashi Takiji

Bōsetsurin & Fuzai jinushi. Tokyo: Iwanami, 2010.
The Cannery Boat and other Japanese Short Stories. Translator anonymous [William Maxwell "Max" Bickerton]. New York: International, 1933.
The Factory Ship & The Absentee Landlord. Translated by Frank Motofuji. Tokyo: Tokyo University Press, 1973.
Kani kōsen & Tōseikatsusha. Tokyo: Shinchō bunko, 2004.
Kōjō saibō & Yasuko. Tokyo: Shin Nihon, 1994.
1928-nen 3-gatsu 15-nichi & Higashi Kutchan kō. Tokyo: Shin Nihon, 1994.
Numajiri-mura. Tokyo: Horubu, 1980.
Orugu. Tokyo: Horubu, 1980.

About the Translator

ŽELJKO CIPRIŠ was born in Zagreb (Croatia, former Yugoslavia), obtained a doctorate from Columbia University's Graduate School of Arts and Sciences, taught at five universities, and is presently an associate professor of Asian Studies and Japanese at the University of the Pacific in Stockton, California. He is co-author with Shoko Hamano of *Making Sense of Japanese Grammar,* and translator of Ishikawa Tatsuzō's novel *Soldiers Alive* and Kuroshima Denji's *A Flock of Swirling Crows & Other Proletarian Writings,* all published by the University of Hawai'i Press. Željko (also known as Jake) is currently working on a translation of selected short stories and plays by his renowned compatriot Miroslav Krleža—a project that the collaboration of Jake's sons Ljubomir Ryu and Shane Satori makes enormously enjoyable.

production notes for...

Kobayashi / *The Crab Cannery Ship* and Other Novels of Struggle

Book and cover design by Julie Matsuo-Chun with display type in Neuzon and text type in Minion Pro

Printing and binding by Edwards Brothers, Inc.

Printed on 50# Arbor, 512 ppi